Preacher Man

Preacher Man

Ted Darling crime series

'their blood shall be upon them'

L. M. Krier

Cover design DMR Creative
© Can Stock Photo / SAKhanPhotograph

PREACHER MAN

ISBN 978-2-901773-09-2

Contents

About the Author

L M Krier is the pen name of former journalist (court reporter) and freelance copywriter, Lesley Tither, who also writes travel memoirs under the name Tottie Limejuice. Lesley also worked as a case tracker for the Crown Prosecution Service.

The Ted Darling series of crime novels comprises: *The First Time Ever, Baby's Got Blue Eyes, Two Little Boys, When I'm Old and Grey, Shut Up and Drive, Only the Lonely, Wild Thing, Walk on By, Preacher Man.*

All books in the series are available in Kindle and paperback format and are also available to read free with Kindle Unlimited.

Contact Details

If you would like to get in touch, please do so at:

tottielimejuice@gmail.com

facebook.com/LMKrier

facebook.com/groups/1450797141836111/

https://twitter.com/tottielimejuice

For a light-hearted look at Ted and the other characters, please consider joining the We Love Ted Darling group on Facebook.

Discover the DI Ted Darling series

If you've enjoyed meeting Ted Darling, you may like to discover the other books in the series:

The First Time Ever
Baby's Got Blue Eyes
Two Little Boys
When I'm Old and Grey
Shut Up and Drive
Only the Lonely
Wild Thing
Walk on By
Preacher Man

Acknowledgements

I would just like to thank the people who have helped me bring Ted Darling to life, beta readers: Jill Pennington, Kate Pill, Karen Corcoran, Jill Evans, Alison Sabedoria, Emma Heath, Police consultants – The Three Karens

To my friend Pat

go easy on the green tea!

Chapter One

Brad Allison was having a good evening. And it wasn't over yet, if he played his cards right. His girlfriend, Bernie, looked cosy and contented in the front passenger seat next to him. The meal had been excellent, if pricey, the wine so good he'd risked a second glass, even though he was driving.

Every time he changed gear, which was often on the narrow, twisty, country roads, he put his hand on Bernie's thigh and gave it a gentle squeeze. It was promising that she made only a token gesture of pushing his hand away with hers.

As they rounded a particularly tight bend, a flash of white emerging from the darkness at the side of the road caught Brad's eye as it lurched towards the path his car was taking.

'Bloody hell!' he shouted, as he stamped on the brakes.

He'd learned that there were certain things he couldn't get away with in front of Bernadette Marie Theresa O'Hanlon. Strong language and blasphemy were two of them.

Advanced Swedish technology brought the car to a halt without it deviating so much as a centimetre from its route. The whiteness revealed itself to be a young man, barely out of his teens, who was now slumping over the front of the car on the passenger side. He was completely naked, his eyes wild and haunted, dark circled. His mouth was forming words, inaudible from the safe cocoon of the vehicle.

Brad turned to check through his rear window as he jammed the car into reverse and started to pull away. The naked figure staggered, deprived of the support of the car bonnet.

'What are you doing?'

Bernie's voice was shrill, her tone horrified. Brad tried to keep his measured, reasonable, as he replied, still backing away, 'I'm getting us out of here, away from that nutter.'

'Stop the car, Bradley. I mean it. We can't leave him like that.'

It was her teacher's tone. The one which could instantly silence a class of rebellious primary school children.

He slowed the Volvo to a crawl, still anxious to put distance between them and the apparition, which was now tottering towards them, arms outstretched imploringly.

'We can call the police to help him. Let's just get to a safe place. We don't know anything about what's going on. It could be a trap. An ambush.'

'Stop!'

Bernie's hand was already on the door handle before he'd fully brought the car to a halt and pulled on the handbrake.

'Have you got a coat or something we can put round him?'

Bernie was half out of the car, clearly concerned only with the welfare of the young man in the road. Brad was terrified and not ashamed to admit it. He was sure it was a set-up. That any minute now, an accomplice was going to jump out of the darkness and do something. What, he didn't know, and he couldn't decide what he feared the most. Losing his car? His girlfriend? His life?

He got out as well, discovering that his legs were trembling with the shock of it all. Bernie was walking forward fearlessly, speaking reassuringly. Now Brad could hear the words tumbling from the lips of the figure in the road, the voice harsh, strained. None of it made much sense to him, and it was being repeated in a toneless loop.

'If a man also lie with mankind, as he lieth with a woman, both of them have committed an abomination: they shall surely be put to death; their blood shall be upon them.

'For this cause God gave them up unto vile affections: for

even their women did change the natural use into that which is against nature: And likewise also the men, leaving the natural use of the woman, burned in their lust one toward another; men with men working that which is unseemly, and receiving in themselves that recompense of their error which was meet.'

'Don't be afraid. I'm Bernie, this is Brad. We'd like to help you. Can you tell me your name?'

'If a man also lie with mankind, as he lieth with a woman, both of them have committed an abomination: they shall surely be put to death; their blood shall be upon them.'

'Brad, where's that coat? And phone an ambulance.'

Brad looked wistfully at the cashmere overcoat he kept on the back seat. It had cost him a fortune, even in the sales. He hated the idea of giving it to this stranger, although clearly they couldn't leave him naked. Close to, he could see that the young man was also trembling, his eyes imploring. He was pitifully thin, his cheeks hollow.

'Do you live near here? Can you give us your name and address?'

Bernie was still trying, in her most persuasive voice. Brad came closer, warily holding out his coat. He thought it best to let Bernie try to put it on him. He got his mobile phone out and reluctantly dialled 999. Surely even two large glasses of wine would still be under the limit?

'Yes, an ambulance please, as quick as you can. Perhaps the police too. I'm not sure.'

He explained as much as he knew, trying to be economical with the details in front of the young man, who was still repeating the same phrases over and over. Clearly something religious but Brad had no idea what. Bernie would probably know, but she was busy trying to reassure the stranger, gently putting the overcoat round his shoulders and leading him towards the safety of the car.

Brad sighed as he went to put on the four-way flashers and get out the warning triangle. There was not much traffic on this road but he didn't want to risk anything which was out and about coming hurtling round that bend and smashing into the back of them.

He was convinced they were dealing with a runaway psychiatric patient. He just hoped neither of them would be murdered before the emergency services arrived, whenever that might be.

Bernie had helped the young man into the rear seat of the car and got back into the front passenger seat herself, still talking calmly to him, trying to get him to respond. He said nothing other than the endlessly repeated biblical phrases.

Brad was about to go and get back in the car himself when the effects of the shock and the adrenaline surge hit him. He rushed to the verge just in time to bring up his expensive meal and probably most of the wine as well. At least that was one problem sorted.

As he slid into the Volvo next to Bernie, he was aware that their unexpected passenger stank to high heaven. Of rancid sweat. Of urine and excrement. And the strange coppery smell of blood. He somehow knew that even if he had the overcoat dry cleaned, he could never bear to wear it again.

'Has he said anything that makes sense? Who he is, or what he's doing here?'

'I can't seem to get through to him. He just keeps repeating the same phrases from the Bible, over and over. His poor lips are so cracked and dry. Do you think we should give him a drink of water?'

She knew Brad always kept a few bottles of mineral water in the car. His job as an IT consultant kept him on the road a lot, which was why he'd invested in a reliable car, one that handled well whatever the road conditions.

'I don't think we should give him anything until the paramedics have seen him. Perhaps he might speak to me? Bloke to bloke?'

He turned round in his seat and smiled in what he hoped

was a reassuring way through the gap between the front seats.

'All right, mate? What are you doing out here in your birthday suit? Is there someone we can call for you? Someone to come and get you?'

The younger man's voice became almost a scream, his face crumbling in panic as he began babbling repeatedly, 'For this cause God gave them up unto vile affections.'

'Hey, calm down, pal, I'm not going to do anything to you. We just want to help.'

Brad didn't think he would feel such relief at the arrival of the police. But as the flashing blue lights of an area car finally came into sight around the corner, he offered up a silent prayer of his own and got out of his vehicle to go and greet them.

Two officers got out, a man and a woman. The man came towards him first, the woman waiting by the car. He explained all the details he knew so far, hoping that his breath now smelt of vomit rather than wine.

The PC listened to what he had to say then turned back towards his partner.

'Do you think we need to treat this as a crime scene until we know what's what, Sarge? Will you call it in, and see if you can hurry that ambulance up?'

Sergeant Emma McCluskey used her radio to contact the station. She agreed with her younger colleague, pleased with how he was starting to shape up. Until they knew exactly what they were dealing with, it would be best to preserve the scene.

She wasn't aware of any recently reported missing persons who would fit the details she'd been given so far. It could be someone with mental health issues needing help. But there was no telling what might be behind the incident or if anyone else was involved. Better to play it cautiously, call up a Senior Investigating Officer to decide how things needed to be handled.

'This is a bit of an odd one, on the face of it. I think it's maybe one we should inform DCI Darling about. It could be one for his team.'

Detective Chief Inspector Ted Darling was enjoying a quiet evening at home, for once, with his partner, Trevor. Both were sitting comfortably on the sofa, feet up on the leg rests, bodies buried under purring cats. Trev had his arm round Ted and his head leaning his shoulder as they watched one of the classic films Trev enjoyed so much. This time, it was Hitchcock's *Rear Window.* They'd both seen it before, many times, but Trev was someone who could watch the same film endlessly and never tire of it.

When their peace was interrupted by Ted's mobile ringing, Trev reached automatically for the remote to mute the sound.

Ted gave him an apologetic look as he picked up the call. His was not a nine-to-five job.

'DCI Darling.'

Trev studied his face as he listened, trying to work out whether it was a call-out or if he was just being kept in the loop about something.

'Yes, thanks, it sounds like I'd better at least go and take a look. Can you let them know I should be there within half an hour.'

'Trouble at t'mill?' Trev asked him with a smile.

'Yes, sorry, I'm going to have to go. It sounds like a strange one, something I ought to go and take a look at. I'll just call Mike to pick me up, then get changed quickly. Sorry to abandon you, and I've no idea how long I'll be, not until I get there.'

He carefully transferred his share of their six cats to Trev as he got to his feet, already calling up one of his two sergeants from the team. Mike Hallam lived close by so was the obvious choice to pick the boss up.

'Is it a body?'

'Not this time. A young man found wandering in suspicious circumstances. The sergeant on call thinks there's something not right about it all so I'd better go and see what's what for myself.'

Ted filled in DS Mike Hallam on the little he knew as they drove out seemingly into the middle of nowhere, beyond Mellor. They were heading for a quiet lane, a cut-through which mostly only the locals knew. When they arrived, a second area car was on the scene and Police tape had closed off the road from both ends. A car was parked roughly half-way between the two lots of tape.

Sgt McCluskey came over as soon as she saw the two plain-clothes officers approaching. She addressed Ted, nodding to Mike Hallam as she greeted them.

'Sorry to disturb your evening, sir, especially going into the weekend. I just thought there might be more to this than meets the eye, and I thought I'd better preserve the scene until I was told otherwise.'

'No need to apologise. You did exactly the right thing. Tell me your thinking.'

'Well, sir, I may be over-reacting because I've just done a course on the Modern Slavery Act. But the lad showed signs of having been tied up and he was really thin. Malnourished, I would say. Also I don't know if English is his first language or not. He was just parroting these strange phrases which I assume were from the Bible or somewhere. But he didn't respond to any questions. I couldn't be sure if he understood English, or if he could speak any. And he doesn't immediately correspond to any of the recent missing persons reports. I checked with the station.'

Ted was looking round carefully, to see what he could deduce from his first glance at the potential crime scene.

'Is he on his way to hospital?'

'Yes, sir, we got lucky and got an ambulance here pretty sharpish. He'd come stumbling out from the side of the road and may have made contact with that Volvo there, so I left it there. I thought there may be fingerprints or DNA to help identify him, if we can't find out any other way who he is.'

'Excellent, good work. Makes our job easier. What about the driver of the car?'

'We've got him in our car, sir, with his girlfriend. She's quite calm, he's very shaken up. We breathalysed him, to be on the safe side. He was just under the limit and he told us he'd been sick, so I reckon he'd probably had a bit too much and was lucky to get away with it.'

'Had he hit the person?'

'No, sir, he stopped the car in time.'

'So what injuries did the young man have?'

'The ambulance crew said he appeared to be dehydrated and in severe shock. When we got here he just had the driver's coat round him. When the paramedics arrived changed that for a space blanket and gave him a thorough examination before they moved him. They told me he was black and blue, sir. Looked as if he'd had a right going over, and more than once. Some of the marks were old. There were burn marks, too.'

She paused, looking slightly awkward, then continued, 'I noticed he had some kind of burns, perhaps chemical burns, round his mouth. And the paramedics told me that his testicles appeared very discoloured and swollen. I didn't want to jump to any conclusions, sir, but it made me wonder, from the injuries they were describing, if he'd been tortured, perhaps over a long period of time.'

Ted exchanged a look with Mike. He didn't like the sound of this one, not on his patch.

'Thank you, Sergeant, you've done an excellent job. You did absolutely the right thing. DS Hallam and I will take charge of the scene now, if you and your officers can keep the road closed off until further notice.

'Mike, can you get someone from forensics in to check out the vehicle and immediate surroundings. I'll go and have a word with the driver and his girlfriend, then we should arrange a car to take them home. He'll have to manage without his own car until we've finished with it. Give the hospital a call, too, see when they might be able to give us any info.'

Ted walked over to the nearer of the two area cars where he could see two people sitting in the back seat. The young PC who had been with Sgt McCluskey was standing outside the car and snapped smartly to attention when the DCI approached. He may have been below average height and looked insignificant but Ted commanded a lot of respect from officers he worked alongside. He was unfailingly polite, for one thing, which was a bit of a rarity.

'I just wanted to have a word with the witnesses, Constable. What are their names, please?'

'Bradley Allison and Bernadette O'Hanlon, sir. Bernie, she said she likes to be called.'

He knew who Ted was but he hadn't encountered him in person before. He was impressed by the please.

Ted opened the front passenger door and slid into the seat, taking out his warrant card to show to the young couple in the back seat. The interior light was on so they could see it and he would be able to see them. He liked to look at faces while he was talking to witnesses. They often gave away a lot of useful information.

'I'm sorry we've had to delay you like this, and that we will need to hang on to your car until we're finished looking for any traces,' he began, twisting right round in the seat so he could see the two of them clearly while he spoke to them. 'We'll also need full statements from each of you, but you can come into the station, perhaps tomorrow, to do that. I'd just like your initial impressions. Please tell me what you saw, what you remember.'

'I was just scared I was going to hit him. He came out of nowhere. Luckily I wasn't speeding or I could have killed him.'

The man spoke first. He was clearly still shaken.

'Can you tell me what he said?'

'I couldn't make head nor tail of it. He just kept repeating something about men lying with men and being put to death for it, I think. It freaked me out. He just kept saying it over and over. We couldn't get him to say anything else. I've no idea what any of it meant.'

'It's a passage from the Bible. Leviticus, I think,' his girlfriend put in. 'I've been on social media groups where people argue about whether or not the Bible forbids homosexuality, and that's the passage which always gets quoted.

'I don't know what's been happening to the poor young man but I know one thing. He looked terrified for his life.'

Chapter Two

Once he'd finished speaking to the couple, Ted went in search of Mike to find out how things were progressing. Although he knew the area well enough, his knowledge didn't include whether there might be somewhere close to the young man could have come from. He didn't like to think of some institution or medical facility restraining him in a way to leave marks and injuries, but there were stories of such things happening.

At some point he'd need to check in with one or other of his senior officers, if it looked as if this was a case for him and his team. As if through some psychic connection, his mobile phone announced an incoming call. When he checked the screen he saw it was from one of them, Superintendent Debra Caldwell.

'Ma'am,' he answered formally, aware that he was in earshot of one of the uniformed constables. He and the Ice Queen, as she was known, would sometimes lapse into first name terms in the privacy of her office, but never in public.

'Chief Inspector,' she replied with similar formality. 'What can you tell me about this case so far? Is it one for you and your team or is it something Uniform can wrap up?'

'I'm not sure yet, ma'am. I'd prefer to keep an open mind at this stage, at least until we find a way of identifying the young man involved.'

He told her all the available details so far. He could hear the distaste in her voice as she replied. She had two teenage sons of her own.

'That poor young man. I don't like the sound of this, not one bit. Please keep me posted, and let me know what personnel you need to wind it up as quickly as possible.'

These days, it always came down to budget, Ted thought as he ended the call. Constant pressure to up the detection rate, in the face of ceaseless cuts in hours and numbers. It didn't make his job any easier.

'Forensics are on their way to check over the car, boss. Do you want anyone else from our team in on it at this stage?' Mike asked him.

'If we knew who he was it might help. What did the hospital say?'

'He's only just being seen so they couldn't tell me anything. They said we'd have to call back later.'

'We could probably do worse than swing by there on our way back, once we pack up here. Who's on the rota tomorrow?'

'Jo and Rob are still up in Bolton on that racial assault but they should get that sorted by Monday. I've got Maurice and Steve down to work tomorrow, and I can go in as well if we need to pick this one up and start running with it.'

'I think we might do. I don't like the possible torture angle at all. If he's been in some sort of hospital or unit where that's been going on, we need to get it investigated as soon as possible. If this was a case of kidnap and torture by an individual, or perhaps more than one person, I'm not sure if that makes it better or worse.'

'Boss, just a thought, but what if this isn't a crime, as such? What if it's consensual?'

'Explain.'

'Well, you do hear sometimes of people doing the most horrendous stuff to one another within a relationship yet if anyone tries to intervene, they'll side together and say it's none of anyone else's business. Maybe this started like that and just got out of hand?'

'We don't know the lad's age yet. If he's a minor, it can't be consensual and it is a crime. I'd rather go on that assumption for now, until we have more info. If I have to finish up justifying the hours on my budget, that's one for me to worry about, not you. You have kids, Mike. Think how you'd feel if it was one of yours.'

'There'd be a more serious crime if it was. I'd want to kill the bastard who did it, with my bare hands.'

'Right, so let's run with it for now, at least until we know who he is and exactly what happened. I want photos of the scene and some video footage. Let's get the tyre marks checked. If we know at exactly what point the driver started braking, it may give us a better idea of where he first saw the lad. That might help with where he came from, and we're clutching at any straws available for now.

'Once forensics are happy they've got whatever they can here, get the car recovered and thoroughly tested for any trace of the victim to see if we can ID him that way. See if Uniform can help with any more bodies at this stage for some initial house-to-house. And check if anyone at the station knows this area well, knows where he might have come from. We need someone with detailed local knowledge. Are there any CSOs out here?

'Doubt it, boss, not many left anywhere. I'll see if I can trace any, or even any former ones.'

Police Community Support Officers had always been a vital source of local knowledge. Budgetary cuts had seen their numbers drastically reduced.

'If you've got shoe covers and gloves in the car, I might just have a poke about myself, before forensics get here. Can you also sort out someone to take the driver and his girlfriend home, too. No point them hanging around; they don't seem to be involved.'

Ted slipped covers over his shoes and put on gloves. He

didn't intend to trample over a potential crime scene but he wanted to have a look around for himself to see if he could get some idea of where the young man had come from. From what he'd been told about the state he was in, he didn't see how he could have walked far.

'Oh, and Mike, I doubt there's any CCTV near here but can you check, please? Just in case he was dumped nearby from a vehicle and we may get lucky enough to have some footage of it.'

It was a long shot that Ted would spot anything which the forensic team didn't. But he was a hands-on copper. Always had been. Even though he trusted his team, he still liked to have eyes on a scene himself. It often gave him ideas at a tangent. The dreaded 'thinking outside the box' phrase which he disliked so much.

He was busy thinking about Mike's earlier suggestions. He knew, of course, that there were relationships based on pain and fear, although he couldn't comprehend them. The mere idea that anyone could willingly inflict harm on someone they professed to care for was beyond him.

He was interrupted by another phone call. Even if the caller ID hadn't been displayed, he would have recognised the hesitant, quiet voice of the local newspaper reporter.

'Erm, Chief Inspector?'

'Hello, Penny. What can I do for you?'

'I heard you'd been called out to an incident. I wondered if you could tell me a bit about it?'

Like her predecessor, she clearly had her contacts who tipped her off about anything happening within her circulation area. She hadn't been with the paper for long. Just long enough to know that she was unlikely to get anything out of Ted, unless it suited his agenda. He gave her full marks for her determination in always trying.

'Nothing at all at the moment, I'm afraid, Penny. With a bit of luck I might be able to let you have a statement in the morning. And I promise I will do so, as soon as there's anything I can release.'

'Erm, I've been told it's an escaped psychiatric patient wandering about naked. Can you confirm that, please?'

Ted fervently wished he knew who the mole was who was leaking such detailed information to the press. He'd have a few choice words to say to them.

'I can't confirm or deny anything at this stage, Penny, and I think you probably know that I'm not going to, certainly not without authority. As I said, I will let you know as soon as I have anything but for now, I need to get on. Thanks for your call.'

It was getting late when Ted called time for him and Mike at the scene and stood down most of the officers from Uniform. To date they'd found nothing of any great use. He got everyone together for a few words of encouragement before they dispersed. He was always keen to make sure officers felt valued for their efforts, even if they hadn't produced the results they wanted. He found they tended to work better for him that way.

He doubted they'd learn anything from a visit to the hospital but he felt they at least needed to try. Mike had been on the phone non-stop since their arrival but they were still no further forward in finding out who the young man was. There was an outside chance that he might have been able to say something coherent at the hospital, but Ted wasn't holding his breath for a miracle on that score.

Even at that hour of the evening, the hospital's Accident and Emergency Department was packed, clearly stretched to its limits. Ted wondered how the front-line staff managed to stay civil when so many people he could see seemed to be the worse for drink. He'd long since stopped drinking altogether and he found it had reduced his tolerance to those who clearly couldn't control their intake, or their behaviour on the wrong side of it.

He and Mike went to the reception desk, showing their ID, and Ted asked if it would be possible to speak to someone about the person who'd been brought in earlier.

The young woman on duty studied her computer before replying.

'It was Mr Khan who saw him. I'll try to see if he's free to talk to you but as you can see, we are busy and I can't promise how soon it'll be.'

'I understand that, of course, but we are anxious to identify the young man as soon as possible. We can't go much further with our enquiries until we do. We won't take up much of his time, we just need a few words as soon as possible.'

'If you'd like to take a seat, I'll see what I can do for you.'

There wasn't anywhere left to sit. Neither of them felt much like doing so anyway. They moved away from the desk and stood, waiting patiently, in the limited space left.

Eventually a man came into the reception area, spoke to the person on the desk, who nodded towards Ted and Mike. The doctor came over to them.

'I'm Mr Khan, the A&E consultant on duty tonight. Sorry to have kept you waiting but, as you can see, we are very busy. I can't give you long, but if you come with me we can find a quiet office and I'll tell you what I know which isn't, unfortunately, very much at this stage.'

'Would it be possible for us to see him? Perhaps try talking to him?' Ted asked.

'Not at all, I'm afraid,' he replied, opening a door and standing aside to let them go first into a small room. 'He was extremely agitated, so we've had to sedate him before finding him a bed in a side room. With luck, he'll sleep for several hours now. He was severely dehydrated and suffering from hypothermia, so we have him on a drip and we're slowly raising his body temperature.'

'Can you tell us anything at all which may help us to identify him, please? Could you estimate his age, for instance?'

The consultant's tone, when he replied, was patient and polite, which stopped his words from sounding patronising.

'I'm sorry, Inspector, but he's not a horse. We can't just look at his teeth and tell you how old he is If I had to guess, I would say mid to late teens. But because of his physical condition, especially because of the fact that he is clearly seriously underweight for his height, it's really very hard to tell with any accuracy.'

Ted wasn't one to correct him on using the wrong rank, although he suspected that it might have been different had he called the consultant Dr Khan instead of Mr Khan.

'Thank you, that's helpful. And what can you tell me about his injuries at this stage please?'

'Disturbing, in a word. Their cause is your department, not mine, but I can list what we've found so far, and I don't think it is yet an exhaustive list. There are numerous burns, some second degree. Some look like cigarette burns, others appear to be chemical. Some I'm not sure about, they're not something I've seen before. Larger, round, almost like from where something like an electrode has been placed against the skin. There are some in and around his mouth which appear indicative of ingesting some sort of corrosive liquid. They're possibly the most concerning at this stage as we don't yet know what we're dealing with, nor its potential level of toxicity.'

'What about drugs or alcohol?'

'We've done a tox screen as routine, but we won't have the results immediately. In addition to everything else, he has marks around his wrists and ankles which appear to indicate that he's been tied up for prolonged periods of time.'

'Has he said anything? Anything at all which might help us to find out who he is or where he's from?'

'He was talking non-stop until we sedated him, clearly very agitated. He just kept repeating a few phrases. Something about men lying with men and being put to death for it. I assume it's something biblical but I don't know it. I can tell you it's not from the Koran, though.'

'Thank you, Mr Khan, you've been helpful, and I appreciate you sparing us the time. One more thing. What are his chances, would you say? Is his life in any danger?'

'Clearly, without the benefit of the toxicology results, and not knowing what he might have ingested, I can only give the most guarded of responses. The official line would be something like, at the present moment I do not believe his life is in danger, if that helps you at all?'

'It does, thank you. Just before I let you go, I'd like to send an officer to sit with him, hopefully someone to be there by the time he wakes up.'

Seeing that the consultant was about to raise an objection, Ted hurried on.

'This would be a specialist officer, a parent himself, someone extremely good at talking to victims of crime. Someone to whom they are often happy to talk, even before they might open up to their family or friends.'

'All right, but they must be prepared to leave immediately if my patient shows any sign of being distressed, or if asked to do so by a member of stuff.'

As Ted and Mike walked back across the car park, the DS turned and asked, 'Maurice, boss?'

'Maurice indeed. Can you think of anyone better?'

Midnight had passed by the time Mike dropped Ted off at the end of his short road and he walked down to his house. He could hear the television on when he let himself in. It was on a French news channel, he saw when he went into the living room. Trev was still sprawled on the sofa buried under cats, much as Ted had left him, but had nodded off.

Ted bent over to kiss him on the top of his black curls. His partner stirred, opening sleepy blue eyes, then stretched his long, lithe frame with the same feline grace as his companions.

'Hey, you. How did it go? Did you catch the bad guys?'

'I'm just going to make myself a cuppa then I'll tell you about it. As much as I can. Do you want anything?'

'No thanks, I have wine.'

Trev reached out a languid arm to pick up a half-full glass of red as Ted headed for the kitchen, automatically picking up the trail of detritus Trev invariably left behind him. Trev was an excellent cook and could iron shirts as well as a professional valet. He kept the house immaculately clean, but he lived in a permanent state of disorder. They'd eaten together before Ted had been called out but Trev had clearly fancied a snack and more than one mug of tea.

Ted retrieved a plate covered in cake crumbs from the floor, a dirty knife from the kitchen table and three abandoned mugs, some still with cold tea in them, strong enough to stain the china with tannin. Another dirty wine glass had made it as far as the work surface next to the sink. Somehow Trev had never mastered the art of rinsing anything, far less of putting it into the dishwasher.

Ted returned with a mug of green tea, bending over the sofa where a small black cat was occupying his usual place.

'Barcelona, my love, would you mind budging up a bit so I can sit down, please? It's been a long day.'

Trev smiled fondly as he picked the cat up and added it to the pile of those already occupying his own chest and lap. He wondered, as he often did, what Ted's team would think if they could hear how soppy their exacting boss was in the sanctuary of his own home.

Ted sank down into the vacant space with a grateful sigh and stretched his legs out in front of him on the footrest.

'Tough one?'

'Nasty one, though not a murder. At least, hopefully not, although the victim isn't out of the woods yet. You know I can't tell you much, and I don't know that much yet. But a young man found wandering naked, spouting biblical phrases and covered in burns and other wounds. It looks as if he may have been held prisoner somewhere and possibly tortured.'

'What sort of phrases?'

'Something about men lying with men as they do with women.'

Trev gave a harsh, hollow laugh.

'Oh yes, Leviticus 20:13. I know it well. "If a man also lie with mankind, as he lieth with a woman, both of them have committed an abomination: they shall surely be put to death; their blood shall be upon them." It's one of the things my father threw at me just before he kicked me out of the family home and told me never to darken his doors again.'

Chapter Three

'Right, everyone, listen up, please.'

It was Ted's familiar call to order for morning briefing. On a Saturday morning, there was only a skeleton staff on duty, himself, DS Hallam, DCs Maurice Brown and Steve Ellis.

'You'll notice there's nothing on the board yet. That's because we don't have much detail at present, and still no name for our victim.'

He brought Maurice and Steve up to date on what he and Mike had found out the night before, then added, 'So today's priority is to identify the victim and find out where he came from. Steve, that's one for you. Get on to all the Missing Persons' alerts. All we know so far is that he's a young man, probably somewhere between mid and late teens. And before you say it, I know that's not a lot to go on.

'Maurice, you go to the hospital. Sit with him. See what, if anything, he says. He's going to take very careful handling, that's why this is going to be one for you. If he'll talk to anyone, it will probably be you. Record anything he does say. So far, all he's said to anyone is a passage from the Bible. I'm told it's Leviticus 20:13. Something about homosexuality. Steve, can we have a printout of that for the board, please?'

Steve's fingers flew over his keyboard, then the nearby printer whirred into life, spitting out the document requested, which he handed to the boss.

Ted put on his reading glasses and read the first part of the quotation to them, before looking at them over the top of his specs.

'If a man also lie with mankind, as he lieth with a woman, both of them have committed an abomination: they shall surely be put to death; their blood shall be upon them.

'We don't at the moment know what the significance of it is, but it appears to be important to our victim because so far that seems to be all he's said to anyone.'

'Sir?' Steve's voice was always hesitant, although he had become less self-conscious about speaking up than when he'd first joined the team. 'Could we call him something other than the victim? It seems a bit impersonal. Just give him a name until we know what his real name is? Like Tina always used to do.'

He was referring to a former team member who had been killed. Tina had always given names, claiming it dehumanised people to refer to them as 'the victim' when their name was unknown.

'All right, I don't have a problem with that. What would you suggest?'

'Leviticus?' Mike Hallam proposed.

'That's a bit of a bloody mouthful, Sarge. Couldn't we just call him Levi for now?' Maurice grunted.

'Fair enough. Right, Maurice, you go and sit with Levi and keep us posted. The consultant did warn me that he might still be very agitated and you might be asked to leave the room. But see if you can work your usual magic, and please keep me posted at all times.

'Mike, can you carry on trying to find out about any institutions, or whatever they're called these days, which might have lost a patient. They should be obliged to report it but I suppose that if there's any question of abuse having gone on, they might try to keep it quiet. But he must have come from somewhere, so we need to find out where and get Levi back where he belongs. Can you also liaise with Uniform about some more door-to-door. Widen the area slightly. I'll leave you in charge of that.

'A point to bear in mind, for all of us. Sgt McCluskey raised it last night. Because he's only been heard reciting that one passage, we can't be sure at this stage whether English is his native language. If he's been taught to parrot a phrase, it might be all he can say in English. So, Steve, don't dismiss anyone as unlikely on grounds of ethnicity. And with that in mind, perhaps check any contacts with the refugee or immigrant communities. Either official channels, or under the radar. Anyone who might know of a young man who's gone missing. Although I know that's going to be another very long shot.

'Can you also see if you can find any reports of similar cases anywhere else. Just in case this isn't a one-off.

'Let's make it our goal for today to at least find out who he is and let his family, if he has one, know where he is now. I suppose it's possible that they're responsible for what happened to him, but I'm hoping not.'

Detective Constable Maurice Brown was the first to admit he was not the best copper in the force. He was the oldest member of Ted's team and the longest serving. He'd been a DC for years and had no ambition to go any further. His ex-wife had always complained he was nothing but a big kid at heart and it was true, to a degree. He didn't want responsibility. He left that to the boss. He was happy keeping his head down and jogging along, doing the minimum possible to keep his job and never missing any chance to skive.

But Maurice had a gift. The boss knew it, and it had earned and kept him his place on the team. He was one of the most kind-hearted people it was possible to meet and he was brilliant with anyone who was hurt or in trouble.

He'd done various courses on Victim Support and interviewing vulnerable witnesses. He wasn't good in an academic setting so he'd never excelled in course work or classroom stuff. Once he sat down in a one-to-one situation, even fellow officers and course tutors found he inspired such trust in them they were happy to tell him things they wouldn't dream of mentioning in normal circumstances, not even to close friends or family.

He would do anything to help anyone in need. Several of the team, and even the formidable Ice Queen herself, had found what a comfort he could be when necessary.

When he got to the hospital, he followed the directions he'd been given to find the room where their latest victim, Levi, was being kept. A nurse was checking him when he got there. Maurice introduced himself and showed his warrant card.

'How's he doing?'

'He woke up a couple of times during the night, still very agitated, so we had to give him more sedation. He's had some not long ago so he's likely to stay asleep for a bit. You can sit here with him, but if he gets disturbed again, just press that red button and someone will come.

'We've got him in here because he was so distressed and also, as you'll notice, he's not very fragrant at the moment. We've been more concerned with getting him rehydrated and stabilised than dealing with his personal hygiene issues.'

Maurice looked at the bruised and battered figure in the bed. He looked younger than he had imagined, nothing more than a boy.

'Eh, bonny lad, what have they done to you?' he asked quietly. 'Has he said anything? Given any indication of who he might be?'

'He just keeps repeating the same thing over and over, from the scriptures. We've not heard him say anything else at all yet. We're not even sure if he understands what's said to him.'

'I'll just sit here with him, then, see if he wakes up again. Would it be all right to touch him? To hold his hand, perhaps? It might be reassuring, if he's very frightened.'

The nurse looked unsure.

'I don't know about that. He seems to panic when he's touched. That's why we've had to keep him sedated.'

'I'm a dad. I have twin girls. I'm good with kids. I operate on their level. I'll see how I get on, but I'll just sit here quietly for now.'

'I'll let Mr Khan's registrar know you're here and if he gets a moment he can perhaps come and have a word with you about him. We're busy and short-staffed, as usual, but if I get chance, I'll try to find someone to bring you a cup of tea at some point, if you'd like? Or coffee?'

Maurice pulled up a chair and put it next to the bed.

'Tea would be marvellous, thank you. No sugar.' He patted his waistline self-consciously. 'I'm meant to be losing weight.'

The nurse left them. Maurice sat down next to the bed, one of his big hands on top of the covers, next to one of Levi's. The young man was asleep, twitching slightly, his head occasionally moving from side to side. Close up, Maurice could see more of his injuries. His mouth and lips looked cracked and burnt. And the nurse hadn't been exaggerating about the smell. He clearly hadn't been cleaned up in some time.

Time passed slowly. There was nothing Maurice could do except wait. He was a patient man. As he saw the young man slowly seemed to be moving into a lighter phase of sleep, he spoke quietly to him, meaningless words, soothing.

Levi's eyelids were fluttering but not opening, not really making any attempt to. It was almost as if he'd found a safe place to take himself to and wasn't ready to come back from it. Not just yet, anyway.

Slowly, Maurice moved his hand nearer, until it was just short of touching Levi's. The weight of it on the covers made the young man's hand slide slightly closer. Softly, almost under his breath, Maurice began to sing as he had so often to his girls when they were little.

'Come here, maw little Jacky
Now aw've smoked me baccy
Let's hev a bit o'cracky
Till the boat comes in
Dance ti' thy daddy, sing ti' thy mammy,
Dance ti' thy daddy, ti' thy mammy sing;
Thou shall hev a fishy on a little dishy,
Thou shall hev a fishy when the boat comes in.'

When the nurse came back in some time later, with the promised cup of tea, she stopped in her tracks just inside the door.

'Good gracious, that's amazing,' she said, keeping her voice down.

The young man was sleeping, seemingly peacefully. The finger and thumb of his hand were wrapped round Maurice's little finger, holding on tightly.

Maurice turned his head and smiled at her, keeping his voice quiet.

'I told you I was good with kids. And this poor young man looks no more than a kid, lying there like that. He must have been to hell and back.'

Drinking his tea was tricky, being held as he was. He kept singing, in between mouthfuls, and was still doing so when the registrar came into the room and introduced himself.

'It's nice to see him sleeping calmly. But I'm afraid I'm going to have to ask you to leave for a moment. I need to run some more tests, to see how he's doing, and we should give him some privacy for that. Some of his injuries aren't very pleasant.'

'I'm a policeman, doctor. There's not a lot I haven't seen. And I do need to know details of his injuries, for my report.'

'I appreciate that, and I will give you all the details. But I do think he needs a moment of privacy while I see to him. I'll be as quick as I can. Especially as you already seem to be doing such a good job of calming him down.'

Maurice took the chance of a leg stretch, a visit to the gents and another cup of tea from the vending machine. He called the boss, while he was waiting outside the door of Levi's room.

'Just checking in, boss. There's nothing much to report yet. He's mostly sleeping, still under sedation, but I've been talking to him, and singing, so he gets used to my voice.'

'We've nothing to report here, yet, either. Steve's still trawling MissPers to see if we can find a match. I'll let you know as soon as we do.'

The door opened and the registrar came out.

'You can go back in now, officer. I've lightened his sedation so he may start to wake up shortly. We've had the toxicology results and there's nothing concerning there. I know Mr Khan was worried about what he might have swallowed to cause the burns to his mouth. But whatever it was hasn't shown up on the tests so he might not have swallowed it. Or he perhaps vomited it back up.

'One thing which is currently causing him some pain and distress is the amount of bruising and swelling to the testicles.'

Maurice couldn't retain the involuntary wince, nor the need to shift his weight slightly as he stood listening.

'From what I can see, it looks almost as if they've been clamped in something, partly crushed. It would certainly explain his level of discomfort and agitation. I imagine either of us would react in pretty much the same way if anyone did that to us.'

It was mid-afternoon when there was a quiet knock on Ted's door and Steve's head appeared in the gap as he opened it slightly when instructed to. Just a short time before, the two of them and Mike had been sitting together companionably, having a drink and a sandwich in the nearby pub, The Grapes. Yet in the work setting, Steve always seemed to be in awe of the boss.

'Come in, Steve. Have you got something for me?' Ted asked, seeing the printed sheet in Steve's hand.

'A possible ID, sir. It's a young man, Darren Lee, who went missing in Preston six months ago, and no reported sightings of him since.'

Ted nodded to him to sit down as he took the sheet of paper and studied the details and the photograph.

'You'll need to get this over to Maurice to see if he recognises him.'

'Already done, sir. Maurice says it could be but it's hard to tell. Levi's very bruised and battered and also thin. But the age would fit, just seventeen. There's something else which makes me think it could be our Levi.'

He hesitated. It was always a bit like pulling teeth, getting Steve to say what was on his mind, although he was an astute and intelligent officer who was often right. Ted encouraged him to go on.

'Darren went missing after going out with friends. He was last seen going to a gay bar.'

He hesitated again.

'It's fine, Steve, you can say gay bar. It's not politically incorrect.'

'Yes, sir. It just got me thinking, though. Levi is reciting biblical text relating to homosexuality. Darren Lee disappeared after visiting a gay bar. Levi appears to have been tortured, possibly electric shocks, maybe having to drink something corrosive. Or wash his mouth out with it. Do you think this is someone's idea of the so-called gay conversion therapy?'

Ted leaned back in his chair to consider his answer.

'Firstly, good work in finding this. Secondly, your theory is interesting, but we need to be cautious about getting ahead of ourselves. It is one possible explanation, but it might take us off in the wrong direction, if we're not careful.

'Right, what I'd like you to do now is first to check with someone at Preston that there's no update on this Darren Lee.

We don't want to be approaching his next of kin if he's been found alive or, even worse, if there's not been a good outcome. You know sometimes these things don't get updated as soon as they should so check first, please.

'After that, speak to the next of kin, as tactfully as possible. Warn them that it might not be Darren, then see about getting them here, as soon as they can come. If they're not mobile, get Preston to arrange a car. And yes, they will tell you they don't have the resources. Be as assertive as you can, but if you get nowhere, let me know and I'll sort it.'

The young man in the bed was starting to stir again. He was once again holding on to Maurice's finger as if his life depended on it. Maurice had been talking and singing to him quietly the whole time as he sat beside the bed. Now instead of the platitudes he'd been repeating, he started telling him, 'You're fine, bonny lad. You're safe. You're in hospital and I'm here to protect you. My name's Maurice. I'm a policeman. No one can hurt you now. I won't let them. You're safe. You can wake up whenever you want to. Nothing bad's going to happen to you, not now. Not while I'm with you.'

He tried using the name Steve had given him, to see if that had any effect.

'Darren? Is it Darren? Are you from Preston? Preston? Does that mean anything to you? You're in Stockport now. In Stepping Hill Hospital. And you're quite safe. I won't let anyone hurt you now. Do you want to tell me who you are, where you come from? Tell me what's happened to you?'

The grip on Maurice's finger tightened in a spasm. The youth's eyelids suddenly snapped open revealing staring mid-brown eyes, which immediately filled with tears.

'Dal,' he said, his voice weak and cracked. 'Dal. Dal, Dal, Dal,'

It was going up in tone now, starting to sound hysterical again.

'It's all right, lad, it's all right. I'm here. Nothing's going to happen now.'

'Daaaaaal!'

It was almost a scream. Reluctantly, Maurice reached across and pressed the red call button. He desperately wanted to talk to the young man, to find out more. But he couldn't let him get as distressed as he was doing. He also hadn't a clue what 'Dal' meant, or even what language it was in. He'd have to let the medics sedate him again for his own good and then try again later.

For once, Maurice the skiver wasn't looking for an excuse to take an early dart and sneak home before his usual time. He felt he'd been making some progress with the young man, whoever he turned out to be, and he wanted to build on that.

Chapter Four

'And you're sure the word is Dal? You've no idea what it means?'

'Not a Scooby, boss,' Maurice replied cheerfully. He'd called the boss with the latest update. 'I don't even know if it's an English word. But it clearly means something important to our lad. He was most insistent, trying to make me understand.'

'Steve's had no luck trying to trace the mother of this Darren Lee yet. Local officers know her. They say she's likely to be on a pub crawl somewhere so they're trying to find her. Darren Lee is English, though. Stay with him for now, see if he says anything else and I'll let you know if we find out any more at this end.

'I'll get Steve to see if he can find what Dal might mean. I'll ask Trev, too. See if it means something in any of the languages he speaks. How's the lad doing, other than that?'

Maurice repeated what the registrar had told him. 'They've got him in a quiet side room for the moment until he stabilises. He stinks to high heaven. I hope they might be able to clean him up a bit before his mum sees him, if he is this Darren and they do manage to find her.'

'Did you record him saying it?'

'Sorry, no. He took me a bit by surprise. It was just the word Dal, though.'

'There's just the possibility that there's an inflection in the word he's saying which might mean something to someone who knew the language, if it isn't English. Good job, though,

Maurice, stay with him and keep me updated.'

He ended the call then immediately dialled another number.

'What does the word Dal mean to you?'

'Indian food,' Trev replied promptly. 'Is that a hint about what you'd like to eat tonight?'

'It wasn't, but it would be nice. I'm not sure what time I'll get home, though. Does it signify anything else?'

'Delta Air Lines? An airfield in Texas, I think. Dallas Love, or something like that. Have I won a prize?'

Ted chuckled. 'Play your cards right when I do finally get home and you might just get lucky.'

He could hear piped music in the background so he asked, 'Where are you?'

'Shopping. It's what police grass widows do when their husbands desert them. It's all going on your card and I'm in Cheshire, so it's going to be expensive. I'm actually meeting Bizzie shortly for coffee. Things are hotting up on the Douglas front so she needs more outfits and I am now her official stylist.'

Ted was still smiling to himself as he rang off. Trev was famous for his improbable friendships. Professor Nelson, the forensic pathologist with whom Ted often worked, had become a big fan of Trev's and especially of his Triumph Bonneville motorbike, on which he'd taken her out for a spin on several occasions. She was now once again dating her childhood sweetheart, Douglas Campbell, a cardiac consultant, and had turned to Trev for wardrobe advice. He never needed any excuse to go shopping, especially as Ted hated it and had to be dragged under sufferance.

Ted went back into the main office to find Steve.

'Any word from Preston on the mother, yet?'

'Not yet, sir, they're still looking. They did warn me that even if they find her today she may not be fit for anything, certainly not coming here.'

'It might not actually be a bad thing if it has to wait until tomorrow. Give the hospital chance to get him more settled and clean him up a bit before the mother sees him, if that's who he is.

'Maurice seems to be working his usual charms and Levi appears to be calmer, at least when Maurice is with him. He's also started saying something else, just one word. Dal. Can you see if you can find out what it might mean? Also did you find any similar cases anywhere else? We'd have heard if it was within our force area, but see if there's been anything else further afield. It might just help us. Thanks, Steve.'

'Nothing yet, sir, but I'll keep looking.'

It wasn't long before Steve came tapping on his door once more.

'Sir, I've found a very similar case, in Humberside. Young lad, seventeen, disappeared after going out with friends. He was found wandering naked, a few months later, repeating biblical phrases and showing evidence of having been tortured.

'I spoke to a DS in Hull who was involved in the case. It's still an open case. No one was ever found or convicted for it. The DS offered to come over tomorrow for a face-to-face meeting, rather than a conference call. He said he can't come over in the morning, he's going to church with his family, but he could come in the afternoon, with all the case notes, if that suits you, boss?'

Ted went quiet, long enough for Steve to shift uncomfortably.

'Was that not right, boss?'

'You did the right thing, Steve. And that's exactly what he said to you?'

When Steve nodded, he said, 'Can you give me the contact details for this DS, please? I'd like a word with him.'

When Steve had brought him the details, Ted made the call.

'DS Groves? This is DCI Darling from Stockport. I believe you've been talking to one of my DCs, Steve Ellis, about a case?'

'Hello, sir, yes, that's right. I'm coming over tomorrow afternoon with copies of all our case files. It's still open, no arrests yet, not even any suspects.'

'And you can't come in the morning because you're going to church, I understand?'

There was a slight pause before the DS replied, 'That's right, sir. But I hope to be with you about one o'clock, if that suits you?'

'I appreciate your offer to come in person when you're not under any obligation to do so. But can I just explain to you why that doesn't suit me. I've got a seriously injured young man lying in a hospital bed, who would no doubt like to be spending Sunday morning with his family, too. Your case sounds, on the face of it, identical to mine, and I would very much like to get my hands on whatever sick piece of work is doing this sort of thing to young men. So it would suit me much better if you could forget your usual weekend routine and get yourself over here first thing in the morning. Either that or can you scan and send the files now then we'll conference call once I've read them, later today.'

There was an even longer pause before the DS replied, his tone measured, 'Sir, I apologise if I've given you the impression of being less than cooperative. To be fair, I'm not on the rota to work at all tomorrow and I clearly misunderstood from your DC the urgency of my visit. I understood from him that you would prefer to meet in person, which is why I offered to come myself. I will, of course, come first thing in the morning. Is nine o'clock better for you? I'll try to make it earlier if I possibly can.'

'Thank you, Sergeant. Nine o'clock. Please don't be late.'

He ended the call abruptly, feeling angry and realising it was irrational. The DS clearly hadn't appreciated the urgency, it was nothing more than that. Nor was he under any obligation to come. So much was done by conference call these days. But Ted was burning with a desire to get his hands on whoever had done this, especially if this was not the first such case.

He was not a big fan of organised religion. He realised that might have been slanting his view. His mother had always been a chapel-goer. She'd insisted on taking him along every Sunday when he was small, largely to hear him sing. He had a good voice. But his father had been an atheist and Ted felt closer to his way of thinking, having been brought up by him for much of his life.

It was getting time to let the team go home for the day. He'd arranged a quick catch-up with Mike and Steve before they left, so he wanted to phone Maurice for any further update.

'Nothing new here, boss. He's been sleeping again a lot of the time. Any news on his mother, if it is the right person?'

'That looks like being tomorrow now, from what Preston say. We're just going to have a debrief then pack up here. There's not a lot we can usefully do for now. There's a similar case in Humberside, unsolved. Their DS is coming over in the morning so we can compare notes. What time are you planning on knocking off there? I think Megan's on tomorrow, isn't she? Perhaps she could sit with him?'

'No worries, boss, I'll come in. I feel I've made a bit of a connection and I'd like to carry on with it. And don't worry about the overtime. You don't need to log it, if it's difficult.'

Ted smiled to himself. Maurice the skiver volunteering for unpaid overtime. It was typical of the man he really was, behind the stereotypical façade.

'You're a good man, Maurice. I'll see you tomorrow.'

Something in the kitchen smelt delicious as Ted let himself into the house. He'd sent Trev a text to let him know roughly what time he would be back. He realised how hungry he was as he savoured the aromas. He went over to where Trev was stirring pans on the cooker and kissed him on the cheek.

'Here you go, tarka dal, with no otters in it, despite the

name. With naan bread, sag aloo and some spicy chicken.'

'Wow, I'm impressed. Where did you find the time to do this, if you shopped until you dropped with Bizzie?'

Trev laughed as he turned the heat off under the pans.

'I cheated. It came from a posh deli. I just put it in pans to heat it up. I was going to pass it off as all my own work but I can't lie to you, officer. You have me bang to rights.'

Because Trev had been out most of the day, the kitchen table was free from its usual chaos. He started to lay it, ready for them to eat as Ted gratefully pulled off his tie and undid the top button of his shirt. He took his jacket off and hung it on the back of his chair.

'It's ready, but I can hold it back a moment if you want to shower and change first?'

'I'd like to eat now, if that suits. It smells good and I'm hungrier than I thought. Did you have a good time? Will I be overdrawn when I get the credit card bill?'

Trev began dishing up, putting the plates on the table.

'Probably. But you like me to look nice. Anyway, I've hidden the receipts for the worst of it. How was your day? Did you make any progress?'

'We've found another, case with a similar MO, from Humberside. A DS from there is coming in the morning to compare notes. I may have got off on the wrong foot with him.'

'That's not like you. Is the case getting to you already?'

Ted was savouring his first mouthful of the curry. He nodded his appreciation.

'This is good. Nearly as good as yours. It's a tough case, yes, but I'm trying to leave work at the nick.'

'Good, because, if I remember rightly from what you said earlier, I'm on a promise tonight and I don't want anything distracting your attention.'

'There's a DS Groves down here for you, sir. Do you want me to send him up?'

Bill was on duty at the front desk. He and Ted went way back and were usually on first name terms. If he was calling him sir, it was because there was a DS from another station within earshot.

'Thanks, Bill, and no, don't worry, I'll come down. I want to make him feel welcome since he went to some lengths to tell me I've spoilt his day off by getting him to come over here.'

The DS was standing at the front desk, making small-talk with Bill, when Ted went downstairs. He turned to greet Ted, his hand held out.

'DCI Darling? I'm DS Groves, sir. Ben. We spoke on the phone.'

'Thank you for coming, and for being prompt,' Ted told him as he shook his hand. 'If you'd like to follow me up to my office, I'll put the kettle on before we begin.'

The message was clear. They'd talk once in private, not before.

On their way through the main office, Ted introduced the DS to his team members who were on duty for the day. Mike Hallam was in again, DCs Megan Jennings and Sal Ahmed had replaced Steve and Maurice. Mike was making sure they were up to speed.

True to his word, Ted headed first to put the kettle on.

'I have coffee or green tea. If you want anything else, I can get someone to get it for you.'

He turned in time to see Groves wrinkle his nose at the suggestion of green tea.

'Coffee will be fine, sir. Black, one sugar. Thank you. I'm not a green tea sort of person.'

'It's my zen drink. Helps calm me down. I think we got off on the wrong foot yesterday and I wanted to apologise. I was wanting to get ahead with this case and I was feeling frustrated. I shouldn't have taken it out on you. You were under no obligation to come here at all, certainly not on your day off.'

'My fault entirely, sir. I didn't appreciate how soon you

wanted my input. I look forward to helping in any way I can. Although I have to say at the outset, we didn't make much progress at all.'

Ted produced the drinks and the two men sat down on opposite sides of the desk.

'Tell me everything you can about your case.'

'A young lad, Robbie Mitchell, seventeen, went out for drinks with mates one evening, as he often did, but never came back. His parents reported him missing almost immediately. A good lad, never been in any trouble, worked hard at school, completely out of character. We searched, did house to house, radio and television appeals, local papers, social media, posters up, the works.

'He turned up one night, wandering about stark naked in a quiet lane out in the sticks. He was in a bad way, malnourished, dehydrated and showing visible signs of having been restrained and tortured. He couldn't, or wouldn't, say anything at all, except for a passage from the Bible.'

'Let me guess. Leviticus 20:13?'

'No, sir, Luke 4, verses 5-8. From the King James version.

'And the devil, taking him up into an high mountain, shewed unto him all the kingdoms of the world in a moment of time.

'And the devil said unto him, All this power will I give thee, and the glory of them: for that is delivered unto me; and to whomsoever I will I give it.

'If thou therefore wilt worship me, all shall be thine.

'And Jesus answered and said unto him, Get thee behind me, Satan: for it is written, Thou shalt worship the Lord thy God, and him only shalt thou serve.'

'So nothing there about homosexuality? And was this lad, this Robbie, going to gay bars or anything like that? Was he known to be gay? Our victim had been to a gay bar and he was quoting a passage about homosexuality.'

'Talking to his parents, it seems Robbie hadn't quite made

up his mind about whether or not he was gay and he did sometimes go to gay bars. Sometimes young lads get a bit of an idea about that sort of thing, don't they, but then they grow out of it. From what his mother said, I formed the impression he was a bit sensitive, quiet, into music and the arts rather than stuff the other lads of his age liked, football, bikes, that sort of thing.'

There was a prolonged silence. Anyone who knew Ted would instantly see it as a warning signal. DS Groves had never met him before and had clearly not done his homework in finding out anything about him.

Finally, Ted spoke, his voice quiet, as ever, his tone level, measured.

'There's no reason why you should know, DS Groves, but I'm gay. I've known since I was a small boy. It's not something you make your mind up about. I'm not into football either but I have black belts in four martial arts and I was an SFO. My partner, who's as gay as I am, unsurprisingly, part owns a motorbike dealership and rides a Triumph Bonneville.'

It was the DS's turn to stay silent. He looked stricken. Eventually he spoke.

'Sir, I am so sorry, that came out completely wrong. I didn't know, but it's no excuse. I can only apologise. It was completely crass of me. I didn't mean any stereotyping. I really didn't.'

'You're not the first, and you won't be the last, sadly. It's just that it might be significant. So was he ever able to say anything about where he'd been? What had happened to him? Did he give any explanation at all?'

'Nothing at all, sir. Once the hospital had finished with his physical injuries, they tried to get him a bed in a psychiatric unit, as clearly he was very disturbed. But you know what it's like for young people. There just aren't the beds available anywhere.

'They discharged him home, into the care of his parents.

But they really couldn't cope at all. He'd changed completely. He was nothing like their Robbie. They couldn't even communicate with him properly. He would scream with terror if anyone got too near to him or tried to touch him, especially a man. Even his father, and they'd always got on well.'

'Would he talk to us, do you think? We have a specialist officer who's already making a lot of progress gaining the trust of our victim.'

'I'm afraid not, sir. I'm sorry, I thought you knew. Robbie died. He became depressed and suicidal. He really needed to be sectioned but there was still no bed available. There were a few incidents where we had to send someone round to try to calm him down when he was trying to do away with himself.

'One night it was very bad. He'd found his dad's Stanley knife and locked himself in his room with it. Two officers went round, ones who knew him, who'd been able to help before, but he was worse than ever.

'He jumped out of the window, onto the garage roof, then down into the garden. He ran straight out of the driveway into the path of a lorry. Killed outright. I'm really sorry, sir, I thought you knew.

'I've made you a full copy of the file, everything we had.'

The DS took a folder out of his briefcase and put it on the desk in front of Ted who reached for his reading glasses and started to look through it.

'How long was he missing for?'

'About six months, sir.'

'About?' Ted queried, looking again at the notes.

'Sorry sir, it was exactly six months, to the day.'

'Is that significant, I wonder?'

He got out his notes on the case his team were working on.

'Now this is very interesting. Your Robbie was missing for exactly six months. And our victim, Darren, if that's who it is, disappeared exactly six months to the day after Robbie reappeared. So that gives us three blocks of six months. Could that be significant, I wonder?

‘And then we have the biblical texts, one about the sins of homosexuality, the other about … what, exactly? Temptation? Overcoming it?

‘Tell me, DS Groves, you’re clearly a religious man. Is there any biblical significance to the number six?’

‘It’s supposed to signify man and human weakness, the evils of Satan and the manifestation of sin. Man was created on the sixth day and men are appointed to labour for six days and worship on the seventh, according to the scriptures.’

The DS hesitated, pausing to drink some of his coffee.

‘There’s something else, sir, which is probably going to sound completely crazy. There is a significance to the numbers six six six. The number of the beast.’

‘I knew there was something about that. I saw *The Omen* and the sequel, *Damien*. My partner’s a real film buff. It’s in that, isn’t it? Damien the Antichrist? He had three sixes on his head. So you’re suggesting not just some possible religious fanatic but, what? A devil worshipper?’

‘It could be a coincidence, sir.’

‘I don’t like coincidences, Sergeant. They make me nervous.’

Chapter Five

'Did you look into other, similar, cases, during this investigation?'

'We didn't, sir. You know our track record on Humberside isn't brilliant and I'm not proud of it. It's not for want of trying by some of us. And please don't take this as an excuse, or as blame-shifting. But my gaffer at the time – he's retired now – was after an easy life. His line was that a teenage lad of that age going missing, even if it wasn't usual, wasn't necessarily anything sinister. He may just have had enough of being the perfect teen and gone off the rails.'

'But we now know he didn't, don't we? Was there never a case review, if this was sitting on the files without result for as long as that?'

The DS shifted in his seat, looking awkward.

'Things haven't always been done quite as they should. A few of us did try to make noises, sir, but we were constantly being told about budgets and lack of designated, experienced officers. I'm sure you've heard similar arguments. And I'm really not trying to make excuses. I have children of my own. It upset me that we didn't do better. Especially when we found out what had happened to Robbie. The problem was that we couldn't talk to him and we had nothing else to go on.'

Ted picked up his desk phone and buzzed through to Sal in the main office.

'Sal, where are you up to with finding any other similar cases, please? We need that information. I'm praying there aren't. Two is too many, but let's check every angle.'

He'd no sooner put the phone down than it rang again.

'Right, thank you for the heads up.'

He looked across the desk at DS Groves.

'That was Preston to say that Darren Lee's mother is on her way. I'll talk to her here first. I'm anxious not to subject her to seeing the lad in hospital if we can rule out definitely that he's her son. It wouldn't be a pleasant experience for her if we got it wrong. They'll be here in under an hour.

'What I want to do next is to read right through your file looking for similarities and differences. My hierarchy here is a little complex. I'm answerable to our own Superintendent in this station, but also to Detective Superintendent Baker if we pick up a case which takes us out of our own division.

'I'm not promising that we can do any better than your team did, but if there's any chance that we can make some sort of progress, it would probably be useful for us to share information. Subject to what my bosses and yours say, I would propose that you, or whoever else worked and is still working on your case, might join some of our briefings. We'd also need to bring someone from Preston on board, whoever was handling the disappearance of our victim. I'm not wanting to tread on any toes, and it's just an idea at the moment.

'I think we'd both agree that whichever of us managed to put their hands on whoever is doing this would be doing an important public service.'

He stood up as he finished speaking.

'I'd like to thank you again for coming over, and to apologise again for sounding a bit tetchy. I hope between us we may be able to make a bit of progress.'

After the DS had left, Ted went to speak to Megan Jennings. He wanted her to sit in while he talked to Mrs Lee, once she arrived from Preston. The presence of another woman might be comforting for her. He noticed Megan was looking decidedly peaky, not on her usual form.

'Are you all right, Megan? You don't look well.'

'Sorry boss. I think it's Maurice's cooking. He tries, bless him, but I think having Friday night's efforts reheated for supper last night was not such a good idea. It was bad enough the first time round. I'll be fine to be with Mrs Lee, I'm sure.'

'I'll send the Preston car back and we'll sort out how to get her home when the time comes. They won't want one of their cars tied up here on taxi service, I've no doubt. They're also bringing us copies of their full file on Darren Lee's disappearance. Perhaps you'd be kind enough to collect Mrs Lee from the front desk when she arrives and bring her up to my office, then get the case files brought up here.'

Ted mentally reproached himself when Megan opened his door and let Mrs Lee enter first. He'd had a mental image of what he was expecting, based on the information from Preston, and he was wrong. He'd been judgemental in his preconceptions, something he hated in others.

The woman who came into his office as he stood up to greet her was around forty. Her clothes were neat and clean though not an expensive make. Her hair and make-up had been done with care but not enough expertise to disguise the dark rings under her brown eyes, and the premature wrinkles. He noticed the slight tremor as she took his proffered hand. She looked like what she probably was – an ordinary person trying the only way she knew to get through the heartache of extraordinary circumstances.

'Is it him? Is it my Dal?' she asked hopefully, as she took the seat Ted offered. He'd found a spare chair and put it next to her for Megan to sit down.

'Dal?'

'It's what he likes to call himself. His initials, you see. Darren Anderton Lee. Darren Anderton?'

She looked at Ted as if she thought the name ought to mean something to him.

'He played for Spurs. And England. Dal's dad was mad

about football. He wanted his son to be the same. Used to drag him off to matches, United mostly, until he was old enough to start refusing.'

Ted had no interest in most team sports, certainly not football. The name meant nothing to him.

'Dal was never interested. He was always a bit, well, girly in his interests, you might say. He's always wanted to be a fashion designer. His dad blamed me. Said I was too soft with him and he should man up. That's why we split up, him and me. Dal stayed with me. Is it really him?'

'Mrs Lee, would you please excuse me for just one moment while I make a quick phone call? Megan, can you make a cup of tea for Mrs Lee, please?'

Ted went out into the main office and called Maurice at the hospital.

'Maurice? Dal. It's his nickname, it's what he calls himself. His initials. Is he awake? Could you try it on him, please, and let me know how he reacts. Then I'll know whether or not to bring Mrs Lee to see him.'

He heard a noise which he imagined was the phone being put down on the bed, then Maurice's voice, calm, quiet, soothing.

'Dal? Is that you, bonny lad? Is your name Dal? That's what you were trying to tell me?'

A sound like a wail of desolation, then loud, ragged sobbing.

'It's all right, lad. It's all right now. Everything's all right. You're safe now and your mam's coming. She's on her way now. Hush, now, it's fine.'

There was a crackle as Maurice picked up the phone.

'I think you got your answer, boss. This is Darren Lee.'

Megan drove Ted's official car to the hospital with Mrs Lee sitting stiff and quiet in the front seat and Ted in the back.

'I need to warn you, Mrs Lee, that Darren, if it is him, is

very distressed. He's clearly been through a lot. I have a trained officer sitting with him who's helped enormously, but it's possible Darren may not be willing or even able to talk to you. I should prepare you by mentioning too that he's clearly been living in very poor conditions for some time and the nursing staff might not yet have been able to do much to clean him up.'

'If it is my Dal I won't care what he looks like. I just want to give him a big hug …'

Her voice broke. Ted wisely said no more, to give her the time to recover.

He'd phoned ahead to let Maurice know they were on their way with Mrs Lee. He let Megan lead the way into the room. The young man in the bed seemed to be sleeping. His eyes were closed, his body still, though tense. His hand was again clutching on to Maurice's.

Maurice nodded as the others appeared, not wanting to let go, although he did stop the gentle, quiet murmuring and singing he had been doing.

Mrs Lee stood transfixed, staring at the wounded body in the bed. Some sort of an attempt had been made to clean him up a bit but there was still a strong fetid smell coming from him.

'Oh Dal. My lovely Dal. Whatever has happened to you?'

His eyelids twitched at the sound of a familiar voice, then opened fully. His eyes still appeared terrified, panic-stricken. His mother looked towards Maurice, her expression clearly seeking some sign from him that it was all right to approach.

Maurice got carefully to his feet, allowing the grip on his hand to remain unbroken.

'Your mam's here now, Dal, lad. Here she is. She's come to see you.'

Maurice nodded to her to move closer. He took her hand in his large spare one and gently laid it over his where Dal was clinging to it.

The boy turned his head towards her, unfocused eyes

flooding with tears, sobs wracking the emaciated body.

'Dal,' was all he managed to articulate.

'Yes, my darling boy. Yes, Dal. You're safe now. Your mum's here.'

Megan was dabbing her eyes and blowing her nose as she and Ted walked back to the car. They'd arranged with the hospital that Mrs Lee would stay there for the time being. Megan had offered to get her a few basic toiletries and essentials and drop them off when she went back to collect Maurice at the end of their shift. The two of them were spending a lot more time in each other's company and things seemed to be going well between them.

'Sorry, boss, you must think I'm a right soppy thing but that really got to me. I couldn't help thinking how I would feel if anything like that ever happened to my son Felix.'

Now that they had a positive ID on their victim, Ted could start to take the case forward. He'd need to talk in detail to Jim Baker and the Super, to see what involvement with other forces there would be and who would be leading the enquiry. He'd called them both to ask for an early morning meeting the following day, Monday, before he briefed his team.

Once he was back from the hospital he got his first chance to discuss with Mike, Sal and Megan the coincidence of the number six which had shown up from his earlier talks with the Humberside DS. It sounded even more far-fetched when he said it aloud in a team briefing, but it was something they couldn't overlook.

'I'll need someone to go over the full file from Preston on their handling of Darren's disappearance and give me a detailed summing up of the main points until I get chance to read it myself. And let's start up a proper board, now we have his name.'

Sal had his head down, reading through the notes on his desk. Then he looked up and spoke.

'Boss, I was just going to say, there was another one. Further back. The first we know of so far. I got the details shortly before you got back. In Lincolnshire. Exactly the same thing. Another young lad disappeared, after a night out in Gainsborough. Tim Phillips. He was found wandering in a lane near to Market Rasen. And yes, I just checked, following on from what you were saying. He was missing for exactly six months and Robbie Mitchell, from Humberside, disappeared six months to the day from when Tim Phillips was found.'

'So now we have five lots of six. A total of thirty. Tim Phillips, missing for six months, then a six-month break. Robbie Mitchell, missing for six months then another break of six months. Then Darren missing for six months. What does that mean? Is there some significance to five times six? Or does that mean there are more to uncover and we've just not found them yet?'

Trev had been out all day with friends, getting in not long before Ted. He was all too familiar with being left on his own because of Ted's job and had learnt to deal with it. He was the gregarious one of the two, always wanting company when Ted wasn't around. Ted was more solitary by nature but he didn't expect Trev to sit around alone waiting for him. Their long-standing relationship was based on trust and understanding. It was almost certainly why it had lasted a lot longer than that of many coppers Ted knew.

'Just as well I bought plenty yesterday. I've not had time to make anything so it's reheated leftovers, I'm afraid. Is that all right?'

'Perfect. Anything. As long as it's safe. Poor Megan was looking green today after eating Maurice's leftovers.'

Trev laughed. 'That sounds gruesome. I imagine you mean leftover food Maurice had cooked? It won't take long, if you want to change first.'

'I will do, thanks. You know how much I hate wearing a

suit, especially at the weekend. How was your day? What did you get up to?'

'Went out with a bunch of bikers to get drunk, stoned and have free love in the park.'

'I am listening, you don't have to test me to check.'

Trev laughed again. 'How do you know it's not true? And I know what you're like when you're on a case. I'm lucky to get half of your attention. I hope you're making progress, though?'

'We're just starting out and it's going to be a tough one. I need to sort out the logistics of it first with Jim and the Ice Queen as it involves other forces. I can't promise being much company while it lasts. And remember I've got that big trial coming up too. Our teenage serial killer. I'm called as a witness so I'm going to be stuck in court until I've given my evidence.'

'Just as long as I have your full attention and total slavish devotion when you do manage to get home. Go. Get changed. This won't be long.'

As Ted obediently headed for the stairs, he called after him, 'And phone your mother. I was speaking to her earlier and she said you haven't phoned her.'

'Six six six and devil worship? Seriously, Ted?' Detective Superintendent Jim Baker was clearly sceptical once Ted had finished outlining to him and his own Super the information they had so far.

They were in the Ice Queen's office, enjoying her freshly-brewed coffee, as Ted brought them up to speed on the case in their own area and the possible links to others.

'It's too much of a coincidence to ignore, having three cases to date where the intervals are exactly six months to the day in each case.'

'I agree that it appears to be too strong not to have some sort of significance. So are you suggesting a pooling of resources with the other forces involved?' Superintendent

Debra Caldwell asked.

'If it's the same person carrying out these attacks that would surely make sense. The Humberside victim sadly died so that trail has gone cold. I don't yet know anything about the Lincolnshire one until I get the files. I'll send someone over there to find out more. So far, we've not been able to question Darren Lee about what happened to him, although we do now have a positive ID on him. I'm hopeful that between Maurice and Darren's mother, we may get something there.'

'This is an assault, albeit a serious one. Is it something which Uniform could wrap up, with just a couple of your team to steer the enquiry?'

'It's more than an assault, Jim, it's systematic torture over a prolonged period of time. On possibly more than one occasion. Surely that comes within my team's Serious and Serial remit? Even though not all the related crimes took place within our force area.'

'You've got the serial killer case coming up in court. That's going to tie you up for quite some time, in all probability. I just don't want you stretching yourself too thin.'

'Jo and Rob will be back tomorrow, that puts us back up to full strength. This is something we should be able to get somewhere with, and if we can bring someone in, it's a good result.'

Ted was far too astute to miss the look which passed between his two senior officers when he mentioned team numbers. He looked suspiciously from one to the other.

'What's going on? What do you two know about that I don't?'

The Ice Queen replied so quickly it only served to make him more suspicious.

'Absolutely nothing at all. Nothing concrete. But you know full well that Superintendent Baker and I are constantly coming under pressure over staffing levels and making best use of all available resources.'

'So we have some sick pervert kidnapping and torturing young men and leaving them too damaged to tell anyone what's happened to them and we can't do anything about it as we don't have enough officers for the case?'

'Wind your neck in, Ted,' Jim Baker told him. 'There's nothing definite yet. Just that we need to be even more careful than usual about what resources are used and where. I would suggest that you go over the files from Humberside and Lincolnshire, then get someone from Preston to come here for a discussion on theirs. Then we'll review what we've got and what resources we need to throw at it.'

'I would just remind you, Chief Inspector, that as well as your big court case coming up, there's also the matter of ADRs to be carried out before too much longer.'

Ted groaned inwardly. As far as he was concerned Annual Development Reviews were yet another exercise in box-ticking. He spent enough time with his team to know which members were doing their jobs correctly and if they were happy in their work.

He'd do his inspector, Jo Rodriguez's review himself, but hopefully Jo could do most of the others and just let Ted look over the results to make sure all was well. He knew it had to be done but between the ADRs and his court appearance, he was worried he wouldn't have as much time as he wanted to work on this case.

He badly wanted to get his hands on whoever was carrying out such acts on young men, and soon. If the number theory was correct, they may have up to six months before the attacker struck again. Unless whatever was motivating them escalated and prompted them to act again sooner.

Chapter Six

All the team members were in on time when Ted went back upstairs to brief them. Those who'd worked the weekend would claw back some hours in the week, if it was possible. Maurice had come in to report before going back to the hospital.

'Dal's a bit more settled now he's got his mam with him, though he's still not saying much that makes any sense. Mrs Lee is planning on staying as long as it takes. She works as a cleaner. She's phoned her regulars to let them know what's happened.'

'What are the doctors saying?'

'Physically he's doing a bit better, boss. They need to get him eating a bit. He's clearly not had very much while he's been missing so they need to take it gently. It will be difficult for him to start with. Mentally, they're a bit more guarded. He's not even said much to his mam, apart from just repeating his name and occasionally still spouting the bible stuff. They're trying to get a psych consult for him but they just wanted to stabilise him a bit more first.

'I was planning to go back as soon as we've finished up here, if that's all right? Just to see if I can get anything out of him?'

Ted nodded. 'That's what I was going to suggest. You've clearly made a good start at gaining his trust, so let's build on that.

'Jo, are you and Rob finished up in Bolton now?'

'All over bar the shouting and a bit of paperwork, which one of us can handle, boss,' DI Jo Rodriguez, Ted's right hand man, informed him. 'Do you want me on this case, if I leave Rob to dot the i's and cross the t's on the Bolton one?'

'I'd like you coordinating house to house near where Darren was found. Ask Inspector Turner what Uniform officers he can spare you and take some of our team with you as well,'

He looked round the room to see who would be best suited for which role.

'Megan, you're with Jo. I want every property anywhere near where Darren turned up to be visited and the occupants questioned. Steve and Sal, brief Océane on what information you've found so far then you're with Jo, too. Océane, can you look further and see if you can find anything else similar anywhere? Also let's look at previous offenders with anything like this kind of form. Don't discount anyone who's still inside. There's the possibility they may have boasted to another inmate who's since been released and gone on to commit copycat crimes.

'I'm hoping to have something more up your specialised street to get stuck into, Océane. I want to find out about mobile phones belonging to our victims. Were they were ever found, and how thoroughly were their contents gone over? There's a chance someone may have overlooked the possibility that these young men were taken by someone they all knew, someone they were already in contact with. So we need to get hold of those phones and get you to dig out all their secrets, even anything which may have been deleted, if that's possible. They may never have been traced, of course, but let's check in all cases.'

Océane nodded in understanding. She was their civilian computer expert. Ted liked to split Steve up from her when he could. They spent a lot of their off duty time together. So far they were both being professional about it, but Steve was the youngest member of the team and the least experienced. It was good to get him out doing some legwork and not just to separate him from computers and Océane for a time.

'Right, I need someone to go over to Lincolnshire to talk to them and to get the full file on their victim. Also to ask about the phone in that case.' Ted slipped his reading glasses on to check his notes for the name. 'Tim Phillips. Disappeared from Gainsborough, found near Market Rasen, so start with a phone call to Gainsborough to see who's been dealing with it.'

'I could go and talk to the Yeller Bellies, boss?' DC Jezza Vine offered.

Ted gave her a stern look over the top of his glasses. He wouldn't allow any hint of disrespect from his team members and that sounded to him as if it might be on a par with calling Uniform officers Woodentops.

Correctly interpreting his look, Jezza reassured him. 'It's not offensive, it's a nickname for people from Lincolnshire.'

Jezza was a walking edition of Trivial Pursuit. It was one of the main obsessions of her younger brother, Tommy, who was autistic.

'Right, fair enough, just as long as no disrespect was intended. You take the Lincolnshire case for now, bring us back all the available details. And ask about the phone in that case, too, please. Bring it back with you if you can unearth it, or get it sent over to us soon as. Sal, how are you getting on with the file from Preston? Is there anything there that helps us at all? Anything about a phone?'

'Not finished it yet, boss, and so far nothing more than you told us from his mother. Darren seems to have been a diligent student, not in any trouble, and nothing at all to indicate if he went off with someone of his own free will or was forcibly taken. I'm still going through it all, making notes. I'll give Preston a call and find out about a mobile phone.'

'I'm doing the same with the Humberside files on Robbie Mitchell. We need a get-together at the end of play today to pool our resources from the day. Virgil, I haven't forgotten you. We need someone to stay relatively free for anything else which comes our way while we're all on this case. Can you also help Océane to trawl previous offenders, cold cases, anything at all, for any similar pattern. And give DS Groves at Humberside a ring about the mobile phone in that case, if it was ever found. We need it.

'For the time being, Darren Lee is our number one priority. We need to find who's done this to him and stop them before they think of doing it again.'

It would take Jezza a couple of hours to get over to Lincolnshire in her Golf Limited Edition, sticking carefully to the speed limits. If ever it got back to the boss that she'd picked up a speeding ticket whilst on duty she would be in deep trouble. He expected his team members to set an example by obeying the law – all of the laws.

She'd spoken by phone to the local police and had been told to go to the county headquarters building in Nettleham and to ask for a DS Streeter who was handling the file on the victim from Gainsborough.

Jezza hadn't visited the area before and went with a preconception that the whole of Lincolnshire was as flat as a pancake and probably rather dull and grey. She was surprised to discover that Nettleham itself was an attractive, quintessentially English village with warm red-tiled roofs, a square-towered church and a red brick pub which looked as if it might do a decent lunch.

By contrast, the police headquarters building was an uninspired slab of grey concrete which was hopefully more functional than it was attractive.

She made her way to the front desk, warrant card held up ready, where an older uniformed PC greeted her with a 'Yes, duck?'

Jezza had a tendency to be prickly. She'd encountered enough sexism in her career to date, although the official line was that it had been rigorously stamped out. She scrutinised the man's face to see if there was any implied meaning behind the word, but he was smiling pleasantly enough so she assumed it must be a local expression.

'I'm DC Vine, from Stockport. I'm here to see DS Streeter.'

'Right you are, duck. I'll let her know you're here, and we'll get you signed in.'

He made a phone call while Jezza signed herself in, then he smiled at her again.

'The DS said to go straight up. Those stairs over there, up to the next floor, along the corridor and it's the room at the end on the right.'

There were three male officers sitting at desks in the open-plan office which Jezza entered without knocking, knowing she was expected. She was wearing her photo ID round her neck. The men looked up at her with varying degrees of interest, though none of them greeted her.

'I'm looking for DS Streeter?'

One of them nodded towards a desk at the far end of the room, up against a window. Jezza suspected there might be a nice view from there on a fine day. Its occupant raised a hand and waved at her, then stood up as Jezza crossed the room. She was short, smaller than Jezza, her build sporty, hair pulled back into neat cornrows.

'I'm DC Vine, Sarge, from Stockport. Jezza.'

'I'm DS Streeter. You can carry on calling me Sarge,' she said, then her face cracked into an infectious smile, showing dazzling white teeth with a pronounced gap between the front upper incisors. 'Only kidding. Call me Bryony, if you like. Park yourself,' she indicated a chair, then raised her voice to address one of the other officers. 'One of you lazy gits go and get some drinks for my visitor and me.'

The youngest-looking of the other officers, glancing round at the others and seeing no signs of movement, got reluctantly to his feet.

'Coffee?'

'Thanks for telling us in advance what it's going to be, Nigel. I can never tell from what you produce. How do you take it, Jezza?'

'Cautiously, by the sound of it. Could I have a tea, no sugar, please?'

'You can ask for whatever you want. I can guarantee you won't be able to tell from the taste what it is,' the sergeant told her. Then she smiled again as she explained, 'You have to jump on them from time to time, to stop them getting above themselves. Especially being a woman, as short as me, and black, to boot. All in good fun, of course, they know that. They love me really.

'Now, how can I help you? I wasn't on the case, it was before I was transferred here to keep this lot in check, but I've got the file and one of my crew is making you a copy to take back with you. I flicked through it when I heard you were coming over. I gather you've had something similar in your neck of the woods?'

Jezza gave her the brief details of their case and as much as she knew about the one in Humberside.

Bryony was nodding as Jezza spoke.

'Sounds very similar to this one. Tim Phillips, sixteen when he disappeared, had his seventeenth birthday while he was missing, poor sod. Found six months later, wandering naked in a village near Market Rasen. Initially the first responders thought he was off his face on something because he just kept reciting the same thing over and again. On closer examination, they found marks on his body indicating he'd been kept tied up and subjected to some pretty nasty goings on.'

'What was he reciting?'

The DS looked at the notes in front of her.

'Yea, though I walk through the valley of the shadow of death, I will fear no evil: for thou art with me; thy rod and thy staff they comfort me.'

'The Lord is my shepherd? I sang in a school choir for a bit, believe it or not. That's the only reason I know it.'

'If you say so,' the DS said with a grin. 'I know nothing of that stuff. But yes, it says that here in the notes: Psalm 23, The Lord is my shepherd, KJV, whatever that means. There was another bit he kept saying, too:

'He restoreth my soul: he leadeth me in the paths of righteousness for his name's sake.'

'KJV is King James Version of the Bible.' When the DS looked at her inquisitively, Jezza explained, 'I'm not into religion but I live with a kid brother who's mad about Trivial Pursuit. He's making up his own set of questions as he knows the answers to all of the published editions.

'Did Tim Phillips ever say anything about what had happened to him? Where is he now? Would I be able to speak to him?'

'So many questions! Anyone would think you were a detective or something.'

The DS certainly liked a touch of humour. She was about to answer when Nigel reappeared with two mugs of seemingly identical dark brown liquid.

'Ah, this is the office initiation test,' the DS said. 'If you can tell which is meant to be your tea, you win a prize. Go on, then, Nigel, give us a clue. Which is which?'

'Dunno, Sarge. Taste them and see,' the officer said helpfully as he headed back to his desk.

'They'll both be crap, I'm warning you. Just pick whichever you fancy. Or whichever repels you the least.

'Now, our young man, Tim Phillips. No, to my knowledge, he never said anything about what happened. From the notes, it looks as if they really did try everything, including a consultant forensic psychologist. His report is included. In a nutshell, it says that whatever happened to him was so dark he shut it away in a corner of his brain and he may never let it out again.

'Where is he now? I'm not sure. The last mention of him on the file he was in some seedy squat on the edge of Lincoln. Would you be able to speak to him? First we'd have to find him, which won't be easy. Secondly, again from the notes, the last record of him suggests he became a total smackhead, refused to have anything to do with his family or anyone from his past.'

'How does he find the money to fund his habit?'

Again, the DS flicked through the notes in front of her.

'No idea but maybe he's on the rob. Or pimping himself out? He was a nice-looking boy, from the before photos.'

'Is he gay?'

She was again consulting the file. 'Is that significant?'

'I'm not sure. Just that our lad, Darren Lee, had apparently been to a gay bar with friends on the night he was taken and he reappeared spouting verses about homosexuality. What was the nature of Tim's injuries? What was done to him?'

Bryony raised her voice again, addressing the other officers who were studiously ignoring the two of them, getting on with their own work.

'Close your ears, boys, you don't want the visitor to see you with tears in your eyes. According to the medical report, some very nasty things were done to him involving, from the hypothesis in the report, feet in a bowl of water and something like a cattle prod or electric fence unit being applied to his delicate bits. Probably repeatedly, over a prolonged period of time, and he was missing for six months. You can understand why he wouldn't be feeling all that talkative after something like that.

'I've freed up a bit of time today when I heard you were coming so we could go for a drive around the seedy side of the city, just on the off-chance that we might find Tim. It's a long shot, and an even longer one to expect that we might get anything out of him where others have failed. Perhaps if we could find him and if you could get him to understand that what happened to him is still going on, he might just tell us something useful.

'From what I've seen of the file there's absolutely nothing for anyone to go on about his actual disappearance. No one saw him vanish, no one ever found where he'd been held for all that time, and no one saw how he reappeared. No CCTV or anything anywhere. His mobile phone was found near to where it's assumed he disappeared from, so there was no means of tracking his movements from that. Incredibly, it was handed in, but that's perhaps because it was found in a churchyard where probably only the righteous and honest would venture.'

'What happened to the phone? Can I get hold of it? We have a CFI who's brilliant at digging out any secrets that others may have overlooked.'

The DS looked impressed. 'You have your own CFI on tap? I've heard on the grapevine that you've got a good team over there, with an outstanding track record. It must certainly help having the right resources at your disposal.'

'What about family? What happened to him when he left hospital?'

'By all accounts he should have been placed in a secure psychiatric unit and helped to get over it. But, typically, there was nothing available for someone of his age. People don't realise but the mental health services have seen some of the worst cuts in recent years, especially for younger people. I've had some personal experience of that, so I've been looking at the statistics.

'The hospital couldn't put him anywhere with adult males. He'd go hysterical near any man he didn't know and there was simply nowhere else to put him.

'His mother was a single parent. The father had long since disappeared off the scene and she clearly couldn't cope on her own, which seems to be why Tim went off to sofa-surf with anyone who'd have him, or to live in squats with other young drop-outs whilst pickling what was left of his brain.

'Right, so if you've finished your absolutely delightful drink – thank you, Nigel, you truly excelled yourself this time – we'll get the car and I'll give you the guided tour. I'm not promising anything and I'm not holding out much hope. But with luck, by the time we get back, Vinnie will have finished copying the file for you and you can take it with you. Nigel, your punishment for a worse than usual drink is to track down the mobile phone from the Tim Phillips case and have it on my desk by the time Jezza and I get back from our little outing.'

Jezza spent an interesting if depressing few hours with the DS, doing the rounds of back streets, occasionally knocking on doors to ask if anyone knew of Tim Phillips' whereabouts. A few of those they spoke to claimed to know who he was but said they hadn't seen him recently. It wasn't much for Jezza to take back to the next briefing, but at least she now had the full file on the case. Nigel had also managed to recover Tim Phillips' phone from somewhere and that too was waiting for her when she and DS Streeter returned to the HQ building. Jezza suspected that despite her flippant humour, the DS ran a tight ship and when she said jump, her team members asked only how high.

Bryony shook her hand as Jezza started gathering up all the items relating to the case.

'It was nice to meet you, Jezza, and I hope you get somewhere with the cases. It was a pleasant change to have some female company. I love the boys dearly,' she threw an ironic glance at the other officers, still working at their desks, now having been joined by another DC who had been introduced to her as the Vinnie who had copied the files for her, 'but the smell of your perfume makes a pleasant change from testosterone and sweaty feet. Dior's Poison, is it?'

'You're very perceptive, Sarge. Anyone would think you were a detective or something,' Jezza jokingly used the DS's own line back to her. Bryony laughed.

‘We’ll keep an eye out for Tim Phillips and I’ll let you know if we do track him down anywhere. Though like I said, I wouldn’t be too optimistic about getting anything out of him. It was bad enough immediately after the incident. I would say that your chances now are somewhere between nil and bugger all.’

Chapter Seven

It was Thursday before Ted could bring together everyone he wanted for a full briefing between officers from the three forces involved to date in their enquiry. He'd left the complex negotiations required for a joint operation to his bosses. There had been lengthy conference calls between senior officers from all three forces before they could go ahead.

At least it gave them a bit of respite for Jo to start ADRs on the team and for Ted to go over the case files they had to date to make sure he had all the available information at his fingertips.

He'd arranged to use the downstairs conference room to accommodate the larger than usual numbers. He wanted his full team there, with the exception of Virgil. He was leaving him free to pick up anything else which came in. Océane was working on the phones which had now been recovered near the point at which the victims were last seen.

Maurice was in and would go back to the hospital after the briefing. Both he and Darren's mother were getting anxious because the hospital staff were making noises about discharging him. They felt they were close to doing all they could for his physical injuries and he had so far refused to have anything to do with anyone from the psychiatric unit.

Darren was still saying little, even to his mother. He hadn't spoken directly to Maurice, apart from repeating his own nickname, but Maurice's presence didn't seem to produce the same level of panic which the appearance of a male psychiatrist had done. He would still sometimes fall asleep holding on to Maurice's hand, clearly finding some comfort with him there.

DS Streeter had come over from Lincolnshire, bringing Nigel, the maker of bad drinks, with her. DS Groves from Humberside was present, with a DC he introduced as Ruth Fleming. She'd been involved in family liaison with the parents of their victim, Robbie Mitchell, so would bring valuable first-hand knowledge of him and his background.

Two Uniform officers from Preston, who had handled the disappearance of Darren Lee, had also come, Sergeant Janine Walsh and PC Alfie Ridgeway.

Ted had expected either Jim Baker or Superintendent Caldwell, possibly both, to sit in, but the two of them had been called away to yet another budgetary meeting up at Central Park.

Ted called the briefing to order and welcomed the visitors.

'Thank you all for coming. I confess to being the old-fashioned sort who likes to meet in the flesh at least once. After today we should be able to manage any joint briefings via video link.

'I think if we all pool what information we have and compare notes, we might have a much better chance of making some progress. I'm particularly looking for similarities between the cases. If we can establish a pattern between them, it might help us going forward.'

He'd started a whiteboard, with photos of the three young men, their names and details, plus the dates of the cases, clearly showing the six-month intervals.

'So, can we list similarities and differences, please. And we'll need a scribe. Rob? Your handwriting is usually legible. For our visitors, these briefings are informal, a place to kick ideas around. Please feel free to put in anything which comes to you, as and when. And don't worry that it might sound far-fetched. Let's face it, we've got the possibility of 666, the Number of the Beast, being relevant, so I think it's safe to say anything goes.'

'The ages are around the same, boss. Two were seventeen, Tim Phillips was sixteen when taken, seventeen when found.'

'From their photos, they look quite young,' Jezza said, studying the pictures on the board. 'You could perhaps take them all for fifteen, going on sixteen.'

'They're all nice looking boys, too, sir,' DS Streeter commented. 'Now I see the other two next to our Tim, it's striking.'

'Sir, you mentioned that Darren Lee had been to a gay bar the night he went missing. I rather clumsily said to you previously that Robbie's parents had some doubts over his sexuality. DC Fleming was the one who spoke to them at length. Ruth?'

'Sir, we never really established much about that side of Robbie's life at the time. He was last seen by his friends at a club in Hull, but not a gay club, so that question never really arose. After the Sarge said you'd brought up that subject, I went back to talk to some of his friends again, to explore that angle a bit more.

'Robbie was a really nice lad, according to everyone who knew him. And he was a very good friend. He wasn't gay, but one of his close friends was. There'd been some trouble in town with attacks on young men going to gay bars and clubs. Robbie arranged for a group of his mates always to hang around with the one who was gay to make sure nothing happened to him.

'So yes, he was going to gay hang-outs, but not for himself. He seems to have been quite shy and reserved. He wasn't seeing anyone in particular, just going out in a group of friends, although there was apparently a girl at his school he used to sit and talk to sometimes.'

Ted looked at the two officers from Lincolnshire.

'What about Tim Phillips? Do we know anything about his sexuality?'

'It didn't really come up in our enquiry either, sir,' DS Streeter told him. 'Tim went missing after an evening out at the cinema with friends, a group of boys and girls from the same school. He wasn't with anyone in particular, but they weren't all in couples. Tim was younger than the other victims, sixteen, and he barely looked that. He'd have had problems getting into even some of the less particular pubs and clubs looking that young and without ID.'

Ted nodded. 'Good point. Thank you. Is that significant? The fact that these boys all looked younger and were all quite strikingly good looking? What did Tim's mother say about him? Did she know if he was seeing anyone?'

DS Streeter gave Nigel a nudge with her elbow as she said, 'DC Willis was lucky enough to talk to the mother. Definitely not the sharpest knife in the drawer, sir. More interested in going out drinking and playing bingo than making sure Tim was all right.'

'Sir, yes, the mother is known to us. She has a couple of public order offences and wasn't the best parent the lad could have had, especially as a single parent. It was never going to work, sending Tim home to live with her when he was as damaged as that. She'd never really been able to cope as a mother and by all accounts, Tim wasn't a bad lad. He was doing surprisingly well at school.'

'So that's another similarity between the three boys. All good students, not in any trouble. Can you flag that up, please, Rob? Darren's interest was fashions, wasn't it?'

The two Preston officers nodded and the sergeant put in, 'Very good at art and design, hoping to go on to college to take it further, sir.'

'And other than him going to gay bars, what else did you find out about Darren?'

'Not involved with anyone in particular. His friends said he was a bit of a flirt, but definitely interested in boys rather than girls for dating. He was close friends with some of the girls he was at school with though, sir.'

'Robbie, DS Groves? What were his academic interests?'

'Music and the arts, sir.'

'And Tim?'

'Engineering, sir. His ambition was to join the Navy to learn it as a trade.'

Ted was studying the board, trying to see what might link the three victims directly.

'Now we know we almost certainly have three victims of the same attacker, we need to look at what other connections there are between these three. Did they ever meet? Have their paths crossed? And did their abductor get to know them through some shared interest they may have had?'

'Social media, boss,' Jezza put in. 'If there's anything on their phones about which ones they used, Océane might be able to find the common denominator. I'll flag it up for her. Laptops, too. The viewing history would give us a clue if the three had any common interests. Have they been examined? Perhaps they were into World of Warcraft or something, like our Steve.'

Ted looked at the officers from Preston, Lincoln and Humberside.

'Laptops? Were they examined at the time, and did they reveal anything? And can we get them couriered over here, please, as soon as. We're lucky enough to have a CFI on site so we might as well make good use of her. She may find things which a summary search overlooked.

'So, back to the phones. All three were dumped, it seems. Luckily all three were found, against the odds. Tim Phillips' one probably because it had been left in a churchyard, so it was less likely to be picked up and pocketed.'

'Robbie Mitchell's was, too, sir,' DS Groves put in. 'It was found on a shelf in the porch of a church not far from where he was last seen.'

'There's one of your biggest connections then, sir,'

Sergeant Walsh put in. 'Darren's phone turned up at a church and was handed in. It was actually inside the church, left on a pew.'

Ted frowned, looking at the information Rob was writing up on the board.

'Why haven't we picked up this link before? Is the church the factor which links all three of them to their attacker?'

'Sir,' Steve sounded more hesitant than usual, with strangers present. 'This really will sound far-fetched. But with the 666 link suggesting something Satanic, surely the abductor wouldn't be frequenting churches to leave the phones there? Certainly not going inside one.'

'But why would the victims themselves finish up at a church after their night out, and why would they leave their phones behind?'

'Boss, perhaps the church is the link, though? Some kind of church organisation? Something which might see them going to an event where they could all have met?' Jo Rodriguez suggested.

'Were any of them religious in any way?'

Blank looks all round. Then DS Groves spoke.

'With respect, sir, it's not the kind of question that tends to get asked in a Missing Persons' enquiry, unless someone disappeared from a church.'

'It was a question, not a criticism, DS Groves. But now we have a possible link, can we please look into it, everyone? Find out if any of the three of them attended church or any kind of activity connected to church or religion.

'DS Groves, you might be able to help us. Would there be some sort of activity which could conceivably have seen three of them, from three different areas, meet up somewhere?'

'Yes, sir, it's possible. There are various youth movements connected to churches. Scouting, Rangers, that type of thing springs to mind. And they often have area meet-ups, camps, all kinds of things. Which also gives the possibility of the abductor being involved. A Scout leader, perhaps?'

'Right, everyone, that's another important angle we need to look at, please. Someone the three of them might know. Or at least someone whose appearance wouldn't give them any cause for concern, so they might willingly go off with them.'

'The most obvious person with the church connection would be a vicar then, boss,' Mike Hallam suggested. 'Or at least someone wearing a dog collar and looking like one.'

'Then why the 666, the Number of the Beast?' DS Groves asked.

'Because he thinks the lads are sinners? Perhaps he thought they were all gay and was trying to cure them. Some of the injuries inflicted appear to be similar to the kind of things you hear of being done on these gay cure programmes.'

'I take it we're assuming the abductor is a man? I have to confess I'm struggling to imagine a woman inflicting injuries like these on young men. Will you be getting a psychological profiler in, sir, to give us more of a clue?'

Ted gave a wry smile. 'My team will tell you, DS Groves, that I'm not big on the idea of psychological profilers.'

There was a small ripple of mirth from Ted's team members. They knew he had always resisted the idea of bringing in anyone like a profiler to work on his cases.

'I will, of course, do anything which I think might advance our case, within our budget. So as I said what we need to do is to find the principle link, the common denominator between these three young men.'

Ted walked over to the whiteboard as he spoke. 'It's quite a wide area, geographically, so the internet is the likely place to start. But we also need to be thinking of someone who might have had contact with all three of them. The Scouting suggestion is a good one. A vicar isn't grabbing me quite as much, unless someone can give me a reason he might have met up with three people over such a wide area. What else? We're missing something.'

'A careers advisor?' DS Groves suggested. 'My kids are too young yet but do they still have such people who visit the schools?'

'A concert, sir?' Steve suggested. 'We know Robbie liked music. Océane will be able to see from their laptops what their musical taste was. Perhaps they'd all met up at a gig somewhere at some point? And possibly met their abductor there at the same time?'

'The three of them may never have met up, but all three could have met their future abductor at something like that,' Jezza put in.

'We need to find that link,' Ted stressed. 'Let's start again with background checks on all three victims, see if we can't find some places in their lives where there's an overlap. Thanks, everyone, I think we're done here. Please keep me informed at all times of any new information, and we'll catch up via conference call before the end of the week. Megan, could you please show our visitors where they can get a coffee before they go back? And Sal, have you got a minute, please?'

As soon as they were alone, Sal started to speak.

'Boss, I know what you're going to say and I'm sorry. I should have checked, when I phoned Preston and Humberside, where the phones in their cases had been found. We should have been on to that link much sooner and I missed it. I can only apologise.'

'It's not like you, Sal. You're the last person I would expect to miss a detail like that. Is everything all right? Anything I should know about?'

Sal was one of his most meticulous officers. He'd worked in Fraud before joining Ted's team and never usually missed a single detail.

'Nothing, boss. It was just a slip. It won't happen again.'

'See that it doesn't, please.

While he was downstairs, Ted decided to put his head round

the door of Inspector Kevin Turner's office for a quick catch-up. He found no one there. He was about to go to see the Ice Queen to let her know how the joint briefing had gone when he heard voices from her office which told him where Kevin was. He could hear through the closed door that Kevin's voice was rising, cut across by the lower, measured tones of the Super. He couldn't hear what was being said and he didn't want to lurk in the corridor eavesdropping. No doubt Kevin would be straight on the phone to him when he took his leave to have a rant about whatever it was that had caused such a heated debate.

Ted had just had time to make himself a green tea and drink half of it back in his office when his desk phone rang. He expected it to be Kevin. Instead it was a royal summons – his turn to be called to the Super's office to hear whatever she had to say. He would have liked to find out first from Kevin what was going on but she made it clear she was expecting him immediately.

Whatever it was, it was unlikely to be good news, he thought, as he gulped the rest of his tea then made his way down the stairs.

'Come in, Chief Inspector.'

Her formal greeting set the tone. Ted instinctively knew that whatever she had to say was not going to please him. He waited to be invited to sit down. She didn't offer coffee. That of itself meant this was something serious.

'I won't beat about the bush. Superintendent Baker and I, as you know, have been at Central Park discussing budgets yet again. I must say at the outset that this is no reflection on you or your team. But cuts have to be made and so far you have escaped. Not this time, I'm afraid. We both fought long and hard to plead your case and were at least successful in damage limitation.

'Nevertheless, your team will have to be reduced by one Detective Constable and I'm afraid the decision as to who that should be is up to you. In addition, your CFI and her very expensive computer are to be transferred up to Central Park. A centralising of resources. You will, of course, still have access to her skills, but no longer exclusive use of her talents. You'll have to join the queue like everyone else.

'Superintendent Baker and I really did the very best we could for you. You could easily have lost your DI or one of your sergeants, which would have been a bigger saving. We managed to limit the cut to one DC, which was a small triumph.

'I am going to need your decision by end of play tomorrow. You could see if anyone is interested in transferring voluntarily to another division which may have a vacancy, or even to another force. There is also the possibility of an attractive redundancy package for someone with sufficient length of service.'

'You mean Maurice, ma'am? He's the only one with enough years for that to apply to. You know why I want to keep him on the team. You've seen at first hand what he can do. He's invaluable at the moment with the Darren Lee case. He's the only man Darren has shown any connection with at all. You want me to get rid of him?'

'Believe me, Chief Inspector, it could have been a lot worse. And I would suggest you don't complain to Inspector Turner until you hear what he is facing in terms of cuts to his uniformed officers and CSOs. I understand why you want to hold on to DC Brown but our hands are tied. Someone has to go. It's your team, so the decision as to who that will be has to be yours, and it needs to be made quickly. Rumours will soon start flying round the station and it's not fair to your team members to leave them with uncertainty hanging over them as to who is to go.

'It's not an easy choice to make, but I would suggest you start from the point of what the ADRs show up in terms of personal development and performance. Try to analyse which team member contributes the least to performance overall, rather than to focus on individual skills.

'As I said, I need your decision by the end of the day tomorrow. These changes need to come into force as soon as possible. Your CFI will be transferring on Monday. She is aware. She's been informed by HR so that is at least one task you won't have to undertake.

'But I do need your decision by tomorrow, or sooner if at all possible. Thank you, Chief Inspector. That will be all.'

Chapter Eight

Ted took the stairs back up to his office two at a time. He was not in the best of moods. He'd not managed to get to either the self-defence club or his judo session the night before. His martial arts usually provided him with an invaluable safety valve, a way of dealing with the pent-up frustrations and emotions of the job. It didn't help that when he went into the main office, Virgil had clearly just cracked a joke as there was some laughter from the team members working at their desks.

'Am I to understand by the laughter that there's been some sort of a breakthrough on the case?'

Heads immediately bowed back over work. It was rare for the boss to speak sharply. It meant they took more notice when he did. Rob O'Connell, as the senior officer present, awarded himself the short straw of answering, although he suspected the question had been rhetorical.

'Nothing new to report yet, sir,' he opted for formality, sensing the boss's mood was not good. 'But we are working on it.'

'Well, can we have more work and less hilarity. We need to start seeing some results. We also need to think about prevention. Our abductor may go quiet for a time, if he follows his previous MO. If not, we need to be on the lookout for any similar cases in the making. I want to be kept informed of any young teenage boys who go missing, especially if they match the profiles of the three we know about. Young, sixteen or seventeen, good students, trouble-free. Anywhere in the country. Let's get something circulated and see if we can't stop another one from happening. Steve, you're in charge of that.'

DC Jezza Vine was the one brave enough to put her head above the parapet to voice what they were all thinking.

'Er, boss, that risks being an awful lot of false alarms to be checked out.'

'I'm well aware of that, DC Vine. Thank you for pointing it out. But what do you suggest? We wait until the next victim turns up? Remember all three of these young men have been held and systematically tortured for six months.

'Can we please all just focus on what it must have been like for Tim, Robbie and Darren being held like that, not knowing if they were ever going to get out alive. And keep in mind the state they were in when they were found. So yes, this is going to mean extra work for all of us. But please think of the alternative.'

Ted headed for the office which Jo Rodriguez shared with Mike Hallam. Jo was at his desk, Mike was out somewhere. Ted sat down in the spare chair.

'This is confidential. It goes no further for now.'

Jo looked up from his paperwork.

'You have my undivided attention, boss.'

'We have to lose a team member. A DC. Orders from on high. You know we've done well to escape the axe so far. Our luck just ran out. So, from ADRs, do you have any recommendations? Or has anyone shown any signs of wanting to spread their wings and move on? I really would prefer to do this on a voluntary basis.'

Jo sat back in his seat and looked at the boss.

'What more do they want from us? We've had some brilliant results. Isn't that enough?'

'Nothing we can do about it, sadly. We've been lucky so far. I need to make a decision, and the Super needs it by end of play tomorrow. So, ADRs? Anything there to help?'

'Well, we both know, without a review to tell us, that

Maurice is a plodder. He does the bare minimum required to scrape by. We also both know what he brings to the team which no one else can. He's the longest-serving and has the least ambition. No plans at all to try for promotion or to stretch himself.

'Sal, on the other hand, is ambitious. He's putting in for his sergeant's exams, which he's bound to waltz through. He should have done them long ago. And then that will present another problem, as surely the team can't justify three DSs?'

'Not remotely. We're lucky to be keeping two. If we suddenly got a major breakthrough on this current case, it might just win us a stay of execution. But that's me clutching at straws, in a big way.'

'So how are you going to pick someone, boss?'

'I wish I knew. I gather Kevin Turner is facing a harder job than me. I'll buy him a consolation pint later on, after work. In the meantime, if you have any bright ideas, Jo, I'd welcome them. And like I said, this is confidential. I don't want people getting worried.'

Ted decided to leave it until later in the day to go and talk to Kevin Turner. He knew he would be taking the news of further cuts to his officers hard. He was on a rant the moment that Ted walked into his office, after a cursory knock.

'If you've come in here to whinge about how hard things are for you then don't. Just bloody don't. I'm dealing with shit here and I've no idea how I'm going to manage. So whatever it is you want to moan about, you can just piss off. Sir.'

It was a measure of how wound up he was that he made the reference to their difference in rank, even in a tone dripping with sarcasm. He and Ted had known one another for years and got usually on well together, working with a mutual respect which made their jobs easier for both of them.

'I was actually coming to suggest I buy you a drink after work. It sounds as if you need it.'

Kevin was rubbing his stomach, a sign that his ulcers were

playing up again. It was no surprise, with the stress he was currently under.

'Yes, sorry, Ted. That would be good. I'll phone the missus and tell her I'll be late, again. She's starting to forget what I look like.'

'Six o'clock in The Grapes, then. My shout.'

Ted got his phone out on the way back upstairs to call Trev.

'I'm going to be late again tonight. Sorry. Are you teaching? You probably told me and I forgot.'

'I did and I am. What time will you be back? I'm just doing a one-hour slot at six, so I won't be late back.'

'No idea, at the moment. I'll text you when I'm leaving. Eat when you're ready, though, don't wait for me. I don't want to spoil your evening if I get back too tired to feel hungry.'

When he returned to the main office, Ted noticed all the team members had their heads down, working. He didn't like doing it, but the odd sharp reminder didn't do them any harm, especially on a case as complex as this one.

'Another thing I want compiling is a detailed list of the injuries each of our victims sustained, and a cross-reference of similarities and differences. Let's look in detail at whether our attacker's methods have changed over the course of the three abductions. Virgil, unless anything else turns up to occupy you, you've got that one.'

'On it, boss.'

'Evening, Ted. Your usual, is it?' Dave, the landlord of The Grapes greeted him as he arrived at the bar ahead of Kevin Turner.

Ted rested his hands against the counter and leaned forward, his weight against his straight arms.

'Not tonight, Dave. Tonight I think I need …'

He let his voice tail off as he bowed his head, struggling for control.

Dave had never seen Ted drink alcohol in all the time he'd

known him. He didn't know his reasons and had never considered it his place to ask. But he could recognise the signs of a man fighting inner demons. He liked Ted. He and his team were good customers, no trouble, always polite. He reached for the makings of Ted's trademark Gunner – ginger beer, ginger ale and lime juice. Ted always insisted on no Angosturas to keep it one hundred per cent alcohol-free.

'Tell me to mind my own business, but I think probably your usual would be a good idea. I'll put some ice in it and an extra slice of lime, just to liven it up a bit.'

Before Ted could reply, Kevin arrived at his side.

'And whatever Kevin's having, please, Dave.'

'Scotch. Double.'

'Take a seat, gents, I'll bring them over. I can see it's been a hard day.'

'Hard day? He doesn't know the bloody half of it,' Kevin commented as the two of them found a quiet table in a far corner.

Ted, the former Specialist Firearms Officer, instinctively took the seat with his back to the wall, facing the door, in a position to see anything going on around him and particularly any trouble approaching him.

'Sorry about earlier, Ted. I'd just about had a bellyful,' Kevin began after Dave had brought their drinks. His double Scotch barely touched the sides on the way down, then he lifted the empty glass in Dave's direction to ask for another, pointing to Ted's barely-touched soft drink to line up another of them for later.

'Leave your car at the station and I'll run you home,' Ted told him. 'I'm not drinking. And go easy on your ulcers. I hear I got off lightly in comparison to you. I have to lose a DC and I've no idea who to pick, but I think you're facing much worse.'

'Apart from having to lose more officers and CSOs by whatever means I can find, I've got to find a way to persuade

Bill to take his retirement.'

'Shit. What the hell is he going to do if he hasn't got his work to live for? It's going to kill him.'

Bill had been a desk sergeant ever since Ted had first transferred to Stockport. He was a widower whose wife had died young. He still lived alone, apart from his profane parrot, Father Jack. His job was what kept him going and he was always picking up any extra shifts available to him.

'They're cutting down on opening hours to the public. It's one way to make crime figures appear better than they are, to discourage people from coming in to report them. I suppose we should be grateful they've not shut our old nick completely, centralised everything somewhere else. That bit of a refurb they gave it probably saved its bacon.

'But how the hell are any of us meant to solve crimes with fewer numbers and our resources being slashed all the time? It makes me seriously wonder whether I want to carry on. And this sick pervert you're after at the moment. What if he takes someone else and you just haven't got enough officers to go after him? It doesn't bear thinking about.'

They talked for a long time. It didn't solve either of their problems but it made them both feel better. Ted liked and needed the company of other coppers from time to time. He tried not to take his work home with him and there were aspects of his job Trev could never begin to understand, though he was always supportive.

It was a drunk and unsteady Kevin whom Ted delivered home to his long-suffering wife later that evening.

'It could have been worse, I suppose,' she sighed as she headed for the kettle, leaving Ted to help a now laughing Kevin to a seat in the kitchen. 'At least he didn't try to drive home. Thanks for bringing him back safely, Ted. I'd offer you a cuppa but I'm sure you're anxious to get back home to your Trevor.'

For once, Ted wasn't sure himself what he wanted to do.

He was always glad to get home to the sanctuary of the house. He deliberately avoided taking any of his worries back to the home setting, to keep it as a place of escape. He would normally be looking forward to a welcoming hug from his partner and purrs of greeting from the cats. This evening, he felt scratchy, irritable. He would have liked to get his day pack and his hill-walking boots and disappear for hours over the tops of the High Peak. Whatever he did, the decision would still be there, waiting for him. Tomorrow he was going to have to pick which member of his team he was prepared to lose.

Trev was at the kitchen table, which was strewn with his English teaching papers. The untidy piles spilled over on to the other chairs and even the work surfaces. It looked as if he had eaten his supper in several stages, judging by the number of dirty plates, bowls, mugs and glasses littered about.

'Hey, you. I got fired up with enthusiasm after the class tonight so I thought I'd start prepping for the next one, while I still had the ideas in my head. Are you hungry? I can soon heat something up for you, if you just give me a minute.'

'And where am I supposed to sit? How can you work in such chaos?'

Ted started clearing up the dirty dishes, running them under hot water so he could move them to the dishwasher.

'Could you not at least rinse things and load them, even if you can't manage to run the cycle?'

He caught sight of the bewildered look Trev was giving him, his blue eyes clearly hurt. He stopped what he was doing, wrenched open the back door and stormed out into the garden. He'd lost it and he was ashamed of himself. It wasn't Trev's fault he'd had a bitch of a day. He'd allowed himself to become the clichéd copper, lashing out at the person he cared for most after the frustrations of work.

Ted was no gardener. The one thing he did love to grow was highly scented lilies. His grandmother had always had them in her garden and he'd been intoxicated by the smell of them on a summer's evening when he was a small boy. He grew them in pots inside a construction like a fruit cage, to keep the cats away from the toxic pollen.

He let himself into the enclosure now, ready to wage war on the dreaded lily beetles which would be starting to ravage the first tender shoots appearing from the bulbs at this time of year. They might not be about at this time of evening, but there may be some greenfly. And crushing living things between his finger and thumb seemed like quite an inviting thing to be doing, feeling as he was. He took a clean handkerchief from his pocket to wipe his hands on as he worked. He didn't want squashed beetle juice on his work suit.

Trev wisely left it some time before he let himself quietly out of the house and walked across the lawn to the lily cage.

'Are you coming out or is it safe for me to come in?'

Ted wiped his hands clean on the handkerchief then let himself out of the mesh enclosure, avoiding eye contact with his partner, feeling wretched.

'I'm sorry I snapped. I've not had a good day, but I shouldn't have bitten your head off.'

'I'm sorry for the mess. I didn't realise it bothered you so much. You've never said anything before, not in all the years you've put up with me.'

'It doesn't. Not really. Well, maybe if you just rinsed things and put them in the dishwasher occasionally?'

'What can I say? I'm a total slob. I grew up with servants.'

Ted was looking round the garden, still avoiding eye contact, still angry – with himself, with the system, with their attacker.

'I think I'll mow the lawn.'

'At this time of night? You can't do that. The neighbours will report you for antisocial behaviour.'

'I'm feeling pretty antisocial.'

'Is it the latest case? Can I help?'

'I don't like bringing work home, you know that. And it's

not the case. It's just admin stuff. I hate it. I've got to make big decisions and I don't want to.'

'Could you talk to Jim about it if you won't talk to me?'

'He'll just tell me it's part of my job and to suck it up. It's just that on days like this, I'm not sure I want to keep doing this job.'

Trev hesitated for a moment, watching his partner closely.

'What would you do if you didn't do the job you have now?'

Ted turned away to look round the garden.

'Anti-terrorism is the one branch of the force which doesn't seem to be facing endless cuts. And I'm a good shot.'

'Ted, you're not serious? Don't even think about it. Please. Look, there must be something I can do to help. We could take the bike and go out somewhere. Go walking. You need something. You're wound up as tight as a spring. Let me help. For better or worse, remember. I know we didn't say those exact words but I certainly meant them and I hoped you did too.'

'I'm not very good company tonight. Sorry.'

'Which is why you need to do something. Let some of the anger out. Pad work, then? Look, go and get changed. I'll get the pads. Half an hour or so of something fast and physical might help.'

He was right. Nearly forty minutes of controlled, energetic martial arts training, aiming jabs and kicks at the pads Trev held, had Ted sweating and breathing hard, but feeling better for it. It was what he needed. He was still no nearer to reaching a decision but the earlier anger and frustration had largely left him. He felt calmer, more in control after a long shared shower, as the two of them lay in bed together.

'Will you be able to get any time off at the weekend? You need a break before the trial. It's Tuesday it starts, isn't it? I'll sort out the right shirt and tie and get everything ready for you on Monday evening. I imagine the press and TV will be there, so you'll want to look nice. Your mother might get a glimpse of you on telly, and you want to show the jury what a good policeman you are and how they can safely believe everything you say.'

'It's not a fashion show,' Ted replied, but there was warmth and affection in his voice. Trev always made such a big deal about how he looked when it was the least of Ted's concerns. 'I doubt I'll get much time off this weekend. We've not made much progress so far on this latest case and we're under pressure to do so.

'I'm sorry about earlier. Really. I shouldn't have lashed out at you. It's been a tough day and tomorrow risks being worse. I'll try to take a half-day at the weekend, at least, if I can. What did you have in mind?'

'We could take the bike, go to the Peaks. Do some strenuous yomping, have a picnic and make mad passionate love in the open air.'

Finally, Ted laughed.

'It sounds tempting. But with such a big trial coming up and our chances of conviction depending in a large degree to how credible the jury find me and my evidence, I'm not sure it's the best time for me to get myself arrested on a public order offence.'

Chapter Nine

'Where's Megan?' Ted asked, looking round the room before starting morning briefing.

'Medical appointment, boss,' Jo told him. 'She rang me first thing to clear it. Apologised profusely for the timing, said it was the best slot she could get. She said she'd be here as soon as she could, depending on waiting times.'

'And Maurice?'

'He went straight to the hospital. They're wanting to discharge Darren today. They seem to like to get rid of the tricky ones before the weekend and they're saying there's nothing else useful they can do for him at the moment. His mother's in bits, worried about how she's going to cope, especially as she has to go out to work.'

'Has Darren said anything at all yet?'

'Nothing so far, boss. Maurice is worried that once he's discharged it's going to be even harder to get anything out of him, unless he's receiving the right sort of support. But at the moment, there's nothing available. Maurice will try to talk to someone from Adolescent Mental Health Services in Preston and see what can be done but again, he's not hopeful.'

Ted wished Maurice wasn't doing such a good job with Darren. He wished he could have caught him out skiving. Not being at the hospital when he was supposed to be. Not doing the job he'd been allocated. It would have made his decision much easier. But he knew that when it came to anyone in pain, emotionally or physically, especially someone young, Maurice would go to the ends of the earth to help them. That sentiment had nearly cost him his life on a recent case.

‘Right, so what progress to date. Anyone?’

‘Sir, before we start, can I just ask a question?’

Rob O’Connell’s formality told Ted exactly what the question was likely to be. It was not something he wanted to touch on, not until all the team members were present, and until after he’d let the person he’d selected know in private that they were off the team.

‘You can, Rob, but if it’s the question I suspect it is, I might not be in a position to answer at this stage.’

‘You know nothing stays secret in the nick. It’s a real rumour mill. Word is going round that you have to lose at least one of the team, maybe more. We need to know who it is, boss. Some of us will want to talk to Federation reps, find out how we’re fixed. The uncertainty is worrying. I have to say, as a newly promoted DS, I’m worried that I’ll be first in line.’

‘I imagine Megan will also be worried in case it’s last in, first out,’ Jezza put in.

‘And I’m worried in case it’s me, now I’ve got a new baby to support. I’ve taken out a mortgage on a nice little place. I’m not looking forward to having to relocate, or facing a longer journey to commute, boss,’ Virgil added.

‘All right, everyone, listen. I understand your concerns. I don’t want to keep you waiting any longer than I have to. But it wouldn’t be fair to discuss this without Maurice and Megan here. You have my word that as soon as I can say anything about what’s happening, I will do.’

Océane was looking at Ted and gave an almost imperceptible nod. He guessed she wanted to let them know that she was one of those who was leaving.

‘I can tell you that Océane will be leaving us and going to Central Park. We’ll be sorry to lose you, Océane.’

The look of surprise on Steve’s face told Ted she hadn’t yet put him in the picture. He admired her for keeping it to herself until the news was official.

'And I'll be sorry to go, boss. I've been made welcome here. But Baby and I are being recalled to be based at HQ, although I'll still keep in contact with you all, and I hope to be able to carry on helping you in the future. Just not exclusively.'

Steve's expression when she mentioned Baby was so comical that Ted almost smiled. Except he didn't feel he had a lot to smile about at the moment. The rest of the team reflected the shock, in differing degrees.

Océane saw it too and grinned at them all.

'Baby is my computer. It's being recalled and I have to go with it.'

'But she's not the only one?' Rob persisted.

'Rob, like I said, I can't say any more at the moment, but I will as soon as I can. So can we all please focus on the case in hand for now.'

The team members were clearly not happy, no more than Ted was. But he was not prepared to continue the discussion. The news would have to be delivered in private to the person affected, before the rest of the team could be made aware.

'You'd be surprised how many teenage boys are reported missing daily, boss,' Jezza told him, trying hard to get the tone of the briefing back to normal. 'I'm trying to follow them up as soon as they come in. So far nothing remotely like the profile of our three.'

Ted nodded. 'Keep on it. Ask for help if you need it with the volume of the reports. We need to be ready at the first sign of something by our attacker.

'Virgil. Injuries?'

'Yes, boss. Thanks for that. It gave me nightmares reading through all of that in detail. I've prepared a summary of everything I found out. You all have a copy. It would seem, from the medical reports, that The Preacher is refining his art somewhat. The injuries to his first victim, Tim Phillips, were somewhat crude but no doubt effective. By the time he got to

Darren Lee, he seemed to have got slightly better at it.'

'The Preacher?'

'We have to call him something, boss, and that seemed as good as any.'

'All right, but let's not get fixated on the religious angle. It could be a red herring which might distract us from the direction we should be going in. Although that does seem unlikely.'

'Looking at the injuries it occurred to me, stating the obvious, that these young lads were likely to have been making a lot of noise while they were being tortured. I mean screaming for mercy, unless they were gagged. Even so, The Preacher couldn't risk them being heard. So wherever he was keeping them would probably be sound-proofed or isolated from any other properties. Possibly both. I can't believe he would have taken the risk of moving them around, so he's probably had them concealed somewhere for the whole six months. It might be useful to bear that in mind when looking for places, unless Darren can finally tell us something.

'The other main difference between the three is that Darren was dumped quite a bit further from where he was taken than the other two were. That could be significant as it might be part of the psychological torture. Alone, naked, dumped in an unfamiliar place. That of itself could finish off the work he'd already done in breaking their minds, if that really was his intention.'

There was a brief silence while the team members digested what he was saying.

'I've included it all in the report but it was about twenty miles for Tim and Robbie, just over forty for Darren. That's a significant change in pattern, which might signal that he's altering his behaviour. And if he's changing in that respect, might it also mean he's going to change his time patterns too? If we knew for sure about the 666 theory, that would help.'

'Sir,' Steve put in. 'What's the significance of the places

where our victims were found? There's a possible, unproven as yet, link to Christianity with the bible passages and the phones left in churches. Then there's the possible Satanic significance of the 666. So what if the places they were dumped is also meant to mean something? What if there's something there like … I don't know … ancient places of worship? Or pagan burial sites or something? Is that worth looking at?'

'Now that is starting to sound a bit far-fetched,' Mike Hallam sounded sceptical.

'The trouble is that all of it sounds beyond belief. So I think anything is worth exploring. Steve, spend a couple of hours, no more, on in-depth research of where they were found. We'll need another get-together at the end of the day so report back then.'

Ted was clearly ready to break up the briefing so Virgil put it, 'Boss, just one more thing. We're more used to dealing with bodies than survivors and in a sense, that's easier. We get DNA and other clues at post-mortem. I know it's a very long shot, especially now, a week on, but what if there are still some traces on Darren's body which could help tell us where he's been? I know Maurice said they hadn't yet succeeded in getting him cleaned up, or persuading him to take a shower.

'Is it worth trying to find out, perhaps before he leaves hospital? He could have evidence still under his fingernails. His toenails too, if he's been barefoot all this time. Maybe even rope fibres from where he's been tied up?'

'You're right, Virgil, we should have picked up on that earlier on. The problem is, of course, that he's so resistant to anyone touching him, unless he's completely sedated. We'd need his mother's consent, because he's under eighteen. I'm sure she'd agree with anything which might help to identify who's done this to Darren. But would we achieve anything in trying, other than to disturb him still further?

'I'll talk to one of the forensics team, see what they think, and I'll give Maurice a bell, see how feasible he thinks it would be.

'Thanks, everyone. I'm sorry to keep you waiting further for news and I will let you know as soon as I can.'

Back in his office, Ted dialled Maurice's number with a heavy heart. It went straight to voicemail.

'Maurice, it's the boss. Call me as soon as you can, please. We need to talk.'

His next call was to one of the forensics team. He chose to call Doug directly as they had a common interest in cats which often got him special favours. Especially as he was always prepared to spend a few minutes talking felines before asking for what he needed.

'Morning Doug, how's Cadfael doing? Did you get to that show last week?'

'Morning, boss, we did and he won. I was very pleased; stiff competition, including another male who's beaten him on every outing so far. But Cadfael's looking really good at the moment, he's really matured and filled out.'

Doug was rightly proud of the British Shorthairs he bred and exhibited. Ted's tribe were just moggies but he loved them no less.

'One of my queens has recently had kittens; only two as she's young still. One is a little belter, a real champion in the making, hopefully. But the other one of them is a really ugly little bugger. He's like a changeling, something the goblins left behind. A male, so he's going to be no use for breeding or showing, looking like he does. I wondered if you and your Trev were interested in another one? I should just put him to sleep but you know I'm too soft to.'

Ted knew that Trev would jump at the idea. But now he was out teaching so much, was it fair to bring another cat into their household, especially a kitten? He promised to think about it, then got down to the business in hand. He explained about their victim and their belated thought that there may still be some salvageable forensic evidence on his body. He stressed the problems involved with getting anywhere near Darren and finished up with, 'I just wondered, before we even consider it, if it's even feasible, Doug?'

'Not remotely, boss,' the forensics officer replied breezily. 'Even if we could get anywhere near him without scaring the young lad half to death, any forensic traces would be hopelessly contaminated by now, totally inadmissible in court.'

'If we can get consent, would you a least consider it? Even if we could never use them as evidence, it might give us a clue as to where he's been held. It would need to be done today, though, before he's discharged. Let me speak to Maurice to ask what he thinks about the idea, then I'll come back to you. Can we leave it like that?'

'Today? So I'm already flat out with trying to clear a backlog before the weekend and you want me to add to it by doing the impossible? I'll tell you what, I'll think about it, if you think about rehoming the kitten. He's too young to be weaned yet, so you have some time to think. Deal?'

'Deal,' Ted said reluctantly, realising he'd been well and truly stitched up.

There was still no word from Maurice by the time Megan got back to the station from her medical appointment. Ted wasn't sure if his silence was connected to that. He hoped it wasn't bad news. His timing couldn't be worse if it was. But it wasn't like Maurice to be out of touch. That was one thing about which he was usually reliable.

Maurice was good at some aspects of his job. He was methodical, good at wading through data to find things. But he was slower than anyone else, often had to be chased for routine paperwork and if he could combine legwork with a sneaky drink or even a coffee, he never wasted an opportunity to do so.

There was a quiet knock at Ted's door. When he replied, the door opened and Megan came in.

'Boss, I'm really sorry about missing morning briefing. I had to go for a scan and it was the best slot they could give me.'

Ted nodded to her to sit down, searching her face anxiously to try to read whether the news was good or bad.

'I hope it went well,' he said guardedly.

'It did, boss. It went very well.' She couldn't contain herself any longer and her face broke into a beaming smile. 'I'm pregnant.'

'Congratulations. I'm pleased for you, if it's what you want. We'll need to talk about maternity leave at some point, and keeping your job open for you to return to.'

'No need, boss. I've already been making enquiries. I've got myself a nice cushy little admin job at Central Park, all lined up for me to start whenever I want. As soon as I realised, I started asking around. I'm sorry to spring it all on you like this, but I needed to get the scan out of the way first, so I'd know about dates. And something else as well.'

'Are you sure that's what you want to do? I thought you were happy with the team?'

'I am, boss. I love it here, and you're the best boss I've ever worked with.' She was looking at him shrewdly as she spoke. She had an open, direct way of studying people and she didn't miss much. It's what made her a good detective and a valuable addition to the team.

'You're asking me if I'm opting to move to protect Maurice's job, aren't you? I love him to bits, but not enough to sacrifice my career for him. And I know he's the most likely to be in line to get shunted off the team. No, it's just that I'm going to need to take it much easier. I'm expecting twins.'

'That really is fantastic news. Congratulations again, twice over, in fact. I think we should all go for a swift one in The Grapes after work, to wet the babies' heads. Was Maurice with you for the scan? Is that why I haven't been able to get hold of him?'

Ted was genuinely pleased for her and Maurice. But he was a boss first and foremost and if Maurice had taken time off without telling him, he would need to explain himself even if it looked likely that Ted could now keep him in post.

'No, boss, he wasn't. I know Maurice has his faults but he missed the chance to get his first look at his new babies because he needed to be with Darren and his mother. I just had time to pop in quickly to show him the scan, and that's all.'

'Another set of twins, though, eh? I bet he's pleased?'

'Thrilled. You know how much he loves kids. And it was always a possibility. Lots of twins on Maurice's side and I have twin second cousins, too. His grandmother was twin and Maurice is a twin himself. Did you know that?'

'I didn't, and I've known him for years.'

'He fell out with his brother. Doesn't talk to him or about him much. Malcolm was going out with Barbara before Maurice met and then married her. It caused a massive rift between them, as you can imagine. Anyway, I better go and get on. I hope me leaving means Maurice can stay?'

'You know I can't say anything until I've spoken to the Super. But I'll let you and the others know as soon as I can.'

He phoned the Ice Queen, rather than go downstairs, to tell her the latest development.

'So is that enough? If DC Jennings is going voluntarily, does that mean I don't need to let anyone else go?'

'I think DC Brown may well have a double reason to celebrate today. I imagine that is who you had decided upon to be the one to go?'

'As it's hopefully academic now, ma'am, I'd rather not say.'

'Not entirely academic, Chief Inspector,' she responded in her driest tone. 'It would have been a valuable insight into your management skills to know who you had picked. However, in answer to your question, yes, one DC is sufficient, especially as it's been painlessly accomplished on a voluntary basis.

Please pass on my congratulations to DC Jennings.'

As soon as he ended the call, his phone rang again. Maurice.

'You wanted to talk to me, boss?'

'I did, DC Brown. I suppose you've been deliberately avoiding me until Megan had spoken to me, which she has now done, as no doubt she's told you.' Then he relaxed his attempt at sounding stern. 'I have to say, Maurice, you are one jammy bastard. I only needed to lose one team member and it was touch and go for a while there. But you're safe. For now. Just make sure that you up your game to keep your place because, sadly, I fear this won't be the last of the cuts we're facing.'

He ended the call and made another quick one before he went back out into the main office.

'I've had a better day than I expected, so I'll take you out to dinner tonight, if you like, and if you're not teaching. Book somewhere nice. Anywhere you like.'

Trev sounded delighted. 'That's dangerous. You know I like expensive.'

'Seriously, whatever takes your fancy. I owe it to you. I've been crap company, but even though we've not got much further on the case, the rest of the day has been good.'

Everyone was still in, which was ideal. He asked Jo and Mike to come out of their shared office and join them all.

'Right, everyone. I'm sorry it's taken a while, and I don't like having made you all sweat. But we have good news, so we'll have a swift one after the end of day briefing. Megan is voluntarily leaving the team because … Megan?'

She was grinning broadly round at the others.

'I'm taking a quiet admin job because I'm pregnant. And it's a double celebration because it's twins.'

Maurice phoned again later in the day.

'Right, boss, it's settled. They're kicking him out shortly. Doug came over after he'd spoken to you again. He couldn't do anything, couldn't even get near him, so he talked me through what to do and Darren let me take some scrapings from under his finger and toenails. He seems to trust me. He tried to say something a bit more to me while I was doing that. It wasn't very clear, but I think he was trying to say dark. Just repeated, over and over, like he did before with his name. If that's what he was trying to say it seems like the bastard kept him in darkness, as well as everything else he was doing to him.

'I'm going to run him and his mam home and stay with them until Darren is settled, as much as he's likely to be. Don't worry about the mileage, boss, I won't claim it. I know the budget is tight.'

'We're all going for a drink after work, to wet your babies' heads, Maurice. And you'll be missing that because you're too busy seeing to that family. You can be a lazy sod at times but when it comes to anything like this, you earn your place on the team.'

Chapter Ten

'So, Steve. What have you found out about the places where our victims were left?'

'This is going to sound crazy, sir,' Steve began apologetically, 'but these places might mean something to The Preacher, so I'm just flagging it up.

'First of all, the Lincolnshire one. Tim Phillips. I narrowed down from the reports exactly where he was found. We just had it as near to Market Rasen, but in fact it was about six miles out. He was found wandering in a quiet lane near to a very small village called Stainton-le-Vale. What's interesting is that Stainton has a place called Lud Well which is supposed to be a healing spring.'

'So first he breaks them and then he puts them somewhere to be healed?' Mike Hallam sounded more sceptical than ever.

Steve went pink, as he had a tendency to do, but he was getting better at speaking up for himself.

'It's just a theory, Sarge. The sites might mean something, and the DCI did tell me to look into it. Lud Well also has a rag well, although that may just be a more modern tradition; they're usually found in Celtic sites.'

'Rag well?' Ted asked, interested in spite of himself.

'They're also called clootie wells, usually in Scotland, sir. It's a place where people hang strips of cloth as part of a healing ritual.'

'Right, so there's a possible link to healing with the Lincolnshire one. We'll bear that in mind. Next?'

'Ours, here, boss. Again, from the precise location where he was found, it was not all that far from Ludworth Moor where there's evidence of a possible Bronze Age Druidic circle. Druids were a high order and featured, among other things, medical professionals, so there's a possible link there to healing again. There's also another Celtic connection as the area was believed to have been inhabited by Celtic Brigantes. Plus we now have two references to Lud, who seems to have been a Celtic deity. Lud Well and Ludworth, although I've not yet had time to research any connection other than by the name.'

'And the Humberside one?'

'Barrows, sir. Bronze Age cemeteries. Not far from where he was found. That's as far as I had chance to go with researching. So a possible healing link with two of them, and also a possible connection in that these are pre-Christian sites, so we might be back to a religious significance, perhaps.'

Most of the team were looking dubious by this point. It didn't amount to anything concrete.

'Good work, Steve, well done. Put it all in writing and it's something we can look at in more detail. You're right in thinking that although we can't see the link, the sites The Preacher picked were probably not random and had some significance to him. If we could find that out, it might lead us somewhere.'

'Boss, something else occurred to me, looking at what we have so far,' Jezza put in.

'All theories are welcome at this point. It's something we're a bit short of.'

'Preston said that Darren's phone was found inside a church, on a pew, not outside like the other two were.'

She looked around at the others who didn't appear to be on the same wavelength. Jezza was the lateral thinker of the team. She sometimes had to keep the irritation out of her voice when the others were slow to follow her on a tangent. She clearly thought whatever she was thinking of should have been obvious to everyone.'

'Well how did it get in there? How many churches are left unlocked these days? Surely most are locked up tight except during services because of theft, and probably squatters. It was night-time when Darren was taken so how did The Preacher put it in there? Did he do it when he took Darren or did he go back and plant it there afterwards? Does that mean that it's someone who has keys to a church, and if so, who would that include?'

Jo was the churchgoer of the team. All eyes instinctively turned towards him.

'I only know about Catholic churches. Was this C of E? I'm not familiar with their protocol but I imagine it's similar. I'd hazard a guess at the parish priest, the curate, if they have one, sacristan, maybe sidesmen, someone in charge of who does the flowers. That sort of thing.'

'Good idea, Jezza, that's certainly worth following up. You're in tomorrow, aren't you? I think it would do then.'

'I don't want to jump to any conclusions, boss, but if it was a vicar, for instance, is it just possible that Darren might have known him and been happy to go off with him? After all, we've got no CCTV or reports of any sort of a struggle involving him, so it might well be someone he knew, at least by sight. Or perhaps the sight of someone in a dog collar wouldn't worry him.'

'Check that out with Preston, too. Do vicars still visit schools? Were Darren or his mother ever churchgoers? It's a line of enquiry, and we're certainly a bit short of those at the moment. Can you also liaise with Humberside and your friends at Gainsborough to find out more about the churches there. I know the phones weren't inside them in those two cases but is there anything which links the churches in some way? Same vicar? Curate? What about an organist? Might they need to have a key to come and go to practise?

'Steve, that's a good start and it's still a theory of interest. Can you do a bit more research please, in particular let's have the exact distance from the places you mentioned to where our victims were found. In fact, I'll take a risk with the budget here, but I'd like you to visit all three sites. Liaise with someone local for more detail. Have a look for yourself. Walk the distance, see how long it would take, bearing in mind the condition the lads were found in. Talk to locals, if you get the chance. There'll be nothing to see at the earlier sites by now, of course, but go back to Mellor and look for yourself. You're observant, see what you can spot.

'Jo, how far afield was the house-to-house carried out?'

'Certainly not out as far as Ludworth Moor, boss, I don't think. I didn't even know about it until Steve mentioned it. I'll liaise with Steve on the exact area that's been covered to date.'

'Right, let's see if we can make some sort of progress between us over the weekend. I've got a meeting with the Big Boss and the Super first thing on Monday and no doubt I'm going to have to justify every resource to date and address our lack of any real lead.

'If only Darren would finally say something to Maurice, that would be the break we need. But now, even though Maurice isn't with us, we need to go and toast his and Megan's good news, and say our goodbyes to Océane and Baby. Let's wind up here and meet in The Grapes in fifteen minutes.'

Ted went back to his office to get his things together and lock them in the boot of his car before he went for the drink. He was just about to shut his computer down when a ping told him he had mail. Before he had chance to open it, Océane appeared round his door after a brief knock.

'Boss, I just sent you a link to a news article. You asked me recently about Diaz Beach, near Cape Town. It brought back some good memories, so I set up an alert for anything about it. Remember me telling you it's a dangerous place to swim? The article is about someone who seems to have drowned there.

The local police think it might have been a British tourist as there was a pair of British army-issue boots with the clothing they found. What a coincidence, eh?'

Ted was studying the article on the screen. He didn't like coincidences. He never trusted them. The last message he'd had from his martial arts and survival skills trainer, Green, had been a single photo of the beach he was now looking at on screen.

'Thanks, Océane. I'll see you in the pub in a few minutes.'

He read the article through in detail, although the information was brief. It was assumed that a tourist, not knowing the risks of the area, had gone for a swim on a deserted beach, got into difficulties and was presumed drowned. The presence of the boots and of a polo shirt with a British label led the local police to assume the person who had disappeared was a British tourist. No other personal possessions were mentioned, and no vehicle had been found parked anywhere nearby which could have belonged to a missing person.

Ted didn't like any of what he was reading. He knew Green was an accomplished swimmer, who'd represented his Army regiment at national level on more than one occasion. He'd been contemptuous of Ted's fear of deep water on one training exercise which had required those taking part to cross a wide lake whilst keeping rifles aloft. Nor was he someone who ever took unnecessary risks. He taught survival and all the training he delivered was based on being able to live to fight another day.

Above all, Ted didn't like the presence of the boots and the shirt label. It all smacked to him of scene-setting. Whatever was going on, he'd have bet a month's salary that wherever Green was now, it was not at the bottom of the ocean. He had good reason to want to disappear from sight. Ted wondered when, and where, he would reappear.

He shut down his computer. Thoughts were niggling at the

back of his brain. But right now he had a round of drinks to buy, then a meal to take Trev out for. After that he would devote most of his weekend to a concerted effort at finding out who the mysterious Preacher was and how they were going to stop him from striking again.

Steve didn't currently have his own car. He'd been lodging for some time with Maurice, after a serious assault on him in his previous flat had left him anxious about living alone. It had also left him with hefty bills for dental work which he was still paying off.

Now that Maurice and Megan were spending so much time together and expecting twins, Steve knew he should be looking for a place of his own to give them space. Megan had a young son, Felix, and when Maurice had his twin girls for the weekend, the house was crowded. Steve had to share with Felix, unless he could escape to Jezza's luxury flat. They were good friends and he always found a welcome there, as long as she wasn't entertaining her increasingly steady boyfriend, Nathan. Steve was starting to feel a bit of a gooseberry wherever he went.

He was wondering if he should pluck up the courage to ask Océane if they might get a place together. He knew it was a bit soon, although he spent a lot of time at the flat she shared with a friend. He didn't want to put her off by appearing too keen.

He took a pool car to do the rounds, setting off early on Saturday morning. He had a lot of miles to cover and he wanted to do a good job. He'd been surprised and pleased that the boss had picked him for the work and he had every intention of showing him he was up to it.

He decided to start with the Humberside case which found him driving round country lanes heading towards a place called Market Weighton. He had the exact grid reference of where Robbie Mitchell, the Humberside victim, had been found. He spent an interesting but largely fruitless hour or more wandering around trying to track a route Robbie may have walked from any of the Bronze Age burial sites to where he was found.

The walking did give him time to think of other angles. Despite being the techie one of the team, Steve always liked to keep a written back-up of his thoughts in a conventional pocket book. Having had his computer destroyed when he was assaulted had drummed that precaution into him. He took it out now to scribble himself a note.

'Any link between the people who found the three victims? Were they random/innocent?'

Next he headed south, crossing the Humber Bridge into North Lincolnshire, then following the satnav's guidance towards the Lincolnshire Wolds. His research had told him it was a designated Area of Outstanding Natural Beauty. He was certainly pleasantly surprised.

Stainton le Vale was a small village, more of a hamlet really. As Steve turned off the B road his research had told him was an old Roman road, he passed a few houses at the bottom of a long hill, where he turned right before coming to a large farmyard near to where, the instructions told him, there was a footpath which would take him to Lud Well. He parked the car on a grass verge, well out of the way of any tractors which might want to pass, and set off on a path which went behind a pair of semi-detached red brick cottages facing the farmyard.

As he passed the second one, a border collie in the garden started to bark and jumped up at the gate as he drew near. It appeared friendly enough, its tail waving in greeting. A woman in the garden, weeding the border, paused in her work to look at him.

'Hello,' she greeted him then, seeing his hesitation, 'are you lost?'

Steve had his phone in his hand and was consulting the screen.

'Hello. I'm looking for somewhere called Lud Well.'

‘You’re nearly there,’ she told him. ‘But it’s on private land. You’re not officially allowed to go there, although people do come to try to find it. There was one young man from Russia once.’

She was looking him up and down critically as she continued, ‘You’re not really dressed for it, not in those shoes, and a suit. Is that really what you’re looking for? You’re not an egger, are you?’

‘I’m afraid I don’t even know what that is.’

‘Someone who steals birds’ eggs from nests. Especially rare ones. It’s the wrong time of year for eggs, of course, but you might be looking out for nesting places. I don’t like eggers. I report them to the police if I spot anyone who looks like one.’

‘Actually, I am a police officer,’ Steve got his card out to prove his point. ‘You get a lot of people coming looking for Lud Well, then?’

‘Not a lot, no, but some do come. Why are the police interested in it?’

Steve thought it best to evade her question.

‘Would you notice if anyone came at night, for instance? If someone was poking about looking for it after dark?’

‘Definitely. Mott would bark,’ she indicated the dog, ‘and we have security lights front and back of the cottage. My husband works for the farm estate. They’ve had a few thefts from the yard opposite and it’s part of his job, and the next door neighbour, who also works for them, to keep an eye out. Which station are you from, then?’

‘Erm,’ Steve didn’t want to give her too much information but couldn’t see a polite way to refuse to answer. ‘I’m actually from Stockport, but it’s in relation to case which Gainsborough have been investigating. I wonder if you could just point out to me where the well is? I don’t need to go to it, just to see where it is in relation to this footpath.’

‘Mott, lie down. Stay.’

She wiped her hands on her jeans, stepped over the now

recumbent collie and let herself out of the gate, closing it firmly behind her. She only walked a few paces on the path before stepping off it to the left, battling the undergrowth for a few more yards then pointing down a hill which appeared to get steeper the further down it went.

'The rag well, the yew tree on the stream bank with all the ribbons and things in it, is more or less straight ahead, down there. Then if you walk up the actual stream bed to the right for a good few yards, you come to like a punchbowl shape in the side of a hill, where the springs rise. There are supposed to be seven springs, and seven is some sort of mystic number.

'I often tell people it's a bit like Narnia as you can't always find your way to it easily, even though it's not far and you may have been before. Depending on the time of year and the state of the undergrowth, it's not always easy to get to and, like I said, it's on private land so people aren't supposed to go down there.'

Steve thanked her, politely refusing her offer of a cup of tea. He'd pick up a coffee and a sandwich somewhere on his way back over the Pennines to Stockport. He walked the distance from where he was to where Tim had been found but he was struggling to imagine someone in a weakened state, naked, terrified, managing to get themselves to or from the Well itself. The dog would surely have heard someone crashing about in the undergrowth and barked a warning to wake its owners.

So far, his theory wasn't looking very promising. He hoped he hadn't been wasting everyone's time, and the budget, with wild ideas. Perhaps he might get lucky with the third one, back on home ground. It was the most recent of the three, so there was still a possibility there might be some traces of activity. He might even find an eyewitness which would be their biggest break to date.

He chose the motorway route to get over to where Darren was found. It would still take him more than two hours, but it gave him thinking time. He made a mental note to do some further digging into the name Lud, having just left Lud Well and now heading towards Ludworth Moor. There was probably a connection there somewhere, if he could just dig it up.

He'd studied maps and satellite views in preparation for his exploratory trip to Ludworth Moor. He headed for what appeared to be a farm track ending in a footpath going up over the moor itself. There was a small, isolated cottage at the end of the track, and what looked like a bigger building, probably a farm, further up. He parked the car and set off on foot in the direction of what was thought to be the remains of a stone circle. At least it wasn't raining and the ground was dry underfoot, he thought to himself. He wasn't ideally dressed, he realised, in his work suit and shoes. It was getting on for late afternoon by now but he didn't really want to check in with the boss until he had something to report.

As he trudged up the track, he saw a large, hairy, ginger-coloured dog trotting towards him, followed by a woman in walking gear. Steve eyed the dog warily. He was relieved when the woman called out, 'Timber, stop,' and the animal obediently immediately sank to its haunches, watching the oncoming stranger.

'Good afternoon,' the woman greeted Steve. 'He won't touch you, unless I tell him to.'

He hoped she was joking as he returned her greeting. The dog was even larger, close up. Some sort of German Shepherd Dog or some similar breed, he thought.

'I was looking for the stone circle,' he added, thinking some explanation of his presence might be in order.

'You're going in the right direction then. You're not ideally dressed for it though,' she replied, looking him up and down critically. 'I've seen worse, it has to be said. Sometimes people come traipsing up here in summer shoes and sandals and it can get a bit blowy on the top, even on what passes for a summer's day.'

Steve decided it might be a good point at which to produce his ID.

'Do you live near here?'

'The cottage lower down the track.'

'Do vehicles come up here sometimes? Other than farm traffic, I mean?'

'From time to time. Some bright sparks try to drive right up to the top of the moor and usually manage to get themselves stuck. We sometimes get the odd ones, hippy types, going up there for the summer solstice. Not so much the winter one.'

'And do you notice when cars go past? I'm thinking especially after dark. Your cottage is a bit isolated. Does it not worry you?'

She smiled indulgently.

'Would you like me to release Timber from his stay and show you why it doesn't?'

No, thank you, I'll take your word for it. Did you happen to notice anyone at the end of last week? Driving past, I mean?'

Now her expression was shrewd.

'You're asking me specifically about the Friday, aren't you? I saw on the news about that poor young man found wandering not far from here. You think he might have been here at some point?'

'Did you see or hear anything on the Friday?'

'As it happens, a car did go past, but I didn't make the connection. It just went up to the end of the track, past the farm. Timber barked as it was passing. I looked out and saw the rear lights disappearing. Then he barked again and I saw it was the car coming back. Somebody took a wrong turn, I imagine. It happens, with those satellite things. They're always sending people the wrong way. Absolute menace. Can't be doing with them.'

'And did Timber bark again at any time? You didn't see anyone coming down the track on foot, later on?'

'So you do think the young man was here? I wish I'd

known, I could perhaps have helped him. And yes, Timber did bark again shortly afterwards, but I didn't see anything. It was very dark by then.'

'I just need to make a phone call to my boss, then may I come to the cottage to get a statement from you, please, Mrs...?'

'You may indeed, Constable. It's Miss, Miss Harrington. I'll have the kettle on.'

Chapter Eleven

'Excellent work, Steve. Really well done,' Ted said after he'd listened to Steve's detailed report of what he'd found out so far. 'It's the first real lead we've had. It's a long shot, after eight days, but I'll get SOCO out to look at where the car turned round. The weather's not been too bad, and as long as tractors or other vehicles haven't driven over the wheelings, there might still be something to show for it. I'll get someone from Uniform to close off the site until we know if there's anything to see.

'I'll come out myself, too. It's no reflection on you. You seem to be handling things well, but it's my case so I ought to put in an appearance, at least. In the meantime, you're my eyes and ears on the scene so please note everything. You go and talk to your witness, find out everything she can tell you. We'll need to ask at the farm, too, in case they saw or heard anything. Good job, Steve, I'll see you soon.'

It was a long shot that they would find anything, Ted knew. But it was something. Finally. He was going to have to present Jim Baker and his own Super with some reason, in their meeting on Monday morning, not to scale the enquiry down. His team had already put in a lot of hours on the case. Up to now, with nothing to show for it. If there was the slightest possibility that Steve had found where Darren had been dumped, they could at least localise the search for any sign of the vehicle which had left him there.

There would be no CCTV out there in the wilds, but there

may well be traffic cameras further down, nearer to civilisation. If they could pinpoint an approximate time when Darren had been dumped, they could at least start looking at camera footage to see if they could pick up on anything.

Ted decided to take his official car. He was constantly being reminded that if he didn't use it, it risked being clawed back. He'd phoned forensics to see if he could get someone to the scene as soon as possible. Doug wasn't on duty. Ted remembered he'd said he would be at another cat show. At least it saved him being put under pressure about the kitten. He'd also sent an area car on ahead of him. When he arrived, the officers were already on site, taping the lane off from the road end. He'd need to talk to the people at the farm as soon as possible to warn them of the disruption.

He didn't want to appear to cramp Steve's style. He was an excellent detective in the making, though with much yet to learn. His weakness was talking to people, so Ted wanted to be there while he was interviewing potential witnesses, just so he didn't miss anything through lack of experience or being too embarrassed to ask awkward questions.

Ted unlatched the gate to the cottage at the end of the lane, walked up to the front door and tapped with the brass knocker. As soon as he did there was an explosion of frenzied barking and a thud against the door. The top half of it was partly glazed with frosted glass through which Ted could see a looming light-coloured shape which seemed intent on ripping the door off its hinges to get at him. He wasn't comfortable with dogs, especially large ones. It was with relief that he heard a woman's voice issue a sharp, stern command and the dog immediately disappeared from view.

The top part of the stable-style door opened and a grey-haired woman looked out at Ted. He had his warrant card ready in his hand and showed it as he introduced himself.

'Miss Harrington? I'm Detective Chief Inspector Darling, from Stockport. I believe you've been talking to my DC?'

'Yes, indeed, what a very polite young man. Please, come in. I've shut Timber in the kitchen so it's perfectly safe. Your officer explained that you don't like dogs.'

She opened both parts of the door wide and stood aside to let him enter the narrow hallway.

'Not dislike so much as fear,' he told her candidly with a disarming smile. 'I'm a cat person.'

'Dreadful creatures,' she snorted with thinly veiled contempt. 'Always off slaughtering birds. They should be banned, in my opinion.'

Ted wisely kept his counsel as he followed her into a small living room dominated by a surprisingly large inglenook fireplace. Steve was sitting in an armchair next to it, his phone, for recording, on one arm of it, his notebook on his leg, a mug of tea in the hand which wasn't holding a pen. He made to rise when his senior officer came in but Ted waved him down. He took his place on the matching two-seater settee Miss Harrington indicated as she went to resume her own chair opposite Steve.

'Sorry to interrupt you, Steve, and please excuse me, Miss Harrington, if I ask you just to give me a quick recap of what you've already told Steve.'

'Would you like some tea, before we begin? There's still some in the pot which shouldn't be too stewed.'

'That's very kind but no thank you. If you could just give me the main points again, please?'

'It was definitely Friday of last week because I'd watched a series I've been following on Friday evenings. I let Timber out at the back to spend a penny before *News at Ten* while I made myself a hot drink. Everything was quiet then or he would have barked. After the news I was looking for something engaging but it was mostly chat shows and utter rubbish so I did a bit of channel hopping and found an old film.

'I can't have watched more than about half an hour when Timber started barking. I looked out of the window and a car was passing. As I've already told the young man, I couldn't see much detail, just the rear lights as it passed. It was a car though, not a big 4x4 or anything like that because I remembered thinking it was going to get bogged down if it tried to go too far. We'd had rain that day and the track was quite wet higher up.

'I'd not long sat back down and settled Timber when he started barking again and I heard the car coming back. I looked out of the window to see it going past but again, no detail. Timber had a bit of another woof shortly afterwards so I thought he'd perhaps heard it again turning round somewhere else. It was probably someone completely lost.'

'Could it have been going to the farm when you first saw it?'

'I doubt it, at that time of night. They go to bed early. They're up before dawn for the livestock. I doubt they would have noticed the car.'

'How much further can you drive, past the farm?'

'In a car, just a few yards, and you'd have to reverse back to the farm gates to turn round. You can get all the way to the top in something like a Land Rover but it's still a rough ride.'

'You've been very helpful, Miss Harrington, thank you. One last thing. Could you form any impression of the car? Its colour, perhaps? Anything at all?'

'Dark, I think. I imagine if it had been light-coloured I would have noticed that.'

'And the size? Roughly?'

'Cars really aren't my thing at all, I'm afraid. They're just a means to get to the shops. I have a Fiat Panda and it looked bigger than that, if that's any help?'

Ted could see that more tapes had gone up and SOCO were installed further up the lane, as he and Steve left the cottage.

'I didn't want to tread on your toes in there, Steve, I just wanted a summary. Right, let's go and see what, if anything,

SOCO can retrieve for us, and then we need to talk to the people at the farm.'

The forensics officer in charge of the scene was grumbling loud and long when Ted and Steve walked up the lane towards him.

After barely a cursory greeting, he launched into a tirade.

'We're not going to get anything of any use here. Eight days on and god knows what's been over the tyre tracks since then. There are hoof prints, cow pats or something, rabbit droppings. You name it, it's contaminating the scene.'

'Even if you can't get me anything I can use in court, can you at least try to give me something. If there's any chance of identifying the type of car, from the tracks, that would be a huge help,' Ted said patiently. 'I'd even settle for a best guess. I wouldn't be asking for the impossible if I wasn't desperate, but I am. And if you think it's a waste of time, I'd be happy to forward you the report on the injuries this victim sustained, as did the other two before him. So just do your best, please.'

It was as close as Ted came to a public reprimand. He knew he was asking for miracles but they were what they needed right now.

'Have you walked the distance yet, Steve? From here to where Darren was found?'

'Not yet, sir, I was just going to do it when I ran into Miss Harrington.'

'Do it now, please, then come back and find me here. I better go and have a word with the farmer. He doesn't look too thrilled by our presence.'

A uniformed constable was trying patiently to talk to a man about to get into his tractor. He appeared to be giving her a hard time. Ted went into the yard to see if he could defuse the situation. The PC looked relieved to see a senior officer arriving.

'Thank you, Constable, I'll take over here,' he told her, reaching for his badge to show the man.

'I'm Detective Chief Inspector Darling, I'm the Senior Investigating Officer on this case, Mr …?'

'Mellor,' the man told him, 'and yes, I've heard all the remarks about being named after where I live and so on. Darling, did you say? I expect you know all about cracks about names, then.'

He was tall and thin, his complexion weather-beaten, a tweed cap protecting his head from the elements. He was looking down at Ted, clearly not impressed by his short, slight stature. Ted had turned forty but looked ten years younger. His dirty blonde hair was the sort which didn't show grey. None of it helped much in giving him any gravitas.

'You're in charge?' He made no attempt to keep the note of incredulity out of his voice.

'I am, Mr Mellor. I wanted to apologise for any inconvenience we're causing you, and to assure you that we will be as quick as possible in our investigations.'

'I've got livestock to see to, cattle to bring in. How am I meant to do that with you lot blocking the track? What's it all about, anyway? What crime?'

'A serious assault.'

'And it happened here? Right outside my gate? When was this?'

'I'm not saying the assault happened here, Mr Mellor. We have reason to believe a vehicle which is of interest to us may have driven up this lane and turned round outside your gate. This was a week ago. On a Friday evening. Did you see or hear anything?'

'What do you call evening?'

'Probably somewhere between ten-thirty and eleven.'

Mellor snorted. 'I can tell you've never farmed. I'd call that the middle of the night. I get up before five most days so at that time I'm in my bed asleep. I wouldn't have heard anything.'

'Do you live with anyone? Might they have heard?' Ted's questions were always carefully gender-neutral.

'Wife's as deaf as a post. She wouldn't hear anything once she's in bed asleep.'

'Do you have dogs? Would they bark if someone drove past in the night, or turned round outside?'

'Working dogs, aye. They sleep in the barn. Even if they kicked off, at that time of night, I could well have slept through it. So what's this about, again? An assault?'

'You've been very helpful, Mr Mellor, thank you for your time. Once again, my apologies for any disruption and we'll try to keep it to a minimum.'

Ted brushed smoothly over the man's questions and went back outside the gate to see how SOCO were getting on. It wasn't long before Steve came walking back up the lane to find him.

'No more than fifteen minutes, sir, even walking slowly as I'm sure Darren would have been doing, if he was dumped up here. There's a track directly opposite the end of this lane which cuts through some fields and comes out right near where Darren was found.'

'Steve, you've played a blinder. You get back to the nick now. It's well past your knocking off time. I'll hang on here a bit, just in case anything shows up. But well done.'

'Now we have a possible idea of where Darren was left, we need to consider whether he was kept near there. There are certainly some remote places up on the moor where no one would hear anything. We're going to need to use mapping to identify likely places.'

It was Sunday morning. Ted was talking to the team members who were on the rota for the day. By the time he'd got back from Ludworth the evening before, there was not much more to be done constructively and the rest of the team had already called it a day.

Ted was under strict orders from Trev to finish work by early afternoon at the latest to give himself something of a break before his important meeting with his two bosses the following morning, then the start of the big trial on Tuesday. Ted was supposed to have had a date later in the day with Walter. That was the name of the fat, placid cob a friend of friends had been lending to him, with something livelier and more exciting for Trev, to go out for the occasional hack.

No one was more surprised than Ted that, after a lifetime of being afraid of horses, he'd not only managed to learn to ride to a modest standard, but was also enjoying his jaunts with Walter. He'd even survived his first fall, when he ambitiously pointed him at a tree trunk the cob had wisely decided was beyond his capabilities. Ted's martial arts training gave him excellent balance and he broke the fall easily, standing up to pat Walter on the neck and concede that the horse had probably been right in his decision.

He'd promised to take the time off but had asked Trev if they could take a rain check on the riding and go walking instead. He hadn't dared tell him that while they were walking about, seemingly fascinated by Bronze Age remains on Ludworth Moor, Ted was actually going to be on the look-out for possible places The Preacher might have held Darren before releasing him.

'I need something for tomorrow morning which looks like a solid lead to follow up,' he told the team. 'I'm worried I'm going to be asked to scale things down, so what I need from you all today is whatever grind it takes to find something that looks like tangible progress. So that means checking out isolated buildings online then getting someone round to look at them. Liaise with Uniform for extra bodies. It also means looking at any and every camera near the two locations, where Darren was found and where we now think he was dumped, and flagging up any vehicle which may need further investigation.

'I'm going to go up to Ludworth myself later on, to have a walk round the whole area and see if I can see anything which might be of interest. I'll keep in contact if I do find anything.

'Maurice, any update on Darren?'

'I went to see him yesterday, boss. And don't worry, I wasn't on the rota so I'm not claiming for it. He does seem to trust me, though, so I don't want to lose touch. His mam managed to help him get cleaned up a bit after I left them on Friday. He still keeps repeating 'dark'. She said once she got him to bed in his old room, as soon as she switched off the light he started screaming and became hysterical so she had to leave it on all night. He wet the bed too, she said.

'I told her to try to find a radio station with something quiet and soothing, maybe classical music, and leave that playing in the background. That used to work a treat to calm the twins if they were frightened in the night, or had bad dreams.'

'Good, thanks, Maurice. The problem is that now he's back home it's going to be harder for me to justify the cost of keep sending you up there to talk to him. I know you're the one he's most likely to talk to, and we need his testimony. But you all know how things are currently with budgets. Every penny spent has to be accounted for and justified.'

'I'll keep going in my own time if I have to, boss. I'm not letting that wee lad down.'

'I appreciate it. Just don't forget that Megan needs you as well, especially now.

'Right, the rest of you. A bit of a grunt, I know, but back to traffic cameras. Now we know roughly what time The Preacher's car may have been in the area, we need to look again for anything which looks possible.'

'Boss, we've been over most of it already,' Rob O'Connell pointed out.

'I know you have, Rob. But before, we were going on the basis that Darren might have been brought here from Preston. Now we need to consider that The Preacher was actually holding him in this area before he released him. So you need to check cameras from different directions, and spread out wider.

Somewhere out there might be the footage we need, which will finally give us an ID on The Preacher.'

Maurice's mobile phone interrupted them.

'Sorry, boss, it's Darren's mam. I'd better take it.'

He picked up the call but instead of speaking he listened then asked, 'Dal? Is that you Dal? It's all right. You're cold? Is your mam there? Can I speak to her?'

He listened again then spoke, looking at the boss for his approval. 'You're scared? It's all right, bonny lad. Don't be scared. I'll come, straight away. I'll be there in an hour. Hang on, lad, Maurice is coming.'

'You gave them your direct number?'

'What was I supposed to do, boss? There's no one to help that lad. I'm all he's got at the moment. And he's trying to talk. He told me he was cold and scared. So can I go, or not?'

'Go. Let me know if he says anything else, anything to help us.'

'So what is this place and why have we come here walking?' Trev asked curiously, looking round the seemingly uninteresting moorland.

'Ludworth Moor. There are supposed to be some Bronze Age remains here. Traces of what might have been a Druidic stone circle. I thought it might be nice to discover some of the ancient history on our own doorstep.'

He'd found a map online of a walking route so that it looked less suspicious, bringing Trev along.

'Besides, it's got Celtic connections, and you have Celtic blood, so I thought it might interest you. It's a nice day for a walk, and not too far to drive.'

'Ted Darling you are possibly the worst liar I've ever encountered. I've never heard such a load of utter bullshit. Since when were you ever interested in ancient history? I bet you don't even know the dates of the Bronze Age. Do you?'

'A long time ago,' Ted replied evasively, looking all round

him as they walked. He was interested in more recent constructions. He thought there may well be old farm buildings, perhaps shepherds' huts or the like, remote, isolated. The perfect place for someone to be held captive without being heard by anyone nearby.

'Is this to do with a case? Have you brought me to a crime scene? Oh my god, Ted, tell me we aren't looking for buried bodies?'

'No, it's nothing like that, honestly. I just needed to have a look about to see if there are any old, abandoned buildings up here. I'm sorry for the subterfuge. I wasn't sure you'd give up the chance of going riding if I said it was work. I should have let you go off riding without me. At least you could have been having some fun while I was working.'

'Oh, I'm sure we can find a way to have some fun. And this is going to cost you, big time. If you thought Friday's meal was expensive, you wait until you get the bill for making this up to me.'

Chapter Twelve

'Darren Lee is just starting to try to talk, but only to Maurice. Not even to his mother. Maurice went up to see him again yesterday. Darren's repeating "cold, dark and scared", but so far nothing else.'

Jim Baker grunted at this. 'I think we could all have worked out for ourselves that he would have been cold and scared, being kept the way he was, without paying man-hours to hear that.

'Thank you, Debs,' he added, as the Super put coffees in front of them all. She clearly thought it was a meeting in which they would have need of them.

'He went on Saturday in his own time and at his own expense though, to be fair. It was just yesterday's trip which came out of my budget. I authorised him to go because Darren actually phoned him. Just as well he did as when Maurice got up there, the mother had been drinking and had passed out cold.'

'He managed to phone him?'

'It just shows how important Maurice is to him. The first person he thought of.'

'It's not an ideal situation that Darren is in now, at all,' Superintendent Caldwell observed as she sat down behind her desk, opposite the other two. 'We all know that the best thing for him would be to be placed in a special unit somewhere until he recovers sufficiently to live at home. The mother clearly needs help, too. But we also know realistically that the cutbacks in services, particularly in adolescent mental health care, mean that's just not going to happen.

'The problem for Superintendent Baker and myself is, of course, the cost of all this. Not just who pays for what but also the dreaded ROI. What return can we show the purse-holders on all our invested personnel hours?'

She was always more politically correct and gender-neutral than Jim Baker, a self-confessed dinosaur. He meant no harm by what he said. He just insisted he was getting too set in his ways to cope with change.

She took a sip of coffee before continuing. 'The ideal solution would be a Family Liaison Officer from Preston, so the hours were coming out of their budget, to spend time with him to gain his trust and hopefully to encourage him to talk.'

Ted shook his head. 'He's made a connection with Maurice. Like I said, that's demonstrated by the fact that it was Maurice he tried to contact when his mother was unconscious. It's probably because it was Maurice's voice he heard most of when he was sedated in hospital.'

'The ideal thing would be to do it gradually. I think our budget could stand a few of DC Brown's hours to work alongside an FLO until Darren felt as comfortable with that person as he currently does with DC Brown.'

'The thing with Maurice, for all his faults, is that he inspires trust. Even a trained FLO might not achieve as much with Darren as he's done, and we desperately need to get Darren to the point where he can say enough to help us move the case forward.'

'This is in no way a criticism of you or your team,' Superintendent Caldwell continued, looking directly at Ted, 'but for all the hours invested so far, we still have little to show for it.'

'We're hampered most by the fact that although we have two surviving victims, neither has been able to talk about what happened to them. Lincolnshire are still looking for Tim

Phillips, so far to no avail. He never has spoken about it, as far as we know, and it's doubtful he will now. But we have to keep trying.'

'What about connections between the three cases? Any links between the victims?'

'Nothing as yet, boss, but we are still looking.'

Jim Baker had been Ted's boss for a long time and using the informal address came naturally to him. He tended to call the Ice Queen ma'am more often than by her first name, unless they were alone. Their relationship was not the same and probably never would be.

'And what about suspects? Neither of us is wishing to put you under any undue pressure but Superintendent Baker and I have another budgetary meeting this afternoon, to report back on the staffing reductions that have been put in place here. Clearly this case is going to come up in the course of that meeting. It would be helpful to have some crumb to throw on the table before the top brass. Even the vague promise of a break-through to come.'

'We're liaising with Preston to get them to find out who would have had a key to the church where Darren's phone was left. DC Vine was the one to point out that it's unusual for churches to be left unlocked in this day and age. As there's a likelihood it was left there at night, it makes it more probable that someone had the means to let themselves in.'

'She's a bright lass, young Jezza,' Jim Baker said admiringly. 'I take it she wasn't on your hit list to get rid of? I suppose it would have had to be Maurice if Megan hadn't given him the get out of jail free card, the jammy bastard.'

'The Chief Inspector has been very coy and refused to tell me who he had lined up,' the Ice Queen said dryly.

'Come on, Ted, it's academic now. Debs and I need to know what management decision you reached. We all know you have a soft spot for Maurice, so would you have had the balls to get rid of him? Sorry, Debs, just an expression, nothing meant by it,' he added hastily.

It was Ted's turn to buy time by drinking his coffee. It was Maurice he'd decided on. He had seen no other choice. His performance, although invaluable in some areas, was below par in others, compared to the other members of the team.

'I'm glad it's turned out as it has. And yes, even though I didn't and don't want to lose him, given the choice between all the current team members, it's Maurice I would have moved on.'

'Sound management choice,' Superintendent Caldwell nodded her approval. 'I hope you will impress upon him what a narrow escape he had and that we will see a consequent improvement in his performance across the board, not just in his specialist field.

'Now, as there's no telling how long you'll be tied in up court this week, presumably you'll be leaving DI Rodriguez in charge of this ongoing investigation?'

'Probably not, ma'am. There's no telling what else will come in. We've had a quiet week last week but who knows when something serious will kick off again. Mike Hallam is perfectly capable of running this one and I'm going to let him do that. That leaves Jo free for anything else that comes in, from anywhere else.'

Both nodded their satisfaction at his reasoning.

'Bloody good job, Ted,' Jim told him. 'Now that my patch is about as big as it's possible to get without giving me offshore islands as well, I need someone strong on your little Sweeney if I want to send anyone elsewhere.'

Jim Baker was in charge of Serious and Serial cases for an increasingly large part of the force area. He used Ted's team as his first resource to send out to lead enquiries where there was no one local sufficiently experienced to do so. He jokingly called them The Sweeney, from the Cockney rhyming slang phrase, Sweeney Todd, for the Metropolitan Police's Flying Squad, although the remit of the two units was different.

'That applies especially if you get stuck in court for days on end. We both know that's likely as the defence will want to unpick every part of your investigation. I hope you have all your facts memorised and all your answers off pat because we know already that the defence barrister doesn't take prisoners. He'll be going for your jugular. I doubt he can avoid a conviction but he might be able to sway the court not to pass too long a term of imprisonment when sentencing.'

'Right, well if you gentleman have finished your coffee, I think we can wind our meeting up and allow the Chief Inspector to go and brief his team. If there's any new information we should have, please let me know before lunchtime, when I'll be leaving for Central Park. Jim, will you be making your own way there?'

Jim was getting awkwardly to his feet, leaning heavily on a stick to help him. His ankle seemed to be taking the devil's own time to heal after a recent bad break and subsequent operation.

'Yes, I have other places to visit before then so I'll see you there, Debs.'

'You all know that the Morgane Edwards trial starts tomorrow and that I'll be tied up with that, possibly for some time. Mike, I want you to take over the Preacher abduction cases, leaving Jo to pick up anything else which may come in.

'Jezza, chase up your Lincolnshire friends for news of Tim Phillips. Maurice, if Tim is found, you'll probably need to be the one to go and try talking to him initially. Mike, a priority for you to sort, please, is to get on to Preston and see if there's an FLO available to help with Darren. And before you interrupt, Maurice, we just can't justify the cost of you keep going up there. What I have managed to get is agreement for you to work in parallel with an FLO until Darren learns to trust them.

'Steve, you mentioned a good point to me on Saturday, so

you can see that it's followed up. Let's just check that the people who found the three lads really are just innocent passers-by and there's no link between them.

'Jezza, how did you get on with finding out who has access to the church?'

'Preston were going to check it out for me, boss, and let me know today. I'll chase them up if I don't hear anything from them.'

'Good, because that's a good point and something we do need to follow up.

'Rob, traffic cameras? Anything?'

'Nothing as yet boss, but we are still looking. Sal's been helping me. There's a lot to trawl through.'

'Megan, we still have a week of your valuable presence so perhaps you can do searches for anyone that needs help? Now we no longer have Océane and Baby on tap, could you do some of that to free others up? It's work you can do sitting down, if you need to.'

She smiled at him. 'Thanks, boss, that's a kind thought but I'm not quite at that stage yet. Sarge, just throw anything my way as you need to.'

'Please keep me updated at all times, especially of any new possible leads. Other than that, I need time to go over all the notes I'll need for this trial, so I'd appreciate some time to get on with that. I'm also going to try to get away at a reasonable hour this evening, to do more of the same at home. We desperately need a good result in court on this one after all the work we've put into it.'

Ted made himself a mug of green tea before he sat down with his notes. He'd been over them endless times already but he needed to be word perfect on this one. He was always a good witness, giving faultless performances in court. This would be the toughest court case he'd ever been involved in and he couldn't afford to be off his game.

Trev was teaching again that Monday evening but had promised to be back by about seven-thirty, eight at the latest. He was not just Bizzie's stylist but Ted's too and would enjoying fussing over which shirt and tie he should wear. They'd discussed the upcoming big day on Sunday evening.

'That sounds fine. I should be back before you, with any luck, although I'll need to bring work home with me. I'll pick up a takeaway on my way home and keep it on a low light. Let me know when you're on your way and I'll have it ready for when you get in. What do you fancy?'

'Not Indian. You won't give a good impression in court if you stink of curry. Something subtle. Thai, perhaps? Or Chinese? I'll probably grab a quick snack when I get home to change to keep me going. I don't want my students to be put off by the sound of my stomach rumbling all through the lesson.'

Ted had smiled at him fondly. 'I've no idea how you stay so slim, the amount you put away.'

'I get plenty of exercise,' Trev had told him, shamelessly preening, sucking in his already non-existent waist to show off the hardened six-pack. 'Especially of the horizontal kind.'

The memory made Ted smile again as he started on the job in hand. He knew he was lucky with his relationship. Coppers didn't make the best partners and many a police marriage had ended as a result of it. Ted worked hard to make sure Trev was happy because having a loving and stable home life was essential for him to concentrate on the job in hand.

He'd asked the team for some quiet time and they'd largely left him alone, apart from a brief visit later in the day from Jezza and Mike.

'Boss, sorry to disturb you but I thought we'd better run this one by you because it might be significant. Jezza's had the list from Preston now of people known to have a key to the church. One of them is, of course, the vicar. But, and here's the part which may be of interest to us. He's relatively new to the parish, took it on just over three years ago.'

Jezza broke in impatiently. 'And three years adds up to Tim Phillips, missing six months and followed by a six-month break. Ditto Robbie Mitchell. And ditto again for Darren Lee. Three twelves, thirty-six months, which is three years.'

'Thank you, DC Vine, I'm not too bad at maths. But yes, it is interesting. We don't want to go rushing over there half-cocked harassing a man of the cloth without a bit more to go on, though. So please get Preston to find out everything they can about him and his previous history. Then discuss it in detail with me or Sgt Hallam before you take any further action. Or Jo, if I'm not around for any reason. This is not a decision for you to make on your own.

'I'll be coming into work before and after trial times for as long as I'm needed there so keep me up to speed at all times. And don't get too carried away. It may be nothing more than a coincidence.'

'But you don't like coincidences, boss, you're always telling us that.'

Sometimes, Ted thought to himself as the two of them left his office, Jezza was only just the right side of being a smartarse.

He was surprised he hadn't heard from Trev by eight o'clock that evening. He'd bought the takeaway as promised and put it on a low light. He'd give it a quick boost as soon as he heard his partner was on his way home. It made a pleasant change for him to be the one dishing up the supper. The kitchen was relatively tidy, which was an unexpected bonus. Trev had clearly grabbed a quick snack before he went back out but he had at least rinsed his mug and plate and had attempted to load them in the dishwasher, although it was not how Ted liked them to be stacked. He'd made an effort though and Ted was touched.

When he still hadn't heard anything by eight-thirty, he

decided to phone, worried the meal was going to be dried up by the time Trev got back. Trev loved company, loved to chat. His classes often ran on as he was so enthusiastic and his students were usually having so much fun they didn't want to go. His call when straight to voicemail.

'I'm just wondering when to dish up but I expect you've just run on. Give me a quick call to say when you're on your way and I'll have it on the table ready.'

Nine o'clock and still no word. That wasn't like him. If nothing else, Trev should be starving by now, the earlier snack a distant memory, his stomach thinking his throat was cut.

Ted turned the oven off completely. He'd just have to flash the meal in the microwave when his partner finally got home. The *popty ping* as Trev had taken to calling it, now he was learning Welsh from Ted's mother. He'd loved the quirkiness of the Welsh expression, ping oven, for a microwave.

Ted took the opportunity to phone his mother, reproaching himself that he didn't do it often enough.

'Sorry I haven't had much chance to phone you of late. Work's been a bit full on,' he said guiltily when his mother answered the phone.

'Don't worry, *bach*, I understand about your job. Trev phones me most days. He is such a lovely young man, very kind and thoughtful.'

'Have you spoken to him today?' Ted tried to make the question sound casual, mundane. But his mother was perceptive.

'Yes, he phoned me before he went out teaching. He does love it, doesn't he? The teaching, I mean. Is there something wrong? Have you two had a row?'

'No, no, nothing at all. I just wondered. I've not caught up with him yet but he'll be back any minute. I'd better go and sort him out some supper. *Nos da, mam.*'

'*Nos da*, Teddy *bach*.'

Trev was in a good mood. As he strode through the streets to where he'd left his Triumph motorbike parked and safely locked up, he was still grinning his pleasure at how the evening class had gone. He'd been teaching a particular group for some time now and they were making excellent progress. So much so that this evening they'd been learning to use the present continuous tense to express future mood.

'What are you doing tomorrow? I'm working, then I'm going out for a meal, then I'm watching television.'

He'd always ask the same question of each person in the class, encouraging them and helping as necessary with the answer, until they all felt confident in how to form a reply. There was one young woman who had so far not uttered a single word in any of the lessons. She hadn't even raised her head to make eye contact with him when he asked her questions, nor with any of the other students in the group.

Trev didn't know much about the background of the people he was teaching. It wasn't relevant, and it was up to them what they wanted to disclose about themselves. He knew some were refugees, often from war-torn regions. They would frequently be reluctant to talk much about their backgrounds. All were united in wanting to learn English to make a better life for themselves in their adoptive country.

He assumed the young woman was from a Muslim country as she always wore a hijab. He was more tactful and careful of how he addressed her, all too aware that her discomfort might be cultural, at being addressed by a strange man. She'd been to every single class since the first evening of, 'Hello, my name is Trevor. What's your name?'

She sat there quietly, eyes downcast, but she studiously copied down everything he wrote on the board and tucked away into her file all the handouts he prepared, though never took them directly from his hand.

It was now just for form's sake that he addressed to her the same question as to everyone else in the class and waited a moment to give her the chance to respond, should she want to, before moving on to the next person.

This evening, she had looked up for the first time, taking his breath away with the brilliance of her shy smile as she said, 'Hello, my name is Aalia. I am from Syria.'

There was a stunned silence from the other students, then everyone broke out into a spontaneous round of applause. Trev would have loved to give her one of his famous hugs but knew it would cause all sorts of problems. Instead, he returned her smile and replied, 'Hello, Aalia, and thank you. Pleased to meet you.'

He was still smiling his delight as he reached the dark side-street where his red bike was waiting for him. He was concentrating on the memory, savouring it again to share with Ted when he got home, taking no notice of his surroundings.

Then the pain hit him. The back of his head appeared to explode. He had a fleeting moment in which to register that this was worse, much worse, than the most severe hangover he could ever remember having, and he'd known a few.

He knew nothing more after that brief thought. He was certainly unaware of his legs buckling beneath him, or of the thwack as the side of his face came into contact with the brutal, unyielding roughness of the paving stones.

Chapter Thirteen

By ten o'clock, Ted had given up on the meal and put it on the side to congeal in its foil containers. Until he knew where Trev was and that he was all right, he didn't have much of an appetite. It was only a couple of hours but it wasn't like him. He always got in touch if he was going to be later than planned. He knew Ted's job made him worry more than most and he was simply too well-mannered not to at least let him know if he was going to be late.

Once eleven o'clock had passed with no news, Ted got the car back out and went looking for him. He realised he was going to look stupid if his partner had simply gone for a drink and lost track of time. But Ted's nerves were on edge with all that he had going on and he decided he would rather look foolish than appear uncaring.

The centre where the classes were held was locked up and in darkness, clearly long since, as he had suspected it would be. There wasn't a pub close to where Trev might have gone for a drink with students or friends and Ted knew that the nearest one would have called time by now.

He parked his car and went for a walk round the side-streets to see if he could see any signs of anything. He kept telling himself that he wasn't worried, not really. Just being neurotic. Trev could take care of himself. Everything would be fine. Any minute now he was going to bump into his partner, walking back from wherever he'd been, full of excuses that he'd lost track of time.

It was when he found the Triumph still parked up that Ted started to get really concerned. He knew Trev didn't like leaving his precious bike parked in these back-streets for longer than he needed to, always worried it would be stolen, even when locked up securely. If he'd gone off somewhere, he'd usually have taken it with him and parked it where he could keep an eye on it.

Ted stopped in his tracks and let practised eyes survey the scene with a professional detachment. Was that a blood stain on the pavement? Recent? Connected? Or was his policeman's brain jumping to conclusions when there was a simple explanation? Seeing crime scenes where they didn't exist.

He tried Trev's phone once more. Straight to voicemail. Then he called the friend who had first got Trev started on the English lessons.

'Mark? It's Ted, Trev's partner. I'm sorry to call you so late. It's just that Trev hasn't got back from teaching yet and I can't get hold of him. Do you happen to know if he was going anywhere afterwards? Drinks with the students or anything like that?'

Mark was pleasant, polite, but he clearly thought Ted was either some kind of neurotic fusspot, or someone insanely jealous of who his partner might be seeing. Either way, he couldn't offer any help with his present whereabouts.

Ted phoned the hospital, shamelessly using his credentials to see if he could find out anything. No one called Trevor Armstrong had been logged into the computer system that evening and no one answering Trev's description had either been seen or was waiting in the A&E department.

He rang the station next. No news there either. No incidents reported which remotely helped him with his search. The officer he spoke to was kind and sympathetic, promising to keep the DCI informed if they got a report of anything which might be relevant.

Midnight now. Ted decided he'd better go home, in case

for some reason Trev had gone there without the bike. Although why he wouldn't have phoned when he knew Ted was probably worried sick by now, he couldn't imagine.

Occam's Razor, he kept reminding himself. Where there were two possible explanations for something, the simpler of the two was more likely to be the correct one. The simplest one of all was that Trev had gone for drinks with someone after the class, had one too many to risk the bike and gone straight home. He hadn't called because he'd lost his phone. Or the battery was flat. Or he knew Ted would give him a hard time for drinking too much when he'd had the bike.

That would be it. When Ted got back, Trev would be there, nursing a sore head, full of apologies and promising all sorts in exchange for forgiveness.

Ted decided to take the bike back with him. He'd brought the keys, just in case Trev had been drinking, not wanting to leave it where it might get stolen. Especially not before he'd finished paying for it. It might teach Trev a valuable lesson if he came back and found it missing. Perhaps then he would listen to Ted's constant reminders not to drink if he had the bike with him. It might also save him from getting arrested for drink-driving which would be disastrous in his line of work.

If Trev's helmet was in the box, he could use that to stay legal. He could safely leave his car. No self-respecting thief or even joyrider would bother stealing anything as modest as his far from new Renault if he locked it up securely. Although he had lost its predecessor when he'd left it open with the keys in.

Whatever time his partner rolled in and in whatever state, he was going to have some serious explaining to do.

'What the hell have you been up to? You look like something one of your cats dragged in through the flap and then rejected,' Jim Baker growled, eyeing Ted up and down critically and clearly finding him wanting. 'Have you forgotten how important today is? Did you sleep in that suit?'

Ted made a half-heartened attempt to do up his collar button and straighten his tie. Not that it made a lot of difference to the overall effect.

'I haven't slept. Trev didn't come home last night and I can't get in touch with him. I found the bike parked where he left it but I can't find out where he is or what's happened to him. I've been out looking for him half the night.'

'There'll be a perfectly simple explanation for it. Have you had a row or something? It won't be the first time your Trev has flounced off.'

'Not without telling me. Never. He's very good at staying in touch. That's why I'm worried. I've rung everyone I can think of, including the hospital, but there's still no trace.'

'Right, well, I know it's worrying for you but I'm sure there's really nothing to get het up about. He'll have gone for a drink, had one too many and be sleeping it off somewhere, with one of his mates. You're always saying it takes a bomb going off to wake him of a morning. And he's probably feeling embarrassed, if that's what's happened.

'But for god's sake, Ted, you know how important this case is and you know as well as I do the defence are gunning for you. If they see you looking like that, they're going to go digging into your background looking for traces of drug or alcohol abuse and goodness knows what else.'

'He's bloody legged it!'

'What are you talking about?' the man who answered his mobile phone kept his voice down, turning to face a wall, anxious that no one should hear what he was saying or lip-read his conversation. 'You mean you've lost him?'

'You didn't say he was some sort of fucking Kung Fu fighter. We didn't tie his legs, just his arms 'cos you never warned us. Anyway he went on the attack, kicked the shit out of the pair of us and managed to get away. We both got badly injured. We went after him but we lost him.'

The man swore comprehensively. 'You pair of incompetent bastards! Surely two of you could have managed to keep hold of him?'

'He was like a madman, I'm telling you. High kicking and everything. We'd been giving him that stuff like you said to keep him sleepy but he bloody woke up all right, with a vengeance. I've never seen nothing like it. I'm telling you, we both got injured.'

'When did this happen?'

'Couple of hours ago now.'

'A couple of hours? And you've only just thought to tell me? You really are a special kind of stupid, aren't you?'

'Don't call me stupid or I'll come and find you, you arrogant prick, as soon as we get back from this godforsaken place.'

'Well, good luck with that. I'm currently surrounded by police. Did you at least get the photo like I told you to, you useless shit for brains?'

'I said don't call me names! You should have warned us what he was capable of. And yes, we got it. Before he woke up.'

'Well send it to the number I gave you, and do it now.'

'What about the rest of our money? You said half up front and half after delivery.'

'You haven't delivered, you dickhead. The goods were lost in transit. Send that text now and we'll talk about it. But send it right fucking now. And I will know immediately if you have done.'

Two things happened in rapid succession. First, a ping told Ted he had an incoming text message on his mobile phone. He grabbed it from his pocket and opened it. He was just about to show it to Jim when he saw a man walking towards him along the corridor of the courthouse.

Clive Edwards. The father of the teenage girl Ted had put

in court today on five charges of murder and one of arson with intent to endanger life. As soon as Ted saw the smirk on the man's face, he knew. Without a shadow of a doubt.

Jim Baker may have been hampered by his dodgy ankle, but there was nothing wrong with his reactions. As soon as he sensed, rather than saw, Ted start to launch himself towards Edwards, he swung his walking stick up and across Ted's midriff, landing him a belt that briefly winded him. For a moment he looked into Ted's eyes and wasn't sure if his long-time friend was going to lamp him one.

Two constables in uniform were nearby and hurried over, looking awkward at the prospect of breaking up some sort of a scrap developing between two senior officers. Both had a hand on their batons, one was also reaching for his spray.

Jim Baker barked orders at them. 'You! Escort the DCI outside and stay with him until I come out. Arrest him if you have to but keep him there. And you. Once I've just had a little word with Mr Edwards, take him and deliver him to the defence team and ask them, with my compliments, to keep him out of harm's way.

'Right, Mr Edwards, would you mind telling me what that little exchange was about?'

'How should I know? Your Chief Inspector is clearly volatile and somewhat irrational. I think it's obvious to anyone who witnessed that incident that he has serious issues, not least of which is showing a lack of judgement. Hardly the sort of behaviour one would expect from a Senior Investigating Officer. It's no wonder this entire enquiry was mishandled and we're now facing this farcical miscarriage of judgement.'

'Well, we'll just have to see what the jury decide, won't we, Mr Edwards? For now, please go with the PC and I strongly advise you to avoid all contact with DCI Darling during the trial. It's highly irregular for you to have any contact with a key prosecution witness anyway.'

Edwards smirked again. 'I think you'll find it was he who

was trying to make contact with me. Clearly a disturbed and dangerous man.'

Jim turned on the heel of his good leg and limped off in search of Ted, outside the courthouse. He found him pacing up and down, clearly beside himself, while the young PC watched him warily.

'Back inside now, Constable. I'll take over here. You wait around, unless you're needed in court straight away, and if anyone is looking for me or the DCI, for any reason, you come and find me immediately. I'll be just round the corner. Clear?'

'Sir.' The officer snapped to attention as he spoke then did an almost parade-ground pivot before marching thankfully back inside. Almost everyone in the force knew about Ted and his martial arts black belts. He was something of a legend. The PC was heartily relieved not to have had to find out the hard way if the stories about his prowess were true.

Ted opened his mouth to speak but Jim grabbed him by the arm, none too gently, and hustled him away from the entrance and around the corner.

'For god's sake, Ted, there's press crawling all round everywhere for the Edwards' trial, in case you've forgotten. You've already behaved like a complete idiot, fortunately out of their sight. Don't give them or the defence team any more ammunition to question your competency. And what, precisely, was that all about anyway?'

Wordlessly, Ted handed over his mobile phone, open at the photo he had received just as Edwards had come striding down the corridor smiling.

'Bloody hell,' the Big Boss grunted, looking at the picture of Trev lying, eyes closed, blood and bruising visible on the side of his face, his long legs pulled up so his body could be accommodated in the boot of a car.

'I don't even know if he's alive, Jim.'

Jim handed the phone back and put on his stern expression. 'Of course he's bloody alive. Stop thinking like his boyfriend and think like a proper detective. Whoever it is, they've got him because they want a hold over you. As long as he's alive, they've got one. Let anything at all happen to him and they lose their power over you. So he's alive. His face looks a bit sore but it's probably nothing. He may be asleep rather than unconscious. Maybe they gave him something.

'The thing to focus on is that he's alive, he's not left you or done anything daft. He's being held somewhere. You know your Trev, if there's a way to escape from them, he'll take it. In the meantime, we can start pulling all the stops out to find him. Forward that to Ocean,' he never managed to get her name quite right, 'and I'll authorise her to drop whatever else she's doing to make that a priority.

'But for god's sake, Ted, pull yourself together. You look a mess. You probably won't be called today but the defence will have their eye on you all the time. They'll be looking for any weakness which favours their case, which is clearly going to be that the investigation was flawed because of you and your character.

'I know it's hard. I can only imagine what you must be feeling. But you know Trev would expect you to go on as normal. He knows how important this case is. So please, go to the gents and do something to smarten yourself up a bit. Look like a copper who's more than capable of running a sound investigation, which you are. And I promise I will put every possible effort into finding Trev.'

Trev woke with difficulty. Someone appeared to have welded his eyelids together whilst he was sleeping, by the feel of it. They were certainly resisting all his efforts to prise them apart. The pain in his head was beyond description and belief. He tried to move, discovering that his hands appeared to be tightly tied behind his back. His legs were folded up and cramping badly, but there was no room to stretch them out. He started, gingerly, to tense and relax the muscles, using martial arts training to focus his concentration on one area at a time.

He finally managed to force his eyes to open but it wasn't a great help. Everything was dark all around him. Noisy, too. And there was movement. He realised he was squashed into the boot of a car. That would explain why he was feeling sick. From the bitter taste in his mouth and the smell in the confined space, he'd clearly already been sick at some point. He struggled to remember what he was wearing. He moved his bound hands. His Kevlar jacket, then. At least that would be easier to clean than his leathers.

But what was he doing in a car boot? More importantly, how the hell was he going to get himself out of there?

He had no impression of how much time might have elapsed. His only clue was that his bladder felt full to bursting, a sensation made worse by every jolt and bump in the car's progress. Several hours at least, then. He remembered he was wearing his new Diesel jeans, the ones for which he'd hidden the receipt from Ted, who would have complained at spending that amount on a made-to-measure suit for a special occasion, let alone for a pair of jeans. It made him determined that, full bladder or not, he was not going to lose control and wet them.

For a brief moment, he felt his eyes welling up, thinking of the worry Ted must be experiencing, not knowing where Trev was or what had happened to him. Trev himself didn't know where he was, just that he had to do everything in his power to get himself out of there as soon as possible. With that in mind, he started to prepare himself, exercising his body as much as he could in the tight confines. If only he could have the advantage of surprise when they stopped and whoever his captors were came and opened the boot, as they surely must do at some point.

After what seemed like an eternity, he felt the car starting to slow down. The sound of the tyres changing from the smooth noise of tarmac to a crunching sound which he thought must have been gravel. They hadn't turned off, though, so he wondered if they'd pulled into a lay-by at the side of the road. Once the engine had been cut, there was hardly a sound outside. He thought he detected a sheep bleating somewhere not far away but that was all.

He'd flexed every muscle in his body that he could manage to repeatedly since he'd woken up. He was cramped, fighting pins and needles, but he was as ready as he was going to be. He'd decided his best bet was to give no sign that he was awake, to lull whoever was holding him into a false sense of security. He was only going to get one chance at escaping, he felt sure, so he had to make the most of it.

The boot lid opened slowly, warily. Low early morning sunlight hit Trev's closed eyelids, sending further lancing pains through his head, but he forced himself to remain motionless.

'Shit, he's not dead, is he?' a man's voice asked.

He felt movement as someone leaned against the car, breath on his face as the person looked at him more closely.

'No, his eyes are twitching. Still out cold. Rapid Eye Movement they call that. It's a sign of deep sleep. Like when you dream.'

'Well, get a photo of him, then. It's coming up time to send it and this place is about as quiet as it gets. We're nearer to a town or something up ahead so we can't be opening up the boot there.'

Trev heard clicks as photos were taken.

'Right, shut the boot again and let's get on the way.'

He didn't want them to shut the boot. This could be his only chance of escape and he was determined to try for it. He stirred and made a long, low groaning sound.

'Shit! Is he all right?'

'Just coming round a bit, I think. Should we give him some more stuff?'

'We're not meant to kill him, remember, and he's had two lots already. We could just gag him with something and risk it?'

'What if he's sick and chokes to death? It stinks like he's already thrown up in here.'

The same feeling of the car dipping slightly, as if someone was bending over him again. Trev knew that this was his one chance and he had to take it, come what may.

His eyes snapped open at the same time as his feet shot out with all the force he could put behind them. He could barely feel his legs and feet so he doubted it would have had the same effect as he could produce in the dojo, but he was rewarded by the satisfying crunch of bone and the sight of blood spurting from the face of one of his assailants.

The movement had brought his legs over the rim of the boot so he allowed his own weight to take him down to the ground. Pointless to try to stand yet and risk falling over. Down on his side, he kicked out again and again with powerful legs. The first man was down already, clutching his face and showing no signs of wanting to get up. Trev's flailing legs took the other one down to land in a heap on top of him.

Trev forced himself to his feet, hampered by his bound hands. His legs were rubbery, the circulation compromised, but he made himself ignore the feelings. He kicked one man squarely in the stomach, another in the side, before staggering away as fast as he could down the road, looking for somewhere to plunge off into whatever cover he could find while he tried to shake off his kidnappers. At least he had a head start on them. They took their time to get their wind back, get to their feet, then limp painfully behind him.

Ted had spent some time, just for amusement, teaching Trev some of the evasion techniques he'd learned with Green on various survival courses. Trev used every one he could remember and was finally rewarded by shaking his pursuers off completely. He'd no idea how long it had taken him, or how much good it had done him. He just knew that after a lot of scrambling about through fields and what appeared to be open moorland, he found himself looking at a distant road below him and watching the two battered and dejected men making their painful way back down the steep hill towards it.

Trev couldn't hear them from his distant vantage point, but he could see their actions. One of them took out his mobile phone, mopping blood from his shattered nose with the back of his hand.

'He's bloody legged it!'

Chapter Fourteen

The men had headed for the road so it was clear to Trev that he couldn't go in that direction himself. He needed help, and soon, not least so he could relieve himself without ruining his expensive jeans. But he couldn't take the risk of being seen by his kidnappers and taken prisoner once again. He had no idea who they were or why they'd taken him. He hadn't recognised them. Their accents suggested Greater Manchester but, looking around at the scenery, he guessed he was some way away from there by now. Perhaps Snowdonia or further south in Wales. Nowhere he recognised, certainly.

He was not in the best condition to carry on dodging them. His head throbbed mercilessly and he was surprisingly hungry, despite still feeling sick. He'd heard the men mention having given him something and wondered if that explained the lingering bitter taste in his mouth as much as having been sick did.

He struggled to his feet and made his way carefully to the top of the hill to see if he could glimpse any hope of rescue. He could see an expanse of water some way in the distance but in between there seemed to be nothing but endless rough grazing, broken into a patchwork by old drystone walls and stock fences. He sank to his knees in despair beside some rocks. A small puddle of rainwater had collected in a hole worn in the top of one of them by the remorseless effect of water over many years.

His mouth was dry and tasted foul but he didn't want to

add to the contents of his bladder which already felt as if it were about to burst. He wondered what his kidneys would think of the abuse he was currently putting them through. He sucked up a cautious mouthful, swilled it round and spat it out, then took more and allowed himself a small swallow. Then he rested the good side of his face, the one which wasn't sore and stinging from contact with something he couldn't remember, against the rocks and allowed a few tears to leak out of his blue eyes. Then he shook himself, as much as his splitting head allowed, and gave himself a sharp talking to.

'For goodness sake get a grip of yourself, Trevor Patrick Costello Armstrong. Since when did girly crying do anyone any good?'

Ted sometimes called him by his full name, especially in tender moments, like when he had proposed to him. Ted. He would be beside himself with worry by now. Trev needed to find a way to contact him, and soon. He would be at the court today. If he had to start presenting his evidence before he knew his partner was safe, he was not going to give the flawless performance he was capable of and that which the prosecution case depended on.

Trev couldn't feel the weight of his phone or his wallet in his jacket pocket. He couldn't have used the phone anyway with his hands tied behind him, unless he'd found a way to get it out of his pocket, if it had still been in there. That was just ridiculous wishful thinking, the stuff which only happened in fiction. He needed to find someone to help him.

He stood up again, straining his eyes to look as far as he could. Then he saw it, partly hidden among some trees. A roof. There was a house down there, in the opposite direction to the lake. A house might mean people. Filled with a new resolve, he set off down the hill towards it, away from where he last saw the men.

He was approaching the house from the side, across the fields, which was why he had not immediately seen the drive running from the front of the building towards a road. As he got near he could see that it appeared to be a farmhouse, a reasonable size, with outbuildings. He skirted round so he could arrive up the driveway from the road. He didn't want to start with annoying a farmer by tramping across their fields, although there was no sign of any livestock about.

A Land Rover Defender was parked in front of the house. A man in a waxed jacket and a pair of overalls, topped off with a tweed hat, had the back door open and was just lifting a shotgun out, the barrels broken. A sable and white collie dog, hearing Trev's stumbling approach, ran towards him barking, showing impressively sharp white teeth.

'Excuse me please, but could you help me? I've been kidnapped and managed to get away. I'm tied up. Look,' Trev turned round as he spoke, showing his bound hands, trying to mask the desperation in his voice. 'Please. It sounds mad, but I really need your help.'

The dog had reached him now and was circling him, eyeing up his legs.

'That'll do, Cap,' the man ordered, and the dog returned to his side in a flash. Its master was looking at Trev with open suspicion. He cradled the gun under his arm but to Trev's relief, he saw him reach into the pocket of his overalls and pull out a folding knife which he opened. Then he approached, warily.

Trev kept his back turned, his bound hands held up. He willed his bladder to hold on just a moment longer, mortified at the thought of losing control now.

'Just be careful, laddie. I've got a gun as well as this knife and Cap is trained to grip livestock when I tell him to so he won't hesitate.'

As soon as he felt the bindings on his wrists give, Trev leapt forward and sprinted a few yards down the drive, wrestling desperately with his flies. There was neat fencing the length of the driveway with climbing plants growing up it. He hoped they would survive him peeing up against them, but he really couldn't hold on any longer. As he ran, Cap sprang after him and had a taste of his calf before his master could call him back.

Trev could see, as he relieved himself, that there was a sign at the road end of the drive offering B&B. At least he could probably get a meal and a clean-up there. Without his wallet, he couldn't pay them in cash but as soon as he could make a phone call to Ted, he'd be able to transfer some money to them and they could hopefully arrange for him to get back home from wherever he was.

He made himself decent before he turned back and approached the man again, wisely not offering to shake his hand.

'I'm so sorry about that, sir,' he used his most polite and persuasive voice and manner. 'I've no idea how long I've been tied up and I was bursting. And I've no idea where I am. Is this Wales?'

The man's look was one of even greater suspicion now. He mentioned a place name which meant absolutely nothing to Trev who looked at him blankly.

'You're in the Scottish Highlands. Nearest town is Fort William.'

'Scotland? I had no idea. Please may I use your phone? I've lost my mobile, and my wallet. I think they were stolen when I was kidnapped.'

Before he could answer, the front door of the house opened and a woman came out. She was wearing an apron and wiping her hands on a teacloth.

'Andrew? Have we got a visitor? Don't keep the young man standing outside.'

'I'm so sorry to turn up like this. My name's Trevor Armstrong. I've been kidnapped. I know that sounds completely unbelievable, but it's honestly the truth. Please may I use your phone? I've lost mine.'

'Oh, you poor thing! And look at your face. That looks sore. Come away in. Of course you can use the telephone. Would you like a nice cup of tea?'

She led the way into a bright inviting kitchen where a range was alight, a kettle simmering on the side and a pan of bacon sizzling away. Trev suddenly realised how hungry he was.

The man had followed them in, pausing to remove his Wellingtons in the porch and to order the dog to remain outside. He pointedly kept the shotgun under his arm.

'I'm so sorry but I don't have any money on me. I need to phone my partner urgently, he'll be going frantic. He's a policeman.'

'He?' the man asked. 'So you're one of those …'

'Andrew!' his wife chided. 'It's absolutely fine, there's the phone, just go ahead. I'll make you some tea. I'm just making Andrew's second breakfast. Would you like some?'

'I'm absolutely starving,' Trev admitted gratefully. 'That would be fantastic. Thanks so much. I'll just phone Ted. He can arrange to transfer some money so I can pay you for a meal, and for me to get back home.'

Trev picked up the phone and started to punch in the number. Zero seven ... Then he stopped and looked at the woman, anguished.

'I can't remember it. I can't remember his number. It's saved on my phone. I never have to dial it.'

'Don't worry, dear, you look as if you've have a nasty bump so your memory will be a bit fuzzy. Can you ring his office?'

'Yes, of course, sorry, I was being stupid and panicky. Can I use your computer to look the number up, please?'

'I'm sorry, dear, we don't have one. We just take phone bookings for the B&B, although our sons keep telling us we should have a website. They've moved on though and I don't think I'd be able to manage it.'

'I'll phone Angus. He can find it for you. He's our local

policeman. Where is it your man works?'

'Stockport.' Seeing the man's blank look, Trev supplied, 'It's in Greater Manchester. The GMP is the police force.'

The man took the phone and made a call of his own.

'Angus? It's Andrew. Aye, I went too. Prices were disappointing, especially ram lambs.'

'Andrew! You're supposed to be helping this young man, not talking livestock prices.'

After another brief exchange, the man handed Trev a piece of paper where he'd scribbled the number.

Trev nearly cried with relief when he finally got through to the station and recognised the familiar voice of Bill, the desk sergeant.

'Bill? It's Trev. Ted's partner. Please can you get a message to him urgently to tell him I'm fine. I'm all right, but I'm up in Scotland with no mobile and no money and no idea of how I'm going to get back home or when.'

'Well, you look marginally more human,' Jim Baker commented as Ted returned from the gents. 'At least with your colouring your five o'clock shadow doesn't show up too much.'

The Big Boss had sat down again, stretching his bad leg out in front of him. Ted knew it still gave him trouble from time to time. He'd done his best at a wash and brush-up within the limitations available to him.

The two PCs who had intervened earlier were still hovering nearby, waiting to be called for whichever case they were involved with. Jim beckoned one of them over and felt in his pocket for some loose change.

'Go and get a couple of coffees from somewhere for me and the DCI, there's a good lad. Sugar in his, none in mine. He and I are in conference.'

He was probably breaking all sorts of rules of political correctness, but the young PC seemed amiable enough. They both needed coffee and they certainly needed to talk.

'Right, Ted, listen to me carefully. I understand. I really do. You forget that my daughter was missing for years. So if anyone feels what you're going through, it's me. I know how hard it was for me every day to keep going in to work not knowing if the next phone call about a body was going to be Rosalie.'

'God, Jim, I'm so sorry. I'm being a self-centred shit, I never thought of what you went through all those years. I'm just going crazy with the worry of it.'

'Never mind, I understand. But you now know who's behind it all and that he's alive. Hold on to that thought. It's unlikely that you'll be called today, but we're going to need a meeting with the prosecution team as soon as court has finished for the day. They're going to want to talk about the defence's opening remarks and what that means for our case. For you in particular.

'During the lunch break, I suggest you buy yourself a disposable razor and some toothpaste from somewhere and sort yourself out properly. We've gone into this prosecution assuring the CPS that our case is watertight because you ran a faultless enquiry, by the book. Now we both know that's true, but looking at you now, our own side is going to have doubts. So sort yourself out, for god's sake. And have faith. Trev is going to be fine.'

The PC appeared with their coffees, carrying them carefully so as not to spill any or scald himself. They sat in companionable silence, drinking them. The two men had been through a lot together, shared many highs and lows. If anyone could help Ted through this, Jim could.

When eventually the mobile in Ted's pocket vibrated, he grabbed it so quickly he nearly dropped his now empty cup. It was the station. Ted dreaded what the news might be.

'Ted? Bill here. Good news. Your Trev's been in touch. He's fine, but he's marooned in the Scottish Highlands with no money and no phone. He told me to tell you not to worry. And I'm not repeating the rest of it, it's too soppy.'

Somehow, Ted got through the rest of the day. At lunchtime, he made a quick call to the number Bill had given him. A woman answered and he asked to speak to Trevor Armstrong.

'You must be Ted, I suppose?' She sounded polite, friendly. 'I've sent him up for a lie down. He's fine, though, don't worry. He'd just had a nasty bang on the head, which I've seen to. I don't think he should travel this evening, not overnight, so he can stay here and my husband will take him to Fort William tomorrow and put him on a train. He'll be in Stockport by half past seven.'

'If you let me have your bank details I can transfer all the money we owe you. I can't thank you enough for taking such good care of him.'

'It's been my pleasure. He's absolutely delightful. Please can we keep him?'

Ted laughed. 'I'd rather you sent him back, if you don't mind.'

'Oh, and don't worry about the cost of anything. Your sergeant at Stockport has already sorted everything out between him and Trevor. He's been kind and helpful, too.'

Promising to call again later that evening, when he'd finished work, Ted ended his call.

If Edwards' plan had been to rattle him to the point of making him appear an unreliable witness, he had nearly succeeded. Now Ted knew his partner was safe and being well looked after, he could put all his attention back where it belonged, in dealing with the case.

He'd rallied by the time of the briefing with the prosecution once court had risen for the day. He looked tired but he was back almost to top form. After a brief discussion, Ted was told that he was unlikely to be needed before afternoon of the following day at the earliest. That suited him fine. He had things to sort and places to be.

He headed back to the station from court. He'd asked for a catch-up with Jo and Mike, to be brought up to speed with anything which had happened in his absence. Most of the team had gone but Jezza was still there, looking anxious.

'Is Trev all right, boss? And are you?' she asked as soon as he walked through the door.

He knew Bill wouldn't have breathed a word of what was going on in his personal life. But the nick was always a gossip factory. Word had probably got out when Ted had contacted the station the night before.

'He's fine, thank you. Marooned in Scotland until tomorrow evening, but otherwise all right. His abduction does appear to be linked to the Edwards case, though, so we'll need to open a file on it. Jo, I'm putting you in charge of that. I'll give you all the detail I know so far, then I'll arrange for Trev to come in and talk to you at some point.

'So, what progress with The Preacher?'

'Boss, Preston think they've found an FLO to help with Darren. Maurice is going up tomorrow morning to meet her first then they'll go and try to see Darren together, see if it works out.'

'Thanks, Mike. Has Darren said anything else?'

'His mam told Maurice he's at least stopped spouting the scriptures. He's added in hungry to the list of words he's saying, but nothing other than that. Nothing that helps us, at least.'

'Boss, Bryony from Lincolnshire contacted me. They've had a more promising lead on where Tim Phillips might be squatting now. They've not found him yet, but it is at least a sighting and it's the first they've had for a while.

'I've had details from Preston about key-holders to the church, too. The vicar who's been there for the past three years has come up squeaky clean so far. The others are all more or less the ones we thought about. The vicar's wife is in charge of flowers, she uses the vicarage spare key to let in whoever's turn it is to do them. The organist checks out, too. He joined the church about the same time as the vicar.'

Ted frowned. 'Is there anything unusual in that? A change of vicar and organist at the same time? Some sort of church politics?'

Jezza shook her head. 'It all seems innocent enough on the face of it. The former vicar died in an accident. Fell down the stairs at the vicarage. He was apparently known to be fond of a drink and he had been drinking that evening, the post-mortem showed. It was recorded as an accidental death. It was his son who was the previous organist. He lived with his father, a widower, at the vicarage, so after his father's death, he had to move out, of course, and he moved away. There doesn't seem to be anything sinister in it.'

'Right, thank you. Good work, everyone. I'm probably not needed in court until tomorrow afternoon, but there's somewhere I need to be in the morning, first thing, if I can. I'll pop in when I get a moment and you can of course contact me by phone if there's anything that needs my attention urgently.'

'But you'll be wanting to get home at a decent time tomorrow if your Trevor is coming back, eh, boss?' Jezza asked him with a cheeky grin.

Ted had found time earlier in the day to phone Trev's long-suffering business partner Geoff to explain that he'd had to go away suddenly but would hopefully be back at work on Thursday.

When he got home at the end of a long day following a night with no sleep, he was set upon by reproachful cats demanding food and attention. It was usually Trev who saw to them in the evenings. He'd remembered to put the takeaway in the fridge away from their inquisitive noses, and managed to resurrect bits of it which were not too dried out to make himself a bit of supper. His meal was interrupted by his phone.

'Where's my brother? He was supposed to phone me last night to help me with a French project and I can't get hold of him.'

'Hello, Ted, how are you? I'm fine, thank you, Siobhan, and you?' Ted chided her gently. Trev's younger sister could be haughty and demanding.

'Yes, whatevs, but where is he?'

'He had to go away unexpectedly for a couple of nights and he's lost his mobile.'

'Oh my god, Trev's right, you are a rubbish liar, Ted. Where is he really and what's happened?'

He managed to persuade her that all was well, Trev would be back tomorrow and he would make sure that he called her as soon as he could. Then he finally got time to speak to Trev himself.

The same woman he'd spoken to earlier answered his call, then he heard her hand the phone to Trev and suggest he take the phone upstairs to his room for a bit of privacy.

'Are you all right? What happened?'

'Somebody clobbered me over the back of the head, stuffed me in the boot of a car and drove me up to the wilds of the Highlands. Luckily, I found this B&B which is blissful. Andrew and Jean have been looking after me ever so well, and Bill has sorted everything for me. You'll need to square up with him. My wallet's gone so I've neither cash nor cards. I've no idea who did it, though, have you? Is it something to do with your work?'

'There's a possibility it might be connected to the court case. Someone trying to intimidate me as a witness. Something like that.'

'There were two men, Greater Manchester accents. I may just have broken one of their noses when I escaped. Does that mean you'll have to arrest me, officer, and put me in handcuffs?'

'Behave yourself.'

'That's not what you usually say. I'm sprawled across a lovely big double bed here so guess what I'm thinking about?'

'You're impossible. I'll see you tomorrow. All being well, I'll be there to meet you off the train.'

'Love you.'

'I love you, too.'

More than you can possibly imagine, Ted thought to himself as he ended the call.

Chapter Fifteen

'The ACC will see you now, Chief Inspector, if you'd like to go in.'

Ted nodded his thanks to the Assistant Chief Constable's personal assistant and walked into Russell Evans' office. He was not at all sure he was doing the right thing. The two of them usually got on well, treated one another with mutual respect. But Ted felt himself burning up with a grievance and he needed to voice it to someone.

'Morning, Ted, to what do I owe this unexpected pleasure? I should just warn you that I'm between meetings but my PA said it was important so I can give you ten minutes.'

'Thank you,' Ted took a deep breath, trying to keep control, but before he could stop himself, he blurted out, 'You set me up.'

Evans spread his hands in feigned innocence.

'Set you up? In what way? What's this about?'

'The commendation. The reception. The press photos. I've always kept my private life separate from the job, but that put my partner in the limelight for the first and only time and now he's been kidnapped.'

'Yes, I heard about that on the grapevine.' Ted wondered if there was anyone who hadn't heard. 'But as for setting you up, I did nothing of the kind. I put you forward for a bravery award because you deserved it for your actions. And you know these things always happen at a function and there's always some publicity out of them.'

'But I was the only recipient who was photographed with their partner. The only gay officer present and the only one to appear in the paper with their significant other. It put him at risk. It was a publicity stunt, a cynical way to show how inclusive the force is.'

Evans held up a hand. 'Let me just stop you right there, Chief Inspector. And let me remind you, although I shouldn't have to. We're both at work. I'm in uniform. I outrank you, quite considerably. So you should be calling me sir. I should also point out that your tone is only just the right side of impertinent.

'If you've come here looking for some sort of ego massage, for me to tell you how much you're valued and assure you it has nothing whatsoever to do with your sexuality, then you're wasting your time and mine. You've had a promotion and subsequent increase in salary. That should tell you that you are valued within the force.

'And let me just assure you that there was no brief to get you both in the publicity shots. If it wasn't what you wanted, you were at liberty to refuse, as was your partner.'

He paused to take a breath, then his tone softened.

'I'm sorry about what happened to your Trevor, I really am, and I was equally relieved to hear that he's turned up and appears unharmed. But to come in here accusing me of some sort of conspiracy to use you as a marketing tool is frankly ridiculous and unworthy of you.

'I can imagine you've been under a lot of stress while he was missing. I'm going to put this exchange down to that. I thought you were meant to be in court today? The Edwards trial? So I'm going to let you get back to that and, because you are a good officer, and a valued one, I'm going to pretend this interview never took place.'

Ted was still standing in front of the ACC's desk, having not been invited to sit. His anger had evaporated and he was left feeling stupid. He'd been angry, furious over what had happened to Trev. He was starting to realise that most of his anger was directed at himself. He should never have allowed Trev to appear in a press photo with him. He'd exposed him to the risk. He'd just needed someone else to blame, to lash out at. He hoped that what he could now recognise as a monumental error of judgement was not going to be a bad career move for him.

'Sir.'

'Seriously, Ted, just go. It's fine. It's forgotten. We all do and say unwise things in moments of stress. I'll put it down to that.'

'Thank you, sir.'

As soon as Ted left his office, the ACC picked up the phone to make a call.

'Chief? We have a small problem. Ted Darling. Not a happy bunny.'

Ted was looking totally different to the way he had the day before when got back to the station in time to catch part of the morning briefing Jo and Mike were running in his absence. Despite all the tension he'd slept better than he expected to, now he knew Trev was safe. He was wearing the shirt and tie Trev had planned for him for the first day of court. He'd not worn it the day before because he was too anxious to think of changing after his night without sleep. He had on just enough but not too much of the expensive cologne Trev had bought for him.

He was back to looking like someone in control, after his earlier outburst, which he now bitterly regretted. It was a stupid thing to have done. Especially to go running up to HQ to do it. He'd made himself the feeble excuse of wanting to talk to Océane, which he could have done by phone, and she hadn't even been there. She'd been away on some course or another. He knew that Trev was his Achilles heel. He cared for him so deeply it sometimes affected his judgement. But now he was once again looking and feeling like someone more than capable of running complex cases and bringing them to a successful conclusion.

He stopped at the front desk on his way up to his office to thank Bill for all his help and to settle up with him.

'I've noted the total and my bank details, Ted. Just transfer it when you have a moment. I'm glad your Trev is all right. You'd be lost without him. Have you time to go for a drink sometime soon? I'd be glad of someone to talk to, if I'm honest. You know I'm for the chop? They seem to think I should be raring to get out, now I'm just about to turn fifty-five. They gave me notice a year ago and I applied for an extension. I thought I'd get it, no worries, but they're using the cost-cutting as a reason not to renew.'

'I will, Bill, but not tonight. Trev's coming home and I promised to try to pick him up from the station. But as soon as I can after that, promise. Why don't you stay on as a civvy? There must be an opening for someone of your experience.'

'They've said I could do that but there's no vacancy for another three months after my official retirement date. But honestly, what else do I have in my life, other than work? What am I supposed to do with myself for three months?'

'There's always NARPO.'

The National Association of Retired Police Officers offered companionship and something of a social life to former serving police officers. Most of them were glad of the chance to retire. Bill was an exception in that he had no one, other than his work colleagues and his parrot. His wife had died young, there were no children and he had never remarried. Never even been out with anyone, as far as Ted was aware, and the two of them talked a lot. Bill had known Ted since he'd first arrived in Stockport. His first post as a detective after he gave up firearms at Trev's insistence. He'd been keen – too keen – but still green. Bill had probably given him more help than anyone else and a genuine friendship had grown between the two as a result.

'What, playing dominoes and drinking pints with other boring, lonely old farts like me? I'd go mad inside a week.'

'I will do that drink as soon as I can, Bill, I promise. But right now I have two places to be at once and I need to start by sending a grovelling email of apology to the ACC. I made a bit of a prat of myself there this morning. Soon. Count on it.'

Mike gave the boss a quick resumé before the end of the briefing. Ted had questions to ask, wanting to be on top of this case as well as the Edwards one. He knew his team could work without him, but it was his head on the block if things went wrong.

'Are we happy Preston have dug deep enough looking at the key-holders for the church? What about any former ones? Could they have kept theirs? The previous organist, for a start? Has he been spoken to?'

'Boss, the current vicar says all the keys were accounted for when he took over. There was an inventory and everything tallied. No keys missing for any of the locks for the church or the vicarage,' Mike told him.

'And is there a link to the church from Darren? Did he go there ever? Would he have known anyone from there, or from somewhere other than church itself? Jezza's point is a valid one. For the mobile to be left inside, someone must have had access to the church, either with a key or by going when it was open, for a service or something. Can we pin down exactly when it was found and by whom? Rob, I think it would be worth a couple of hours of your time to go up to Preston yourself and double check everything.

'At the moment we're relying on another force to do our legwork for us and we don't know if they're as thorough as one of you would be. See if you can find this former vicar's son. Just on the off-chance he knows of someone in the past who might have had a key which for some reason isn't on the inventory. I'm assuming a key to a church door would be a biggish thing? Not the sort of thing you could easily get a copy made at one of these on-the-spot places? Can you find that out, too, please? Perhaps a quick visit to the church? See if it is left open, check times of service, that sort of thing. While you're up there already.'

'No worries, boss, I'll get up there as soon as we've finished here.'

'Boss, Lincolnshire have pinned down where Tim Phillips is staying but before they do anything else, they want to know what they're supposed to do with him,' Jezza told him. 'They've seen his file, they know his issues and the state he's likely to be in. They're worried that taking him to the nick could tip him over the edge. Then there's his addiction problem. He really needs to be in a secure unit now.'

'What age is he now, nineteen? Does that mean a place might be easier to find for him, if he's classed as an adult?'

'If he's anything like Darren, he'd flip at being put with adult men,' Maurice warned. 'I think it's fairly obvious that whoever is doing this is a man so there's a big risk in putting anyone as damaged as these lads are in a unit with adult males.'

'Maurice has a point, boss,' Megan put in. 'I've a friend who works in this area. She once told me a lot of young people go on to self-harm after something like this and it's often something they learn to do much more efficiently because of being put somewhere where there are already self-harmers. You'd be surprised where they can hide things with which to do themselves serious damage. It starts a vicious circle that's often hard to break. And that would be the last thing either Tim or Darren need now. Tim would need to be on the highest level of monitoring, I imagine, to keep him safe.'

'This is going to sound crazy, boss, and it is just an idea,' Virgil began.

'Whatever it is, let's hear it, Virgil. It's high time we started making some progress on this.'

'Is there any way you could arrange for Tim and Darren to meet? Maybe if they could each see that someone else has been through the same thing, they may find they could communicate with one another and we might get something out of it.'

'Risky, I would say. I'd want the opinion of a psychologist before we did something like that,' Ted replied. 'In fact, I should be seeing the one who did the report on Morgane Edwards during this trial. It's something I could ask him about. If we don't handle it very carefully, we could finish up making both of them worse than they are now and losing all hope of getting any information out of either of them. At the moment, they're our main hope of anything to go on.'

'Might some of Darren's friends be able to talk to him, boss?' Jezza suggested. 'Perhaps he would feel more at ease talking to them.'

Maurice shook his head. 'I wouldn't recommend it. It might be upsetting for them all. I'm not sure how much Darren is truly aware of but I doubt if he'd want people to see him as he is now. Maybe if he gets a bit better, it would be worth trying. I know it means waiting longer.'

'I'd certainly like the friends spoken to again, of all three victims, see if there's anything else at all they can tell us that would help. Anyone they can think of who the lads would have gone off with. Sal, can you go over their statements again then phone them and ask. Start off with Darren and work back from there. And let's keep on looking for links between the schools and colleges our three victims attended.

'Any news from SOCO about the tyre tracks from Ludworth Moor?'

'Not yet, boss, and yes, I will chase it up.' Mike Hallam's hand was already on his phone.

'Steve, did you get any further with your theory about the sites being connected? And with whoever this Lud character is?'

'Nothing, sir, sorry. I'm sure there is something there that makes sense to The Preacher but I can't get into the same mindset as him to see it just at the moment. I'll keep trying. It might help.'

'Right, you help Sal. Perhaps one of you checking out the friends, the other looking for anything at all which links the three victims.

'Is there anything else that's come in that I need to know about?'

'Virgil and I are just off out on a nice little spate of burglaries with assault as a side order, boss,' Jo told him. 'From initial reports, we should hopefully be able to wrap it up fairly quickly.'

'Right, I'll just clear some paperwork then I'll be off back to court. I'll call in again at the end of the day to see what's new.'

'What time does Trev get back from his adventures, boss? Do you want one of us to get a bunch of flowers for you?' Jezza asked him teasingly.

'Keep it up, DC Vine. I'm sure I can find a nice stack of filing to occupy you if you're getting bored.'

'You certainly look a lot more presentable than you did yesterday. Nice scent, too,' Jim Baker greeted Ted as he arrived at the Crown Court later. Jim wasn't required to give evidence but he had been in overall charge of the case, above Ted, so he was keeping an anxious eye on how the proceedings were going, when he could spare the time. 'You'd probably convince a jury that you're a reasonable policeman, looking like that. How are things with the other cases? Any news of what happened with Trev, or who's behind that? I know you're convinced it's Edwards but have you looked at other possibilities?'

'He gets home this evening so I'll do an initial interview …'

'I bet you will, but I don't need to know about that,' Jim

said jokingly. Ted was surprised. The Big Boss was usually careful to avoid anything which made him think about Ted's private life. He guessed his friend was probably relieved that it had ended well.

'If Edwards farmed the job out to anyone of the same intellect as the toe-rag who ran me off the road during that enquiry, we shouldn't have any problems tracking them down. As far as The Preacher goes, we're focusing on trying to find anything which links the three victims. It could all be random but I thought we'd start with the simplest explanation first.'

'You and bloody Occam's Razor. You're obsessed with it. I spoke to the prosecution team again earlier. They think you might possibly get called later this afternoon, but it may not be until tomorrow morning. The defence QC wants the ins and outs of a duck's arse from every witness so far. He's leaving no stone unturned, so keep your focus.'

Ted didn't get chance to find out what the QC was like. By the time he was next to be called it was getting late in the afternoon so the judge decided to adjourn until the following morning. It gave Ted chance to get back to the team for any updates.

'Boss, we have a possible link between the three victims,' Sal told him when they got together at the end of the day. 'We think it's possible that all three did NCS through their schools.'

The name meant nothing to Ted. He looked to Jo for enlightenment. He and Virgil were already back from the other case, reporting that it was mostly concluded apart from statement-taking, which they'd left to the local officers. Jo had six children. He was the office mine of information on anything to do with schools or children of any age.

'National Citizen Service, boss. Two of mine have done it so far, most of the others are mithering to do the same because George and Sophie liked it so much. It's a personal development scheme, government-backed. They do stuff like adventure training, social skills, leadership. It involves staying away from home, which was blissful in a large family like mine. A bit of peace and quiet while they're away.'

'Did all three of our lads do it? Is it affordable? Tim's mum was a single parent, wasn't she, and doesn't appear to have had the money to look after the lad let alone pay for stuff like that.'

'We're not sure yet if they all did it, boss, we're still looking at that,' Sal told him. 'But certainly it was on offer at all the schools they attended. And it's made affordable and accessible to anyone so yes, he could have. And it's something which would have looked good on his application to join the Navy. Steve's chasing up a list of participants at each school.'

'But surely anyone involved with young people through a scheme like that would need DBS checks? There'd have to be a thorough screening process?'

'Just because someone has no previous, it doesn't mean they won't go on to offend, Mike. It's certainly worth looking into. Keep me posted. I'm giving evidence tomorrow and from what's been seen of the defence QC in action so far, I expect I'll be there for most of the day, if not longer.'

'Make sure you get plenty of sleep tonight then, boss – if you can,' Jezza told him with a wicked grin. She had more respect for Ted than for any other senior officer she'd ever served under. Her teasing of him was her way of showing her estimation and affection.

'Point duty, DC Vine. I'm sure Inspector Turner would be glad of an officer of your calibre to help with the smooth running of traffic around the town.'

Ted went straight to the railway station from work, pausing only to pick up a takeaway so there'd be something to offer Trev to eat when he got back. Knowing him, he'd be starving. He knew his partner had two changes to make on his journey, once at Glasgow and once at Preston, and that he had less than ten minutes to make his connection at Preston. Ted was on pins waiting for him, especially when the Preston train was running late.

Then finally the train came trundling towards him, brakes squealing. As soon as the doors were released, Trev erupted out of one of them and came sprinting up the platform, crushing Ted in a bear hug which nearly lifted him off his feet. He was grinning from ear to ear.

'What larks, Pip! Apart from being bashed over the head, shut in a car boot and scared half to death, I've had such an adventure. But I've been so well looked after. Jean even washed all my clothes for me because they had puke on them and these are my good jeans.'

'They're very nice, too. You look good in them. Are they new?'

'Oh Ted, you are hopeless! You never notice what I'm wearing. I've had these old things for ages,' Trev lied shamelessly. 'Come on, take me home, and once I've finished showing you how glad I am to be back, I'll tell you all about it.'

Chapter Sixteen

'If you spit on your hanky and start rubbing marks off my face with it, that's the point at which you and I might just cease to be friends, Jim,' Ted told the Big Boss, who was looking him over intently before he was called into court.

Jim Baker wasn't appearing as a witness in this case so he would be sitting inside the court as Ted was giving his evidence. He clearly wanted him to be looking his best. They'd had a lengthy discussion earlier with the prosecution team who wanted to stress how important it was that, no matter how much the defence counsel needled him, Ted remain calm and professional, without rising to the bait.

'I don't want to put any more pressure on you, Ted, but there's a lot riding on this. I know you can do it. Just keep your cool and don't let him provoke you.'

'Yes, boss,' Ted smiled patiently.

There were a lot of press and public attending the trial. The judge had, as was normal in such cases, made an order prohibiting the reporting of anything which might identify the defendant because she was a young offender. There was a possibility that the order could be reversed if she was found guilty. It was a high profile case because of the age of the defendant and the severity of the crimes.

When Ted was called and Jim slipped quietly into a seat from where he could watch the proceedings, Ted was surprised to see that the defendant, Morgane Edwards, gave him a beaming smile, as if he was an old friend she was delighted to see at a social occasion. Her fine blonde hair was pulled back into a neat French plait, she wasn't wearing any make-up and she looked about twelve instead of her real age of sixteen. Ted could almost sense that she already had the jury feeling sorry for her with her little girl lost appearance.

Ted always declined the oath, preferring instead to affirm. He wasn't religious at all and he refused to be a hypocrite.

The prosecuting counsel took him through his evidence which he presented clearly and concisely. Then the defence QC rose to cross-examine him. He was tall and good-looking, well-spoken, with an air of privilege about him and a self-assurance bordering on arrogance in his bearing and his way of posing questions. Ted had earlier given his credentials but he knew the man now facing him had a vested interest in bringing them and everything about him into question.

'Chief Inspector, you haven't always been a plain clothes criminal investigator, have you? Would you tell the court what your police role was before that.'

'Most of us started out in uniform in the days when I joined. It's different now. I'm a former SFO, a Specialist Firearms Officer, Your Honour.'

Although the barrister was posing the questions, it was to the judge that Ted correctly directed his answers.

'Firearms. I see. So you shot people. Did you actually kill anyone whilst in that role?'

The prosecuting counsel was going to get plenty of exercise for this phase of the trial with the number of times he would leap to his feet to object to a line of questioning. On this, his first attempt, he was not successful.

'I did, Your Honour. It was part of my job.'

'What sort of personality is required to shoot people as part of a job?'

'A trained police firearms officer's personality, Your Honour.'

'Would you describe yourself as a violent man, Chief

Inspector?'

'No, Your Honour, I would not.'

'But you are a practitioner of martial arts, are you not? Holding several black belts?'

'I am, Your Honour, which is why I would not describe myself as violent. Martial arts training teaches self-control, the opposite of violence.'

'But is it not, in fact, the case that on the first day of this trial, Tuesday, to be precise, when you saw Mr Edwards, the defendant's father, approaching you in this court building, you lunged violently towards him? And that you had to be restrained by a senior officer wielding a walking stick and two Police Constables in uniform, preparing to use batons and sprays?'

'That's not exactly how it happened, Your Honour. I did stand up rather suddenly to speak to Mr Edwards on another matter, totally unrelated to the trial. My Superintendent advised me against doing so, so I left the building with one of the PCs.'

'He advised you with his walking stick, did he not, Chief Inspector? With a blow to your midriff? Does that not rather indicate that he feared you were about to carry out an act of violence?'

'I can't speak for what was going through my Superintendent's mind, Your Honour.'

The prosecutor was still trying valiantly to get the line of questioning changed. The judge indicated that he wanted to see it move on significantly before much longer.

'And what about obsessive, Chief Inspector? Would you describe yourself as an obsessive man?'

'I would say no more so than any police officer dealing with a difficult and complex case, Your Honour.'

'Paranoid, then? Do you consider yourself to be paranoid?'

'Not in the slightest.'

'But it is true, is it not, that during the course of your investigations following the death of the defendant's mother,

Stephanie Mason, you went to see her father, Clive Edwards, to accuse him of hiring someone to try to kill you?'

The exchange went on remorselessly. Ted played some racquet games when he got the chance - badminton, squash. He was starting to feel as if he was on the end of a long and vicious rally with a player of a higher calibre. He felt he was only just managing to return the shots.

When the judge called a halt for a lunch recess, the prosecuting counsel, looking daggers, jerked his head in Ted's direction, a silent but clear summons to another briefing. Ted groaned inwardly. He wanted to check his phone, which had been switched off whilst he was in court, but Jim Baker caught him by the arm and hustled him along to the office the prosecuting team were using. There was a table laid with coffee and sandwiches waiting for them. It would be a working lunch, but at least they were going to be able to eat something.

As soon as the door closed behind them all, the senior prosecutor rounded on Ted.

'You were about to attack a defence witness in a public place and had to be beaten off with a walking stick? For god's sake, Ted, when were you going to share that nugget with us? And what's all this about accusing him of taking out a contract on you? Why is this the first we're hearing of any of this?'

'It wasn't like that at all, it's been blown out of all proportion,' Jim Baker put in, hurrying to defuse the situation. 'I didn't think for a moment Ted was going to attack him. I thought he was going to speak to him and that it was ill-advised. I'm not very swift on my pins since my accident so I stuck my stick out to deter him. I certainly wasn't beating him off.'

'But the damage has probably already been done. The jury now clearly think the enquiry has been run by a violent maniac with paranoid delusions. We are going to have to work like hell to airbrush that impression out of their minds.'

It took a long time to smooth feathers and find common

ground going forward to the afternoon session. Ted was itching to check his messages, to see what progress was being made on The Preacher case and if there was yet any word from Océane on who was behind Trev's kidnapping.

He only had a few moments on his way to the gents to prepare for the afternoon's grilling. Jim Baker fell into step behind him, growling ominously.

'That's the last time I dig you out of the shit on this one, Ted. Whatever you think is going on between you and Edwards, for god's sake find some evidence of it or shut up about it. Even I'm starting to think you're getting paranoid on the subject.'

He finally got a few brief moments to call Océane. As he'd hoped, she had left a message for him to do so as soon as he could.

'Good news and bad news, boss. Which would you like first?'

'Save the best for the last, please. I've not had a good morning.'

'Okay, the bad is that it's highly unlikely we'll ever be able to trace the mobile that sent you the photo of Trev. It's an unregistered pay as you go. It could possibly be done eventually but it would take forever and make all kinds of a hole in your budget.'

'And the good news?'

'Is very good. Because we now know roughly where Trev was taken to, up in the Highlands, we were able to look at mobile phone traffic in that area. And there's very little of it. I assume sheep don't have their own smartphones and the human population seems low. Anyway, shortly before you received that message, we picked up a trace of a call from the same place. But not from the same phone number.'

Ted could tell she was dragging it out for the dramatic impact. He felt like shouting at her to hurry up. But he didn't. For one thing, he couldn't afford anyone to see any display of temper or loss of control on his part. He knew that he would be being closely watched and that was not paranoia on his part.

'Luckily for us, our kidnapper doesn't seem to be the sharpest knife in the drawer. It shouldn't be long now before I can tell you exactly who he is, because it seems he stupidly used his own phone for the earlier call. With luck, I can also tell you exactly who he was calling.'

'Océane, that is what I call very good news. Thank you so much. I owe you a drink, if not a meal.'

Rob was enjoying the chance of a run out up to Preston. He had the radio on full blast and was singing along. He'd had an anxious few days, with rumours of cuts rife in the station. He knew his position, as a newly promoted DS, could have put him at risk of being moved on and it was the last thing he wanted. He was engaged now and he and his fiancée Sally were making plans to get married.

She had a good job in Stockport as an RSPCA inspector and neither of them wanted to move to a new area. They wanted to settle down and start a family. Not of their own, as Sally couldn't. But having spent some time in foster care himself, Rob was keen to foster and possibly to go on to adopt. Now he knew they were staying put, at least for the time being, they could take their plans to the next level.

He found the church he was looking for with no difficulty. It was a short distance outside Preston and was as he imagined it would be. An old-fashioned 'proper' church which probably dated back a few centuries and had a churchyard which looked as if it would be a creepy place to find oneself after dark.

As he'd thought, the building was locked firmly and the boss had been right. It must have been a big key to fit that lock and turn the mechanism. A notice in the porch gave him the times of service. He took a photo of it on his mobile.

He decided to take a walk round the outside of the building, to see what he could find out. He'd phoned ahead to find out if the vicar would be available to talk to him and had been given a slot. He was slightly early so he had time to kill.

Around the far side of the church, he found a much smaller door, a side entrance of some sort. Rob didn't know anything much about churches but vaguely knew they had something called a vestry and he supposed this was the way into it. He noticed that this door had a modern Yale lock. That would make the possibility of having a duplicate key made much easier. He took a photo of that too. Then he headed off to find the vicarage, a short distance away.

He passed an impressively large detached house which he assumed must once have been the vicarage before he came to a much smaller modern building, built on land which looked as if it could previously have been part of the old vicarage grounds. More signs of cost-cutting and down-sizing, he supposed.

A woman answered the door when he rang the bell. He showed her his ID and she led him into a light and pleasant sitting room.

'I'll just let my husband know you're here. He's upstairs in his study. Please take a seat. Would you like some tea? Or some coffee?'

'Coffee, thank you, very kind.'

Rob wasn't sure what he was expecting a vicar to look like. The man who bounced through the door didn't fit any preconceived ideas he had. He was probably in his forties, though looked younger. With his rather wild hair and somewhat eccentric clothing he looked more like a hippy than a cleric. He wasn't wearing a dog collar either, as Rob had expected him to be.

'Hi, I'm Gabriel Clegg. Please call me Gabe,' the vicar said breezily, extending a hand. 'Yes, really, like the archangel. You can tell my parents had a certain path mapped out for me. What can I do for you?'

'I'm just checking a bit further about access to the church. As I said on the phone, it's about the phone which was found there. I'm trying to find out who might have had a key as it was left there outside times when the church was open. I know you've already given a list to the police here in Preston but I wondered if you could think of anyone else who might have a key for any reason? I noticed there's a side door with a Yale lock. Could someone have had a spare key cut for that, without you knowing?'

They were briefly interrupted by the vicar's wife bringing in the coffee on a tray which she put on the low table between them, instructing Rob to help himself to milk, sugar and biscuits.

'Well, I suppose that's possible, but I can't think why anyone would want to.'

'Can you tell me briefly about the former vicar? I understand his son used to be the organist here.'

'Yes that's right. Robert Spencer was vicar here for many years. He used to live in the old vicarage. You probably noticed it as you walked past. It was sold off as the diocese needed the money so they kept a part of the garden and built this smaller one. He died in an accident, as I'm sure you've heard.

'His son Peter was indeed the organist but he moved on soon after his father died. That would be more than three years now, I think.'

'Do you know where Peter Spencer is now? I was wondering if he might remember someone from his father's time here who might perhaps have had a duplicate key.'

'I'm sorry but I don't. I might have an address for him somewhere but I've no idea if it's still current. Might I ask what this is all about, officer?'

Rob hesitated. He didn't want to say too much about an ongoing enquiry but he thought he could probably trust a vicar.

'The phone belonged to a young man who was kidnapped in Preston, about six months ago. You may perhaps have seen details in the local paper? Darren Lee.'

'Yes indeed, I've been keeping him in my prayers. Is there any news of him?'

'He's been found, although not in a very good way. His phone being found inside the church here is the last trace of him so far. That's why we're trying to find out who may have left it in the church, if he didn't do so himself. Who might have had access to do so and presumably Darren wouldn't have.'

'I certainly won't have Peter Spencer's contact details in my phone. But I would imagine he will be quite easy to track down. His profession is not very common. He's an IBO accredited church organ tuner, and there aren't many of those to the pound.'

Seeing Rob's querying look, he continued, 'Institute of British Organ Building. They'd probably have contact details for him, if he's still doing that. He was also a freelance teacher of organ and piano so once again, you might be able to track him down through that. There's probably a register of those, too.'

By the time court was finished for the day, Ted felt as if he'd done a twenty-mile forced march followed by an hour of Krava Maga with Green. The defence's tactics were a relentless attack on everything Ted had done and said throughout the enquiry. He was just thanking his lucky stars that no one had dug deep enough to discover that he had been seeing a therapist, on and off, for some time to deal with things from his past. That could potentially have put the nail in his coffin as a reliable person to have run a balanced enquiry.

But at least they had finished with him for now so, unless he was recalled for some reason, he could get back to the station and get on with being a copper. He had to put up with another lecture from Jim about keeping well away from Edwards and not doing anything to rock the boat until the trial was over and sentence handed down if Morgane was convicted. There was always the possibility of an appeal and he was certain that Clive Edwards would move heaven and earth to lodge one if he could.

He decided to phone Océane again for any news before he left Manchester, in case he needed to swing by Central Park on his way back to Stockport. Although he was not looking forward to doing so, in case he bumped into the ACC again. He was still feeling stupid about his behaviour, bitterly regretting his impulsive action in storming up there to see him.

There was another message from Océane when he turned his phone back on, asking him to phone when he could. He hoped it was good news. He could certainly do with some.

'Do you want the good news or the good news, boss?'

'I want the best news I can get, please, after the day I've just had. So go on, make my day.'

'I have the contact details for the registered owner of the phone which made the call. A certain Tony Barlow. And I can tell you exactly to whom the call was made.'

There was a pause. He could tell she was enjoying the suspense. He wasn't.

'I'll forward you all the details but the recipient phone is registered to a Mr Clive Edwards. Is that good news, boss?'

'That is bloody marvellous news, Océane. Thank you. But it's also a poisoned chalice because I haven't a clue what I can do with it just at the moment.'

'I've finished in court but I need to go back to the nick now and I don't know what time I'll be finished. Sorry. Don't wait to eat. I'll grab something when I can. How are you? How's the head?'

'I'm fine. You know me, as bouncy as Tigger. I still don't get what it was all about, though. Why would anyone kidnap me? It's not as if you're loaded, and you didn't get a ransom demand. And if it's to do with your work, how would they know about me, and where to find me?'

'I might just have a few answers for you by the time I get

back. Just please be careful. Keep an eye out all the time. I can't guarantee yet that this is over. You're sure you're all right?'

'I'm fine, don't fuss. Just try not to be too late home. Then I can show you how fine I am.'

Chapter Seventeen

'How did it go at court, Ted? You look a bit frazzled.'

'Frazzled? The jury now think I'm a gun-toting, high-kicking psychopath with a grudge, so I'd say frazzled is the least of it, Bill.'

'They've about got your measure then,' Bill laughed. 'What about that drink tonight? Perhaps a ginger beer might perk you up a bit.'

'I can't tonight, Bill, I'm sorry. I've no idea what time I'm going to finish. When's your end date?'

'Friday of next week. Then an enforced extended holiday until they can throw me the lifeline of some pen-pushing job to keep me going.'

'As soon as that?' Ted was surprised. 'I'm really sorry, Bill. Tomorrow evening then, promise. Surely I'll have caught up with myself by then. I suppose there's a leaving do next week?'

'I'm not supposed to know. It's a surprise party. I hate those bloody things. How old am I, for god's sake? But Kevin will wheel me over to The Grapes on the pretence of a quiet pint and I'll have to pretend to be surprised and pleased in equal measure when half the station is there making out that they care that I'm not going to be behind this desk any more.

'I'll hold you to your promise for tomorrow, then, Ted. Don't let me down.'

Ted took the stairs two at a time, as much to burn off some energy as anything else. He hadn't managed any martial arts to speak of, except for a bit of pad work and a few kata sessions in the garden with Trev, for a couple of weeks now. It always showed. He needed both the release and the controlled discipline of martial arts to help him through his work.

The first thing he noticed when he went into the main office was that Megan Jennings was looking a decidedly unhealthy colour. He hoped it wasn't a sign of something serious.

'Are you all right, Megan? You don't look too brilliant.'

'It's not the babies, boss, it's a new case. The front desk asked for a female officer to attend and I drew the short straw. My first case of FGM.'

Ted gave an involuntary wince at the thought. He'd heard of Female Genital Mutilation going on. It seemed to be rife in some areas amongst certain immigrant populations. This was the first case he'd heard about on his patch. It was certainly the first one his team would be involved in.

'Are you all right with that?'

'Yes, fine. I'd like to at least start it before I go off to my nice desk job. I've taken lengthy statements already. I'll pass my notes over to Jezza, shall I?'

Ted nodded. 'I'll just catch up on messages and then we need a get-together. The full team. Can you make sure everyone knows and get them together in, say, half an hour? A bit longer if anyone's out further afield.'

Rob had done an internet search for church organ tuners as soon as he'd finished talking to the vicar. He found Peter Spencer easily enough, the only accredited tuner listed in Lancashire, with an address not far from Preston and a mobile phone number. Rob rang it, but it went straight to voicemail. He left a brief and somewhat vague message, asking the man to contact him as soon as possible, not sure if he would get a response.

He was back at the station, writing up his notes from the

morning before he did.

‘Is that Sergeant O’Connell? I’m Peter Spencer, the organ tuner. As you’re a policeman, I’m assuming you don’t have a church organ at the station which needs tuning, so how can I help you?’

‘Thank you for calling me back, Mr Spencer. It’s just an ongoing enquiry, and the church where your father was the vicar is a subject of interest to us. I wondered if you might remember who would have had a key to the church back when you were there?’

‘Please call me Peter. And gracious me, that’s a strange question, but let me see. There was Miss Moneypenny, of course.’

‘Miss Moneypenny?’

‘Father and I were very bad for giving everyone nicknames. She was called Miss Dean, in fact, but she was always talking about having to count the pennies to make her pension last so the name rather stuck. She was in charge of the flower rota and she was quite a dragon. Heaven help any of the ladies who put a wilted bloom on the altar.’

‘I believe it’s the new vicar’s wife who does that now, so perhaps she’s retired?’

‘Oh good gracious, she won’t like that! She’s probably making effigies of her usurper out of candle-wax and sticking pins in it,’ Spencer laughed then went on hurriedly, ‘Oh, heck, that was a bit tactless. I do hope it’s not a serious case you’re investigating?’

‘How old was Miss Dean?’ Rob neatly avoided his question.

‘She must have been in her eighties, I think. Quite a character. Had a manky old cat which always had something or other wrong with it and had to wear one of those big collars, like a cone. She thought it looked like a chorister’s collar. She always told us Buttons was in the choir again. I don’t even know if she would still be in the land of the living.’

'I'll check up, thank you. Anyone else?'

'Well, there was Stan the Man.' Spencer laughed again. He had a pleasant voice and a ready laugh. 'You see, there we go again, another nickname. We were very bad. He was some sort of obsessive expert on religions of all kinds, both Christian and pre-Christian. Once he latches on to someone, he's a bit like a stray cat. Give him a saucer of milk and he refuses to go away. Father was kind to him, because he was like that, despite the nicknames. He spent some time with him and after that we were rather haunted by Stan the Man. I think Father eventually let him have a key for a while to fuddle about in the church whenever he wanted to, rather than having to see him all the time to let him in.'

'Can you tell me his full name?'

'It'll come to me in a minute. Stanley … Stanley … Something or another. He's got a few books out, some minor imprint or another, so you might be able to find him on the mighty Amazon. Or there's possibly some mention of him somewhere on the internet. He does talks and things, I think, about his research and his books. Very strange fellow. Scrawny, rather seedy looking somehow, with possibly the worst comb-over you could imagine. Father and I were awful about him, honestly, but never to his face, of course. Father used to say that if Stan was a scoutmaster, anyone with sons wouldn't want them to go off camping with him, if you understand me.

'Stanley Harrison, that was it!'

'Did your father give people the key to the church door?'

'Heavens no! Far too big and clunky and very difficult to get replacements if they lost them. No, he'd let them have a key to the vestry door. That's a Yale lock. But he was always very careful to keep track of them. They all had to go on an inventory and be accounted for to the diocese. They always kept a very tight grip on the purse-strings.'

'So if it was a Yale key, people could have had a copy of it made?'

'Well, I suppose they could, yes, although I'm not sure who would want to or why. It was never a rich parish, not a lot of money in the collection plates, no rare works of art or anything.'

'Thanks, Peter, you've been very helpful. If you do happen to think of anyone else, it would be great if you could give me a bell.'

'I will do, of course, but I should just warn you that I'm going on holiday in a few days. Another of my very indulgent extended tours round Europe to see some of the finest church organs in the world. It's a little treat I award myself when I can. Because of my credentials, I'm sometimes granted the honour of playing some of them. This trip includes Freiberg, Sion in Switzerland, and Brescia in Italy.'

'Do you still work as a tuner? I understand you teach organ and piano, too.'

'I do, but not as much as previously. This is going to sound highly improbable and will make Father spin in his grave at the very idea but I had a win on the Lottery. One of those instant millionaire things. Incredible. I'd never bought a ticket before but I suddenly decided to try one just after Father died and there you go. Divine intervention, perhaps. I still tune church organs and I've kept on some of the most interesting and talented of my pupils but that's all.'

Something rang a bell in Rob's memory. A music connection.

'By any chance, did you ever have a student called Robbie Mitchell? A lad from Humberside?'

'Humberside? Heavens no. I'll travel a lot for a church organs but for students it was only local to Preston. There's very little money in private teaching like that, certainly not if you have to factor in high mileage. Very occasionally I'd travel as far as northern Greater Manchester or, at a push, into wildest West Yorkshire, but never any further than that.'

'Right, progress reports from everyone, please, and let's see where we're going next. I'm finished in court, for the time being at least, unless I get recalled, so I'm back overseeing.

'Jo, I now have contact details for the person who made a mobile phone call to Clive Edwards' phone from the location where Trev ended up in Scotland shortly before I received the picture of him from a different phone. Tony Barlow. The name's familiar, I think we know him. He needs picking up and interviewing, at length, to see if he can finger Edwards. Get a detailed description and get him to do a likeness. Goodness knows why he used a traceable phone for that call but there's a good chance he wasn't thinking straight. That's because there's a strong possibility that he has a broken nose. He clearly didn't realise that Trev is a karate black belt who was not too happy about being shut in a car boot. I doubt he'd have taken the job if he'd known. Anyway, round him up and see what he says. We want the name of his accomplice and we want Edwards.'

'Bloody hell, boss, that's going to be a political hot potato. You surely can't arrest Edwards in the middle of his daughter's trial? What if the press get hold of that?'

'That's what's worrying me, which is why I've arranged an early meeting with the Super and the Big Boss in the morning. It's a decision they need to take, not me, but if this bloke you're going after delivers him on a plate, we can't ignore it. But bear in mind I had a rough day in court today and the jury have already been fed the idea that I was on some sort of personal vendetta against Edwards.'

Ted paused for a swallow of his green tea. Trev was always telling him he drank too much of it and it would do dire things to him, but right now he felt he needed it and had earned it.

'Right, our first FGM. Megan and Jezza will be interviewing those victims who have already, as well as those who can be persuaded to come forward. We may need interpreters for some?'

He looked to Megan for confirmation and she nodded. 'The one I spoke to came with someone who spoke good English, boss, but I'm not sure that will always be the case. I think now that one has plucked up courage to talk, others might well do the same. And some of them are going to be quite young girls, from the information we have so far.'

'Good, well if we need interpreters, we'll get them. There's a lot of useful information on the West Midlands' force's website. Have a look on there everyone, so we know what we're doing. I imagine if there are any men involved who need to be spoken to that it might be better, from a cultural point of view, if they're interviewed by male officers. Virgil, you work with Jo on that, please.'

'Is it because I is black?' Virgil asked, putting on a heavy accent and with a touch of irony in his voice. 'Seriously, boss, you do know I was born in Salford, don't you? I don't know anything about the culture that does this shit.'

'Right, listen up, everyone. I've not had a good day in court. In fact, I've had a pretty crap day. As a result, if I say anything which gives offence, I apologise, but it's not meant to. I thought you all knew me better than that.'

'I was just messing, boss. Sorry.' Virgil sounded contrite.

'Now The Preacher. What have we got and where are we going?'

Rob recounted his conversation with Peter Spencer, the former vicar's son and one-time organist at the church.

'I've been trying to track down this Stanley Harrison. So far I've found his publisher's details. I have a feeling it may be one of those vanity imprints, where you pay to get your book published. Anyway I've not been able to get hold of them yet so I'll keep trying all means I can think of.

'I did ask Spencer if he ever taught Robbie Phillips, as he teaches piano and organ and we know Robbie was musical. He said not, that he doesn't cover that area.'

'Let's check it out, though. Someone phone Robbie's

parents in the morning, tactfully, please, and ask what instruments he played and who his teacher was. And this Harrison would fit in with your theory, Steve, about the Christian and pre-Christian connection so he's definitely someone we need to find and have a long talk to. Have a dig about as you've already been looking at that angle. It's possible you may even have come across some of his stuff online before we knew he might be of interest to us.'

'Where are we up to with links between the schools or the three victims? Anything on that, yet? What about this NCS line of enquiry. Any links with where they all went for their residential bit of it?'

'Still digging, boss, but something did occur to me today which we've also started to look at as a possible link, and another musical one,' Mike Hallam put it. 'The school prom. My daughter is way too young yet but she's already started designing the dress she wants to wear for it.'

'School prom?' Ted queried. 'Isn't that more an American thing?'

'Meanwhile on twenty-first century Planet Earth,' Jezza said, half under her breath. As she felt the boss's stern look turn her way, she continued, 'Oh, come on, boss, I was just pointing out that, with respect, you don't know an awful lot about teen culture.'

For a brief moment, Jezza wasn't sure if this time she had pushed it too far, especially as she knew how much the boss disliked the phrase 'with respect'. She'd perhaps taken too big a risk, after the day he'd had. Then she saw his face soften and his lips twitch into a smile.

'Absolutely right, DC Vine, guilty as charged. The only thing I know about teens is through Trev's younger sister Siobhan and she moves in the horsey set so it seems to be hunt balls and the like. So tell me about these proms. What is the musical connection? Do they have groups who play? Ones who might have been at all three schools?'

'These days it's often groups of pupils from the school itself, boss,' Jo told him. 'That's getting to be quite a popular idea. But we can easily find out who played at each school, and if our three lads attended a prom at their school.'

'I don't suppose there's much call for church organ music at something like that. But just check if this Peter Spencer plays any other instrument that might be of interest. And what kind of piano does he play? And I don't mean an upright or a grand. I mean might he play the sort of music that would be in demand for a school prom? Seems unlikely, but perhaps he plays keyboard or synthesizer or something.

'Anything else?'

'Boss, I took a message from Doug in forensics,' Sal told him. 'The tyre tracks up at Ludworth Moor didn't give them much at all, they were too indistinct. All he would say was they're a size which could fit anything like a Ford Fiesta, including several models of Fiat. So that doesn't narrow it down for us all that much, especially as Fiesta is the most popular model on the road. He said if we could find a suspect vehicle, they might be able to give us a match that was on the probable side of possible, but that would be best-case scenario. Oh, and he said to ask you "what about the kitten," if that means anything to you.'

Ted decided to pretend to ignore that particular message. He knew that the moment he mentioned a kitten to Trev, he'd want to take it on. They'd had seven cats before and managed. He'd promised Doug that he would think about it and he would. But that might be all he did.

'I'm going to work on a bit this evening, see if I can catch up with what I've missed being away. Perhaps some of you can do the same? Can you sort it out between you, or maybe Jo, you can make executive decisions? We need to crack on with this case. We've still not a lot to show for it.

'If someone fancies going out for something to keep us going, a bit of pizza or something, let me know and I'll put something in the kitty.'

'You're late back. Have you eaten?' Trev asked as Ted flopped next to him on the sofa when he finally got home.

'I had some pizza. Allegedly. If I hadn't been looking at it when I ate it, it could just as easily have been the cardboard box it came in. How's the head?'

'I still have an impressive lump.' Trev bent his head forward. Ted ran a gentle hand carefully over the glossy back curls. It was true, there was still a bump the size of a small egg.

'We might just have the person who did it in our sights.'

'Who was it, and how did they find me?'

Ted hesitated, not sure whether or not to tell him the full story. He tried always to be open and honest but he didn't like discussing case-work outside the station and in a sense, this was work.

'You know that Morgane Edwards' father hired someone to try to scare me off? Before the trial? I think he thought that when that didn't work, he'd turn his attention to you. I think the plan was to hold you captive all the time the court case was on, in the hopes of making me appear flaky, not able to run a proper enquiry.'

'But how did he know about me? Oh, god, it was me posing in that photo with you, at the awards ceremony. That was it, wasn't it? Me being vain and wanting to be in the photos? But how did he track me down? How did he know where to send his thugs to find me?'

'The newspaper article about the English classes. Having seen the photo of us together, with your name in it, he'd only have had to search a bit and he would have found that article with details of where the centre is and that you teach English there.

'Just promise me you'll be very careful because for various reasons, we may not be able to arrest him immediately. So that means he might possibly still send someone after you. Don't take any risks. Always let me know where you are and what time you'll be back. And stay in contact.'

Trev gave him a hug. 'I love it that you care. How was your day, anyway?'

Ted picked up the nearest cat to put on his lap and stroke. Little Barcelona purred her delight at being singled out for special attention.

'You know some of those courtroom dramas you love to watch? Where some intelligent and ruthless barrister is tearing a witness apart in the box? Well, I was on the receiving end of some of that today.'

He gently ran a hand the length of Barcelona's back and she yawned and stretched to show her pleasure.

'Doug's got a kitten he wants to get rid of,' he said, then wished he hadn't when he saw Trev's face light up.

'A kitten? Can we? That would be fantastic. Back up to seven. I'm sure it's a much luckier number than six.'

Chapter Eighteen

'Bloody hell, Ted, this is going to be a right nightmare to sort out,' Jim Baker grumbled, slurping coffee. 'We're going to be damned if we do, damned if we don't. Can you imagine the field day the papers will have if we charge the defendant's father in the middle of the trial?'

'Imagine what will happen if we don't and it comes out later that we had the evidence to do so,' Ted said reasonably.

'But do we have the evidence?' Superintendent Caldwell asked. 'We will clearly have to meet the burden of proof more highly on this one than we usually do. Because as Jim says, there are going to be ramifications if we don't. So what do we have?'

'Jo's going over to find this Tony Barlow this morning, armed with warrants for him, his phone, his property and his vehicle. He's the registered owner of the mobile that made the call to Edwards. With any luck, he'll talk, hoping to do a deal. There may well still be traces of Trev in the boot of his car, and if there are, we've got the beginnings of a solid case.'

'We need more than the beginnings, though. We need a solid middle and a rock-solid end or we're going to looking like a bunch of incompetent pillocks. Sorry, Debs.'

'Jim and I will be at Central Park again first thing on Monday morning talking budgets. So what can we tell them about the ongoing enquiry, the three young men? We're going to start coming under increased pressure to scale the operation down considerably if we don't make some tangible progress soon. Especially if we don't have a realistic chance of doing so. And I'm sure we're all agreed that we must resist that happening. Weekend approaching or not, Chief Inspector, I'm afraid we're going to need you to furnish us with detailed costings to date, and projections for going forward.'

Ted was tempted to retort that he'd be more use working on the case than balancing the books but he knew it was a waste of time. His role was increasingly a management one. He'd oversee the case and its direction but the paperwork left him little time for much more.

'We're trying to find out more about another key-holder for the church where the phone was left inside. He's of particular interest as he's apparently an expert on Christian and pre-Christian holy places, which fits in with Steve's observations.

'And speaking of the budget, something I wanted to ask about was bringing in a forensic psychologist. The one we used on the Edwards case, as he's a specialist with young people. Virgil made a suggestion of letting the two surviving lads meet. Darren and Tim, if Lincolnshire can ever find him. I'm worried about the implications so I'd like expert advice. I'd also like to ask if he would talk to either or both of them, to see what that tells us.'

'He's not exactly low budget,' the Ice Queen said. 'But if it would advance the enquiry we can make a case for it, so it might be worth looking at.'

'I also wonder if we should consider letting the press know that we believe the three cases to be linked.'

Both his senior officers looked at him in surprise. Ted usually avoided the press like the plague.

'I think we need to do it as a warning. It's just possible that The Preacher will strike again, take another young lad and do the same to him as he's done to the others. We surely have a duty to prevent that happening by any means at our disposal?'

'It's going to be a very hard warning to issue though. "Don't go off with anyone, even if you know them and stay away from churches”. It’s likely to cause some degree of fear and also it’s showing our hand with how little we actually know about what’s going on.’

Jim had a point, Ted knew. He just wasn’t sure what else to do.

‘Again, if the press find out we knew the cases were linked and didn’t issue a warning, we’re going to be hung out to dry for that as well.’

‘I’m inclined to agree on this one. I’ll speak to the Press Office to see what sort of a statement we should put out and whether it warrants a full press conference. If it does, you ought to show your face, Ted.’

He’d known she was going to say that. He didn’t like it but if it would help prevent a further crime, he was prepared to put up with it.

Before he went back upstairs after the meeting with his bosses, Ted stopped at the front desk to talk to Bill.

‘All being well, unless something unforeseen happens, I’ll see you in The Grapes later, Bill. Give me a quick bell when you finish your shift and I’ll get myself over there. If I don’t, it’s because something has come up that means I can’t. But I will try, honestly.’

‘Make my day, please, tell me we’re finally making some progress with The Preacher.’

‘Boss, Rob has gone off to talk to this Stanley Harrison, the religious expert. He managed to track him down in the end and we got lucky. Harrison is in Manchester today, doing one of his lectures, so Rob’s gone up to see him,’ Sal told him. ‘DS Hallam’s gone with Uniform to oversee the arrest of this Tony Barlow and the search of his property.

‘We got news of a double homicide while you were in the meeting so Jo’s gone to do the initial work on that. A man took a dim view of his girlfriend sleeping with his best friend so he went round to where they were in bed together, chucked a gallon of petrol over them and lit a match. He waited just long enough before he dialled 999, then he gave himself up to the first attenders, so it should be straightforward to wrap up.'

It was good, logical deployment of team members, giving the homicide to the DI. Ted knew he had a solid and reliable deputy in Jo.

Jezza was still on the phone, just finishing up a call.

'Boss, that was Lincolnshire. They've had a definite sighting of Tim Phillips so they're hoping to follow it up. Who do you want to go over for that? Assuming he will talk to anyone and is in a fit enough state to do so.'

'Maurice, how are things going with Darren? Any progress there? Could you leave him today and go over to see if Tim would talk to you?'

'Darren seems to be starting to accept Amy, the FLO. But yesterday I thought I'd try asking him about church. If he ever went to one, anything like that. He pretty much flipped. It was clear the mention of church meant something to him but that it also scared him badly. We lost a bit of ground, took a few steps back in the progress we'd been making. I'd like to go back again today if I can, boss. Just to get him back on track.'

'I could go to Lincoln, boss? I can certainly make myself look much closer to Tim's age than Maurice possibly could, so maybe we could make a connection that way?'

'He needs to be in no doubt that he's talking to a police officer, though. We don't want to deceive him in any way and risk him losing trust.'

'Understood, boss. It's worth a shot, though? And Lincoln are asking again what they should do with him when they bring him in?'

'Which is the million dollar question. There must be some place of safety where he can be put? See what you can find out about that while you're over there. And I'm putting out feelers about getting a psychologist involved on the case, if only to advise us on how we should be approaching Darren and Tim.

Maurice, you've done a great job. Go up there again today but after that I'm probably going to have to pull you. I have books to balance this weekend and the budget is in danger of shrinking.

'Megan, are you all right on the FGM today without Jezza? If you need extra help, ask Susan Heap from Uniform. She has the training. I'll clear it with Inspector Turner if you need her. I want it wrapped up as soon as possible. Leave people in no doubt that everyone is welcome here but they must live by our laws, and mutilating young girls is against them.

'I'd much rather be doing something practical instead of all this paperwork, but I'm in my office if you need me for anything.'

Stanley Harrison had sounded irritable, tetchy, when he'd replied to the message Rob O'Connell left on his answerphone. He'd grudgingly agreed to a visit from Rob, constantly repeating that he didn't see how he could help.

He was staying in a cheap hotel out near the University. It looked as if it had been a pub in a previous life and managed to retain a lingering smell of cheap beer. Harrison was waiting for him in what had clearly been the bar, now a dining room of sorts. They sat on upright and uncomfortable chairs at a pine table. Rob asked for coffees which were delivered, most of the contents slopped over into the saucers, by a young girl who looked as if she considered that she had far better things to be doing with her morning.

'I still don't see how you think I can help you. What's all this about?'

'It's just routine enquiries at this stage, Mr Harrison.' Rob got his phone out and put it on the table between them. 'Would you have any objection to me recording your answers? It would be much more efficient then me trying to scribble everything down.'

'If you must.'

Rob could see that he was going to have his work cut out with this interview. Harrison was indeed a strange-looking person and Peter Spencer had been right about the comb-over. It did nothing for him. He would have done better to admit defeat and accept his baldness. Rob wondered if it was an image he cultivated to suit the role of the eccentric historian. His clothes were decidedly old-fashioned, perhaps studiously so. He reminded Rob of a portrayal he'd seen in a film about John Reginald Christie, the Rillington Place serial killer.

'We're talking to anyone who may have had a key to a church we're interested in. I understand from Peter Spencer that his father may have given you a key to his church. Is that so?'

'Well, he did, three years or more ago, but I didn't keep it, clearly. I quite liked Robert Spencer. He was intelligent and knowledgeable though he could be incredibly patronising. And intransigent, with some of his ideas. The church itself was of moderate interest to me but I did enjoy the debates with Robert. I didn't take to his successor. Too happy-clappy for my taste. Trying to be all-embracing. I tried discussing theology with him but it was all a bit superficial. Not the same level of intellect at all as Robert.'

'Could you explain a bit about what it is you actually do, Mr Harrison?'

'I research British religions through the ages and places of significance within them. I write about them and give talks on them. I'm occasionally booked to go on cruises for enthusiasts, to deliver lectures there. That's reasonably lucrative, unlike most of the other work, but a hard way to earn a crust if, like me, you suffer from extreme motion sickness.'

'Do you know any churches in or around Gainsborough? And what about Hull?'

'Sergeant – you did say that was your rank, didn't you - churches are part of my speciality. It would probably save us both a lot of time if I told you the ones I haven't visited. I have occasionally been given a key to use for my research purposes but I have always returned them. People may think me odd but that oddity does not include a liking for lurking in churches. I visit them for research purposes, that's all.'

'I understand you're also an expert in pre-Christian worship sites too. Pagan? That sort of thing?'

'That sort of thing, as you put it, is a simplistic and dismissive way of talking about centuries of misunderstood culture, Sergeant, but yes, that is a speciality of mine also.'

'Have you heard of a place called Lud's Well, in Lincolnshire?'

The man's upper lip curled in a sneer. 'Lud Well. Yes. A ridiculous modern imposter. A sham. Probably Victorian in origin. When I visited there was even a Tampax hanging from the yew tree above the so-called rag well. Mercifully not a used one. The real spiritual site is upstream, where the seven springs rise, of course.'

'What about Ludworth Moor, near Stockport? Is there a connection through the name?'

'I know of it. Bronze Age, I think, from memory. What is this line of questioning all about?'

'It's just routine, Mr Harrison, as I said. If I gave you some dates, over the last three years or so, would you be able to tell me what you were doing on those dates?'

Harrison was starting to look suspicious now, his small dark eyes narrowing. 'I think I would want to know more of your reasons for asking me. But yes, I probably could. I keep detailed diaries of all my engagements. For tax purposes as much as anything. Given sufficient notice, I could. But I think I might prefer to take legal advice before I did so, unless you give me more information on why you're asking.'

'You're perfectly entitled to do that, of course, Mr Harrison. But it really is just a matter of routine, at this stage. We're speaking to anyone who visited certain churches, and in particular, anyone who had a key to any of them.'

The man was looking at him with open suspicion, a touch of hostility showing in those small rodent eyes.

'Ah, but there's that phrase. At this stage. I can tell by the way you're looking at me that you have already made a judgement because of my appearance. You're trying to hide it, of course, because that's what you're trained to do, but I can see it. I've seen it so often. I saw it from Robert Spencer and that son of his. I heard them laughing together many times, as soon as I left a room.

'My hairstyle, for example. I'm aware it's the cause of mockery but it's what I choose to do. What else should I do? Shave my head and grow stubble instead, as you have clearly done, when faced with a prematurely receding hairline? Why should I? I am what I am. But it wouldn't be the first time the British police have made a false judgement on someone based purely on their appearance and apparent eccentricity, would it?

'I suppose the Spencers told you I'm a homosexual, too, did they? I know it's what they thought. They both made insinuations and I'm sure the son mentioned me to the new vicar as he was at pains to assure me, when he took over, that the church was inclusive, welcoming everyone of whatever persuasion. I found his words disgusting. I'm not a homosexual. I don't mind what people do in the privacy of their own homes. But the mere thought of any kind of intimacy between men is repugnant to me.

'So if it's all the same to you, Sergeant, I am going to stop here and I would ask that if you want to speak to me further, then you give me more notice so I can arrange for a solicitor to be present.'

With those words, he stood up and left the room, leaving Rob sitting rubbing a hand self-consciously over his shaven head and the stubble on his jaws.

'So I'm sorry if I screwed up, boss. He was quite difficult,' Rob said apologetically as he played his recorded interview back to the team at the end-of-day get-together.

Virgil leaned over to him and patted his head affectionately. 'Never mind, Baldy, it sounds as if you just got off on the wrong foot.'

'That's DS Baldy to you, DC Tibbs.'

Ted let it go. Harmless fun. It was the end of a hard week. He wasn't about to jump on them.

'I think we could do worse than to take a closer look at Mr Harrison. His homophobic views are not, sadly, all that unusual and may mean nothing. But we can't overlook the fact that he does tick a few boxes as regards suspect profile.'

'Already started digging, boss,' Rob told him. 'Nothing so far. Not known to us, at least not as Stanley Harrison. But I suppose as he's an author, that could be a pen-name, so I'm trying to find if he uses any others. I'll keep looking.'

'I think it would also be a good idea to give him that list of dates and arrange another meeting. With his solicitor, if he really does want to go down that route. So let's make it a formal one. Get him to come here. Check the six dates, when each of the lads disappeared and then were found, and see where he was and what he was up to then and in between.

'Anything else, anyone?'

'We have Tony Barlow downstairs, boss. If he was singing any more we could put him in as Britain's entry for the next Eurovision. I'm just giving him a bit of a break and then I'll start questioning him some more. You were right. Not only a badly broken nose but a pair of black eyes a panda would be proud of.'

'I want to see him, hear what he has to say.'

'Not a chance, boss. We've got him on this one, and his oppo. He gave him up straight away. Uniform are just out tracking him down.'

'Just over the monitor. I won't go near him.'

'Still no,' Jo told him firmly. 'I'm putting a total exclusion zone round him as far as you're concerned. If he keeps

Edwards out of it, there's just a chance your friend will pick up the tab for a decent defence lawyer for him. And if said lawyer gets wind that you were even in the same building, he'll claim all sorts of breaches of procedure. Just leave him to me.'

Ted knew he was right. He didn't like it, but he had to accept it.

'Any word from Jezza?'

'Nothing yet, boss, just a quick call to tell us the lead went cold on them. She's on her way back. She decided, wisely, I think, that even if they found Tim, a Friday night was not the best time to be trying to find him somewhere safe. He has no stable home to go back to so he's doubly at risk. The local Uniforms are going to try to keep an eye out for him over the weekend then they'll try again on Monday. At least that gives us a few more days for those concerned to try to find a place of safety for him.'

'And Maurice?'

'He's been up with Darren and Amy all day, boss,' Megan told him. 'Darren's been a bit calmer today. They've not mentioned churches again. Maurice said he's saying a few more words each time. Today it's been mainly "thirsty" which doesn't get us very far but still, it's progress of a sort.'

'Right everyone, I think we've probably all done about as much as we can for now. Megan, it's been great having you on the team. Enjoy your well-earned desk job, and keep in touch with us.'

Ted's phone was ringing as he went back to his office. Bill, to tell him he was clocking off and that he would see him in The Grapes in ten minutes. Ted made a quick call of his own before he cleared his desk.

'I'm going to be a bit late again tonight. Sorry. I've promised to have a quick drink with Bill. He's a bit low. No doubt I'll need to run him home afterwards, but I'll get back as soon as I can. Will you cook or shall I bring a takeaway?'

'It's all ready. Just needs heating up when you're ready for it.'

'If you get hungry, don't wait for me.'

'Are you going to get any time off over the weekend? Walter would like you to take him out for a bit of a pipe-opener, I'm sure. Shall I arrange it?'

'I will if I can, I promise but the Ice Queen's given me a lot of homework. If I can't go, you go for a ride anyway. It's not fair that you keep missing out because of my work.'

Ted was a bit late, though not much, but it was clear from Bill's ruddy complexion that he'd made a start without waiting for him. He was on the whisky already. Ted bought him another without comment. Who was he to criticise? He didn't drink now, but it hadn't always been that way.

'How are you doing, Bill? Really?'

'Really? I'm bricking myself. I know it's only three months, but I have no idea what I'm supposed to do with myself. I find it hard enough when I'm on a day off, never mind that long.'

'Could you take a holiday? I could perhaps look after Jack, if he'd be all right with the cats.'

Bill snorted into his Scotch. 'Jack would be all right, but I couldn't vouch for your cats. And a holiday? I've not been anywhere since Ben died. I wouldn't know what to do or where to go.'

Ben had been his name for his wife, Brenda. Ted knew Bill was lonely, but he probably hadn't realised quite how bad things were.

'I know who I am when I put my uniform on. I'm Bill, the copper. With my medal ribbons. Take that away from me and what am I? I don't know myself, and that's what scares me.'

Chapter Nineteen

Superintendent Debra Caldwell was as demanding of herself as she was of any officer under her command. That's why, on yet another Saturday morning, while her husband and teenage sons had gone off for a weekend's sailing, she was on her way to the station.

The modern police force was supposed to be inclusive; equal rights for all. Things were improving, with more women at executive level than ever before. Neighbouring Lancashire Constabulary had appointed the first woman Chief Constable in the country in the 1990s and the glass ceiling was slowly being chipped away.

In reality, she knew it was harder than it appeared. She'd always found she had to push herself harder, achieve more at a higher level, than any of her male counterparts. It's what had earned her the nickname of the Ice Queen, which even her family knew and used. The boys thought it hilarious and apt since she expected as much respect from them as from officers in her division. Even her husband, Robin, an inspector in Traffic, used it ironically, as well as calling her ma'am affectionately in moments of intimacy.

If it had been hard for her to climb the ranks as a woman in a largely male-dominated world, she couldn't begin to imagine how hard it had been for Ted. She knew he'd had a tough time early on, especially in his SFO days. He'd had to work harder than anyone to be taken seriously and treated with respect, not least because of his small stature and unfortunate surname.

Today she was meeting him to go over the planned press conference details. She'd also been taxed with raising other issues with him. She was not looking forward to that aspect of their meeting. She'd opted for his office rather than her own, thinking he might be more at ease on his own territory. She decided to broach the difficult subject first, over a mug of green tea. Once it was dealt with and out of the way, they could get on with the business in hand.

'How is Trevor now? Has he fully recovered from his ordeal?' she began, keeping her tone as neutral as she could.

'He's fine, luckily, thank you for asking.'

'And you think the fact that he was taken is linked to the photograph from the awards ceremony?'

Ted groaned. 'You've been talking to the ACC? He told me my moment of madness was forgotten. I did a daft thing. I was angry. But yes, that's the only explanation I have to date.'

'In fact it was the Chief himself who phoned me. He and Mr Evans are concerned about you, Ted. They wanted me to check that you're happy in your role and feeling valued.'

'Valued? That's a modern term that's getting a bit overused, don't you think? You know as well as I do that I'm good PR for the force, which is why they took the chance to put me on display, when I've always resisted before. I should have been more responsible. I shouldn't have let Trev put himself in the public eye as my partner. That's what put him at risk, but I needed to rant at someone and I chose the ACC. Not my smartest career move, no doubt.

'But you can assure them both that I'm not thinking of quitting. Not at the moment, anyway. Certainly not when we have someone as dangerous as The Preacher to deal with. So perhaps we should just forget my total lack of judgement and discuss how best to deal with that, ma'am.'

His formality told her the subject was closed as far as he was concerned. He could be prickly about his private life and she knew there was no point in trying to press him. He hadn't quite finished, though.

'But talking of welfare issues, I am worried about Bill. Is there no way he can start his civilian post as soon as he finishes in uniform? He's starting to sound very low at the prospect of not working. He's drinking more than usual, too. His job is all he's got, apart from his parrot, and that's not much company for three months.'

She shook her head firmly. 'Whilst I have every sympathy for Sergeant Baxter, we simply don't have the budget to carry him, even for a relatively short period. He's been promised the new post in twelve weeks' time. Most people would be delighted at the prospect of a break.'

'Bill's not most people.'

'Moving on, what do we need to focus on for Monday's press conference?'

It was her own way of declaring a subject off limits for further discussion. She pressed on.

'We've been incredibly lucky to date that none of the press appear to have picked up on a link between the cases on their own initiative. I'm surprised more wasn't made of the first case, especially with the subsequent death of Robbie Mitchell.'

'I can probably explain that. There's still a school of thought which holds that homosexuality is so perverse that everything about it is aberrant. That instead of it being about loving relationships, it's full of deviant practices. Auto-eroticism, for example.

'Even though Robbie Mitchell wasn't gay, he had been going to gay clubs with a friend. I've read through the press coverage of his inquest, such as it was. There are some passing references to him having been subjected to some form of torture whilst being held against his will prior to his death, but that's all. If I had a fiver for every time I've heard someone say that gay people are more promiscuous than straight ones, I'd be retiring now, never mind Bill.

'I may be wrong, and I hope I am, but the cynical side of

me thinks someone may have looked at the details and decided he was a young lad, experimenting with his sexuality, who got into an abusive relationship which sent him spiralling into depression.

'I've managed so far to fob off our local hack, Penny, with not a lot of detail. But I'll make sure she knows that there's a possibility of a big story coming on Monday, to get her on side.'

'It's up to us to set the record straight about Robbie, and about the others,' the Ice Queen said firmly. 'So, what information do we need to include?'

'I'd like to see the press use photos of the three churches where the phones were found. If not all of them, then at least our last case, Darren Lee. If we can get those three pictures out there in the public's mind, we may just get some information of what could possibly link them.'

Ted's meeting with the Super was over by the time the team members working that day were at their desks and getting started. He asked for an update.

'With the tyre tracks up at Ludworth being identified as possibly Ford Fiesta, I've been looking at what vehicles are driven by anyone who's been on our radar for anything to do with this case. Stanley Harrison doesn't appear to own a vehicle. I know he told me he'd be travelling to Manchester by train when I arranged to meet him. I certainly can't find anyone with his name as the registered owner of a vehicle, nor a driving licence issued to the right Stanley Harrison. I'm still trying to find out if he uses another name for his writing which he might also use for other things. All the historical books by him I can find listed online are under the name of Stanley Harrison. But maybe he does have another name, writing goodness knows what. Romance? Erotica? There might be good reasons why he would keep the two identities separate,' Rob told him

'Fiesta is just one possibility for a tyre match, but I have found Fiestas registered to both the current vicar, Gabriel Clegg, and to the former vicar's son, Peter Spencer. Very different models. Spencer told me about his lottery win so it's not surprising that his is top of the range with all the extras going. Clegg's is older, basic, a model that's not even made any more. Forensics were cagey about whether they could pin the tyre tracks down with any certainty other than being the right size for a Fiesta, so that might not advance us very far. Oh, and there's another message from Doug for you to phone him, boss. About the kitten, he said.'

Ted decided to ignore the further reminder. Kittens were the last thing on his mind at the moment.

'What do we know about the vicar, Gabriel Clegg?'

'Nothing on the radar anywhere. Seems squeaky clean. As far as I can tell he's never come to the attention of the police at any time. Not even a speeding ticket. His only interest to us is that he happens to be the vicar of the church inside which Darren's phone was found and he drives the most common vehicle on the road.'

'Peter Spencer checks out, too, doesn't he, despite the car coincidence? Again, let's dig a little deeper into his background. Any friends or relatives, someone who might have borrowed his key when he was organist and had a copy made, without him knowing?

'Who actually found the phone and handed it in?'

Rob flicked through his notes.

'This famous Miss Dean that Peter Spencer told me about, I've found out since I spoke to him. He and his father used to call her Miss Moneypenny. She's well into her eighties now but still quite sprightly, by all accounts. When Clegg's wife took over the flower rota, the Vicar knew Miss Dean wasn't happy at being pushed out so he offered her some light cleaning and tidying duties in the church. She still has her key from her flower days and she goes in of a morning to have a quick tiffle about. I'm not sure what, exactly. That's how she found the phone. She took it to the vicar who handed it in to the police. She's surely not a suspect though, boss?'

'I think it unlikely. I don't see an elderly lady, no matter how sprightly, overpowering young lads. Nor doing the sort of things which were done to them. But have a dig into her background. She has a key, after all. Does she have any family? Children of her own? A nephew, perhaps? Someone she lets borrow her key. Or perhaps someone who has access to it and could have taken it without her noticing. And does she have a car, which someone may have borrowed?'

'On it, boss.'

'Have you actually had a face to face with Peter Spencer? Might be a good idea to do so, see what opinion you form of him.'

'I haven't yet. I spoke to him on the phone. But he checks out too. He's not on the system anywhere, other than a clean DBS check, which I suppose he needs for giving private lessons to young people.'

'Set up a meeting, just to cover our backs. He's another one who's not very likely but let's do a thorough job. We need to explore every possibility before the budget is cut to the bone.'

'It might be tricky, boss. He's going off on an extended trip round Europe to look at church organs any day now. I'm not sure if he's already left.'

'I'd like him seen and spoken to before he goes away, if it's at all possible, please. See if you can set something up. We don't want him disappearing out of our reach then finding out more reasons why we should look at him more closely.

'Have you checked if the address you have for him is still current?'

Rob looked uncomfortable. 'Not yet, boss,' he admitted. 'I spoke to him on his mobile. He called me back when I left a message. He wasn't trying to avoid contact or anything like that.'

‘Check it out anyway. Ask the local force to find out if he’s still at the address you’ve got for him. Let’s not assume that just because he’s a vicar’s son with a clean disclosure that he’s above board. Not until we’ve established that for ourselves, beyond all doubt.

‘Where are we at with direct links between the three victims?’

‘Nothing much yet, boss,’ Steve told him. ‘I did find out that Darren and Robbie had done the residential part of their NCS at the same place, though not at the same time. I’m currently trawling through people they may both have come into contact with when they were there.’

‘We need to get someone to talk to whoever was in charge at the time that both of them were there. I expect they get so many young people through centres like those that they won’t always remember individuals, unless something out of the ordinary happened. Get on to whichever station is local to them, get them to visit, with photos of the two lads, and do some asking around. Tell them it’s important, so we’d appreciate their help soon as. If you run into any difficulties, ask me or Jo to speak to them.’

Ted knew he had hours of paperwork ahead of him over the weekend. Trev was still keen that he should find time to go riding, for a couple of hours at least. It was looking like a slim chance, unless he got his head down and made some serious inroads into the budget. There were days when he regretted taking the promotion to DCI. It meant he spent more and more time desk-bound and less out there on the job which is what he liked best and what he was good at. There were even times when he missed Firearms, but he knew those days were long gone. Trev would never contemplate him going back to that job.

He was anxious to catch up with Mike Hallam to find out the situation with Tony Barlow, the man arrested for kidnapping Trev. Mike had spoken to CPS and Barlow was now going to be charged. He had a record already so with any luck he would be remanded in custody.

In a way, Ted was hoping that he might be given bail. There was a chance that if he did, the first thing he would try to do would be to contact Clive Edwards, seeking help, and if they could catch him in the act of doing that, it would give them a better chance of a successful prosecution of him.

The verdict on Edwards' daughter, Morgane, was expected around the middle of the week. Whichever way it went, Ted was hoping they would be in a position to order the arrest of Edwards with a reasonable chance of a successful prosecution for intimidation of a witness under the Criminal Justice and Public Order Act 1994. It could land him a prison sentence, up to five years if it was tried on indictment.

Ted was still under strict orders to stay away but he couldn't help himself. He couldn't resist sneaking in to watch Barlow over the monitor while DS Hallam was questioning the man in another room. Mike hadn't been exaggerating about the state of Barlow's injuries. It gave Ted a small feeling of some justice at least having been done. He'd been on the receiving end of kicks from Trev during training sessions. He could imagine what it had been like for the man, not having a clue that the person he had shut in his car boot was a martial arts black belt. Ted almost felt sorry for him. Almost.

'Where do you want to go? You don't want us to go riding round some crime scene or another this time, do you?'

Trev had finally persuaded Ted to take a couple of hours out of work to go for a ride, Ted on broad and placid Walter, Trev on a much bigger and livelier eventer which belonged to friends of their friends Willow and Rupert.

'Anywhere you fancy. But only a couple of hours and nothing too exciting. I've still not finished everything I need to prepare for tomorrow and I don't think the Ice Queen would be impressed if I said sorry, ma'am, I didn't do my homework because I fell off a horse while I was wagging it from work.'

Trev laughed. 'I know just the ride. Two hours, and a nice safe place for you to have a little burn-up. It will do you good, blow the cobwebs away. You need to be looking your best for another press conference. I'll be recording it so I can share it with Annie if it doesn't make the national news. You know she loves to see you on the telly.'

'For once I hope it does hit the nationals,' Ted told him. 'We're going nowhere at the moment on this one and we badly need the public's help, hence my voluntarily calling a press conference.'

The horses fell into step side by side. Ted had been amazed at the calming effect sitting on a moving horse had on him. He'd formed a bond with Walter and trusted him implicitly. Trev's mount, Polaris, was a great dark-coated brute of a thing with a notoriously bad temper. He scared the living daylights out of Ted, even at a distance and he knew he would never feel brave enough to tackle anything like that. He was happy just plodding along with Walter. That was more than he had ever dreamt of doing. He liked the higher vantage point afforded by Walter's wide back, allowing him to see things he might never have noticed when walking along at his own modest height.

'It's amazing how many abandoned old farms and outbuildings there are when you come to look around. I should think some of these have stood empty for years. I wonder if anyone ever goes near them?'

'That sounds to me like Ted the Policeman talking. I thought we weren't looking at crime scenes today?'

'We weren't going to. It's just made me realise what a mammoth task we've got on when we come to start looking for ones in connection with this latest case.'

'The kidnappings?' Trev asked. Ted hadn't told him much about the case, just the bare outlines.

'You could hide someone away in old buildings like these

and it would be completely by chance if anyone found them, I imagine.'

'Wouldn't sound carry though, up here? And if someone needed to get to them by vehicle, surely people would see lights after dark and investigate? They perhaps still belong to someone; a nearby farm maybe? I would think farmers would be keeping an eye out. Is there much rustling going on? Lights up here might be someone coming to steal the sheep?'

'At the moment we don't even know where to start looking. But at least it's given me more ideas.'

They were approaching a long but gentle rise in the ground. Ahead of them a well-trodden track led up to the top of the incline.

'The ideal place for you to discover Walter's top gear. Come on, I'll race you.'

Ted looked at Trev, sitting confidently astride the great dark beast which was Polaris, who would flatten his ears and snake his head to try to take a sneaky bite out of Walter whenever he could.

'We don't stand a chance.'

'Go on, give it a go. We'll give you a head start. Just give it some welly, hold your panic strap and keep your heels down.'

Ted just had time to see Polaris show his disapproval at being restrained by rearing up on his hind legs, then exploding in a series of bucks as soon as all four feet were back on the ground. Trev's laughter told him he was fine and in no danger of being unseated.

Ted hung on for dear life and gave Walter a nudge of encouragement with his heels. The next minute they were away, flying over the turf faster than he'd thought his steady mount capable of. Ted found he was suddenly enjoying himself, feeling the adrenaline rush of watching the short, sheep-cropped grass fly by underneath them, listening to the pound of Walter's hooves and hearing whoops of encouragement from Trev behind him but closing fast.

Their moment of triumph was short-lived as the much longer-legged and by now furious Polaris steamed up and stuck his long neck out in front of them, reaching the end of the gallop first. As they let their mounts walk on a long rein to regain their breath and cool down, Ted's grin almost matched that of Trev.

'I liked that. It was just what I needed. The prospect of more spreadsheets later suddenly doesn't seem quite as bad.'

Chapter Twenty

'So we're hoping that members of the public might be able to help us with any information they may have on these particular three churches.'

Ted was addressing the press conference, in front of a screen showing the churches in question, where the phones of their three victims had been found. Much as Ted disliked taking centre stage, the Super had impressed on him that he was the ideal person to present to the press as he always came across as sincere. People instinctively liked and trusted him, and wanted to help when he asked them to.

'Something connects these three locations and our three victims. We're working hard to find out what it is and we would really appreciate the public's help in doing so.'

With the permission of Robbie Mitchell's parents, his photo was also on view. They were not at this stage releasing those of Darren Lee and Tim Phillips. Their photos had been widely distributed when the boys were missing so the press could find them easily enough if they decided to do a bit of digging.

'We're keen to stress that we are now fairly sure that these three cases are linked and we feel there is a strong possibility that this person may offend again. Which is why we want to make the public aware and ask for their help.'

As soon as he threw the conference open to questions, Ted thankfully handed over to the Ice Queen and the Press Officer. They were much more adept than he was at that sort of thing.

And there were plenty of questions, most of which they had anticipated.

'Why was the connection not picked up earlier?'

'Why were the public not warned sooner?'

'If the connection hadn't been missed might the third victim not have been taken?'

'Is there a suspect?'

'If not, why not?'

'What state are the two surviving victims in?'

'Are you going to reveal their identities?'

'Can we talk to them?'

'What is their prognosis?'

'What information have they been able to give?'

And more of the same. Endlessly, remorselessly. Facing the press was always a double-edged sword. They could be a vital help in getting word out in an appeal for information. But it wouldn't be the first time the press pack had turned such an event into a savaging of the police for their lack of progress on a case.

Ted tried to avoid scowling at those assembled as they posed their questions, as he often did. He knew he needed their help on this. He was also aware of Trev reminding him that his mother would be watching his performance at some point so he tried to keep his face neutral. Trev had also organised his wardrobe for the occasion once again.

The press conference was first thing on the Monday morning. They were anxious to try to catch the lunchtime news. The sooner they put the information out there, the sooner they should start getting some results. There would inevitably be the usual deluge of irrelevant calls, including some timewasters. But somewhere amongst them all, there might just be the one which could start to provide the missing key.

There was the inevitable debrief for Ted with the Super and the Press Officer once the conference was over and the members of the press had left. Overall, they were pleased with how things had gone, optimistic that the press would concentrate more on asking for the public's help than on police bashing. Even if there was just one phone call which gave them a lead, it would take them further forward than they were now.

Ted watched the news item go out at lunchtime from the sanctuary of his own office. It wasn't long before the first call came in, but it was not one they had been expecting at all. Ted heard his name being called from the main office with a degree of urgency. He went out to find Maurice talking on his mobile phone, his tone placating.

'It's all right, Darren, lad. Just calm down. Can you put Amy on, please? Let me talk to Amy, Darren, then I know what's going on.'

Ted and every team member present held their breath, waiting to find out what was the reason for the phone call.

'Amy? What's he trying to tell me?'

Maurice listened for what seemed like a long time. Then he said, 'Right, I'm coming up there. I'll be with you as soon as I can. Tell Darren I'm on my way.

'Boss, I need to get up to Preston. Darren's mam sometimes has the telly on while she's doing the ironing. She takes stuff in for some of her cleaning clients. Darren never takes any notice of it. He's usually glued to his PlayStation. He's been more and more into that as he's started to settle a bit.

'For some reason he just happened to look up as the lunchtime news was on and he saw the church. The one where his phone was left. Amy said he got extremely agitated, he kept repeating the word church over and over. She couldn't settle him, so she let him phone me. I need to go there, boss. It seems like he recognised the place and that's a new word he's not said before. He may just be on the brink of talking to us.'

'Damn, I should have thought of that. The risk of Darren seeing it. I should have made sure Amy was warned and prepared. Yes, you go, Maurice. Keep us posted, please, but stay as long as you need to. I think if Tim Phillips is living in some dodgy squat somewhere, it's highly unlikely that he's seen anything on television. Let's hope he's found today. He needs to be somewhere safe, even if he can't tell us anything.'

'If Darren's seen the conference, he may now know he's not the only one. Let's hope that gets through to him and he realises he may be able to help prevent it happening again,' Jo put in.

'Jo, the state that young lad's in, I doubt he's thinking like that. If he's reacted to seeing the church it's because it's scared him. He's so shut down he's not able to think about anyone else. I need to go. Amy's good with him but for some reason, it's still me he trusts most.'

Jezza wasn't greatly enjoying her tour of the less attractive parts of Lincoln, even with the easy company of DS Bryony Streeter. They were in the DS's car, in convoy with an area car. They weren't sure how easy it would be to pick up Tim Phillips if and when they found him so they'd decided to go prepared for trouble. Depending on where he was and who he was with, things could get a bit ugly. Bryony's risk assessment had been to go with back-up already in place, rather than having to wait for them to come out if they were needed.

'Well, if he's not here, then I don't know where we look next. This is the last place on our list of possibles. Who'd have thought that an addict who's been through what he has could sofa-surf at such speed?' Bryony said brightly as she pulled up outside yet another run-down and partly boarded up house, the front garden full of refuse, the walls spray-painted with graffiti and gang symbols.

'You bring me to all the nicest places, Sarge,' Jezza smiled as the two of them got out of the car. The two uniformed officers also got out but at a word from the DS, they waited by the vehicle.

'I doubt we'll get a warm reception here but they don't usually bite. At least, not as long as they've had their fix. Hide behind me, if you like,' she told Jezza.

'I do kick-boxing. I don't mind going first if you'd prefer me to.'

They were both smiling as they tried the garden gate, which promptly fell off its hinges. They walked up to the front door, paint peeling from it in strips. Bryony knocked firmly on the cracked and dirty glass panel. There was no response.

'Police. Can you open up, please?' she asked as she knocked again. Then she grinned once more at Jezza as she said, 'Not a very welcoming crowd, are they? I don't think we're going to be offered a cup of tea.'

'Looking at the place, I think I'm quite relieved about that. And looking at that door, I think a hearty sneeze would probably open it.'

Bryony pushed gently against the door which gave way immediately, swinging open to reveal a filthy hallway, crammed with litter as well as discarded footwear and outer clothing. The smell hit both of them at the same time. So many different odours, none of them pleasant.

'Police. Anyone home?'

There was a sound of sudden movement, scuffling, the inevitable hiding of anything incriminating following the dreaded knock on the door. After a few moments, a young woman came out of an open doorway on the left. Dark-skinned, dark hair in dreadlocks, clothes which had seen better days, sharp eyes which missed nothing.

'DS Streeter, DC Vine,' Bryony began, as they held up their ID. 'We're looking for Tim Phillips. Is he here?'

'Why?'

'Because we want to talk to him.'

'Tim doesn't talk. Not much, anyway.'

'You know him then? Is he here or not?'

'He doesn't like strangers.'

'Then we'll introduce ourselves to him. And we're not really all that strange. We're quite nice people actually, when you get to know us.'

'What do you want him for?'

'So he's here then? We want to make sure he's all right. We're concerned for his welfare.'

She snorted in contempt. 'Why now, all of a sudden? Do you know how long Tim's been living rough? Why was no one concerned for him before now? Is it about what happened to him?'

'What do you know about that?'

'I've seen his body. I've seen the scars. He hasn't said anything. Like I said, he doesn't talk.'

'Can we see him, then? Look, Tim fell through the system in the past. We're trying to put that right now. We genuinely do want to help him. And we think he may be able to help us.'

'So now you want to help him? Now, when there's something in it for you? Anyway, you won't get him to go anywhere with you. He's terrified of anyone he doesn't know.' She was looking past them now, at the two PCs and the area car outside. 'And he'll flip completely if he thinks you're going to try to put him in a car with two strange men.'

'Are you his girlfriend?'

'I'm his friend. He trusts me.'

'So can we see him? I promise we're not going to arrest him or do anything to frighten him. We really do want to help him. What's your name?'

She was still studying them with open suspicion and hostility. Her eyes settled on Jezza, as if she found her the more sympathetic of the two.

'Storm. What's yours?'

'DC Vine. Jezza. And it's true, we really are here to try to help Tim. I know he's been badly let down in the past and we want to start trying to put that right now. So can we see him?'

She took a moment to weigh things up then jerked her head at them to follow her as she went back into the room she had come out of. There were two young men in there, one of them lying, completely out of it, on a dirty rug in front of a fireplace, curled up, with a ragged blanket thrown over his legs and feet. The other was sitting near the window, in an old armchair from which the stuffing protruded in places. As soon as he saw two strange faces, he pulled his filthy bare feet up on to the chair and wriggled himself as far back as he could, as if trying to pass through the chair's back and hide himself in a dark corner. They both knew immediately that this was Tim Phillips.

First impressions were of how thin he was, almost emaciated. It made his anxious eyes appear even bigger in his gaunt face. If Jezza had ever wondered about the meaning of the phrase 'a haunted expression', it became clear just from looking at Tim Phillips' face.

'Hello, Tim,' the DS said, as gently as she could. 'I'm Bryony and this is Jezza. Would it be all right if we had a little word with you?'

There was no mistaking the terror in those wide eyes. Jezza knew instinctively that they had one chance only to get this right. If they blew it, they'd never again get anywhere near Tim Phillips. Jezza moved a little closer, speaking quietly to the DS as she did so.

'Sarge, let me have a go.'

Bryony moved aside and Jezza squatted on her haunches in front of the cowering young man.

'Tim, I'm Jezza and I really do just want to help you. I'm not going to hurt you, I promise, and I don't want to frighten you. I think you need some help, Tim. Would you let me help you?'

He was looking pleadingly towards the girl, seeking the reassurance of familiarity.

'Tim doesn't trust anyone. Not even me all of the time,' she told them.

Jezza never moved her eyes from his face as she continued to speak gently.

'I understand that, Tim. I know you're very scared. If

Storm comes with us, would you go with us to find someone who can help you? A safe place for you to be until you're well again? Somewhere I promise you that no one will hurt or frighten you. Where you'll be properly looked after until you're better.'

'Why this sudden interest in him now?' the girl began angrily, but the DS silenced her with a gesture. Jezza was still speaking.

'Tim, you've been let down, very badly. You should have had help long ago. I know it's late coming but I promise you, we have found you somewhere where you'll be safe and be looked after. By people who understand your fears. And no one will force you stay. If Storm comes with us, will you let us help you?'

For a moment, Jezza thought he was going to push himself so far back in the chair that he would disappear up over the backrest. But at least he was making eye contact with her, scrutinising her face for some sign, some reassurance he was seeking. Then he gave one quick, almost imperceptible nod of his head, his eyes still locked with Jezza's.

Storm was looking out of the window at the area car again.

'You'll never get him in there, never in a month of Sundays,' she warned.

'We'll take him in my car, then. Will you come with us?' the DS asked.

'Are you really trying to help him? This isn't just some devious way of arresting him on a drugs charge?'

'We really are trying to help him,' Jezza assured her. 'Tim's been abandoned and left to fend for himself ever since what happened to him and he shouldn't have been. It's time to put that right, to give him the care he needs. Tim's a victim here, not a criminal, and he'll be treated as such.'

Storm took his hand and helped him to his feet.

'Come on, then, Tim. I'll go with you and we'll see what these people can do to help you. But I promise you that if they don't help or if they frighten you, I'll get you out of there. Then you and I will go off and find somewhere where no one will ever bother us again. Swear down.'

As she led him from the room, the DS turned to Jezza.

'That was pretty impressive.'

'My kid brother's autistic. He lives with me. He can sometimes go into meltdown for reasons I don't fully understand. I've had to learn ways to get him to calm down. So, where to now?'

'I'd have liked to take him to the nick first, to get him processed through the system. But that will obviously completely freak him out, so we'll go straight to the unit where we've finally managed to find him a place. A couple of years too late, but at least it's better late than never.'

All Jezza's patient work was nearly undone when they got Tim outside and he saw the two male officers in uniform standing next to the area car. It seemed to send him into total panic mode and he turned and tried to bolt back to the sanctuary of the house. This time it was Storm who managed to calm him down. It was clear she genuinely cared for him, but whether there was any sort of relationship between the two was uncertain.

The DS had to tell the two officers to get back in the car and drive round the block to wait for them before Tim would move. Jezza stood back and left Storm to deal with him. She took the time to make a quick phone call to the boss.

'We've found Tim, boss. We're just trying to persuade him to get into DS Streeter's car, but we have at least found him. He's not in a good way. He has a friend with him, a girl, and she says he doesn't talk much. I don't know if we'll get anywhere with him but at least he's going to be in a safe place tonight, and for a few days to come.'

'Excellent, Jezza, good work. We've got news of Darren, too. Maurice has gone up to be with him. It's still him Darren wants when he's upset.'

He told her about Darren having seen part of the press conference and his reaction to the sight of the church.

'It seems that the word church, or the sight of that one in particular, is some sort of trigger word for Darren. He seemed to recognise the one where his phone was left and his reaction was quite extreme. So just watch out for the same happening with Tim.'

'Are we any nearer to getting him, boss? The Preacher, I mean? Do you think so?'

'I honestly don't know yet, Jezza. I think we're nearer than we were, especially now Darren is trying to tell Maurice something. Our best chance so far is if either Tim or Darren say something which advances us. Or if the press conference brings us in any reliable leads. So far we've had the usual run of irrelevant ones but it's early yet. With luck the piece will go out again at least once this evening and then we might really start to get somewhere.'

Chapter Twenty-one

Rob O'Connell was sorting out the list of things the boss wanted him to do, starting with trying to arrange a face-to-face with Peter Spencer. He was annoyed with himself that he hadn't done it without being prompted. He'd just found nothing so far in the man's background which seemed to make him a suspect. He knew the boss liked nothing left to chance so he felt he should have done it without prompting. He knew his concentration wasn't what it should be at the moment, not now he and Sally had started the application process to be foster parents.

He phoned Spencer's mobile, but it went to voicemail. He left a brief message for him to get in touch. Then he called Stanley Harrison. As he suspected, the man was not thrilled to hear from him again, even less so to be asked to present himself at the station either with a solicitor of his own choosing, or to ask for the duty solicitor when he arrived.

'Am I being arrested for something? If so, what?'

'No, not at all, sir,' Rob decided he better be as polite as possible. He was fully expecting Harrison to make a complaint about him at some point. He didn't want to give him any ammunition. 'It's just that it would be helpful to our current enquiries if you could give me an account of your movements on certain dates, as I mentioned at our last meeting.'

'I'm sure my solicitor will advise me to tell you nothing at all until you tell me why you're asking me these questions. Give me the dates which interest you and depending on what my solicitor says, I'll either give you the answers or not. And it will depend on his availability when we can meet. I don't have a car. Could you not travel to see us?'

'I'm prepared to do that, Mr Harrison, if that would be better for you. Let me have your address and tell me when would be more convenient.'

'Oh, I'm not giving you my address. I don't want the police coming round here bothering my mother. You can come to my solicitor's office.'

'Thank you, sir. If it could be as soon as possible that would help us immensely. I think you yourself live in Poulton-le-Fylde? Is that correct, Mr Harrison, so is your solicitor somewhere near there?' Rob said politely, waiting to note the details Harrison gave him.

He couldn't resist dropping into the conversation that he already had the man's address, or at least his last known one.

'How did you know that? Why are you snooping on me?'

'I'm not, Mr Harrison. I'm talking to several people who have any connection with the church I asked you about previously, as well as a couple of others. You don't have a car, you say, but does your mother perhaps?'

'Mother's in her late eighties and registered blind so no, she doesn't have a car. She can't drive. Never has been able to. Neither can I.'

'Is there anyone else at your address? Anyone who perhaps does drive and who might have a car, or have access to one?'

'I think you should wait to put any questions to me until I've taken advice from my solicitor.'

'It's a simple enough question, Mr Harrison. I can easily find the information for myself. But it would be much quicker and more helpful if you could give me the information now.'

Harrison hesitated then made a sound of irritation.

'Very well. Mother's younger brother lives with us. Harold Buckley. Much younger. He's in his sixties. He's what always used to be called backward. He certainly doesn't drive a car.

He can't really do anything much for himself.'

'Thank you, Mr Harrison, you've been most helpful and I appreciate it. If you could let me know as soon as possible when we can meet up.'

It was as well the boss wasn't in the main office to see the coarse gestures Rob was making at his phone when he ended the call. There was only young Steve in the office. He saw and went pink but he was not about to say anything.

Rob caught his expression and laughed.

'Man's a complete wanker, and a creepy one, at that. If you're making coffee, Steve, I wouldn't say no.'

Somehow it was always Steve's turn to make the coffee, as the youngest member of the team, but he got up obligingly and went to do so. There was only him and Rob in at the moment and he would have felt uncomfortable expecting the DS to brew up for him, although the boss wasn't above making drinks for anyone.

Rob had to wait awhile until he heard from Peter Spencer. His mobile showed an incoming call from a number he didn't recognise.

'DS O'Connell? It's Peter Spencer again. You asked me to call you.'

'Thanks for calling me back, Peter. I didn't recognise the number.'

Again the ready laugh that had marked their previous conversation.

'You wouldn't believe the phone troubles I've been having. It could only happen to me. I dropped my smartphone, which was not very smart of me, and it was not smart enough to withstand such abuse. Apart from a cracked screen, I can now just about pick up incoming messages but despite my best intentions plus a few words Father would not have approved of, I can't manage to make any calls or send any texts. Anyway, long story short, I've picked up a cheap pay as you go, which is what I'm calling from, until I can get the other one repaired. What can I do for you?'

'I wonder if I could ask you a few more questions about the church? Preferably before you go off on your trip. And preferably face-to-face, if that's possible?'

'Oh, I'm sorry. I'm actually already on board a ferry, heading for the continent. I could launch a lifeboat and row back to shore, if it's urgent?' There was laughter in his voice again as he spoke. 'I don't know if you can hear me well enough, but I'm not catching everything you say. It's probably this cheap phone.'

'I don't think you need to do anything that drastic. When are you back?'

'Not for two or three months at least, I'm afraid. I've cleared my teaching engagements for three. Look, if it's important for you to see my ugly mug while we're talking, although I can't imagine why you'd want to, I have my laptop with me so as soon as I get to my first hotel, we could perhaps talk via Skype, or something like that?'

'Do you know when that's likely to be?'

'I'm footloose and fancy-free. I have a few firm appointments but the rest of the time I'm going where the wind blows me. I never book anything in advance. I'm a free spirit now, so I make the most of it. I've not even brought the car, so I'll be travelling by train. I'll probably find a hotel this evening, I imagine, unless I decide to board a sleeper train. But I will make contact as soon as I can, I promise.'

Trev's phone went straight to voicemail when Ted phoned him later in the day. He told himself firmly that there was no need to panic. Trev loved to talk. He'd been thrilled at the chance of a brand new phone to replace the one stolen when he'd been kidnapped. He rang his sister, Siobhan, most days as well as Ted's mother, Annie, not to mention his circle of friends. Ted was over-protective since what had happened, he knew. Hopefully now Trev was aware of the danger, he'd be on the alert for any sign of further trouble.

'Hi, it's me. I'm working late again this evening. No idea what time I'll get back so eat when you like. I'll get a takeaway. Not pizza this time. That was inedible. I'll see you later.'

He wanted to work on until Maurice and Jezza got back so he could get an update on Tim Phillips and Darren Lee. There'd just been one brief call from Maurice to say Darren was still agitated but he and Amy were working with him.

Trev didn't keep him waiting long for news.

'I was talking to your mother. I miss knowing she's just round the corner, and I was practising my Welsh with her. She'd seen you on the lunchtime news. So did I. She's so proud of you. She said you looked very handsome and she liked the shirt.'

Ted laughed. 'I'm not sure having a nice shirt on is enough to get us the breakthrough we need on this case. We've not had anything of interest yet. Just the usual round of people wanting to tell us how weird their neighbours are. Are you going out tonight?'

'I've said I'll do an early English class, then I'm meeting Mark and some of the other volunteers to go for a drink or three.'

'Don't take the bike if you're drinking.'

'No, Mother.'

'Give me a bell when you're ready to go home and I can collect you if you like. And be careful – keep your wits about you.'

'Yes, Mother. Love you. Especially when you show how much you care. And phone your own mother! She says she never hears from you unless I nag you.'

Ted was smiling to himself as he ended the call. Touching base with his partner helped him get through the day. Too many police officers had ruined their marriages by not doing that. Trev understood about his job and didn't make unrealistic demands on his time, but he appreciated him keeping in contact whenever it was possible.

The Super had gone straight up to Central Park after the press conference and debrief to talk budgets. Ted hadn't yet heard from her if any more cuts were needed. He sincerely hoped not. He went out into the main office.

'It's likely to be a latish one, for most of us anyway, this evening. So at some point we'll need to order in. Steve, would you mind seeing to that? I fancy Chinese, myself, but I'm happy to go with what everyone wants. Just no more cardboard pizza, please. I want us to take stock of what we've got, once Jezza and Maurice are back, and where we're going next with all the current cases.'

Jezza looked tired when she got back from Lincolnshire. It had been a hard day, emotionally, dealing with the sad wreck of a person that was Tim Phillips. But Maurice looked drained and bone-weary when he stumped slowly up the stairs to join them shortly afterwards.

At first glance, Maurice appeared to be insensitive, about as politically incorrect as it was possible to be, and with as much tact as a steam roller. Even Jezza, who was particularly fond of him, called him a sexist pig from time to time. Anyone who really knew him understood that he was in truth a sensitive man, capable of intense feeling, and with an innate desire to take care of anyone in pain. In his own words, a Daddy Hen.

Ted would normally encourage team members not to get too close to anyone in a case, especially not a victim. He wouldn't generally approve of them giving out personal phone numbers, nor of going to see them on their rest days. But he knew he would be fighting a losing battle ordering Maurice to back off from anyone who needed him. It was the reason he always fought so hard to keep him on the team.

He left Maurice to come to a bit and let Jezza go first.

'Boss, Tim Phillips is now clean, physically, though still

drying out from his addiction, fed and hopefully sleeping in a nice bed for the first time for a long time. He's not saying anything. He's completely shut down, overwhelmed, but at least he's safe. The unit is a nice one, the people are very kind and understanding. They're even letting his friend Storm stay with him as much as possible. They've suggested we give him a day or so to settle then think about talking to him, if he will.

'I had a long talk with Storm to find out what, if anything, he's ever told her about what happened to him. There wasn't much, but she did say sometimes he mentions the name Simon. She doesn't know who Simon is, though.'

Maurice sat up and looked more alert at that.

'Darren's said 'Simon' a few times today, as well. When I got there, he just kept repeating church over and again. In the end I found the photo of the church you released for the press conference and showed it to him again. The one he'd seen on the telly. He got very excited but he kept shaking his head and saying 'other church'. I've no idea what he meant and he gets very frustrated when he can't express himself. It's like he wants to tell me but something's stopped him. Fear of something, but I don't know what.'

'Fear of getting electric shock treatment, I would imagine,' Jezza put in. 'We won't know, unless one or other of them starts to talk, but they've both clearly been subjected to some sort of brainwashing technique. We know they turned up not saying anything other than repeating the bible passages they'd clearly been trained, or conditioned rather, to recite. Let's just suppose for a moment that that's all they were allowed to say. Suppose if they repeated those they got rewards, like something to eat or drink, of perhaps a light being left on for them. If they said anything else which wasn't on the list of what they were allowed to say, that's when the torture happened.

'Six months of that and I suppose it would take them both a

long time to unlearn that technique and realise that they could now say whatever they want to without fear of pain and more suffering.'

'So who is Simon?' Ted asked. 'Steve, Sal, how are we doing with anyone known to have had contact with the three through school, through NCS or anything else? Is there a Simon in common?'

'We can soon cross-check that, boss. Steve can do that easily enough now we've started a database. From memory, we've not yet flagged up any Simons as of interest.'

'And this other church that Darren mentioned? Any thoughts, anyone?'

'Could he have been taken to another church and held there?' Rob suggested. 'Do churches have crypts or anything now? Some sort of underground room where he might have been held?'

'What about the noise, though? These poor lads must have screamed the place down, with what they went through, unless they were gagged the whole time.' When Maurice spoke, the pain on his face showed how deeply the case was affecting him.

Steve was, as usual, sitting in front of his computer the whole time. Although he was paying attention, his fingers would start working from time to time and his eyes would be on the monitor.

'Sir, did you know you can buy a derelict church for under a hundred grand? There's a firm here that seems to specialise in selling them. They've got half a dozen for sale at the moment in the Greater Manchester area alone.'

'Have they, now? That's very interesting. Well done, Steve. There's no point in trying to do anything with that now, it's getting late to get hold of anyone to check it out. But tomorrow, can you contact those agents, and anyone else you can find who sells old churches and get a list of how many they've sold in the last three or four years and who to. Maurice, if Steve lets you have links of any he comes up with, is it worth trying Darren again with some more photos?'

'I'm not sure, boss. He's trying so hard to tell me stuff. I don't want to risk scaring him too much so he stops trying. I don't want to do anything to break his trust in me.'

'I'm meeting with the psychologist we used on the Morgane Edwards case tomorrow. He should hopefully have finished giving his evidence on that case and he's agreed to talk to me about this one. He can either advise us how to proceed or, if he thinks it's worth trying, he's said he would speak to both Darren and to Tim, as long as he's not treading on any toes at the unit he's in.'

They had a lot to get through before Ted was prepared to call a halt for the evening. Steve was despatched to get Chinese takeaway and soft drinks for everyone to keep them going. With so many ongoing cases and a diminished team, they were starting to feel stretched. It was why Ted wanted to oversee everything, so no mistakes were made.

Virgil had been busy helping Uniform with the interviews for the FGM case. It was turning out to be bigger than they thought. Now the first young woman had spoken out, others were being encouraged to come forward and do the same, knowing that they would be listened to and believed. Megan and Jezza had handed over the files they'd started to Susan Heap from Uniform. If they could pull it all together, it would be a good result. Virgil confessed to finding it a hard case to handle. It was something beyond his experience and comprehension, but it was part of his job.

'Peter Spencer called me back, boss, but unfortunately, he's already left on this organ tour of Europe,' Rob said when the boss turned to him for an update. 'He promised me he'd try to Skype me for a face-to-face as soon as he can but he hasn't done so yet. I've also arranged another meeting with Stanley Harrison.'

'Are either of them likely as suspects, do you think? Gut

instinct?'

'Harrison is definitely strange. But then he says he can't drive. He certainly has no licence and we know The Preacher used a vehicle to drop Darren off at Ludworth.'

'We don't know it for sure, though. We're assuming he did. But he could have had an accomplice that we don't yet know about.'

Rob mentally kicked himself. The boss was right, of course. He'd slipped up yet again. He needed to up his game or he could be for the chop in the next round of cuts.

'And don't forget the current vicar. Gabriel Clegg. Just check out the relevant dates with him, too, so we cover all bases.

'Jo, the arson and murder?'

'Nice easy one, boss. He's confessed. Nothing but the paperwork to sort now so that'll be another good, fast result for our stats.'

'And Tony Barlow, Mike?'

'That's sorted too, boss, and we've got his mate. It was Giggsy, so we know him.'

Giggsy was the nickname of a local petty villain, well known to them. With the first name of Ryan, he was always called Giggsy after footballer Ryan Giggs.

'Giggsy? Ryan O'Brien? Kidnap is a bit outside his usual MO, isn't it?'

'I think he thought it would be easy money. He was probably looking for a reason to go back inside anyway. He likes it there. Always says he can make shed-loads more money and more easily inside than out, with his contacts. He's a runner for the big boys, selling drugs and mobiles.'

'Perhaps we should spoil his fun and not press for a custodial sentence. Good, though, some good results. Now all we need to do is get our hands on The Preacher. It feels as if we're making some progress. We just need a breakthrough. Sal, you're in charge of calls. Have they thrown anything up?

What about any previous offenders with similar form? Any traces on our patch?'

'Nothing from the calls yet, boss. Usual load of unhelpful stuff, as you'd expect. Now we have the name Simon mentioned by both Darren and Tim, I'll cross-check through them all to see if there's a Simon there, and the same with previous offenders.'

'Let's hope it's not a nickname. Steve, as well as old churches, maybe we should start taking a look at other isolated buildings like old farms, perhaps. I saw a few when I was out the other day and it made me think. I can't imagine the agents sell many of those, so see if you can find any that have sold in the last three years or so.

'How did you get on with getting someone to talk to staff at this centre the lads were at?'

'A couple of local officers went round today, sir, but it seems it's not open all the time, just weekends and then when it's booked for a group. They're trying to find contact details of someone in charge to talk to, and they'll let me know.'

Ted glanced up at the clock on the wall. It was getting late. They'd probably covered all they could for the day. Maurice in particular looked in need of some rest.

'Right, thank you, everyone. We all have homes to go to so I think that's what we should do for now. Back here bright and early tomorrow. Can someone volunteer to dispose of the remains of our supper, please? We'll have the cleaners complaining it stinks like a Chinese takeaway if we don't.'

Ted didn't feel much like company or being forcibly cheerful with people he didn't know when he went to pick Trev up. He waited outside the pub in the car and sent a text to say he was there. Trev was on top form, smelling of wine, laughing, talkative, happy. Back to his old self.

Ted leaned across to kiss him fondly as he half fell into the passenger seat.

'I should warn you, officer, that I may be just a teeny bit squiffy so I am totally at your mercy.'

Ted smiled as he put the car into gear and drove off.

'That sounds good to me.'

Chapter Twenty-two

'Just a quick catch-up before I go out. You all know what you need to be getting on with. I just wondered if anyone had had a brainwave in the night? A flash of inspiration?'

'Boss ...' Steve began hesitantly.

'Let's hear it, Steve, even if you think it sounds crazy. Your ideas are usually very good.'

'You were saying about Simon possibly being a nickname. It got me thinking.'

Ted tried to stay patient and sound encouraging. He just wished Steve would find a bit more confidence from somewhere to speak up without hesitation.

'And let's not forget you were a big help on the subject of nicknames not so long ago, with Simon the Pieman in the abuse case. So what did you come up with?'

'It's the biblical theme that started me thinking. One of the twelve apostles, the one who was supposedly closest to Christ. He was called Peter, also known as Simon Peter. And he's the one who denied Christ. Three times, I think.'

Several of the team looked towards Rob as Ted said, 'And we do have one Peter that we know of already. Right, Rob, it's becoming more important than it was before that you make contact with Peter Spencer and check out some of his alibis. It could well be total coincidence but we need at least to eliminate him from our enquiries. Steve and Sal, keep an eye out for Peters now, as well as Simons on the staff lists from schools and centres.

'It's a good idea, Steve, but of course it may be completely wrong. Although the denial of Christ idea would fit, too, possibly. The idea of taking them first to a church then leaving them somewhere with a pre-Christian connection. But let's not get too hung up on it, at least until we know if Peter Spencer is out of the frame or not.

'And let's not overlook Gabriel Clegg. A vicar would certainly get the reference to Simon and denying Christ, that sort of thing. Dig deeper into his background. We need to know even more about him and what he was doing before he moved to his current parish.

'I'll be going out later this morning to meet the psychologist and that will hopefully give us an idea of how to proceed with Tim and Darren. Keep me updated on those two in particular. I'll be on the end of the phone if you need me, of course.'

Ted had arranged to meet the forensic psychologist in a small coffee shop he knew, enough of a distance from the Crown Court not to be full of witnesses or lawyers involved in the case. Anthony Hopkins was the last prosecution witness to be called. His evidence was strong, his credentials impressive, and that was what the prosecution team had decided would be the best closing shot. The one which would hopefully stick in the jury members' minds before they started listening to the defence, who were only calling two witnesses.

There was not much of a defence case to make, which was why destroying prosecution witnesses' credibility and tearing their testimonies apart had been such an important part of their strategy. The defendant, Morgane Edwards, had tried to alibi herself for one of the murders but had been outwitted by Ted and by an eager young police sniffer dog called Tally.

All they could really rely on was their own psychological report, which differed significantly from that of Hopkins, plus the girl's father, who was clearly prepared to perjure himself by providing alibis which were questionable for all of the crimes.

'Hello, Anthony, nice to see you again, thanks for agreeing to meet,' Ted stood up to greet the man, remembering to pronounce the H in his name, shaking his hand. 'How did it go in court this morning? Would you like tea? Coffee? Something else?'

'I think a double-shot espresso might be the order of the day, but my palpitations tell me a pot of tea would be far more sensible. I imagine there are fighting pit-bulls of a more amenable temperament than the defence barrister, as you no doubt found out yourself.'

It was waitress service. When the young woman came to take their order, Ted asked for a pot of tea for two, checked with Anthony and then ordered tuna and tomato sandwiches for them both. Then he laughed ruefully.

'I have to agree with you there. He gave me quite a mauling.'

'He is either an extremely diligent defence counsel or he has serious issues he should be addressing. I was almost tempted to give him my card. I was surprised at their choice of expert witness, though. She's quite young, very keen but – although I don't like to boast – I rather outrank her in terms of both qualifications and experience. It just depends on whom the jury are more inclined to believe.'

'What's your gut feeling?'

'Ah, now that is not something in which I usually deal. I prefer a more scientific approach. Morgane Edwards is, of course, a consummate actress. It's part of her condition. She was giving an Oscar-winning performance throughout, flashing those innocent baby-blue eyes at the jury. I would say it's in the balance at the moment. It depends on the performance of the defence witnesses, I would be inclined to say.

'These sandwiches are surprisingly good,' he went on, taking a bite out of the light lunch that had just been brought to their table. 'I've not discovered this place before. Now, you didn't get me here to ply me with tea or discuss Morgane Edwards, and my meter is ticking. So tell me in more detail about this case with which you may require my help.'

Ted always spoke quietly but he lowered his voice more, discussing work in a public place. It was not busy and he'd deliberately picked the quietest corner he could. He'd already outlined the case to Hopkins over the phone when arranging to meet him. But now he was able to give him more detail, anxious for an expert opinion.

'You don't need me to tell you that your kidnapper is seriously disturbed. That much is evident from his actions. I like the theory of your DC, about the brainwashing technique and the boys now being reluctant to say anything for fear of saying the wrong thing. That to me is eminently plausible. Not to be too indelicate, I think if someone was administering electric shocks, even relatively mild ones, to my genitals if I said the wrong thing, I too might be inclined to opt to say as little as possible.

'Will they ever speak openly about their experiences? Impossible to say without me observing them over a period of time, which would cost your budget a lot of money. Should you let them meet? I would advise against it without knowing a great deal more. It could potentially have a catastrophic effect if not handled properly.

'What is your best way forwards from here, with your two victims? The mercenary part of me says employ me, for lots of lucrative hours, and I'll get through to them and get you the information you need. The decent part of me - because believe it or not there is one – says that from what you tell me, you're doing absolutely the right thing, and possibly the only thing you can do with them at the moment.

'I know some of the staff at the unit in Lincolnshire and they're very good. That young man is in the ideal place. As long as the bed remains available for him, you have as good a chance as any of him improving enough to say something.

Your other young man is extremely lucky to have a mother who obviously cares for him and will do her best, despite her own problems. So with her, your liaison officer and your own DC – who incidentally sounds like an absolute gem – again, if there's any chance of him recovering from this, he will, where he is.

'I won't insult your intelligence by telling you that the problems will arise when yet another funding crisis means the withdrawal of financial provision in place for these two young men. That will then inevitably result in the life-raft being pulled out from under them and them being left to paddle their own way back to shore. I suspect at that point they would drift off course never to be brought back.

'Now, shall we have some more of this quite drinkable tea and perhaps a sticky bun, by way of a pudding? I confess to having an appallingly sweet tooth.'

As soon as Ted walked back into the main office after his meeting with Hopkins, he could tell that something significant had happened. Only Jo, Rob and Jezza were in. They had their heads together and were discussing something, their faces serious.

'What's happened?'

Jo spoke, as the senior officer present.

'It may be nothing, boss, and we're hoping it is. But a teenage lad has been reported missing from the centre of Manchester. Seventeen years old, out with friends at a club last night and never went home. Never done anything like it before. Another good lad, serious student, never given his parents any anxious moments so, naturally, they're worried sick. It's not twenty-four hours yet, of course, so he could just be sleeping off a monumental hangover. It's just been flagged up because of the similarities.'

'And the biggest similarity, boss, is that this lad is gay,' Jezza put in. 'He's …'

'If you're about to say openly gay, Jezza, please don't.'

'I wasn't, boss,' she sounded offended. 'I was going to say that he's in a steady relationship. He wasn't out with his boyfriend, though, as the boyfriend's got flu. The lad, Gary Heath, was just with a bunch of mates, doing a few pubs and clubs. After they left the last club, he headed off to go home but he never got there. His mobile phone's missing, too.'

'Sorry, Jezza, I know you better than that. I made a wrong assumption and I apologise. Right, first off, let's cross all our fingers and toes that there's a perfectly innocent explanation to this and that Gary will turn up safe and sound but just slightly hung over. Keep me updated and, it goes without saying, we need to know immediately if his phone turns up anywhere if he doesn't.

'So, Rob, any progress on Peter Spencer? Have you been able to contact him again?'

'Not yet, boss. I've left messages on both his phones but he's not returned my calls yet.'

'Do we actually know if he is in Europe or not? Other than him telling you that he is? Did he mention which ports he was using? Have you checked passenger lists with the ferry companies? What about his car? Have you checked that it wasn't on a ferry, even if he told you he was travelling by train?

Rob was starting to look increasingly uncomfortable.

'I'll do it now, boss.'

'And have we got a photo of him, in case we should need one? If not, let's get hold of one from somewhere. Passport office, perhaps.

'There are several reasons to hope this latest disappearance is not the work of The Preacher. The first and possibly the most significant is the complete change of MO in that this time there's no six month gap. It's just over a couple of weeks, so there's still a good chance that this is something unrelated and hopefully harmless, despite the other similarities.

'Keep me posted on any and all developments. Rob, a word, please.'

Rob had his head down as he followed the boss into his office, shutting the door quickly behind him as he did so, not quite sure what was in store for him.

'Boss, I know what you're going to say and you're right. I completely ballsed this one up.'

Ted had pulled out the spare chair and indicated for Rob to sit down.

'That's not what I was going to say and I certainly wouldn't have put it like that. But yes, this was poor, sloppy work. It's not what I expect from a DS and it's certainly not what I expect from you, Rob. So what I was going to say is what's wrong? Your mind's clearly not on the job so is there anything I should know about? Anything preventing you from doing the job as you should do?'

'There is no excuse, boss, and I can only apologise. I wasn't concentrating, but I can't even claim anything's wrong. Quite the reverse. Me and Sally have applied to be foster parents and we're waiting to hear if we're through to the next stage. I'm sorry. I should have kept my mind on the job.'

'Well, that's good news. I hope you're successful. For what it's worth, I think you'd make great foster parents. If ever you need a reference, I'd be happy to write something to say you're a good officer, most of the time, and if you learn to keep your private life out of work, you've got good career prospects. Just don't let me down again.'

'I won't, boss, and thank you,' Rob scrambled to his feet, glad to have got off lightly.

'Go on, get out of here,' Ted told him, although his tone was good-natured.

Rob talking about foster parents made him think of Doug and the kitten, for some reason. He knew he should call him back, as a courtesy, even if it was to tell him that he didn't think it was the right time for him and Trev to even consider adopting another cat, especially not such a young one.

Doug would often go the extra mile for Ted because he liked him, appreciated his interest in all things feline. He also found it a pleasant change that a DCI was polite enough always to give him the time of day and talk cats, no matter how urgent his enquiry was.

Ted promised himself he'd call him later that day. Or perhaps tomorrow.

Ted was convinced that as soon as he left the office for more than five minutes, paperwork started breeding in his inbox, his in-tray and anywhere else it could. It was not for nothing that the standing joke in many police forces that the most serious line of duty injury a DCI was likely to suffer was a paper cut.

Once he'd made enough of a dent in the latest load he thought he'd take time to nip downstairs and catch a few words with Kevin Turner. He hardly seemed to see him these days. The two of them spent far too much time confined to their respective offices.

As soon as he tapped on the door and went in, he could see from Kev's dishevelled appearance and the mountain of scattered documents surrounding him that he was not in the best of moods.

'Whatever it is you want, Ted, I haven't got it. Not the manpower, not the budget, bugger all. So go and ask some other sod.'

'As good as that, eh?' Ted asked him, ignoring his bad mood and pulling out a spare chair to sit down on.

'Bloody worse,' Kev finally looked up, one hand rubbing his stomach again. The pills seemed to be having less and less effect on his ulcers, with the amount of stress he was under. 'It's getting beyond a joke. How the hell are we supposed to respond even to urgent cases with the force numbers cut to the bare bone? What was it you wanted, anyway? Whatever it is, you can't have it. Not from me, in any case.'

'I'm worried about Bill.'

'Is that it? You're worried about Bill? I'm worried about Bill. I'm worried about rising crime and cuts to resources. I'm worried about global warming. I'm worried about the situation in the Middle East. I've just had to order a car to cease chasing two lads on a moped who assaulted and robbed someone. Little scrotes had no helmets on and you know the new rules mean we mustn't risk them getting injured in a pursuit. Bill gets to put his feet up for a few weeks well-earned rest, counting his pension. Then he's back here again, in civvies, getting paid. What do you expect me to do about it?'

'He's getting very low, Kev. You must have noticed.'

'Noticed? I spend so many hours in here I need a map to get to the car park. I'm sorry for Bill, I really am. I know he loves his job and he thinks of the nick as his home and his colleagues as his family. But seriously, Ted, what can I do? The budget isn't there. He's got to take a three-month break before he can start back. But he can start back. The job's his, it's a firm offer.

'I'll try to keep in touch with him, keep an eye on him. But you know what it's like lately. My wife almost dials 999 when I go home these days. She sees so little of me she doesn't recognise me, thinks I'm a burglar.'

'I know. I do understand. We've got off lightly so far, and we were lucky that Megan wanted to go without me having to pick someone to bin. I just thought I'd flag it up. We need to keep an eye on him between us all, if we can, when he's not coming in here practically every day. He deserves that much, at least.'

'Are you coming to his leaving do on Friday?'

'The surprise party he knows all about and is dreading? I'll be there if I can, you know that.'

This time the tension in the main office was palpable when Ted went back upstairs. Most of the team were now back in, only

Mike and Virgil still tied up on other cases.

'Tell me,' Ted ordered.

'Gary's phone has been found, boss. In a church near Manchester. In the porch again. But another church. And there's still no sign of the lad, and no word from him. His parents saw the press conference on TV so they're beside themselves and they don't even know about the phone and where it was found yet. They're practically camped out at their local nick demanding action.'

'Right, we've got to crank this enquiry up a few notches or we're going to look very bad. We've got to find this lad and soon, before he ends up like the other two. Or worse.

'I just need to talk to the Super and the Big Boss but if they agree I think, Jo, that you and I should go and be a high visibility presence. Talk to this Gary's parents, assure them we're doing everything we possibly can on this, otherwise the press really are going to hang us out to dry.

'I'm going to ask for more officers to be made available, run this as a major ongoing crime, covering all four of the cases we now have. A single unit, working together.

'If we don't take some drastic action and soon we could risk a fatality. The Preacher, if it is him, has changed his pattern. That means anything else could also change. We might be faced with anything, including another death, and not an accidental one, this time. It's just possible that the press conference has pushed The Preacher over the edge. He may be about to take things further. We have to find him and stop him before he does.

'And Rob …'

'I know, boss. Find Peter Spencer.'

Chapter Twenty-three

'CPS are still telling me they're expecting a fairly speedy verdict,' Jim Baker told Ted and the Ice Queen at their early morning conference on what was anticipated to be the last day of the Morgane Edwards trial.

'There's just the father to finish his pack of lies, then the summing up, then the jury will be sent out to consider. At the moment, I'd say it's too close to call but our lot are fairly confident. So we need to discuss - providing you can assure me you have the evidence you need, Ted - the when and the where of arresting the father. Because you don't need me to remind you that if we clap him in handcuffs and drag him out of court just after he's seen his daughter convicted, it's going to make front page news everywhere. And if we've got it wrong, we'll be joining Bill in retirement, though not from choice.'

'My feeling is that if it's a guilty verdict, the father will completely lose it in court. He'll need to be removed and it may need more than an usher. We could legitimately have a couple of Uniform officers at the back on stand-by. If he kicks off, they could quietly remove him and whisk him away. That shouldn't look too suspicious, even to the press pack.'

'And if he doesn't?'

'Then the officers follow him discreetly. If he gets in his car to head home, they pull him over on some minor traffic offence. Tell him he has a tail-light out or something. Then he can be arrested and charged. No doubt his flat will be under press siege so we don't really want to arrest him there until they get bored of waiting and go somewhere else.'

'He will almost certainly be demanding an appeal, so he might well go straight into meetings with the defence team,' Superintendent Caldwell pointed out reasonably.

'Then we play cat and mouse until we can get him somewhere quiet. I've spoken at length to CPS and whatever Edwards says when we question him, they feel we have enough to at least charge him. Tony Barlow and Giggsy have told us everything. They've given us a good description of Edwards, plus we have the phone contact between them.'

'Giggsy?' The Super hadn't been at Stockport as long as Ted and Jim Baker had been so she didn't know the nicknames of all the local villains.

'Ryan O'Brien,' Ted told her. 'He's the accomplice and he's already known to us. Neither he nor Barlow are terribly credible witnesses. But in a sense that works to our advantage because they would be unlikely to come into contact with someone like Edwards unless it was for something a bit dodgy.'

'Right, I'm happy with all of that, as long as Jim is. So now tell us about this latest possible victim of The Preacher.'

'There's still no signs of Gary Heath and no contact from him. The parents are going frantic because it's totally out of character.'

'Sadly, teenage boys often reach a stage in their lives where most of them do something completely out of character.'

The Ice Queen was speaking from experience. The elder of her two sons had given his parents a real fright by doing something stupid at a party. Fortunately he'd lived to tell the tale.

'I'd be happy to put it down to no more than that if his phone hadn't been found in a church porch. That worries me. That's too much of a coincidence and you know I don't like coincidences.

'This is going to blow the budget apart, I'm afraid, but it

needs sorting. Apart from the damage to another young man, the press backlash if we don't crack this case, and soon, is going to be potentially catastrophic. That's why I've called a briefing for mid-morning with officers from all four forces involved; us, Lancashire, Lincolnshire and Humberside. I've got a room sorted at Central Park, as that seemed the logical place. We need to get our heads together on this one and come up with something concrete.'

Both Ted's senior officers were nodding in agreement, which was a good sign. It was up to them to deal with the financial issues involved. That's what they were there for. This wasn't just about the teenagers now. It was about damage limitation. If four forces between them couldn't manage to catch and stop The Preacher, public confidence in the police was going to take a serious knock.

'I need to swing by court first then I'll join you, Ted. If we can't manage to wind this up with four forces and a combined budget, then we deserve to be hung out to dry.'

'And once the briefing is over, I'll go and talk to the parents of Gary Heath, if there's still no sign of him anywhere.'

'I suppose a briefing of this size couldn't realistically happen via a conference call?'

The Super had one last attempt at salvaging the budget. She agreed with Ted. They needed to do something. But if it could be done as effectively at a lower cost, she should at least raise the possibility.

The looks she got from both Ted and Jim told her what they thought of her idea.

'Then let's do it. Let's see if we can't finally get whoever is behind these dreadful cases.'

Jim Baker stood up to leave but Ted lingered a bit. He wanted the chance of a quiet word alone with the Ice Queen about the presumed drowning near Cape Town. She, too, knew Green and had been on some of his training courses.

'You don't really think it was Mr Green, do you?' she

asked after he told her what he knew. 'After all the time he spent shouting at us all about assessing and managing risk before we did anything else, would he really put himself in danger like that?'

'I can't see him of all people taking risks in water. We both know he was an excellent swimmer. My feeling is he's either staged his own disappearance or ...'

'Somebody wanted him out of the way,' she finished for him.

Ted was perching on the edge of a desk near the whiteboard using a pointer to illustrate the information up there. He always preferred not to stand. It only emphasised how short he was.

'We can't really call them suspects at this stage as we don't actually have enough to link them to the cases. But these three, Gabriel Clegg, the current vicar, Peter Spencer, the former organist and son of the previous vicar, and Stanley Harrison, a writer specialising in both Christian and pre-Christian places of worship are at present the three people most of interest to us.

'For those of you who are new to the case, our biggest difficulty to date is that neither of the surviving victims is talking much so we don't have a great deal to go on.

'DC Maurice Brown, from my team, has been spending time with Darren Lee, gaining his trust. Darren has started to attempt to communicate, but it's still not a great deal to go on. Maurice?'

'Boss, I went to see Darren this morning before I came here. Yesterday he was saying 'other church' and using this name, Simon, which so far means nothing much to us. This morning he kept saying the word 'redemption' to me. I don't know what he meant. Probably another part of some of the bible verses he was conditioned into repeating.'

'Sir, DC Brown phoned me to let me know the new words, but we've been specifically asked by the unit where Tim Phillips is being looked after to leave him to settle in for the time being before we try asking him anything which might set him off again,' DS Bryony Streeter, from Lincoln, told the briefing. 'In a sense, Tim is a worse case than Darren because he took to drugs after what happened to him, so the unit needs to deal with getting him off those before he's in a fit state for us to talk to him at all.'

The door opened at that moment and the ACC (Crime) Russell Evans, strode in to the conference room. Ted hadn't been expecting him to attend. He leapt off the desk to stand, still feeling guilty about his previous encounter with him. A few other officers made to rise but not all those assembled. Formality was on the decline within the force as a whole. In some divisions, everyone was on first name terms, nobody was called 'sir' or 'ma'am', except on formal occasions and people no longer stood, except for the highest executive officers. Ted actually preferred the older rank structure and its inherent formality, but he was an old-fashioned sort. At least you knew where you were with it.

'As you were, ladies and gentlemen. I don't want to disturb you. But with the latest victim taken from almost on our doorstep here, I wanted to see the progress of this enquiry. Above all, I just wanted to assure everyone that resources will be found for this case. I don't want anyone to think that this person is going to get away with what he's been doing simply because money's a bit tight.

'Is there any news yet of this latest young lad?'

'Nothing, sir. Because his phone was found at a church, we're treating this as another kidnapping by The Preacher, in the absence of any explanation to the contrary. I'm going to talk to the parents, with DI Rodriguez, once I've finished here.'

'Good, excellent. I like that thinking. Let's show the public we're all over this and no effort will be spared to get the person behind it. I'll just sit at the back here and observe. Ignore me.'

'What I now need from all of you here is help to look at what links these cases. You've now got all the information that we have so far. The main link we have up to this point between two of the victims is that they did part of their National Citizen Service, the residential part, at the same centre, though not at the same time. So naturally we now need to find out if the latest presumed victim, Gary Heath, did the same.

'The other thing I'd like each local force to concentrate on, please, is the possibility that The Preacher keeps his victims in something like an old church. Darren has talked about another church. He reacted to the photo of the church where his phone was found but he still kept talking about another church. We've found that it's often surprisingly inexpensive to buy a decommissioned church. So can you all please check your own areas. Are there any such buildings? Have any been sold in the last three to four years? Can we try and get someone out to take a look at them and see if there's any signs of recent activity there.'

'Vicarages too, sir?' an officer Ted didn't know by sight asked.

'Yes, please, good point. Anything with a church connection. Churches, church halls, vicarages. DS O'Connell is talking to this man,' he used the pointer to indicate Harrison, 'who has visited a great many churches and has seemingly sometimes been given a key for access. We're also digging deeper into the background of the vicar, Gabriel Clegg. Peter Spencer, as far as we are aware, is currently out of the country.'

'Does that mean he's out of the frame, sir? If the latest lad was taken while he was away?'

'He's not out of the frame yet, no. Not until we've established for ourselves, rather than just take his word for it, that he is on the continent. My team are working on that now.'

The ACC was still waiting when the briefing broke up. Ted had hoped to slink away without talking to him but it was clear that he wasn't going to be able to.

'You don't need to hide, Ted. We're good. Moment of

madness, all forgotten. Good briefing, exactly as I'd have run it. Let's get him, and soon. And I meant what I said. For something like this, and as high profile as this, budgets can be stretched. Just ask me.'

'Hello, again, DS O'Connell, Peter Spencer, once more. Contrite, humble, and more than slightly embarrassed as I realise you must now be convinced I'm guilty of something for failing to contact you, as promised. I opted for a homely B&B rather than an impersonal hotel last night so guess what? No Wifi! I hadn't even considered the possibility.'

'Thank you for getting back in touch, Peter. I really do need to ask you about some specific dates, just so I can eliminate you from our enquiries.'

'I doubt I'll have all the answers off the top of my head, but you could email me the dates. I'll check through my diaries and get back to you with the answers as soon as I can, hopefully this evening. I keep such stuff on my laptop. I'll be sure to pick a hotel with Wifi then we can see one another via Skype, although I'm still not sure why you'd want to. My email is organist.peter@gmail.com.'

'Where are you at the moment, Peter?'

'In a small town in Germany. You can probably hear the TV news channel in the background. I've no idea what they're saying. My German is fairly basic, but I can follow the pictures. Hang on, I'll just mute the volume.'

'You didn't take your car, though?'

'No, I much prefer to travel by train. Look, I'm sorry to hurry you but I've just realised the battery is going flat on me. I thought I'd put in on to charge last night but I'm so inept with anything electronic I can't have plugged the lead in properly or something. I'm hopeless!' he laughed.

'Which ferry crossing did you travel on? I've heard the North Sea one is a good route for Germany. Hello? Hello? Peter?'

The phone had gone dead. Rob had no way of knowing whether the man he'd been speaking to was, as he said, simply not technically minded or whether he was giving him the run-around. So far, he hadn't found the man's name listed as a foot passenger on any of the ferries he'd tried. These days, that of itself didn't mean much. With sometimes relaxed border controls in place for travelling within Europe, it wasn't always as easy as it had once been to track people coming and going on the ferries on foot.

'Is that DC Ellis? Steve? Hello, again. This is Hazel, from the estate agent. We spoke before?' The voice at the end of the phone went up at the end of the sentence, making a statement into a question.

'Yes, I remember. Did you have an update for me?' Steve asked.

'I wanted to apologise. When you phoned I wasn't really thinking straight. I'd just found my boyfriend's been cheating on me and … Well, you don't want to hear any of that. I just wasn't really on the ball. You asked about anyone buying any of the old churches and I said no. But then I remembered that someone did rent one of them. They don't sell well, because of the lack of planning permission for residential development use, in many cases.

'I don't have any details for you yet because I deal with sales, rather than rentals. You'd need to speak to my boss, Alison and she's out of the office at the moment. I can't give you the details anyway without checking with her first, but I thought it might just be helpful if you knew that information was coming.'

'That's incredibly helpful, Hazel, thanks so much. I really appreciate it. This could be very important to our enquiries.'

Ted and Jo were not yet back from going to visit Gary Heath's parents. Rob O'Connell and Mike Hallam were both in the office so Steve conveyed the message he'd just received.

'Did she say which church? Where?'

Steve shook his head. 'She didn't have it to hand. It needs to come from her boss and she's out of the office at the moment.'

'We need that information and we need it now. There's just a possibility that The Preacher may be the one who rented the church and that could be where he's holding Gary. Give me details of where the agent is and I'll try to get the nearest station to send someone straight round there. If necessary, I'll sort out a warrant. But we need that information.'

'Is it the same man who's got our Gary, Inspector? The one who did those terrible things we heard about on the telly?'

Gary Heath's mother looked distraught. It wasn't all that long that her son had been missing but she and her husband were clearly not stupid. They'd seen the press conference, they knew the significance of their son's mobile phone having been found at a church, as they'd now been informed.

They'd appeared reassured by two senior officers calling on them in person. At least it showed the police were taking the disappearance of their son seriously, although he'd not been missing for all that long.

'The simple truth is that for now, Mr and Mrs Heath, we don't know and it would be wrong of me to mislead you. There are a number of similarities between the cases, not just involving where the phone was found. Would Gary have done anything like National Citizen Service?'

The couple looked puzzled.

'I don't think we've heard of that Citizen thing,' Gary's father replied. 'Have we, love? Is it something they do through school or college or something?'

'I don't think our Gary did it. I'm sure he'd have told us if he did.'

'Part of it involves going away to something like an outdoor adventure centre. Did Gary ever do anything like that? Or any other sort of Outward Bound things? Scouts or Boys

Brigade, perhaps?'

'That wouldn't really be our Gary's sort of thing. He's not sporty at all. If it was like camping or anything he'd hate it. He's afraid of spiders and daddy long legs, that sort of thing.'

'Is he musical at all? Does he play a musical instrument?'

'He sings beautifully,' she told him. 'Not in a choir or anything, but he's really ever so good. He loves singing but he's a shy lad, he wouldn't do it to an audience.'

'Was he ever in a choir? Are you church-goers at all? Did he perhaps sing at church?'

'We're not religious at all, any of us. Our Gary wouldn't sing in public, not even in church if he ever went. He's very sensitive. He's gay, you know. Did you know that?'

'Yes, I did, Mrs Heath. He has a steady boyfriend, I understand?'

'Yes, Roger. He's a lovely lad. So polite. They make a lovely couple. They're only kids, of course, really. I'd like to think they'd stay together a bit, though, they're so good together.'

'Perhaps you can give us Roger's contact details so we can have a talk with him. Do you happen to know, either of you, if Gary knows anyone called Simon? Has he ever mentioned a Simon?'

'Well, Roger has an older brother called Simon. He's in the Army, he's not home much. I don't think our Gary's actually met him but Roger talks about him quite a lot. I think he's very proud of his brother. Simon has served in Afghanistan, I think it was. He has medals for it.'

'I know you'll have given a recent photo of Gary to the local police to help in the search for him, but do you have one handy that I could just have a look at, please?'

The boy's mother stood up and went over to a bookshelf in the corner of the room. She took a framed photo down from a shelf, gave the glass a little wipe with her sleeve, smiling at the image looking up at her, then handed it to Ted.

'This is our Gary. It was taken last year when he left school, when he was all dressed up for their prom.'

She handed the photo to Ted. He looked down at a fresh, open face, slightly chubby, lingering puppy fat, smiling broadly for the camera. Ginger hair was jelled into submission and he was clearly wearing his best clothes for the occasion.

'Please find him, Inspector,' his mother implored, tears in her eyes and a catch in her voice. 'He's such a good lad. It's just not like him to worry us like this. He's always so considerate. Even if he's just going to be a bit late, he always rings to let us know. Please find him. Please don't let anything happen to him.'

Chapter Twenty-four

There was an air of high anticipation in the courtroom when Ted got there. The jury were still out, so he found Jim Baker, waiting outside, to ask him for news of the case and give him an update on the latest kidnap.

'The jury have been out a couple of hours but our team are still convinced it's going to be a relatively quick decision. I've been watching carefully and my gut feeling is that Morgane's blown it for herself with all that smiling she does. The more she smiles at people, the more it's clear it's nothing but a learned response. Something she knows people do, but she doesn't know the rules of why or when it's appropriate. I've noticed she sometimes makes some members of the jury look a bit uncomfortable. So let's hope that means that the verdict goes in our favour.

'I've got a couple of Uniforms on standby ready to deal with Edwards if he does kick off. In a way it's good that you're here as you're clearly like a red rag to a bull, as far as he's concerned. If anything makes him lose it completely, seeing you here will do, especially as he no doubt knows by now that your Trev is safe.

'So what's happening with the latest missing lad? Has he turned up'

'No, not yet. The longer he's out of touch, the more I think The Preacher has him.'

'Can you find him?'

'We're doing everything we can, Jim. You know that.'

There was a stirring of movement among those waiting outside the room. Word had gone out that the jury were back.

'Well, this is it. Let's see if we've won.'

Ted and Jim slid into seats next to one another. Jim glanced to see if the uniformed officers were in place and they gave him a nod of acknowledgement.

Ted found his mouth was dry. He and the team had worked so hard to bring this case to court. Depending on the whim of twelve complete strangers, it could still all be to no avail.

The forewoman of the jury was asked to stand. It was an encouraging start when she reported that the jury had reached a unanimous verdict. Then the first of the charges was read out and she was asked what the finding was.

'Guilty, Your Honour.'

Clive Edwards, Morgane's father, was on his feet in an instant, his face darkening in fury. It was to Ted he turned, his accusing arm outstretched, as he shouted, 'This is all your fault, you perverted little bastard! You framed her! You framed my little girl. I'll get you for this. I'll bloody get you.'

Before the judge even had time to order his removal, the two police officers, at a gesture of confirmation from Jim Baker, appeared alongside the shouting man and escorted him, swiftly and efficiently, from the courtroom.

It was now just a formality. It was clear the verdict was going to be the same on all counts. It still gave Ted a great deal of satisfaction to hear it announced. Guilty on five charges of murder and one of arson. The court was adjourned for further reports to be prepared before sentencing but, with luck, it was going to be some considerable time before Morgane Edwards would even be considered for release.

Before she was escorted out of the court, she turned her blue-eyed gaze in Ted's direction. He had expected to see naked hate in her expression. Instead, the softness in her eyes and the warmth of the smile she sent his way was one of the most profoundly disturbing things he'd ever seen in more than twenty years as a police officer.

‘Hi, it’s me.’

‘Ted, you say that every time and I know who’s calling me, from the screen,’ Trev told him patiently, as he had so many times before. ‘How did the court case go?’

‘Guilty on all charges, thankfully. Adjourned for sentencing.’

‘That’s good news. It must be a relief. I suppose you’re phoning to say you’ll be late again tonight?’

‘Sorry, yes. We’ve got this live ongoing kidnap so I’m not going to make it to the dojo at all, most likely. Not for self-defence nor for judo. In fact, I’ve no idea what time I’ll be home. It could easily turn into an all-nighter, if we can pin down where the latest young lad is being held.’

‘You could do with a judo session, for sure. But I understand. I hope you can find him.’

‘I’m sorry I’m standing you up yet again. I’ll make it up to you.’

‘Oh, I know you will. I’ll see to it that you do.’

The office was a hive of activity when Ted got back from court. Jo was directing operations while the boss was out. Everyone had their heads down, working hard.

‘Guilty on all counts,’ Ted announced as he walked in. ‘And the father’s been arrested. Has he arrived back here?’

‘Just come in and been processed and Mike’s downstairs interviewing him now, boss.’

‘So, what progress with The Preacher?’

‘A possible lead. We’re checking it now. Steve phoned the agents about any churches sold in the last three to four years. Initially they said there were none, then they came back to him with details of one which they had, in fact, rented out just over three years ago. It’s in a small town out the other side of Rochdale.

'They couldn't give us all the details initially. The person who deals with letting was out of the office, but they did come back to us eventually. The trail's a bit complicated. It was all handled through a law firm. The agents never had direct contact with the tenant. The law firm were acting on behalf of a company. That sort of thing is Sal's area of expertise, as you know, so he's trying to work his way through it now.'

Sal looked up from his computer. 'It's not going to be a speedy answer, I'm afraid, boss. At first glance it's hard to unpick the trail and it looks as if the law firm in question was chosen because they're good at masking identities.'

'Money laundering? Something like that?'

'I would say that's a possibility. Or there's just a chance the person renting could be a celebrity, or someone else who would want their identity kept quiet.'

'Do we know the firm in question?'

'Not that I know of. They're called Parton and Carter, they have an office in Manchester. They seem to specialise in this kind of thing. I can probably follow the trail back to the source but it's likely to take me quite some time, unfortunately.'

'Have we sent anyone round there, to the church, to have a quick look round?'

'I got a local area car to go and have a look. They've reported no signs of any activity there. The place is locked up and quiet,' Jo told him. 'I've tried speaking to the lawyers but they're playing it very close to their chests. Client confidentiality blah-blah-blah. We're going to need court orders.'

'Check back with the Uniform officers again. I want to know exactly what they mean by no activity. Any recent tyre tracks? Are the doors locked? New locks? You know the sort of thing. If they're our eyes on this, they need to be looking at things like one of us would do.

'And Gary Heath is still missing?'

'No word on him at all, boss.'

'Rob, what news of Peter Spencer and Stanley Harrison?'

'I'm seeing Harrison again in the morning. I've spoken to Spencer on the phone again but not yet via Skype. I've still found no trace of him listed as a passenger on a ferry but I don't know if that necessarily proves he didn't cross over to the continent. His excuses for not making visual contact do actually sound plausible, so I really can't decide if he's spinning me a line or not, boss.'

'Where does he claim to be at the moment?'

'In Germany. One of the organs he's supposed to be going to see, and possibly be allowed to play, is in Freiburg.'

'And where else is he supposed to be going?'

'Italy and Switzerland. He said he could be away up to three months.'

'We need to know if he really is where he says he is. I don't want to involve the police in those countries at this stage. It could get complicated and costly if he is over there on a perfectly innocent tour round famous churches and organs. But try this. Trev speaks fluent German, Italian and French. If Spencer is going to be allowed to play these organs, someone must know of him by reputation. Find contact details of the churches, get hold of Trev and ask him to phone and speak to someone there, a priest or whoever. Ask if they're expecting a visit from Spencer. If so when, and ask them to let us know if he turns up. You've got Trev's contact details? But phone him soon, he'll be going to the dojo this evening and he'll have his phone turned off there.'

Trev was friends with some of Ted's team and would occasionally go for a drink with them to talk about big bikes. Using his partner to do any interpreting they needed would save Ted a few bob on his budget, at least.

'Rob, another thing. You said Spencer was able to pick up your message even though his phone was damaged. So that means he had it switched on at some time. Can we trace where the phone was at the time it was on? Can we find him from its location?'

He checked the time. It was getting late in the day.

'See if Océane is still at Central Park and if she can help us on that one. If not her, get one of the other techie types on to it. We need to pin Spencer down. Like you said, it may all be perfectly innocent, but at the moment we can't eliminate him as a possible suspect.

'What about the vicar, Gabriel Clegg?'

'Boringly clean, boss,' Jezza told him. 'Nothing, nada, zippo. Not even a hint of any scandal anywhere. And he has alibis for all of the dates that concern this case. Solid ones. Also, if he is involved and he was the one who handed in Darren's phone, that would be a hell of a double-bluff, surely? I'm pretty sure we could write him off as a suspect, but I'll give you my detailed report of what I've found and you can decide what you think.'

'I've been to see the parents of the latest suspected victim, Gary Heath. Interestingly, but it's possibly not significant, Gary has a boyfriend, Roger Ashton, who has an elder brother called Simon. Army, served in Afghanistan. We don't know if Gary has ever met him but apparently Roger talks about him a lot. He's rather proud of his big brother. And unless you've uncovered anything while I've been out, he's our first Simon. I'll give you the contact details, and he'll need checking out. We need to know where he is and where he's been, in detail, for the past three years. If he's been serving somewhere with his regiment, then he's out of the frame.

'Maurice, is Darren saying anything else? Has he said any more about a Simon?'

'Amy's been keeping me posted since I was up there. He keeps saying the name Simon and he appears to get frustrated when she doesn't understand. He's also now said 'saviour' a few times, so another biblical reference, it seems. But I was wrong about redemption, apparently, or he's being clearer in what he says now. Amy says it's Redemption Song, not redemption. That's a Bob Marley song, not a phrase from the bible.'

'I know that, believe it or not,' Ted told him dryly. 'But how does it help us? Steve, let's have a print-out of the lyrics. It has something about mental slavery, I think. Does that tie in with The Preacher in some way? And does it have any other significance?

'I'll be in my office for a bit, waging war on paper. Keep me posted about any developments. Above all, let me know how it's going with Edwards. I think I'll sleep better tonight if I know he's safely out of harm's way. We need to press for a remand in custody for him, on the grounds of him interfering with witnesses if there is going to be an appeal.'

'Boss, Simon Ashton. Medically discharged from his unit more than three years ago. Parents don't know where he is. The last they heard of him he was living rough. He was diagnosed as suffering from PTSD but he went walkabout and they have no idea where he is now,' Jo explained as they got together for an end of day briefing.

'Gary's parents said Roger often talks about him and how proud he is of him.'

'According to Roger's parents, they decided not to tell him what happened. He idolises his older brother. He's a good bit older. Roger's eighteen, Simon is mid-30s.'

'So why does he not think it strange he never sees or hears from him?' Ted asked.

'They told him he's on a special mission, out of touch, off the radar. From time to time, they tell Roger they've had a quick phone call from Simon, always when Roger's out.'

'And he believes that?'

'He has no reason not to.'

'So now we have a former soldier, suffering from a mental health condition, on the loose somewhere and his name just happens to be Simon. Plus he's the older brother of the latest victim's boyfriend. What do we know about him? Does he have a record?'

'Just some minor stuff as a juvenile, mostly riding in stolen vehicles. The Army were prepared to overlook it and he's been a model soldier since. Up until his last tour, when he saw a close friend killed in front of him when he stood on a land mine. That's when his problems started.'

'Do we have anything yet to link him to the other lads? If he's ex-forces, could he have been involved in things like Outward Bound training anywhere?'

'We're still digging, but it's getting to that time of day when we're not getting replies from anyone. Offices and the like have mostly finished work and closed up until tomorrow. We may just have to give it best for today and start again tomorrow, first thing.'

'I want to get a look inside that church, as soon as possible. I don't like the idea that Gary is somewhere like that and we're being held up searching for him by a paper trail.'

'We're on it. We're all over it. But we need a warrant. We can't just go steaming in. It's going to be tomorrow at the earliest,' Jo told him. 'I was thinking of standing everyone down now. I just don't see what else we can do at this time of the evening. If we all come in early and crack on, we could make the breakthrough we need tomorrow. Oh, and Steve has some interesting news, too.'

'Sir, I was looking for other instances of Redemption Song and I found a group called that. It's a five-piece band. They have a not very good website, saying they're available for all kinds of gigs including proms. There's only an email for contact, which is unusual, so I've sent them a message, from my own private mail, with my own phone number, just asking general questions.'

Ted could see that Steve was holding the best part of his news back for special effect. He nodded at him to continue, eager to hear what he had to say.

'Sir, according to the website the keyboard player is called Simon Saviour.'

'We need to find this group and we need to do it soon. This is definitely one coincidence too many. If Darren's saying Redemption Song and Simon Saviour, it must surely be connected to them. Is there no other way of getting hold of them? Can you find out who's behind the website? And what about this Simon Ashton? Is he musical at all?'

'I asked his parents, once Steve had the information. He did use to have an electronic keyboard in his teens but they said he lost interest in it as he grew up and as far as they know, he hasn't played in years,' Jo replied.

'Rob, what news of Spencer and his whereabouts? Was Trev able to help?'

'He was, boss. Spencer is expected at Freiburg this weekend, so that part of the story is genuine. At least the fact that he's meant to be going there, although I've still not traced how he travelled, if he did. We've not yet been able to pinpoint where his phone was last used and he hasn't called me back, although I've left messages on both phone numbers.'

'So now make my day and tell me Spencer's photo matches one on the website of this group and identifies him as Simon Saviour the keyboard player.'

'I would if I could,' Jo assured him, 'but the website photo is all arty soft focus. The group members could be almost anyone. We haven't yet got a photo of Simon Ashton but we're working on that. Boss, we really have done all we can for now.'

Ted sighed in frustration. He knew Jo was right. There was realistically nothing more they could do until the morning. Far more sensible to let everyone go home, have a rest and come back fresh early the next day. They were going in the right direction, finally. He just hated the idea of Gary spending another night afraid, perhaps alone, not knowing what was happening, if indeed he was now being held by The Preacher.

'All right, time to call it a day, everyone. Early doors tomorrow, please. Let's crack on and put an end to this case.'

It was good to be home before Trev, for once. There would have been no point in Ted going to the dojo. He'd only have caught the last ten minutes or so of the judo session, and it wouldn't have been worth getting changed for that. He was tired, he needed something to eat and a hot shower, then some time to relax and unwind.

Trev had left a casserole in the oven on a low light, so Ted set about laying the table in preparation. Things were reasonably tidy. He checked in the dishwasher. Trev had attempted to rinse and load the crockery and cutlery he'd used for breakfast and for a snack when he got home from work. Ted methodically rearranged everything, smiling to himself. At least he'd tried.

The cats had been fed but denied it, rubbing round Ted's legs, looking for more. He gave himself a mental reminder that he really must speak to Doug and tell him his decision about the kitten. It wasn't fair to keep him waiting.

He heard Trev's bike, then the garage doors open and close when he got back from judo.

'Hey, you're back, I didn't expect you until much later. Did you wind the case up?

Ted shook his head. 'I wish we had but we just hit a brick wall for now.'

'You'll solve it tomorrow. You always do.'

Sometimes Ted wished he shared his partner's confidence in him.

Chapter Twenty-five

'So I want a warrant to get into that church and search it, as soon as possible,' Ted said, finishing his summing up to the Ice Queen in her office. Jim Baker was joining them via conference call. He had other meetings to attend and no time to be there in person.

'You haven't got anything like enough even to apply for a warrant yet and you know it,' Jim grumbled. 'You haven't even got the name of the face behind the paper trail. Without knowing who the premises belong to, how are you going to persuade the magistrates you suspect that a crime has been committed there? You need a hell of a lot more than you've got at the moment before we can make a case for a search. At least one I'd be happy to counter-sign. I can't speak for Debs, of course, but I'd be surprised if she didn't feel the same.'

'We're working on it now. I'm going to speak to the solicitors myself as soon as their office opens at nine-thirty. We have to do something. There's a good chance that, whoever this Simon Saviour is, he could be holding Gary inside that church. If he gets wind of the fact that we're getting close, there's no telling what he might do to him.'

'But that's half the problem. You don't yet know who Simon Saviour is. I'd be happier to go ahead if we knew that much, at least. What do you think, Debs?'

'The police officer in me says we need to follow correct procedure in applying for the warrant, as you say, Jim. The mother in me wants someone to go straight round there with an

Enforcer and break the door down, if there's the slightest chance that Gary may be inside.'

'Get us something concrete, Ted and we'll get you the search warrant. Where are you at with the three suspects?'

'Spencer is still unaccounted for, Rob is talking to Harrison again this morning, with his solicitor, and I'd say Gabriel Clegg is out of the frame, unless we're missing something glaringly obvious. We're just starting on the search for Simon Ashton, but I don't see at the moment how a penniless ex-squaddie with no fixed abode could be connected to renting a church.'

'Could he be sleeping rough there? Or maybe he's been given a few bob to keep an eye on the place. To stop squatters moving in, or to move on any undesirables?' Jim suggested. 'If he's ex-forces, he might be quite handy, a tough guy.'

'We won't know until we can get a look inside it,' Ted retorted. 'I'd better go and get us enough to be sure of that warrant, then.'

Before he went back up to his own office, Ted stopped at the front desk for a quick word with Bill.

'Last day tomorrow, then? Are you all set? Prepared to act surprised at your party?'

'You will be there, won't you, Ted? I need at least one person I can talk to.'

'You know I will if I can, Bill, but we're closing in on this case now. There's just a chance I'll be tied up. But I'll keep in touch. And it won't be long before you're back here. You can always phone me, at any time, if you want to chat. If I can't talk straight away, I'll call you back when I can. Don't feel we've forgotten about you. I mean it. Get in touch whenever you need anything.'

He wished he could have offered more. He knew how much Bill was dreading the enforced break. He hoped he would be all right in the time before he was back at the station, the place he felt most at home.

Sal was at his desk when Ted went upstairs. He'd clearly come in early, ahead of the others, determined to get to the end of the paper trail which was so far masking who was behind renting the old church. He shook his head in response to Ted's question about any progress so far.

'Nothing, boss. The cover-up's been thoroughly done, by someone who's an expert. But that's not to say it's impossible to crack. It just means it will take longer.'

'Keep at it, and let me know when you find something. You can do it if anyone can. I'm just going to make myself some tea before briefing. Do you want anything?'

Ted never considered himself above brewing up for his team members. It was another reason they appreciated him.

'No thanks, I'm on my second coffee already.'

Rob was going straight up to talk to Stanley Harrison so he wouldn't be in until later on. Depending on whether or not Harrison had sound alibis for the days they were interested in, he might be someone else they could cross off their list of possible subjects, together with Gabriel Clegg, the vicar. If that was so, that left them with only Simon Ashton, the homeless ex-serviceman, and Peter Spencer, the organist, neither of whom they had so far been able to trace.

'The priority today is to find Simon Ashton and to trace whoever is behind renting the church,' Ted told the team once they were all in. 'Plus looking further into this group Redemption Song.

'Steve, the young woman you spoke to at the agents. Is it worth you getting back to her, to see if she knows, or can find out, anything for you? If necessary go and see her. Explain that it's urgent, without giving her too much detail.'

'Yeah, Steve, go and use your charm on her,' Jezza teased him.

'Focus on the case, please,' Ted said automatically. 'There's just a possibility that it will be a quicker way to find something out than either Sal unpicking the thread, or me talking to the lawyers, which is what I'm going to do as soon as their office opens.

'We need to get inside that church and soon. But first we need something a bit more which will help us get a warrant to do so.

'Maurice, can you speak to the Ashton parents, see if they might possibly have any idea where their son could be? Him being the brother of the latest suspected victim's boyfriend is a bit too close to home. Unless anything else comes our way in the meantime, I want everyone on this. Jo, I'll leave it to you to allocate roles.

'So far, Central Park haven't been able to come up with any trace of Peter Spencer via his mobile phone. There may be a perfectly innocent explanation for that, of course. While Rob's out, let's have a few more goes at getting hold of Spencer. We need to know about him one way or the other.'

It was nearly ten o'clock before Ted managed to get hold of one of the senior partners in the law firm. If they were uncooperative he'd need court orders to find out who their mysterious client was, unless Sal uncovered the information first. He was hoping that a call from a Senior Investigating Officer might just loosen tongues, although he knew it was unlikely. Solicitors could be tighter than clams when it came to protecting their clients.

'I can put you through to Mr Carter now, Inspector,' a helpful voice at the end of the phone told him, as if she was doing him a huge favour.

'Mr Carter?'

'I'm Jon Carter, yes.'

'Detective Chief Inspector Darling, Greater Manchester Police. I understand your firm acts on behalf of a client who has rented a redundant church near to Rochdale. We need to get in touch with your client as a matter of some urgency, in connection with an ongoing enquiry.'

'I'm sure you can appreciate, Inspector, that client confidentiality is an important part of the work we do. I'm afraid I can't pass on any contact details directly. However if you would like to submit your request in writing, perhaps by email if it's urgent, I can then pass it on to our client and take their instruction.'

'Mr Carter, I need to get a look inside that church, as soon as possible. I have reason to believe that a crime or crimes have been committed on the premises, and that one may be ongoing. I am applying for search warrants. It would be much better and certainly quicker if your client would simply allow us to take a look inside.'

'As you don't seem to know who our clients are, I'm struggling to see how you would have such suspicions relating to them, Inspector.'

'Are you refusing to give me any information, Mr Carter?'

'In the absence of a better reason to do so, I am indeed, at this stage. And I think we both know that I am within my rights. Please put your request in writing and I will forward it to our client as soon as possible.'

'Can you at least tell me if your client is in this country or abroad at the moment? It's important to our enquiry to know that.'

'Good day, Inspector. Please put your request in writing.'

Ted slammed his desk phone back down, hard. Trev was right. He needed an outlet for his pent-up frustration, and soon. In the absence of a better solution, he kicked his waste-paper basket round his office until it too, like many predecessors, was mangled beyond recognition. He knew he was in for a telling off by the woman who had cleaned his office for years and did the same on every such occasion. It was almost worth it, though.

'I have advised my client that he is under no obligation to reply to your questioning, Sergeant, without at least being told more about your reasons for asking. However, Mr Harrison is keen to cooperate with the police in the hopes that he will then be left alone. He has therefore prepared a detailed list of his movements on all of the dates you asked about, which he hopes will help you.'

Stanley Harrison's solicitor was a dry sort, with a clipped accent, wearing an old-fashioned three-piece suit with a bow tie. He was somehow exactly the sort of legal advisor Rob had expected Harrison to engage. He pushed a typed piece of paper across the desk towards Rob, who picked it up and scanned it. He'd need to check them in detail but at first glance, it looked as if Harrison was in the clear. On some of the dates he claimed to have been delivering lectures on his specialist subject, on one occasion on a cruise round the islands of Britain, so they would be easy to check.

'Thank you, Mr Harrison, you've been very helpful.'

Rob was trying to stay polite, despite the waste of time. Harrison could easily have agreed to supply him with the information directly instead of insisting on the trip up to talk to him in the presence of his lawyer. One way or another, Rob was not having much luck with this case. He desperately needed to win himself some Brownie points.

He went back to his car and got his phone out. He tried both of Peter Spencer's numbers again, getting an answering message on both.

'Peter, it's DS Rob O'Connell, again. I'm sorry to be interrupting your holiday like this, but I really do need to talk to you as soon as possible. Would you mind giving me a ring as soon as you get this message, please?'

Next he checked in with the team. He decided not to talk to the boss as once again he had nothing much of any use to report. Instead he phoned Jo.

'Good, you're not far from Blackpool, so you can get round to this Simon Ashton's former regiment and see what you can find out about him. Maurice got the details from his parents.

We need to trace him so we need to find anyone who might still have contact with him. If he was kicked out, he might not have any type of welfare or support. But someone, somewhere, might have an idea of how we might find him. Where do homeless ex-squaddies hang out? His parents have no idea, so anything you can find could help us with The Preacher. Not to mention helping to reunite Simon with his family and get him some help, if it's not him.

'Check back in with me before you set off back here. I might need you to go and talk to the family face to face if we don't get any further than we are now.'

Steve had phoned ahead to arrange to talk to Hazel, from the estate agency. He'd asked if she had a break and if they could meet for coffee somewhere close by. He hoped it didn't sound as if he was trying to ask her out. He remembered she'd had problems with her boyfriend so he suspected she may be vulnerable.

He'd asked her over the phone if she would be able to find out anything from the office files about the company, or the person behind it, who had rented the church. He didn't want to get her into trouble, but they did need the information.

So far, they weren't having much luck making contact with the band, Redemption Song. No one had replied yet to Steve's email and they were still trying to find them through other means. Jezza was checking if the band had played at any of the schools or the residential centres the victims had been at, but it was a slow process.

Steve found the café easily enough, not far from the agency's address. He didn't know what Hazel looked like but he couldn't see any lone females who seemed to be waiting for someone. He ordered himself a coffee and sat down to wait.

After about ten minutes, a young woman came in, looking round expectantly. Steve stood up, smiling, so she approached him.

'Are you DC Ellis? I'm Hazel.'

'Thank you for coming. What can I get you to drink?'

'A tea would be nice, thank you.'

He hoped he wasn't doing his usual trick of blushing. Steve was a bit shy, rather awkward when meeting anyone for the first time. He went to the counter for the tea and managed to carry it back without spilling any.

'I really appreciate you helping me like this. I hope it won't get you into any trouble at work?'

'I don't think so. I sneaked a look at the files while my boss was out. There wasn't an awful lot. The church is being rented by a company called Revelations Recordings. It's some music production company or something like that. They rented it just over three years ago. I wonder if they might have chosen it because the acoustics would be good in a church, perhaps, although I don't really know anything about it. Anyway the only other thing of interest on the file says that they did ask if they could construct some sort of soundproof room or chamber or something within the building. Perhaps that was to avoid any complaints from neighbours about noise. That seems to have been allowed under the terms of the lease.'

'That's fantastically helpful, thank you.'

Now he had the information he needed, Steve wanted to get his phone out to let the boss know straight away. But he saw from Hazel's face that she wanted to chat for a bit and he felt he owed her that much.

Luckily for him, she didn't have long for her break. She insisted on giving him her mobile phone number, looking hopeful. Once she'd left to return to work, Steve was finally able to go back to his car and phone the office. He got through to Mike Hallam.

'Sarge, the church is rented by Revelations Recordings and, get this – they asked for permission to construct some sort of soundproof booth within the building. Do you think that might be where The Preacher has been keeping the lads? And do you think that means that Gary Heath is in there?'

'So another biblical theme. Revelations. Good work, Steve, well done. Sal, we need everything you can find on Revelations Recordings. Who's behind it? Are they connected to this group, Redemption Song? Do they record for them? At least now we should have enough for the search warrant for the premises. I'll get that in motion.

'Rob, what news of our suspects?'

'Harrison's alibis check out for most of the dates I've looked at so far, boss. Apart from being a bit strange and having a criminally bad haircut, I think he's in the clear. I still can't get hold of Peter Spencer, he's not returning my calls.

'I spoke to the adjutant of Simon Ashton's former regiment near Blackpool. He remembered him. He'd been a good soldier, been promoted a couple of times. Then after the incident on active duty he changed completely. He'd become prone to violent outbursts, moody, withdrawn, always getting into trouble. It was put down to PTSD and he was medically discharged. So far, no one knows where he might be but they did promise to put the word out and let me know if they find anything.'

'What about photos of Ashton and Spencer? Could either of them be this Simon Saviour from Redemption Song?'

'Impossible to say with any certainty,' Jo told him. 'The pictures are just mugshots; they could be anyone. And as for comparing them with the band photo from the website, the keyboard player on there could be anyone, too. Both Ashton and Spencer are in their mid-thirties and they're not all that dissimilar. Basically, it could be either of them or neither of them.'

Ted looked at the time.

'Right, I'll get us that search warrant and let's go and have a look inside that church, find out what's been going on there. We may not get it tonight, we may be looking at tomorrow morning now. I don't really want to wait another night but we may have to.

'We need to take some local Uniforms with us so Jo, can you arrange that. I'm definitely coming on this one. I want to be there if there's even an outside chance of coming face to face with The Preacher. Mike, you're with me. Maurice, you too. If there's any chance at all of us finding Gary in there, I want you there to be the one to talk to him first. He's going to need someone who's good at handling anyone who's been through what he has these last few days.'

Chapter Twenty-six

'Tut tut, Chief Inspector. Another waste-paper basket? Temper, temper! Mrs Skinner.'

Despite the seriousness of the day ahead, Ted couldn't help smiling at the reproachful note from the cleaning lady, neatly handwritten and lying in the centre of his tidied and polished desk. He could almost hear her voice saying it to him, as she had done several times before when she'd come in to clean and found him working late. She'd removed the latest casualty and replaced it with a brand new one. Ted would have to pay, as he usually did. He couldn't justify even to himself replacing them out of his stationery budget.

He'd called the team in early. He wanted to be ready to move as soon as they got the search warrant through for the church. Whilst that search was going ahead, he wanted all other available bodies trying to find Peter Spencer and Simon Ashton, as well as tracing anything which might link the four kidnap victims to the group Redemption Song.

Steve had explained that it was unusual for a group not to have a social media presence, especially on Facebook or Instagram. Both were a valuable source of free advertising for groups promoting themselves for hire. So far he'd found nothing but their website and had not yet had any response to his enquiry through it.

Until Ted had the search warrant in his hand, there was nothing he and his team could usefully be doing. He took a moment to talk to Bill, promising again to be back in time for his leaving drinks if he possibly could. Bill was looking more glum with every day as the date for his enforced break crept up on him. A three-month holiday might be some people's idea of bliss. It certainly wasn't Bill's.

Ted had already told both the Super and Jim Baker that he fully intended to go in person to the church to oversee the search. It was not standard procedure for a DCI, who would normally be desk-bound driving the operation, or simply doing the paperwork and leaving it to a DS or possibly a DI, if they had one. They both knew him well enough to know it was pointless arguing the toss with him. Ted was not by nature a maverick or a rule-breaker. He ran his enquiries scrupulously by the book and still got results despite that. But this case was getting to them all. If he felt the need to be there up to the end, they weren't going to try to stop him.

As soon as Ted got word they had the warrant, he and the team went into action. He got Jo to phone ahead to the local station with whom he'd arranged a Uniform presence. He wanted to make sure no one entered or left the building before he and the others got there. But he was anxious not to have to force the door of a church building if there was any way round it.

As Maurice drove Ted's official car, with the blues on to give them clear passage, Ted sat in the passenger seat, with Mike Hallam in the back. He first called the law firm handling the church rental and after having to insist, he was once more put through to Jon Carter.

'DCI Darling here, Mr Carter. This is just a courtesy call to tell you that officers are on the way to gain entry to and search the church building for which your firm handles the lease from the Church Commissioners for your client, Revelations Recordings.'

He was anxious to let the man know how much information they had to date, to leave him in no doubt that the net was closing.

'Now I don't want to have to break into a church if it can be avoided. Perhaps your client, or someone from your firm, could go there to meet us and allow us entry with a key? We'll be there in less than half an hour, but I'm perfectly prepared to wait a few moments before making a forced entry, if I know someone is on the way.'

He could hear the annoyance in the man's voice as he replied.

'This firm doesn't hold a key to the church. We would have no occasion to do so. And our client is currently out of the country and will be for some weeks. Whatever you might think has been going on there, it almost certainly has nothing to do with our client.'

Ted noticed the care he took not to reveal so much as the gender of his client. He hadn't expected to get anywhere with the lawyer, but at least his conscience was clear. He tried the estate agency next. When he asked to speak to the person in charge of rentals he was put through to someone who gave her name as Yvonne Dixon.

Again, he explained briefly what was happening and asked if the agency had a key, to avoid the police having to break open the door.

'I can't allow you access to the property without the permission of the leaseholder or his lawyers. We've never dealt with him direct.'

At least Ted now knew the client was a man. Clearly the agent was not as careful with such information as the lawyer had been.

'Ms Dixon,' Ted began, keeping it neutral.

'It's Mrs,' she corrected him sharply. 'I detest Ms.'

'Excuse me. Mrs Dixon. I'm not actually asking you for permission. I have that already in the shape of a search warrant, lawfully granted. It's just a courtesy call. I would prefer not to have to break down a church door if there was a way to avoid it. But I need to get access to that building, and soon. I have reasonable grounds to believe a crime is taking place there. Now, I'm less than twenty minutes away. I see from your address that if you were to leave now, with the keys, we could meet up there at about the same time. Would you be able to do that, please?'

From her response, she was clearly not happy but said she would see him there.

There were two local area cars and four PCs on site when Maurice pulled the black Ford up as close as he could get. Already one or two people were starting to gather to see what was going on. Ted showed his ID and asked one of the PCs to make sure the watchers stayed well out of the way.

'There's hopefully a key-holder on her way. Is there any sign of anyone on the premises?'

'No, sir, we haven't seen anyone. The church is locked up and there's no vehicle parked close by. Would you like us to start PNC checks of the registration numbers of anything parked in the area?' one of the PCs asked him.

'Please. Let's have one of you on doing that, one on shepherding the rubberneckers and the other two staying here. I want to be sure no one goes in or out until we've thoroughly checked inside. Once we get access, it's a potential crime scene search, so gloves on and please don't handle anything more than you have to.'

He was probably teaching his granny to suck eggs. But he didn't know any of the officers and he didn't want to find out the hard way that any of them made basic procedural errors which would affect his chances of a successful conviction.

Ted went up to the church door, followed by Mike and Maurice. As he'd thought, it was an impressive arched wooden one, solidly built, with black metal hinges and studding, clearly locked by a sizeable key, judging by the hole it would fit. Even if it caused a slight delay, he felt he'd made the right call in asking for a key.

The three of them walked right round the perimeter of the

building. There was no sign of life, not a sound from anywhere. It was frustrating, thinking that Gary Heath could be being held within yards of where they were.

As they got back to the entrance, a sleek silver car was trying to park as near as possible to the church gates, the PC in charge there leaning in at the window to check the driver's identity.

A woman in a neatly-tailored trouser suit teamed with impossibly high heels marched up the path, clearly not happy. Ted stood in front of the church, flanked by Mike and Maurice. All three were wearing their ID visibly but without peering at it closely, it was impossible to tell rank. She addressed herself to Mike, the tallest of the three. People tended to dismiss Ted with his small, slight stature. He was used to it.

'I'm Yvonne Dixon. Are you the detective who phoned me?'

'I'm DS Hallam. This is DCI Darling, who's in charge of this investigation.'

The look she gave Ted said it all.

'Thank you for coming, Mrs Dixon. As I said, it would be a shame to have to break this door down to gain entry. Here's the warrant, if you want to check it. Then I'd be grateful if you could let us in as soon as possible, please.'

She barely glanced at the document he was holding out for her inspection before flouncing up to the door, a bunch of keys in her hand. She selected the largest, inserted it in the keyhole and tried to turn it. It resisted her efforts.

Ted stepped forward, trying to remain calm and polite. In reality he felt like kicking the door down. Gary could be inside and every precious minute lost felt too long.

'May I try?'

With a scornful look and a noise like a tut, she stepped aside. Ted took hold of the heavy ring handle and pulled the door towards him as he tried to turn the key. This time it yielded easily. Before he swung the heavy door inwards to open it, he withdrew the bunch of keys and kept hold of it.

'Thank you, Mrs Dixon. If you wouldn't mind waiting for a few moments, perhaps in your car?'

Whatever they were about to find in the church, he didn't want the woman there to see it. He nodded to one of the uniformed PCs to make sure she was safely out of the way before he and the others made their way through the arched doorway and into the cool of the church's interior.

It was surprisingly impressive, with high pillars and vaulted archways on either side of the nave. In its day, it must have been a fine building and, judging by the number of pews still in place, a popular place of worship. With the rapid decline in church-going, it had clearly become a liability to its owners. It was also, at first glance, empty of any sign of life.

'Where's this soundproof bit then?' Maurice asked, looking all around him. 'Doesn't look like anyone's been in here for ages.'

'We'll search everywhere. Under pews, inside the altar, if it's hollow underneath. Is there a vestry? A bell tower? Spread out, all of you. He must be here somewhere. All the info we have so far points to it being the likeliest place.'

They did as he said. They searched every square inch of the old building, more than once. In the end it was Mike Hallam who told Ted quietly, 'He's not here, boss. There's nowhere else he can be hidden. Unless there's some secret entrance to a crypt or something, under a flagstone with a ring set in it. And that stuff only happens in the Famous Five books.'

Ted was feeling bitterly disappointed. He'd been so sure they were going to find Gary, in time to get him to safety.

'We could get a dog team,' he suggested. 'Just in case there is somewhere underground. They might be able to pick up a trace.'

Mike spoke again, patiently. 'We have to admit it. He's just not here. And it doesn't look as if he ever was. We tried our best, boss, but it's not the right place.'

Ted was just about to give the word, reluctantly, to stand down, then go and hand the keys back to the agent when his mobile phone rang. Steve Ellis calling him.

'Yes, Steve?'

'Sir, have you found him?'

'No. There's no sign, and it doesn't look like anyone's been inside the place for some time.'

'Boss, there's another building. A church hall. It's also part of the lease. Round the back somewhere. Hazel, from the agency, phoned me again. Her boss was bringing the keys over to you and she wanted to chat to me. I hope I didn't give her the wrong impression, inviting her for coffee.'

'Steve, you little belter, that is brilliant news! You be nice to her. Take her out to dinner if you have to. I'll pay. We'll go and look now. And thanks to you both.'

He looked much happier than he had before when he ended the call. They were getting close now, he could sense it.

'Right, everyone, wrong building. There's a church hall somewhere. We need to find that and hope that the key for it is on this keyring.'

They hurried out of the church, looking around. There was no other building in sight. Tall trees around the edge of the graveyard masked anything from their view.

'Do any of you know this place? Do you know where the hall is?'

The local officers were shaking their heads.

'Not a church-goer, sir, never have been,' one of them said.

'Boss, there's a path there that goes off through the graves,' Maurice said, pointing.

They made their way along the narrow gravel walkway. The graves to either side of it were unkempt, overgrown, but the path itself had clearly known feet on it more recently as weeds like plantain were trodden down. It led to a lychgate which Ted opened. In front of them, through the trees, the path continuing straight to its front door, was another building.

Single storey, brick, with a slate roof and a derelict air. They could see from a distance that the diamond-pattern leaded windows were missing a few panes here and there.

The double doors, when they reached them, had what looked like quite a new lock. Ted could see straight away that there was nothing on the bunch of keys which would open it.

Mike spoke again, keeping his voice down, not wanting to say too much in front of officers none of them knew.

'Boss, the warrant is for the church, not for any other buildings.'

Ted was eyeing up the door and its locking mechanism.

'Tell me, DS Hallam, if it was your lad in there, what would you be saying?'

Mike was looking from his diminutive boss to the obstacle confronting them.

'I'd say that lock looks new but the door seems a bit ropey. So it's a good job that no burglar who was an expert at the kick-trick happened to come this way.'

Ted was still studying the woodwork, gauging distance and force.

'That's pretty much what I was thinking, DS Hallam. And church hall is only one word different from church, after all.'

The speed with which Ted's foot shot up and impacted with the door startled the uniformed officers. They'd clearly not heard of Ted's martial arts skills and certainly weren't expecting a visiting DCI to be a man of action.

'Whoops,' Ted commented as the wood split under the impact.

The door didn't quite burst open on the first kick. It took a couple more before it sagged in on its hinges and allowed them access.

It was much more gloomy in the old hall than the church had been. The windows were high up and filthy, green with some sort of mossy growth which obscured the light. The uniformed officers produced high-powered torches and shone them around.

The hall itself was empty apart from a covering of old leaves which had clearly blown in through gaps in the windows. At the far end was a raised area, some sort of stage. On that platform had been constructed something almost like a film set of a room, but closed on all sides, including the top, in some sort of heavy chipboard. It formed an apparently completely sealed unit. There was no sound of anything or anybody.

'We need to get in there.'

Ted led the way across the old and dirty parquet flooring, heading to the side of the stage where three steps led up to it. He could see there was a door in the side of the unit. There was no handle of any description visible on the outside, just a keyhole.

'He's in there, I know he is.'

His first couple of kicks produced nothing. On the third, there was a cracking sound, but it wasn't giving fast enough for Ted's liking.

'Everyone together, shoulders, feet, anything. We have to get inside.'

Finally, under the combined assault, the door was ripped from its hinges, falling flat into the unit with a loud bang. Inside, some kind of harsh lighting was rigged up. The first thing they saw was a naked youth, wide-eyed, clearly terrified, tied to a chair and struggling hard against his bonds, screaming in terror. The sound-proofing panels lining every inch of the room's interior explained why they had heard nothing when they first entered the building.

Then their eyes were drawn to the sight of a man's body, hanging from a rope attached to a hook in the ceiling, a fallen chair near to his feet. The legs were still twitching and jerking as the body swayed slowly from side to side.

Maurice rushed towards the youth but Ted stopped him with a barked order.

'I want this bastard alive, DC Brown. All of you, help take his weight. One of you find something to cut him down with. Get on the radio. I want two ambulances. These two are both going to hospital separately, and I want them kept separate at all times.'

Ted's height was frustrating him. He couldn't do anything to lift the body high enough. It needed the taller officers to do that. Ted could only stand and watch as they took the weight and raised it. One of the PCs found a knife on a nearby workbench then used the chair to get up to cut the rope. As soon as the body was cut down and laid on the floor, Maurice rushed to the boy in the chair, pulling off his jacket to cover him with, speaking soothingly to calm him as he carried on shouting in fear.

'Shush, Gary, you're safe now. I'm Maurice. I'm here to help you, lad. Let's get you untied. He can't hurt you now.'

Ted went closer to him, keeping his own voice quiet and gentle. He crouched down in front of the chair and made eye contact with Gary Heath.

'Can you tell us who he is, Gary? Do you know this man's name?'

'Simon! Redemption Song!' The youth's voice was like a strangled scream. 'It's Simon Saviour.'

Chapter Twenty-seven

Once he'd seen that Gary appeared to be all right other than terrified, Ted turned back to where Mike and one of the uniformed PCs were checking the vital signs of the man they knew only as Simon Saviour.

'Is he alive?'

'No breath sounds, boss, but there's a very weak pulse.'

They had the man on his back. Mike had carefully lifted and positioned the lower jaw to clear his airway. The face looked puffy, an angry red weal around the throat from the rope, the lips with a blueish tinge. It was impossible to recognise the features as either of their remaining suspects.

'Don't lose him, Mike. I want to be able to put this piece of work in the dock for what he's done.'

'I'm just going to try a rescue breath, on the grounds that we've not got much to lose.'

He sealed the man's nose with his hand, covered the mouth with his own then exhaled fully. They watched the chest rise then fall again slowly. There was an agonising pause as nothing happened. Then the man took a ragged, seemingly painful breath of his own and his eyelids fluttered.

'Yes!' Ted exclaimed in triumph. 'Stay with him, Mike. Don't let him go. Has he got any ID on him anywhere?'

Still monitoring the man closely, Mike patted down his pockets looking for something, anything, to tell them who they had their hands on.

'Nothing, boss, unless it's in his back pocket and he's not

stable enough yet to move him, I don't think. It would need a really careful log roll in case of a serious spinal injury and I'd rather not risk that until the paramedics arrive. I'd prefer to keep him like this for now in case he needs more assisted breathing.'

'Sir, there's a set of car keys here on the workbench where I found the knife,' one of the PCs said.

As instructed, he was wearing gloves but he waited for authority from the SIO before touching anything in the crime scene.

'I need you to find that car and get the registration checked. But do it very carefully so you don't contaminate evidence. Slide the keys into an evidence bag, please, then take them outside into the road and point them at any car you find parked nearby. Come back to me when you know who the car belongs to.'

'Sir.'

'Make sure your colleagues know that this is now a confirmed crime scene. No one in or out at all without my authority. Tell them they can let the agent go now. I'll be holding on to the keys but they will be returned in due course.'

The PC went in search of the car. Ted turned to the remaining constable.

'Which is the nearest A&E department to here?'

'They'll probably take them to Fairfield, sir, at Bury.'

Ted nodded his thanks.

'Maurice, I think you should go with Gary in the ambulance. I'll follow on in my car. Mike, you stay here and control the scene. I'll get hold of SOCO next then get some more bodies to seal the whole site off and start searching.

'Gary, I'm going to call your parents now, to let them know you're safe.'

Despite Maurice's jacket, the youth was trembling violently, his teeth chattering so hard he could barely articulate.

'Roger. My boyfriend. Please call him. Or get my mum to.

Please. He'll be worried sick.'

'Yes, of course. Gary, this man, Simon Saviour. Is he Roger's brother Simon?'

The youth looked in astonishment at Ted, as if suddenly doubting he was really a policeman.

'Roger's brother? No, I don't think so.'

'Have you ever met Simon Ashton?'

'No, never. He's away on a special mission. But the house is full of photos of him. That isn't him, I'm sure. That's Simon Saviour. He's the keyboard player in a group, Redemption Song. I've seen him at a couple of gigs. That's why I accepted a lift from him. Why did he do this to me? He started doing things, torturing me. Why?'

Ted was saved from answering by the arrival of a paramedic, a motorbike first responder. Ted introduced himself and explained the situation.

'We'll need two ambulances. The hanging is the presumed perpetrator. He wasn't breathing independently but my sergeant got him back. Gary, over there, is the victim, so obviously I need him kept separate at all times from the other man.'

'You'll be lucky, mate,' the paramedic told him. 'There's a big multi-vehicle accident on the other side of town so they sent me on ahead to triage and assess what's needed. We'll certainly need an ambulance and a spinal board for the hanging but I don't know if we can get two out here quickly.'

'If you can clear the lad for me to transport, I can take him in the car. I need my DC to go with him, whatever happens.'

The paramedic went first to the prone figure on the floor. Simon Saviour's chest was now rising and falling with his own unassisted breathing, although there was a harsh sound in his throat with each laboured breath he took. Mike had stayed with him, keeping his head still, monitoring him constantly.

'Right, that's looking good, you're doing everything right.

I'll just put a cover over him, maintain his body temp, until we can get an ambulance for him. He's definitely going to need one, and as a priority.'

He opened his medical kit, took out a space blanket, undid the wrapping, and laid it over the person lying on the floor. He did a quick check to assess consciousness levels. Then he moved across the room to where Gary was still sitting shivering on the chair, Maurice with a protective arm around his shoulders, comforting him. He squatted down in front of him.

'Hello, I'm Frank. Can you tell me your name?'

'G-Gary.' His teeth were chattering, as much from shock as from cold.

'Gary what, my friend?'

'Gary Heath. Can I go home now? Please?'

'I just need to check you out first, Gary, if that's all right with you? Can you tell me what happened to you?'

Gary jerked his chin towards the figure on the ground. 'He kidnapped me. He brought me here and tied me up. Then he … he did things to me.'

His face crumpled as he dissolved in tears, instinctively turning his head towards Maurice, hiding away against his chest as he sobbed.

Ted nodded to the paramedic to move away so they were out of earshot, then he explained.

'It's likely that he's been held here since late Monday night, perhaps Tuesday morning. He probably won't have had anything to eat in that time and maybe very little to drink. It's also likely that he's had some kind of electric shocks applied to his genital area.'

'Ouch,' Frank said with feeling. 'Well, I need to examine him, if he'll let me, and I need to radio for an ambulance for the other one. Do we have a name for him?'

'We only know him as Simon Saviour which is almost certainly not his real name. He had no ID on him that we could find. We're looking for a vehicle he may have been driving now and hoping to identify him through that. As long as you're happy for me to transport him, I'll get Gary to hospital. I just want to avoid him seeing Simon when he gets there, if that's at all possible.'

'I doubt anything can be guaranteed with a possible ongoing Majax but I'll certainly pass the word along and see what can be done.'

'Hey, is that Steve? This is Michael Marley, from Redemption Song. Sorry it took a while to get back to you. What can I do for you, man?'

There was a hint of a West Indies accent, but whether or not that was for effect, Steve couldn't yet tell. The call had come through on his personal mobile number, the one he had included with his email to the group's website.

'Hi, thanks for calling me. Let me just go somewhere a bit quieter. Hang on.'

His fingers were flying over his keyboard as he spoke. An email to Océane, with the number which had called him, asking for any help she could give with a trace on it.

He went out into the corridor, pulling the door to noisily behind him for effect. He didn't at this stage want to let his caller know he was police. First he wanted to see what information, if any, he could get from the call.

'Sorry about that, I didn't want to talk in front of my mate. I'm planning a surprise.'

'No sweat, man. Like I said, sorry for the delay in contacting you. It's usually Simon, the keyboard player, who does that stuff but he's away for a few weeks. So what can I do for you?'

'If Simon's away, does that mean you're not taking bookings? I was kind of interested in getting him. I've heard he's good.'

'The band does play without him, you can still book us, just there won't be keyboard.'

'I was trying to find out more about him but there's nothing online.'

The man laughed. 'Oh, Simon's a bit shy about his day job. It's not cool for someone playing the gigs we do to admit to mucking around with church organs. Don't tell him I told you that or he'll kill me.'

'Do you know when he's back? Only I'd like to book when he's playing.'

'A few weeks for sure. I'll try to get hold of him for a definite date, then I can call you again when I know.'

Steve thanked him then, as soon as he ended the call he dialled the boss.

'Yes, Steve?'

'Sir, Simon Saviour. It's Peter Spencer. The organ tuner. I've just had confirmation from another band member that Simon Saviour's day job is church organs. It can't be a coincidence, can it, boss?''

'That's great, thanks, Steve. And no, I doubt it's a coincidence. Good news here, too. We've just found Gary Heath, in the church hall. He's going to be all right. The Preacher was here too. He tried to hang himself but we've got him down and he's on his way to hospital shortly. Maurice and I are taking Gary there, too. And we just got confirmation that Peter Spencer's car is parked in the road outside the church hall. Good work, Steve. Let the team know, please, and the Super. And circulate the word to the other forces involved.'

Ted wanted to see the man he was now fairly sure was Peter Spencer loaded into an ambulance and on his way to hospital before he left the site. The rapid responder had been right. There was currently only one ambulance available but after checking Gary over thoroughly, the paramedics had declared him safe to be taken by car. He too was now bundled up in blankets. Ted decided in the end to let Maurice go on ahead with him. He'd follow himself in the ambulance. Now he had his hands on The Preacher, he was anxious not to let him out of his sight.

While the ambulance crew were working to stabilise Spencer before moving him, Ted had calls to make. He wanted more bodies to do a thorough site search and he wanted a full forensics team. That thought gave him a fleeting feeling of guilt, remembering he had not yet phoned Doug to tell him he couldn't take the kitten.

He wanted forensics to check every inch of the church hall, both inside the unit and in the space outside, as well as Spencer's car, for any signs that the other victims had also been brought there. They needed anything which would tie Spencer to all four abductions and tortures. Now they had his car, there was just an outside chance they could get a partial match for the tyre tracks up at Ludworth Moor.

He also wanted to arrange with the local station to have a police presence near to Spencer in hospital all the time, and to make sure everyone connected to his treatment knew that he was a potential suicide risk. More than anything, he wanted to see the man in court for what he'd done, and to find out what had motivated him.

He made a quick call to Trev, while he had the chance.

'Hi, it's me. I'm going to be late tonight.'

'I know. You told me. Bill's leaving do.'

'I'm not going to get to that, unfortunately, and I've no idea what time I'll get back. We just got the bad guy.'

'Well, that's great news. Does that mean I might get to see a bit of you over the weekend? Shame about Bill's do though, he'll miss you. D'you want me to call in at The Grapes on my way home to let him know why you can't be there? More personal than a call.'

'Would you? That would be really kind. I don't deserve you.'

Trev laughed. 'I know you don't. I shall expect to be taken out and wined and dined in thanks.'

‘Just don’t drink this evening if you’re on the bike.’

‘Yes, Mother.’

‘Don’t count on me over the weekend, though. You know that just because we’ve got him it doesn’t mean it’s over. I’ll be up to my neck in paperwork.’

‘Try to find a couple of hours. Who knows, you and Walter might just win next time.’

When he went back, Spencer had been loaded onto a trolley and was being wheeled carefully out to the ambulance. His eyes were open but he showed no signs of being aware of his surroundings.

‘I don’t think he’s going to be doing much talking for a while,’ one of the paramedics told Ted as they carefully transferred their patient to the back of the ambulance.

‘Just as long as I, or one of my team, is with him once he is talking,’ Ted told them as he climbed in and the doors were shut. ‘We’ve been tracking him for a while and we’re going to be very interested in what he has to say for himself.’

Spencer was whisked away to a bay for assessment as soon as he arrived. A uniformed constable was already there and approached Ted to introduce himself, seeing his police ID round his neck.

‘I want you to stay as close to him as you can, Constable. Right outside the door and don’t leave him unattended for any reason. He’s a suicide risk and I don’t want to lose him before I’ve had chance to question him.’

‘Sir.’

‘I’m going to find our victim and see what else he can tell us. Then I’ll be back.’

Ted was directed to a relatives’ room where he found Maurice looking after Gary’s parents, who had been summoned and arrived quickly, and an older teenager who was presumably Roger, Gary’s boyfriend. Ted wasn’t surprised to see that Maurice had supplied everyone with hot chocolate, his cure-all for everything. Maurice stood up to make the introductions.

Gary's father rose to his feet to shake Ted's hand.

'Thank you for finding our lad, Inspector. Do you know who did this to him and why?'

'I'm afraid there's nothing I can tell you at the moment, Mr Heath. As soon as I know anything, I will tell you what I can, I promise.'

'And do you know when we can see our Gary?'

'Someone will come and find you, as soon as they've finished examining him. If you'll excuse me now, please, I need to go and find out what's happening. DC Brown will stay with you until we know more. You're in safe hands with him.'

Ted was anxious to find a doctor to tell him about Spencer's condition and prognosis. They now had The Preacher, but Ted was none the wiser as to why he'd been committing the crimes he had. He wanted to know when they could start interviewing him, to find out his motives.

He finally found a doctor involved with treating Spencer, who had now been moved to a side room, with the police constable on duty outside his door.

Ted showed his ID and asked, 'Are you able to tell me when we can start interviewing Mr Spencer, please?'

'Certainly not for a couple of days yet. There's some damage to his larynx from the noose so he's not going to be able to speak at the moment. This was definitely a suicide attempt, I believe? Not something someone else did to him? And I understand you're anxious that he's kept on suicide watch in case of a further attempt? I'm trying to get someone from psych to come and assess him, for our own records as much as anything else.'

'We're not looking for anyone else in connection with Mr Spencer's injuries, and we're fairly certain that he was responsible for those to the young man who came in at the same time, Gary Heath. There's a good chance that he's also behind similar assaults on three other young men. Even if he can't talk to me, is there any chance I could see him just for a few moments?'

'As long as you promise me that you're not going to do anything to him.'

The doctor sounded suspicious of his motives.

'I can assure you of that, Doctor. I'm not that sort of policeman.'

The constable outside opened the door for Ted to go in. He walked over to the bed to where The Preacher was lying, his eyelids lightly closed. The puffiness was going from his face and his lips had lost their earlier blueish hue. He was starting to look more like the photo they had of Peter Spencer.

Sensing a presence next to him, the man in the bed opened his eyes. They were a light hazel colour, not unlike Ted's own. He looked at the figure standing next to him, then his gaze slid down to take in the ID round Ted's neck.

'I'm Detective Chief Inspector Darling, from Stockport. I've been investigating a series of crimes involving the kidnap and torture of young men. I understand that you aren't able to speak at the moment so I don't intend to attempt to question you. I would be grateful though if you could confirm your identity for me by nodding or shaking your head in response to some questions.

'You're a musician who plays in a band called Redemption Song?'

A cautious nod.

'Your stage name is Simon Saviour?'

Another slight nod, which produced a wince. The movement was clearly painful.

'Your real name is Peter Spencer and you are, by profession, a church organ tuner?'

Spencer nodded twice, barely moving this time, in confirmation of both questions.

'Thank you, Mr Spencer. That will be all for now. There will be a police officer outside your door at all times and as soon as the doctors tell us you are fit to be interviewed, we will want to ask you more questions.'

As Ted turned to go, he felt Spencer's hand catch hold weakly of his arm. He looked back towards the man in the bed. Spencer's lips were moving but no sound was audible. Ted could lip read what he was saying easily enough.

'Thank you.'

Chapter Twenty-eight

'I don't want to ruin everyone's weekend, but as you all know, even with The Preacher safely in hospital, there's still a lot of work to be done before we can charge him.'

Ted had called his full team in for a Saturday morning briefing. He was hoping that between them they could sort out what needed doing so that everyone got some time off before Monday.

'Rob, interviewing Peter Spencer will be your job. Liaise with the hospital, make sure they know you want to talk to him as soon as it's possible. An interview under caution, recorded. There is just a chance he might confess. Yesterday he tried to thank me. Whether that was for not letting him die or stopping him from committing further crimes, I don't know, but it might be a good sign.

'Maurice, I think you need to go and see Darren. Tell him we have Simon Saviour. If you can get him to understand that, he might feel able to talk to you a bit more. We need to prepare for the possibility of a not guilty plea and have all the witness statements we can get. You should also talk to Gary when he's back home, see what he can tell you. He's the least traumatised of them so see what detail you can get from him.

'Jezza, same for you with Tim, please. You seem to have some way of getting through to him. Ask the centre where he's staying if you can go and visit him, tell him the news and see if that prompts him to start talking.'

'Boss, what's going to happen to Tim when the unit needs

the bed? If he's kicked out he's going to be right back where he started from, on the streets and probably on drugs.'

'Not our problem, Jezza,' Ted told her patiently.

'But he's going to be no use to us as a witness if he goes back to living as he was doing before. There must be something we can do for him. It's just plain wrong that a vulnerable victim like that is abandoned by the system. Not to mention the other Simon, Roger's brother.'

'I hear what you say, Jezza, but for now, we need to focus on the case. I agree, there's something broken in society when there are so many homeless people, including ex-servicemen. But that's a political discussion for another time, not during briefing, please.'

It was said pleasantly enough but it left none of them, not even Jezza, in any doubt that the subject was off limits for now.

'Steve, we need to know everything you can find out about Peter Spencer, especially how he came up clear on Disclosure. Also all the other members of this group he plays in, Redemption Song. For a crime like this, it would be highly unusual for The Preacher to be working with an accomplice, but let's make sure. And Sal, I want everything you can find on this company, Revelations Recordings, and how the paperwork trail was handled. I didn't care for this Jon Carter of Parton and Carter. Not one bit. It would be an added bonus if we could dig up anything to rattle his cage, while we're at it.

'Virgil, how's the FGM case? I've left you on that for now.'

'Still a bit of paperwork, boss, but coming along nicely, if I can use that word for a case like this.'

'Talking of paperwork, mine is calling to me. Jo, Mike, over to you to allocate from here. And let's keep up the search for Simon Ashton. If we can at least let his family know where he is, that would be something.'

Ted tried calling Bill around mid-morning, leaving him time to sleep off a hangover. Trev had said that he'd been drinking heavily when he'd called in at The Grapes the evening before and was looking morose, clearly not enjoying either his supposedly surprise party or the prospect of his enforced leave.

'Hi Bill, it's Ted. I imagine you had a good night if you're not awake yet. I just wanted to say sorry, once again, that I couldn't make it last night. I'll try again later, but just call me if you want to chat at any time.'

He didn't get a reply from him at all on Saturday. By mid-morning Sunday, he tried leaving another message on Bill's mobile and on his landline. He was getting slightly concerned. He'd try to call round there at the end of the day, but he didn't seem to be making much progress in clearing his desk. He'd had to cry off going riding, insisting that Trev go by himself so he didn't miss out on having some fun while his partner was working.

It was getting late in the afternoon before his conscience would allow him to call a halt for the day. He was gathering up his briefcase when his mobile beeped with an incoming text message. Bill's number.

'Ted. Please look after Jack. Sorry.'

He felt his heart start to pound. He tried calling Bill but it went straight to answerphone. He called the control room.

'DCI Darling. Get a car round to Bill Baxter's house, now, and call an ambulance. I think he's done something stupid. I'm on my way.'

He took his official car so he could use the blues and twos if he needed to. As it was, he covered the distance up to Marple Bridge in record time, squealing to a halt close to Bill's house. There was no sign of life and the upstairs curtains were closed.

Ted hammered on the front door, a finger pressed against the bell push and not letting go. He lifted the letter flap and shouted through it.

'Bill! Bill! Are you in there? It's Ted. Open up, Bill.'

All he could hear from inside was the shouting of Bill's

foul-tempered cockatoo, Father Jack. The bird was named after the drunken priest in the TV show Father Ted and Bill had taken great delight in teaching him all his catchphrases.

'Feck! Arse! Drink! Girls!'

'Bill! Come on, let me in.'

Ted was still banging on the door as he shouted. The front door of the next house opened and an elderly woman peered out suspiciously.

'What are you doing? Who are you?'

Ted still had his ID round his neck. He held it up towards her.

'I'm police, a work colleague of Bill. I'm worried about him. Have you seen him today?'

'Oh dear. No, no I haven't.'

'You don't know if anyone has a key, do you?'

'Oh I wouldn't think so. He's a very private man.'

An area car arrived at that moment and pulled up behind Ted's car.

'We need to get inside,' Ted told the officers who got out, not bothering with formalities. 'Break in, on my authority. Is there an ambulance on its way?'

'Yes, sir, ETA five minutes.'

One of the PCs drew a baton, broke a pane of glass and reached in to open the lock.

'The sarge needs to do something about his security,' he commented.

Ted thought that was likely to be the least of Bill's worries at the moment as he pushed the door open and hurried inside. It stank like a pub, whisky, and lots of it. Instinctively, Ted knew Bill wouldn't do anything in front of Father Jack, who lived in the kitchen. He had a quick glance inside the front room then sprinted up the stairs, two at a time, the two PCs following him.

He found Bill in the front bedroom, lying across the double bed. He bent over to shake him by the shoulders.

'Bill! Bill, wake up, you silly old bugger. What've you done? Wake up, Bill.'

'Sir, it looks as if he's taken these.'

One of the PCs was looking at an empty container which had clearly had pills in it. There was also an empty bottle, which had contained Bill's favourite brand of Scotch whisky, on the floor next to the bed. Ted was busily checking his vital signs.

'We should turn him, in case he vomits and aspirates. He's breathing and there's a pulse, but it's a bit thready. One of you give me a hand, please.'

They heard the siren as they were turning him. The sound of it seemed to send Father Jack into a frenzy downstairs. They could hear the bird repeatedly screeching 'Feck off!' at the top of its voice.

'One of you go down and put a towel over the parrot's cage. The other show the paramedics in. I'll stay with Sergeant Baxter.'

The two of them exchanged apprehensive looks.

'Does it bite, sir? The bird?'

'It's a parrot. Behind bars. Keep your fingers out of the way and do it,' Ted told them shortly.

'Bill, you silly sod, what were you playing at?' he said quietly to his old friend as the two officers left them alone for a moment. 'Why didn't you talk to me, if things had got this bad? Don't you worry about Jack. I'll take him home with me and take care of him. Trev will probably divorce me. He doesn't like birds. But don't you worry. You just concentrate on getting better and we'll get you some help.'

The first paramedic to walk through the door recognised Ted at once.

'Hello again, Ted. How are you, and how's the hand now?'

He and his team mate had picked up both Maurice and Ted when they had been separately injured in an earlier enquiry. Although he asked the question, he was already focusing on the figure on the bed and asking Ted for any details, mentally noting the information.

'Bill? Can you hear me, Bill? My name's Phil and I'm just going to take a look at you.'

Ted moved out of the way and went to talk to the two PCs as they were coming back upstairs.

'You survived, then?' he asked them dryly. 'One of you outside now, please, keep the spectators away. And can one of you arrange someone to come and secure the house? We don't want him coming home to find he's been burgled. I'll take Father Jack home with me, and I'll follow the ambulance down.'

Phil heard him and came over to the door to talk to him, on his way to get a stretcher, leaving his oppo to carry on seeing to Bill.

'It might be better just to leave it for a while, Ted. Phone the hospital first to see if he's up to visitors. Sometimes, with things like this, people feel a bit reluctant to face even close friends. Was that a parrot shouting its head off downstairs when we arrived?'

'A cockatoo. Father Jack. I'll take him home with me for now. Bill sent me a text asking me to look after Jack. That's how I knew something was wrong.'

'Just as well you acted quickly, looking at what he's taken. Let's hope there weren't many left. So how will your missus react when you turn up at home with a strange bird?'

'He'll be furious. He hates birds at close quarters.'

Trev's motorbike was back in the garage when Ted got back. He'd half been hoping his partner would still be out so he could at least have got Jack into the house and hopefully settled down before Trev saw him. He knew Trev had something of a phobia about flapping wings, and Jack did like his liberty. It was not going to be an easy situation to manage, especially as, at a difficult part of a testing case, Ted was going to be working long hours. That would mean persuading Trev to feed Jack and let him out of his cage for some exercise.

He paused on the doorstep to have a few stern words with the cockatoo.

'Now, this is my house but Trev's in charge. Well, Trev and the cats. So if you want to stay, you have to be polite to Trev and don't attack the cats. All right?'

He kept the cage covered as he opened the door and walked in, heading for the kitchen. Trev was sitting at the table with a mug of tea, his long legs, clad in another recent purchase, expensive riding breeches, stretched out in front of him. His black curls were damp and tousled from having been squashed under his riding hat and he looked as if he'd had an enjoyable time, if the slight smile on his lips and the tuneless humming between mouthfuls of dark tea were anything to go by.

He turned his head with a smile of welcome which froze on his lips as he saw the cage.

'What is that?' he asked in horror.

At the sound of his voice, the bird started up a shouted chorus of 'Feck! Arse!' from under the tea-towel.

Ted was busily setting up the stand for the cage, studiously avoiding Trev's eyes.

'I'm sorry, but I can explain. Bill's been rushed into hospital. He's taken an overdose. I've not yet heard if he's going to be all right. He sent me a text asking me to look after Jack, which is how I knew he'd done something. Thankfully, or he might not have survived. I still don't know if he will, but at least he's in the right place.'

'I'm really sorry about Bill but seriously, Ted? A bird? You know I hate them flapping about. And what about the cats? Won't they get him?'

Ted had taken the towel off the cage. Six inquisitive felines were staring up at the white bird inside who was busily swearing at them. Ted opened the cage door.

'Jack can look after himself. He does like a bit of freedom

though. He won't bother you. He doesn't fly about much. He just hops from place to place. And I'm sure he can take care of himself with the cats. Just please don't leave any windows or the garden door open. I don't want him to escape.'

Seeing the door open to freedom, Jack launched himself through it and fluttered the short distance to land on Trev's shoulder.

'Feck off, cup!' he squawked, tugging viciously at Trev's hair with his curved beak. Then he turned himself round so that, with incredible accuracy, the dropping he did landed right on the leg of Trev's breeches, the white mess trickling down over the suede patches which ran up the inside legs and round his seat at the back.

'He just shat on my best breeches! Has he any idea what these cost me? Ted, hand me my phone. I am going to ring the station to report a murder that's about to happen. Once this creature gets off me, I am so going to kill you.'

Phil the paramedic had been right. When Ted phoned the hospital later, he was told that Bill had regained consciousness but was refusing to see anyone. Ted asked for a message to be passed to him assuring him that his cockatoo was being well looked after and saying he would come and see him as soon as he was up to receiving visitors.

Next he phoned the hospital near Bury for news of The Preacher. After being left on hold for some moments, he was eventually spoken to and told that Peter Spencer was making good progress and was still on suicide watch. The registrar who spoke to him said Spencer could now talk, though still with some difficulty and his voice was weak. He told Ted to call again in the morning and that it might just be possible for someone to speak to Spencer later in the day, though not for long.

It looked as if they might finally be going to get some answers.

Chapter Twenty-nine

'I really am very sorry to hear about Bill. I know you tried to warn us all, but I honestly don't think anyone realised how depressed he was becoming.'

The Ice Queen was repeatedly stirring her coffee as she spoke. Ted often wondered why she bothered as she usually took it black with no sugar. It seemed to be something she did when she needed to measure her words carefully.

'I certainly didn't,' Kevin Turner said glumly. 'And I should have done. I speak to him practically every day. I was selfishly thinking of things from my point of view, not his. Thinking what I wouldn't give for a three-month break right now.'

'Technically, he was no longer a serving officer when he did what he did. I think nevertheless that we need to have a close look at what has happened and see what lessons can be learned from it. What's the latest news on him?'

'I phoned the hospital first thing,' Ted told them both. 'They say he's out of danger, thankfully. He's still refusing to see anyone at all. Not me, and certainly not anyone from psych. Stubborn old bugger. I'm hoping he might let me visit later today. He'll be wanting to know about Jack.'

'Jack?'

'His parrot,' Ted told her. The Super didn't know Bill as well as Ted and Kevin did. 'I've got him staying with me for now. Trev and the cats are not amused. I think they may all leave home. But knowing Bill, what will be worrying him most at the moment is whether this incident will affect his job offer to come back as a civvy. He'll be fine, once he gets back here, where he feels he belongs.'

'There's no reason why it should affect his future post. But in the circumstances, he would need to satisfy HR and Occupational Health that his recent problem was not going to present any further issues. Could you perhaps persuade him to see someone? To accept some help?'

'I can try,' Ted said, his lack of optimism obvious from his tone.

Kevin drained his coffee and rose to go.

'If you'll excuse me, ma'am, I'd better get back to the coalface, if you don't need me for anything else?'

She nodded her agreement. Kev turned to Ted with an ironic grin and a wink as he said, 'Sir.'

It was purely for form's sake, in front of the Super, and they all knew it.

'So, it looks as if your team has had some excellent results. With Clive Edwards and his henchmen all now remanded in custody for your Trevor's kidnapping, and with a strong possibility that you have the right person for these appalling tortures, it's looking good. Not to mention wrapping up this female genital mutilation case. That's an excellent result as it sends a strong message. Please pass on my congratulations to everyone involved.

'If you are able to visit Bill, please send him my best wishes and assure him that as far as I am concerned, his new job is still waiting for him.'

The morning briefing was just a formality. Everyone knew exactly what they needed to be working on. Rob had been told by the hospital that he could go in and interview Peter Spencer at eleven o'clock, once he had been seen by a doctor. He'd been warned that he couldn't stay long and that Spencer might not say a lot but that he appeared to be quite happy about talking to the police.

Sal followed Ted as he went back to his office and asked if he could have a word.

'Yes, Sal, what can I do for you?'

'Boss, I've nearly finished digging through the paperwork on the lease. I've more or less unpicked the trail now and I'll probably be able to submit a report on it later today. But it's made me realise something. This is the sort of stuff I like doing best, and I'm good at it. So I want to go back to Fraud.'

'I'll be sorry to lose you, Sal. You're a good officer. I thought you were happy on the team?'

'I am boss, it's been great working here. But I've put in for my sergeant's exams, as you know, and with Mike and Rob already as DSs, there's no place for me realistically on the team if I get the promotion. I've been talking to some old friends in Fraud and there's a post there coming available. So I'd like to put in for it, but I didn't want to go behind your back.'

'Thank you, I appreciate that. If you need a reference from me, you know it will be a glowing one. Best of luck, Sal. When are you thinking of leaving us?'

'It would be in about a month, if all goes well and if I get the post I'm after.'

Ted shook the DC's hand and watched him leave the office. His mind was busily pondering whether the powers that be would allow him a replacement for Sal or if they would leap on the chance of the further reduction in personnel on his team.

Ted picked up his phone. He needed to speak to SOCO about the crime scene and about the possibility of getting a match on the tyres on Spencer's car. He also needed to speak to Doug about the kitten. He'd put it off long enough.

'Bless me, father, for I have sinned. It has been many years since my last confession.'

The voice was faint, barely above a whisper, but Rob could still detect the ironic note of laughter in what Peter Spencer was saying. He'd cautioned him and told him he was recording the conversation. Spencer was reclining against the raised head of the bed. He'd waived the right to have a solicitor present. He had water in a cup with a straw to ease this throat, which was clearly still painful. Rob had told the uniformed constable at the door to take a quick tea break while he had the chance.

'My name is Peter Spencer. I'm an organ tuner by day and sometimes a keyboard player with a band at night. My late father, Robert Spencer, was a parish priest. My mother died when I was young and I was brought up by my father at the vicarage until he died a little over three years ago.'

He took a sip of the water, swallowing with obvious difficulty.

'My father's bishop was a frequent visitor to the vicarage. He too was something of a musician who played piano and organ to a reasonable level. When I was small and couldn't easily reach the pedals with my feet, the bishop would sit on the piano stool and put me in between his legs so I could play the keys and he could operate the pedals for me.

'I was quite young at this time, far too young to realise why I could always feel something hard and stiff pressing against the back of my buttocks as I sat there playing. My father would be sitting not far away and he appeared to be completely oblivious to what was happening.'

Another drink, and for a moment he rested his head back against the pillows, summoning his strength.

'If at any time you're unable to continue, Mr Spencer, please say so and I can suspend the interview for now.'

'I would like to continue. Confession is good for the soul, they say, and mine is in sore need of relief.

'As I got older, I started to play the organ. Again, the reach and the complexity of the pedals was problematic. My father took to sending me to the church to practise, alone with the bishop. By this time, I was becoming more mature and, I'm sure I don't have to spell it out for you, Sergeant, I was becoming all too aware of what an erection was.

'I had no feelings for men. The mere idea repelled me. I was just starting to discover girls. But at that age, almost anything can be sexually stimulating. The bishop had started touching me, fondling me, aware of the reaction it was provoking in me. I was disgusted. With him, with myself, with my reaction to what was happening, my lack of self control. I decided to speak of it to my father.'

He paused again, drinking more water. It was clearly becoming emotionally as well as physically painful for him to continue. Rob waited, not wanting to press him.

'My father … my father didn't believe me. Not a word of it. The bishop was a man of high repute, widely respected. He wrote theological books. He was heavily involved in charitable works and missions in third world countries. How could I possibly be telling the truth? I was an adolescent boy, a mass of spots and raging hormones, experiencing wet dreams and clearly prone to unhealthy fantasies.

'He told me I was wicked. That I was committing a sin to spread such lies about a holy man. He made me kneel while he prayed for me, great long passages from the King James' Bible, because he was always old-fashioned. He didn't like the scriptures being rendered into modern vernacular. He made me memorise and repeat sections and told me that I must recite them whenever I had impure thoughts of such a nature.

'Then he locked me in the cubbyhole under the stairs, in the dark. I hate the dark. I've always been afraid of it. I think it's because my mother died in the night-time. Even now I sometimes sleep with a light on. I hate spiders, too, and any kind of creepy-crawly. He left me there overnight. I was terrified. I was so afraid I wet myself, to my shame. He refused to let me out until I apologised and promised never again to tell such wicked lies.

'The next time the bishop came to visit, Father sent me to the church with him as if nothing had happened and I'd mentioned nothing to him. So it continued for perhaps two years more. It was only ever touching, no more than that. Intimate touching. But all the time I was playing he would press against me from behind and fondle me and I couldn't control my reactions.

'It went on until the bishop was abruptly moved to a distant diocese. I found out much later that there was a hint of a scandal surrounding him, other complaints from young boys like me, which was hushed up and he was sent away to keep it quiet.'

There was a knock at the door and a nurse came in. Rob paused the recording.

'I just need to check on Mr Spencer, and to make sure he's not getting overtired.'

'I would prefer to go on. In the words of the TV programme, 'I've started so I'll finish.' I haven't a lot more to say.'

She checked his pulse and temperature, adjusted the pillows, smoothed down the sheets.

'As long as you're sure ...'

'I have explained to Mr Spencer that he isn't obliged to say anything at this time,' Rob assured her. 'But he has said to me that he'd like to continue and I think we're nearly finished for now.'

She left the room. Spencer drank more water.

'I thought – and lying here like this, talking to a policeman, I can see now how insane the whole thing was – but I did think that if I could get hold of young men, ones who were gay or thought they were, and show them the error of their ways, perhaps I could stop similar things happening in the future. It seemed right. It seemed as if I was helping them.

'It was easy enough to pick victims. They'd seen me before, at gigs, playing with the group. They had no reason to fear me. And I never had any intention of killing them. Nothing like that. I always meant to let them go. If I could just reprogramme them in some way.

'I think I realised, after the first one, that it was not the right thing to do. But somehow, I couldn't stop myself. I wanted to. I really did. But I couldn't find the strength to do so. I always told myself that if anyone got too close, I would stop. Forever. That's why I had the noose ready. I never intended to walk away. I knew there would have to be a reckoning for what I'd done.'

The fatigue was showing on his face now and his voice was getting weaker.

'Mr Spencer, may I just ask you a couple of questions before we finish?'

Spencer finished drinking and nodded wearily.

'Did you kill your father, Mr Spencer?'

He gave a wan smile.

'To my eternal shame, I didn't. I wanted to. I so badly wanted to. But you could say that I engineered his death. He drank too much. He'd started drinking heavily after my mother died and it got much worse when I tried to tell him about the bishop. He was always critical of me, of everything I did. Nothing was ever good enough, especially since the time I'd tried to talk to him. Things were never the same between us after that.

'I'd thought many times of moving out, of leaving him to rot and going to make a new life for myself somewhere else. I found I didn't have the courage. Nor the financial means.

'One evening we had a row. That was nothing new, but this was a particularly heated one. It was something and nothing. He didn't like the arrangement of something I'd played at a wedding. Said it was too modern, disrespectful. As he was going up the stairs, clearly the worst for wear, I was shouting at him from the hall, provoking him.

'He got to where the stairs made a right-angle turn. He was trying to look back at me, to finish the argument. He slipped and lost his footing. The stairs were polished oak, uncarpeted. Lethal, even if you were sober. He fell heavily all the way to the bottom. His head made rather a satisfying noise as it hit the quarry tiles near to where I was standing.

'I stood and watched him die. I could probably have done something to prevent it. But I did nothing. Then I called the ambulance. I simply told them, and the police who came as well as a matter of routine, that I'd been in the church practising and had come back to find him dead at the foot of the stairs. Everyone believed me. Why wouldn't they? I was the fine, upstanding son of a vicar. I couldn't possibly be telling lies.'

'Thank you, Mr Spencer. And the bishop who abused you. Is he still alive, do you know?'

'He's an old man now, in his eighties, long since retired. I believe he lives in a care home for former clergy. But yes, as far as I know, he is still alive.'

The team were quiet for a moment when Rob finished playing the recorded interview. Jo was the first to speak.

'There is almost some kind of perverted logic behind what he set out to do, I suppose. I don't condone any of it, of course, but after all it's not uncommon for an abuse victim to go on to become an abuser.'

'Good work, Rob. With a bit of luck, he's not going to deny any of it and we should get a good conclusion. He may well be sent to a secure psychiatric unit, at least initially, but he should hopefully be off the streets for some time. Especially if we can get any kind of statement from the three surviving victims. What's the latest on that?'

'Gary's fine now he's back with his family, boss, and they're all very supportive of him. He's starting to talk and he'll make a good witness if we need him. I told Darren we had The Preacher and he cried. He tried to talk a bit so as long as he can get some sort of ongoing help, which is always tricky, I know, he might be able to give us a statement at some point in the future,' Maurice told them.

'Tim is looking loads better but still not saying much,' Jezza put in. 'The problem there is that they're already making noises about moving him on as they need the bed. Then what's going to happen to him, with nowhere to go and no kind of support in place?'

'All we can do is ask Lincolnshire to try to keep an eye on him and see if there's not some sort of support he could tap into – if he'd accept that,' Ted replied. 'Any news of Simon Ashton?'

Head shakes all round. There were now so many homeless ex-serviceman that he was just another statistic and their hopes of tracing him were slim.

'Well done, everyone, good result. Why don't we all try to finish at a reasonable time tonight, get back to our nearest and dearest before the middle of the night, for once. Thanks, all of you, for your hard work on this. It's appreciated. The Super also passed on her thanks.'

'Boss, just one thing, before we knock off,' Rob put in. 'I'd like to start up a historical child abuse enquiry. I want to go after that bishop, while he's still alive. There's no excuse for what Spencer did and he's not using that as an excuse. He accepts full responsibility. But who's to say if Spencer would have turned out that way if he hadn't been interfered with for years, and in particular, if his father hadn't refused to believe him?'

Ted looked at him, considering. He knew it was something Rob was likely to feel deeply about. He'd told Ted in confidence that he'd experienced similar abuse as a boy when he'd been put into temporary foster care.

'You've been given information of a serious crime having been committed and information that the perpetrator is still alive. I think you would be negligent in your duties if you didn't open an enquiry, Rob.'

Chapter Thirty

The curtains were drawn round Bill's bed when Ted got to the ward. He'd been told Bill was still refusing visitors but he'd used his not inconsiderable charm, and his warrant card, to be allowed to see him, on the strict understanding that he kept it brief.

The reception he got was hardly warm. Bill was sitting up in bed, looking paler and older than his actual years. He scowled at Ted and pulled the sheet protectively closer. He was wearing a hospital gown and had a drip in one arm.

'What are you doing here? I said no visitors.'

'I'm not a visitor, I'm a friend, you miserable old bugger. I thought you'd want to know how Jack was doing.'

There was no sign of a chair and perching on the bed felt too much like an invasion of Bill's personal space, so Ted remained standing. The neighbour had been right; he was a private man.

'Is he all right?'

For a moment, his face was less hostile.

'He's all right but Trev is threatening to leave me. He hates birds and Jack made a beeline for him when I let him out and started trying to pull his hair out. And he crapped on his favourite new riding breeches. The cats are afraid of him, too.'

The ghost of a smile passed over Bill's face.

'How are you, anyway?' Ted asked him.

'I have the worst hangover in living memory. Apparently the alcohol poisoning was worse than the pills. I didn't take enough of them to do much harm.'

'Where did you get the pills?'

'The doctor gave me something to help me sleep. I've been fretting about this retirement rubbish for months now. The nearer it got to Monday morning and no job to go to, the more I just couldn't take it. I suppose that sounds daft.'

'Not daft at all. We should all have realised and been more supportive. I'm sorry you were let down, Bill. But the Super says to tell you your new job is waiting for you, as planned, as long as you're well enough to come back.'

Bill lowered his head, looking suddenly emotional.

'Thanks. I'm sorry I was a prick,' he muttered.

'Look, I had an idea. I think you should find a lodger.'

'A lodger? What the bloody hell for? I don't need the money, with my pension and then my new job. And if you think Jack is hard to live with, let me tell you I'm far worse.'

'But I'm not thinking of the benefits to you. You've got a lot to offer, not just a spare room in your house. On this latest case we've come across people who are homeless through no fault of their own. I'm not meaning them specifically but there are lots of people like them. They can't break out of the vicious circle without an address. You're bloody good with people, Bill. Look how much you helped me when I first came to the nick.'

Bill gave a snort of amusement.

'I remember you, the first time you walked through the doors. Bloody full of yourself. Like a little bantam cock, ready to pick a fight with any bigger cockerel who got in your way. Someone had to take you under their wing before you got yourself in serious trouble.'

'Exactly! I'd not have made it, certainly not to DCI, without you keeping an eye on me. So will you at least think of it? You might just be able to help someone turn their life around.'

Ted could hear Trev's voice in the sitting room when he quietly opened the front door and went into the house. The kitchen door was firmly shut and from inside he heard Jack shouting and swearing away at the top of his voice. Ted put his things down in the hall and went into the sitting room. Trev was on his mobile, talking animated French. Ted didn't understand what he was saying but he could imagine what the subject was. He bent down to kiss him and waited for him to finish the call.

'I let the vulture out, like you asked. It tried to savage me so the cats and I have taken refuge in here and I am not going back in that kitchen until the thing has gone. So either you cook or it's takeaways for every meal. How is Bill, by the way?'

'I'm sorry about Jack. I'll go and have a word with him. And Bill's doing much better, you'll be pleased to hear. They're hoping to send him home tomorrow, as long as he accepts a bit of help. I brought you something, to make up for the invasion.'

He went back out into the hall, then returned and plonked a small kitten on Trev's lap. He'd smuggled one of the cat carriers out of the garage when he'd left for work and called on Doug after his visit to the hospital.

'Oh my god, Ted! You said we couldn't have one. Is it a boy or a girl?'

'It's a boy. And I decided you deserved a present after all I've put you through recently.'

Trev gently picked the little cat up and looked at it. Its small pink mouth opened in a soundless meow.

'He is absolutely gorgeous!'

Beauty was truly in the eye of the beholder. Doug had been right about the kitten. He really was an ugly little bugger. He was almost all white, with a great disfiguring splodge of dark colouring across almost half of his head and face. His eyes were different colours and one ear resolutely refused to stand up like the other one. His front legs were somewhat bandy. Ted could hear his mother's voice in his head, saying the cat could never stop a pig in a poke. The physical attributes all added up to making the kitten look rather clown-like. It was easy to see why Doug had said he was not worth showing, despite coming from pedigree stock.

But Trev had him cuddled against his cheek, stroking the soft fur and murmuring gently to him. The kitten clearly knew it had landed on its paws as it was purring away loudly, totally unafraid. The rest of the cats were looking up at this new intruder with a mixture of curiosity and hostility.

'I know I've been neglecting you lately. And I let you be put at risk. I should never have let you appear in that photo with me. Edwards and your two kidnappers are out of harm's way for now and will hopefully go down. But no more appearing with me in public. Not in any photos, certainly, and definitely not with your name in the caption. I don't want anything like that happening to you again.

'CPS think Edwards' own legal team will advise him against appealing Morgane's conviction or sentence, whatever it is. They're bound to tell him his actions are going to go against him. But it's happened once and I'm going to do everything I can to see nothing like that ever happens again.'

What he didn't tell Trev was that he'd arranged for the photo of the two of them together at the awards ceremony to be removed from the GMP site and archives. He'd also sweet-talked the local reporter, Penny Hunter, into getting it removed from the newspaper site, on the promise of plenty of tip-offs to come as a reward. It wouldn't stop anyone really determined from digging into his personal life, but it was at least something.

'What will you call him?'

Trev had transferred the kitten to his lap where it lay on its back, eyes closed in bliss, having its tummy tickled. Queen, the senior cat, had jumped up on to the sofa next to them and was sniffing warily at the newcomer.

'Well if he's coming to join Queen, he has to be called Adam, doesn't he?'

They were both big fans of Queen's music who had accepted Adam Lambert as a good addition to the group on tour.

Ted smiled. It was a fitting name. He was pleased that he seemed to have done the right thing. He would do anything to see Trev happy.

His mobile phone interrupted him. An unknown caller, so he answered with a neutral, 'Hello?'

'We need to talk, Gayboy.'

It was the unmistakable voice of his martial arts and survival skills trainer, Green. Last heard of on a beach in South Africa. The same beach where later a pile of clothing and a pair of British Army boots had suggested the ocean had claimed another victim.

Ted got up and went back out into the hall before he spoke.

'I thought you'd drowned off Cape Town.'

'Then you're even more stupid than I thought you were. We have unfinished business to attend to. I'll be in touch.'

THE END

Lightning Source UK Ltd.
Milton Keynes UK
UKHW041820150719
346204UK00002B/98/P